THE DARK SIDE OF THE MOON

AFTER TWO MONTHS of unconsciousness, Ryan Wratch opened his eyes. Or more accurately, he folded into tight pleats two hundred tiny shutters of dirty purplish-brown tissue and thereupon looked out on a new world.

For perhaps twenty seconds, Wratch stared at delirium made tangible, madness beyond all expression. He heard a high-pitched staccato, a vague somehow familiar shrillness, then once more lost consciousness.

About the Author

Born in 1916 and educated at the University of California, Jack Vance wrote his first story while serving in the US Merchant Navy during the Second World War. His first book, THE DYING EARTH, was published in 1950 and he went on to become one of the acknowledged masters of fantasy and science fiction.

He has enjoyed success both as a screenwriter and author of mystery and suspense novels – THE MAN IN THE CAGE won the coveted Edgar award – and he has won both of the major awards for science fiction, THE DRAGON MASTERS winning the Hugo and THE LAST CASTLE taking both the Hugo and the Nebula. Jack Vance's hobbies include blue-water sailing and early jazz. He lives near Oakland, California.

JACK VANCE

THE DARK SIDE OF THE MOON

NEW ENGLISH LIBRARY
Hodder and Stoughton

Copyright © 1986 by
Jack Vance

First published in the United
States of America in 1986 by
Underwood-Miller

First published in Great Britain
in 1989 by New English
Library Paperbacks

British Library C.I.P.

Vance, Jack, 1916–
    The dark side of the moon.
    I. Title
    813′.54[F]

ISBN 0-450-50257-0

Printed and bound in Great Britain
for Hodder and Stoughton
paperbacks, a division of Hodder and
Stoughton Ltd., Mill Road,
Dunton Green, Sevenoaks, Kent
TN13 2YA (Editorial Office:
47 Bedford Square, London
WC1B 3DP) by Richard Clay,
Bungay, Suffolk.

CONTENTS

INTRODUCTION

INTRODUCTIONS ARE THE BANE of a writer's trade, at least for this writer. I have already composed two for this collection and both have been discarded, on grounds of excessive frivolity. Herewith: the third version.

As I look over the Table of Contents, I move up and down the gamut of emotions, from enthusiasm and pride to indifference. There are stories here forty years old, which I barely remember. Since I refuse to re-read them, my opinions are not to the point.

Well then; as for the stories I do recall:

Planet of the Black Dust was my second story in print. I can remember the mood I wanted to generate but little else. Same with *Phalid's Fate*, my third in print, although I have never forgotten the name of the protagonist 'Ryan Wratch.' I selected this name because I did not want to call him 'Curt Wilson' or 'Kent Stevens' or 'Dirk Weston.' In a sense, I straddled two horses, 'Ryan' being an OK name, while 'Wratch' is overkill. I plead youth, inexperience and good intentions.

DP appeared originally in a magazine called *Avon Science Fiction and Fantasy Reader*. The editor was so affected by the story and believed so fiercely in its thesis, that he added an emotional coda to the last paragraph, thereby beating a very dead horse. I have deleted the editor's extraneous remarks in this present version. The story was written at a quaint little village in the Austrian Tyrol, where, as I vividly recall, I was stung by a bee while sitting on the sunny balcony of·the hotel. Could this have established a mood for the story, which is definitely morose? I think not.

I might mention that Norma and I revisited this village, Fulpmes, last year, and found a graceless modern town lacking every trace of its old romantic atmosphere. Sad to say, the situation is about the same, almost everywhere else in the world. Perhaps it is over-ingenuous to complain that romance is dead; still, I fear that a good case might be made, especially among young people.

Alfred's Ark and *First Star I see Tonight* are two of my favorites. *Alfred's Ark* tells you all you need to know in regard to the human condition. Background for *First Star* was assimilated during my assocation with Palomar astronomer Robert Richardson ('Philip Latham'), during the time we both wrote CAPTAIN VIDEO scripts for television. There are dark and sinister aspects to the astronomer's life of which the public is unaware; this story, so I am told, prompts astronomers to nod in grim corroboration and look over their shoulders.

The Phantom Milkman derives from a rainy evening and several batches of rum punch in an old farm-house behind Kenwood, California, where the Vances and the Frank Herberts had taken up residence prior to departure for Mexico. Someone—or something—had delivered a quart of milk to the doorstep that morning. All day Norma and Beverly had been attempting to resolve the mystery, without success. We discussed the affair long into the night, and at last decided that in the absence of trained and experience investigators, it might be fool-hardy to proceed further.

As for *Parapsyche*: ??? I had been doing some reading in the field of psionics and decided to expatiate upon my own theories, using a story for the vehicle. The theories are as sound as any others in the field—which means that no one will want to use them for pitons while scaling El Capitan. Need I say more? I have quite forgotten the story itself, save that it involves a clergyman.

Before my first sale: *The World-Thinker* (not included here), I wrote an epic novel in the style of E. E. Smith's cosmic chronicles. My own epic was rejected everywhere. I finally broke it into pieces and salvaged a few episodes for short stories. I think that *The Temple of Han* (originally *The God and the Temple Robber*) was one of these altered episodes.

As for the other titles, I can't come up with any recollection or insights, and hence will say nothing whatever.

Just for fun and since I have the chance, I'd like to dedicate this book to the unique and charming

Janet Miller
First lady of Columbia, Pennsylvania

Jack Vance
December 28,1985

THE DARK SIDE OF THE MOON

SULWEN'S PLANET

1

PROFESSOR JASON GENCH, Professor Victor Kosmin, Dr. Lawrence Drewe, and twenty-four others of equal eminence filed from the spaceship to contemplate the scene on Sulwen Plain below. The startled mutterings dwindled to silence.

Even a hollow facetiousness met no response. Professor Gench glanced sidelong toward Professor Kosmin, to encounter Professor Kosmin's bland stare. Gench jerked his gaze away.

Boorish bumbling camel, thought Gench.

Piffling little jackanapes, thought Kosmin.

Each wished the other twelve hundred and four light-years distant: which is to say, back on Earth. Or twelve hundred and five light-years.

The first man on Sulwen Plain had been James Sulwen, an embittered Irish Nationalist turned vagabond space-wanderer. In his memoirs Sulwen wrote: 'To say I was startled, awed, dumbfounded, is like saying the ocean is wet. Oh, but it's a lonesome place, so far away, so dim and cold, the more so for the mystery. I stayed there three days and two nights, taking pictures, wondering about all the histories of the universe. What had happened so long ago? What had brought these strange folk here to die? I became haunted, obsessed; I had to leave . . . .'

Sulwen returned to Earth with his photographs. His discovery was hailed as 'the single most important event in human history.' Public interest reached a level of dizzy excitement; here was cosmic drama at its most vivid: mystery, tragedy, cataclysm.

In such a perfervid atmosphere the 'Sulwen's Plant Survey Commission' was nominated, confirmed, and instructed to perform a brief investigation upon which a full-scale program of research could be based. No one thought to point out that the function of Professor Victor Kosmin, in the field of comparative linguistics, and that of Professor Jason Gench, a philologist, overlapped. The Director of the commission was Dr. Lawrence Drewe, Fellow of Mathematical Philosophy at Vidmar Institute: a mild wry gentleman, superficially inadequate to the job of controlling the personalities of the other members of the commission.

Accompanied by four supply transports with men, materials, and machinery for the construction of a permanent base, the commission departed Earth.

2

Sulwen had grossly understated the desolation of Sulwen Plain. A dwarf white sun cast a wan glare double, or possibly triple, the intensity of full moonlight. Basalt crags rimmed the plain to north and east. A mile from the base of the crags was the first of the seven wrecked spaceships: a collapsed cylinder of black-and-white metal two hundred and forty feet long, a hundred and two feet in diameter. There were five such hulks. In and out of the ships, perfectly preserved in the scant atmosphere of frigid nitrogen, were the corpses of a squat pallid race, something under human size, with four arms, each terminating in but two slender fingers.

The remaining two ships, three times the length and twice the diameter of the black-and-white ships, had been conceived and constructed on a larger, more flamboyant, scale. Big Purple, as one came to be known, was undamaged except for a gash down the length of its dorsal surface. Big Blue, the other, had crashed nose-first to the planet and stood in an attitude of precarious equilibrium, seemingly ready to topple at a touch. The design of Big Purple and Big Blue was eccentric, refined, and captious, implying esthetic intent or some analogous quality. These ships were manned by tall slender blue-black creatures with many-horned heads and delicate pinched faces half-concealed behind tufts of hair. They became known as Wasps and their enemies, the pale creatures, were labeled Sea Cows, though in neither case was the metaphor particularly apt.

Sulwen Plain had been the site of a terrible battle between two spacefaring races: so much was clear. Three questions occurred simultaneously to each of the commissioners:

Where did these peoples originate?

How long ago had the battle occurred?

How did the technology of the 'Wasps' and 'Sea Cows' compare with that of Earth?

There was no immediate answer to the first question. Sulwen's Star controlled no other planets.

As to the time of the battle, a first estimate derived from the deposition of meteoric dust suggested a figure of fifty thousand years. More accurate and technical determinations ultimately put the time at sixty-two thousand years.

The third question was more difficult to answer. In somewhat comparable histories Wasp, Sea Cow, and man had come by different routes to similar ends. In other cases, no comparison was possible.

There was endless speculation as to the course of the battle. The most popular theory envisioned the Sea Cow ships sweeping down upon Sulwen Plain to find Big Blue and Big Purple at rest. Big Blue had lifted perhaps half a mile, only to be crippled and plunge headlong to the surface. Big Purple, with a mortal gash down the back, apparently had never left the ground. Perhaps other ships had been present; there was no way of knowing. By one agency or another five Sea Cow ships had been destroyed in that final encounter.

3

The ships from Earth landed on a rise to the southeast of the battlefield, near to the location where James Sulwen originally had put down. The commissioners, debarking, lumbered out to the nearest Sea Cow ship: Sea Cow D, as it became known. Sulwen's Star hung low to the horizon, casting a stark pallid light. Long black shadows lay across the putty-colored plain.

The commissioners studied the ruptured ship, inspected the twisted Sea Cow corpses, then Sulwen's Star dropped below the horizon. Instant darkness came to the plain, and the commissioners, looking over their shoulders, returned to their own ship.

Later, after the evening meal, Director Drewe addressed the group: 'This is a preliminary survey. I reiterate the obvious because we are scientists: we want to know! We are not so much interested in planning research as in the research itself. Well — we must practice a certain restraint. For most of you, these wrecks will occupy many years to come. I myself, unfortunately! am a formalist, a mathematical theorist, and as such will be denied your first-hand opportunity. Well, then, my personal problems aside: temporarily we must resign ourselves to a state of ignorance. The mystery will remain a mystery, unless Professor Gench or Professor Kosmin is already able to read one of the languages.' Here Drewe chuckled; he had intended the remark jocularly. Noticing the quick, suspicious glance exchanged by Tench and Kosmin, he decided that the remark had not been tactful. 'For a day or two, I suggest a casual inspection of the project, to orient ourselves. There is no pressure on us; we will achieve more if we relax, and try to realize a wide-angle view of the situation. And by all means, everyone be careful of the big blue ship. It looks as if it might topple at a breath!'

Professor Gench smiled bitterly. He was thin as a shrike, with a gaunt crooked face, a crag of a forehead, a black angry gaze. ' "No pressure on us," ' he thought. 'What a joke!'

' "Relax!" ' thought Kosmin, with a sardonic twitch of the lips. 'With that preposterous Gench underfoot? Hah!' In contrast to Gench, Kosmin was massive, almost portly, with a big pale face, a tuft of yellow hair. His cheekbones were heavy, his forehead narrow and back-sloping. He made no effort to project an ingratiating personality; nor did Gench. Of the two, Gench was perhaps the more gregarious, but his approach to any situation, social or professional, tended to be sharp and doctrinaire.

'I will perform some quick and brilliant exposition,' Gench decided. 'I must put Kosmin in his place.'

'One man eventually will direct the linguistic programe,' mused Kosmin to himself. 'Who but a comparative linguist?'

Drewe concluded his remarks. 'I need hardly urge everyone to caution. Be especially careful of your footing; do not venture into closed areas. You naturally will be wearing work-suits; check your regenerators and energy levels before leaving the ship, keep your communications channels open at all times. Another matter: let us try to disturb conditions as little as possible. This is a monumental job, there is no point rushing forth and worrying at it like dogs. Well, then: a good night's rest and tomorrow, we'll have at it!'

4

The commissioners stepped out upon the dreary surface of the plain, approached the wrecked ships. The closest at hand was Sea Cow D, a black-and-white vessel, battered, broken, littered with pale corpses. The metallurgists touched analyzers to various sections of the hull and machinery, reading off alloy compositions; the biologists began to examine the corpses; the physicists and technicians peered into the engine compartments, marveling at the unfamiliar engineering of an alien race. Gench, walking under the hulk, found a strip of white fiber covered with rows of queer smears. As he lifted it, the fiber, brittle from cold and age, fell to pieces.

Kosmin, noticing the effect, shook his head critically. 'Precisely what you must not do!' he told Gench. 'A valuable piece of information is lost forever.'

Gench drew his lips back across his teeth. 'That much is self-evident. Since the basic responsibility is mine, you need not trouble yourself with doubts or anxieties.'

Kosmin ignored Gench's remarks as if he had never spoken. 'In the future, please do not move or disturb an important item without consulting me.'

Gench turned a withering glare upon his ponderous colleague. 'As I interpret the scope of your work, you are to compare the languages after I have deciphered them. You are thus happily able to indulge your curiosity without incurring any immediate responsibility.'

Kosmin did not trouble to refute Gench's proposition. 'Please disturb no further data. You have carelessly destroyed an artifact. Consult me before you touch anything further.' And he moved off across the plain toward Big Purple.

Gench, hissing between his teeth, hesitated, then hastened in pursuit. Left to his own devices, Kosmin was capable of any excess. Gench told himself, 'Two can play that game!'

Most of the group now assembled stood about Big Purple, which, enormous and almost undamaged, dominated Sulwen Plain. The hull was a rough-textured lavender substance striped with four horizontal bands of corroded metal: apparently a component of the drive-system. Only a powdering of dust and crystals of frozen gas gave an intimation of its great age.

The commissioners walked around the hull, but the ports were sealed. The only access was through an opening provided by the gash along the top surface. A metallurgist found exterior rungs recessed into the hull: he tested the structure: they seemed sound. While all watched he climbed to the ruptured spine of the ship, gave a jaunty wave of the hand and disappeared.

Gench glanced covertly at Kosmin, who was considering the recessions with lips pursed in distaste. Gench marched forward and climbed. Kosmin started as if he had been stung. He grimaced, took a step forward, put one of his big legs on the first insert.

Drewe came forward to counsel caution. 'Better not risk it, Professor Kosmin; why take chances? I'll have technicians open the port, then we all can enter in safety. We are in no haste, none whatever.'

Kosmin thought, 'You're in no haste, of course not! And while you dither, that stick-insect walks inside pre-empting the best of everything!'

This indeed was Gench's intent. Clambering down through the torn hull with his suit-light on, he found himself in a marvelous environment of shapes and colors which could only be characterized, if tritely, by the word 'weird.'* Certain functional details resembled those of Earth ships, but with odd distortions and differences of proportion that were subtly jarring and disjunctive. 'Naturally, and to be expected,' Gench told himself. 'We alter environment to the convenience of our needs: the length of our tread, the reach of our arms, the sensitivity of our retinas, many other considerations. And these other races, likewise . . . Fascinating . . . I suspect that a man, confined for any length of time in this strange ship, might become seriously disturbed, if not deranged.' With great interest Gench inspected the Wasp corpses which lay sprawled along the corridors: blue-black husks, chitinous surfaces still glossy where dust had not settled. How long would corpses remain preserved, Gench wondered. Forever? Why not? At 100 degrees K, in an inert atmosphere, it was difficult to imagine changes occurring except those stimulated by cosmic rays . . . But to work. No time now for speculation! He had gained the initiative from the torpid Kosmin, and he meant to make the most of it.

One encouraging matter: there was no lack of native

---

*In Drewe's book, *Sulwen's Planet*, he remarked: 'Color is color and shape is shape; it would seem incorrect to speak of *human* shape and *human* color, and *Wasp* shape and *Wasp* color; but somehow, by some means, the distinction exists. Call me a mystic if you like. . . .'

writing. Everywhere were signs, plaques, notices in angular
interweaving lines which at first glance offered no hope
of easy decipherment. Gench was more pleased that
discouraged. The task would be challenging, but with the
aid of computers, pattern-recognizing devices, keys and
correlations derived from a study of the context in which
the symbols occurred (here indeed lay the decipherer's basic
contribution to the process) the language eventually would
be elucidated. Another matter: aboard a ship of this size
there might well exist not only a library, but rosters,
inventories, service manuals pertaining to the various
mechanisms; a wealth of material! And Gench saw his
problem to be, not the eventual process of decipherment,
but the actual presence of Professor Kosmin.

Gench shook his head fretfully. A damnable nuisance!
He must have a word with Director Drewe. Kosmin
perhaps could be assigned to another task: indexing
material to be transshipped to Earth, something of the sort.

Gench proceeded through the corridors and levels of
Big Purple, trying to locate either a central repository of
written materials or, failing this, the control center. But
the ship's architecture was not instantly comprehensible
and Gench was initially unsuccessful. Wandering back and
forth, he found himself in what appeared to be a storage
hold, stacked with cases and cartons, then, descending
a ramp, he came to the base level and an entry foyer.
The port had been forced; commissioners and technicians
were passing in and out. Gench halted in disgust, then
returned the way he had come: through the storage hold,
along corridors, up and down ramps. He began
encountering other members of the commission, and
hurried his steps to such an extent that his colleagues
turned to look after him in surprise. At last he came to
the control room, though it bore no resemblance to the
corresponding office of any Earth ship, and which in fact
Gench had passed through before without recognizing its
function.

Professor Kosmin, already on hand, glanced around at

Gench, then resumed the examination of what appeared to be a large book.

Gench marched indignantly forward. 'Professor Kosmin, I prefer that you do not disturb the source materials, or move them, as the context in which they are found may be important.'

Kosmin gave Gench a mild glare and returned to his scrutiny of the book.

'Please be extremely careful,' said Professor Gench. 'If any materials are damaged through mishandling — well, they are irreplaceable.' Gench stepped forward. Kosmin moved slightly but somehow contrived to thrust his ample haunch into Gench, and thus barred his way.

Gench glared at his colleague's back, then turned and departed the chamber in an ill-concealed huff.

He shought out Director Drewe. 'Director, may I have a word with you?'

'Certainly.'

'I fear that my investigations, and indeed the success of the entire translation program, are being compromised by the conduct of Professor Kosmin, who insists upon intruding into my scope of operation. I am sorry to trouble you with a complaint of this sort, but I feel that a decisive act now on your part will facilitate my work and ensure the integrity of our projects here.'

Director Drewe sighed. 'Professor Kosmin has taken a similar position. Something indeed must be done. Where is Kosmin now?'

'In the control chamber, thumbing through an absolutely vital element of the investigation, as if it were a discarded magazine.'

Drewe and Gench walked toward the control chamber. Gench remonstrated, 'I suggest that you use Professor Kosmin in some administrative capacity: logging, indexing, compilation, or the like, until the translation program is sufficiently advanced that he may employ his specialized talents. As of now — ha, ha! — there are no language correlatives for him to compare!'

Drewe made no comment. In the control room they found Kosmin still absorbed in the book.

'What have we here?' inquired Drewe mildly.

'Hmmm. Umph .... A highly important find. It appears to be — I may be over-optimistic — a dictionary, a word-book, a correspondence between the languages of the two races!'

'If this is the case,' declared Gench, 'I had better take charge of it at once.'

Drewe heaved a deep sigh. 'Gentlemen, temporarily, at any rate, we must arrange a division of function so that neither you, Professor Kosmin, nor you, Professor Gench, are hampered. There are two races here, two languages. Professor Kosmin, which of the two interests you the more profoundly?'

'That is difficult to say,' rumbled Kosmin. 'I am not yet acquainted with either.'

'What about you, Professor Gench?'

With his eyes fixed on the book, Gench said, 'My first emphasis will be upon the records of this ship, though naturally, when the inquiry is expanded and I assemble a staff, I will devote equal effort to the other ships.'

'Bah!' declared Kosmin, with as much emphasis as he ever permitted himself. 'I will work at this ship,' he told Drewe. 'It is more convenient. On the other hand, I would wish to insure that source material elsewhere is also handled competently. I have already reported the loss of one irreplaceable record.'

Drewe nodded. 'It seems there is no possibility of agreement, let alone cooperation. Very well.' He picked up a small metal disk. 'We will consider this a coin. This side with the two nicks we will call heads. The other will be tails. Professor Gench, be so good as to call heads or tails while the disk is in the air. If you call correctly, you may concentrate your research on the two large ships.'

He tossed the disk.

'Heads,' called Gench.

'The coin is tails,' said Drewe. 'Professor Gench, you

will survey the five black-and-white ships. Professor Kosmin, your responsibility will be the two larger ships. This seems a fair division of effort, and neither will inconvenience the other.'

Kosmin made a guttural sound. Gench scowled and bit his lip. Neither was satisfied with the decision. With each familiar with only half of the program, a third man might be appointed to supervise and coordinate the labors of both.

Drewe said, 'You both must remember that this is a survey expedition. What is required are suggestions as to how the research should be performed, not the research itself.'

Kosmion turned to examine the book he had found. Gench threw his hands in the air and strode furiously away.

5

The season seemed to be an equivalent of summer. Sulwen's Star, a glittering sequin, rose far to the southeast, slanted up into the northern sky, slanted back down into the southwest, as black shadows shifted in consonance around the wrecked hulks. The construction crews erected a pair of polyhedric bubbles as base camp and the commission moved into more comfortable quarters.

On the fourth evening, as Sulwen's Star touched the edge of the plain, Drewe called his fellow commissioners together.

'By now,' he said, 'I think we all have come to grips with the situation. I myself have done little but wander here and there. In fact, I fear I am but excess baggage on the expedition. Well — as I have said before — enough of my personal hopes and fears. What have we learned so far? There seems a consensus that both races were technically more advanced than ourselves, though this may only be an intuition. As to their technical level relative to each other — who knows? But let us have an inventory, an assessment of our mutual findings.'

The physicists expressed astonishment at the radically

different solutions to the problem of space-drive reached by the three races: man, Sea Cow, and Wasp. The chemists speculated as to the probable atmosphere utilized by Wasp and Sea Cow, and commented upon some of the new metalurgic compounds they had encountered aboard the ships. The engineers were somewhat nonplussed, having noticed unorthodox systems not readily susceptible to analysis. The biochemists could provide no immediate insight into the metabolic processes of either Wasp or Sea Cow.

Drewe called for an opinion on the languages, and the possibility of translation. Professor Gench rose to his feet, cleared his throat, only to hear the detested voice of Professor Kosmin issuing from another quarter of the room. 'As of yet,' said Kosmin, 'I have given little attention to the Sea Cow language or system of writing. The Wasps, so I have learned from Professor Hideman and Doctor Miller, lack vocal cords, or equivalent organs. They seem to have produced sound by a scraping of certain bony parts behind a resonating membrane. Their conversation, it has been suggested, sounded like a cheap violin played by an idiot child.' And Kosmin gave one of his rare oily chuckles. 'The writing corresponds to this 'speech' as much as human writing corresponds to human speech. In other words, a vibrating, fluctuating sound is transcribed by a vibrating, fluctuating line: a difficult language to decipher. Naturally, not impossible. I have made one very important find: a compendium or dictionary of Sea Cow pictographs referred to their equivalent in the Wasp written system — a proof, incidentally, that the work of translating both languages must be entrusted to a single agency, and I will formulate a scheme to this end. I welcome the help of all of you; if anyone notices a clear-cut correspondence between symbol and idea, please call it to my attention. I have entrusted to Professor Gench the first cursory examination of the Sea Cow ships, but as of yet I have not checked through his findings.' Kosmin continued a few minutes longer, then Drewe called on

Professor Gench for his report. Gench leapt to his feet, lips twitching. He spoke with great care. 'The program Professor Kosmin mentions is standard procedure. Professor Kosmin, a comparator of known languages, may well be excused for ignorance of deciphering techniques. With two such difficult languages no one need feel shame for working beyond his depth. The dictionary mentioned by Professor Kosmin is a valuable item indeed and I suggest that Director Drewe put it into safe custody or entrust it into my care. We cannot risk its abuse by untrained amateurs and dilettantes. I am even now pressing my search for a similar compendium aboard the Sea Cow ships.

'And I would like to announce a small but significant accomplishment. I have established the Sea Cow numerical system and it is much like our own. An unbroken black rectangle is zero. A single bar is one. A cross-bar is two. An inverted u, unconventionalised perhaps from a triangle, is three. A digit resembling our own two is the Sea Cow four. And so on . . . . Perhaps Professor Kosmin has established the Wasp numeration?'

Kosmin, who had been listening without expression, said, 'I have been busy with the work for which I was appointed: the formation and supervision of a decipherment program. Numbers at the moment are of no great matter.'

'I will look over your formulations,' said Gench. 'If any aspects seem well conceived, I will include them in the master program I am preparing. Here I wish to utter a testimonial to Professor Kosmin. He was urged into the commission against his better judgment; he was assigned a task for which he had no training; nonetheless he has uncomplainingly done his best, even though he is anxious to return to Earth and work he so generously interrupted in our behalf.' And Gench, with a grin and bob of the head, bowed toward Kosmin. From the other members of the commission came a spatter of restrained applause.

Kosmin rose ponderously to his feet. 'Thank you, Professor Gench.' He reflected a moment. 'I have not heard any report on the condition of Big Blue. It seems precariously balanced, but on the other hand it has remained in stasis for thousands of years. I wonder if there has been any decision as to the feasibility of boarding this ship?' He peered toward the engineers.

Director Drew responded: 'I don't think there has been any definite verdict here. For the present, I think we had better stand clear of it.'

'Unfortunate,' said Kosmin. 'It appears that the damage suffered by Big Purple destroyed the chamber which served as a repository of written materials. The corresponding location of Big Blue by some freak is quite undamaged, and I am anxious to investigage.'

Gench sat kneading his long chin.

'In due course, in due course,' said Crewe. 'Yes, Professor Gench?'

Gench frowned, unclenching his hands. He spoke slowly. 'It may interest the commission to learn that aboard Sea Cow B, the ship north of Big Purple, I have located just such a repository of Sea Cow documents, though I haven't checked the contents yet. This repository is in Room Eleven on the second deck from ground level and seems to be the only such repository known to be undamaged.'

'Interesting news,' said Drewe, squinting sidelong toward Gench. 'Interesting indeed. Well, then, on to the drive technicians: what, offhand, do you make of the Wasp and Sea Cow space-drives, vis-à-vis each other and our own?'

The meeting continued another hour. Director Drewe made a final announcement. 'Our primary goal has almost been achieved, and unless there is a pressing reason to the contrary, I think that we will start back to Earth in two days. Kindly base your thinking upon this timetable.'

6

The following morning Professor Gench continued his investigations aboard Sea Cow B. At lunch he appeared highly excited. 'I believe I have located a Wasp-Sea Cow compendium in Room Eleven of Sea Cow B! An amazing document! This afternoon I must check Sea Cow E for a similar storeroom.'

Professor Kosmin, sitting two tables distant, lowered his head over his plate.

7

Gench seemed somewhat nervous, and his fingers trembled as he constricted himself into his work-suit. He stepped out upon the plain. Directly overhead glittered Sulwen's Star. The wrecked ships stood, without human reality or relevance, like models on the bleak, flat plain.

Sea Cow E lay a mile to the south. Gench marched stiffly across the surface, from time to time glancing back at other personnel, unidentifiable in work-suits. His course took him past Big Blue and he veered so as to pass close under the great broken ship. He turned another quick glance over his shoulder: no one in view. He glanced up at the precariously balanced hulk. 'Safe? Safe as mother's milk.' He walked north toward Sea Cow B, and presently stood by the crushed hull. 'The entrance? Yes . . . . To the second deck then . . . . Surprising architecture. What peculiar coloring . . . . Hmm. Room Eleven. The numerals are clear enough. This is the one, the single bar. And here the two.' Kosmin proceeded along the corridor. 'Six . . . seven . . . . Strange. Ten. Where are eight and nine? Well, no matter. Unlucky numbers perhaps. Here is ten, and here eleven. Aha.' Kosmin pushed aside the panel and entered Chamber Eleven.

8

Sulwen's Star slanted down to the gray horizon and past; darkness came almost instantly to the plain. Neither Gench nor Kosmin appeared for the evening meal. The steward called Director Drewe's attention to the fact.

Drewe considered the two empty seats. 'I suppose we must send out to find them. Professor Gench will no doubt be exploring Big Blue. I presume we will find Professor Kosmin hard at work in Sea Cow B.'

9

Professor Gench had suffered a broken collar-bone, contusions, and shock from the blow of the heavy beam which Professor Kosmin — so Gench claimed — had arranged to fall upon whoever might enter Big Blue's control cabin.

'Not so!' boomed Professor Kosmin, both of whose legs had been broken as a result of his fall through the floor of Chamber Eleven on the second deck of Sea Cow B. 'You were warned expressly not to set foot in Big Blue. How could I set a trap in a place you were forbidden to visit? What of the detestable pitfall by which you hoped to kill me? But I am too strong for you! I caught the floor and broke my fall! I survived your worst!'

'You survive your own stupidity,' sneered Gench. 'Sea Cows, with two fingers on each of four arms, use base eight in their enumerations. You went into Chamber Nine, not Chamber Eleven. A person as obtuse and as murderous as yourself has no place in the field of science! I am lucky to be alive!'

'Were my legs still sound I would stomp on you for the roach you are!' shouted Professor Kosmin.

Director Drewe intervened. 'Gentlemen, calm yourselves. Reproaches are futile; remorse is far more appropriate. You must realize that neither of you will head the decipherment program.'

'Indeed? And why not?' snorted Gench.

'Under the circumstances I fear that I can recommend neither of you.'

'Then who will be appointed?' demanded Kosmin. 'The field is not crowded with able men, and who else is available here and now?'

Drewe shrugged. 'As a mathematician, I may say that deciphering appeals to me as a fascinating exercise in logic. I might be persuaded to accept the post myself. To be candid, it is probably my only chance for continued association with the project.' Director Drewe bowed politely and left the room.

Professor Gench and Professor Kosmin were silent for several minutes. Then Gench said, 'Peculiar. Very peculiar indeed. I arranged no pitfall in Chamber Nine. I admit I had noted that the panel could be opened from one direction only, from the corridor . . . . A person venturing into Chamber Nine might find himself in a humiliating position . . . . Strange.'

'Hmm,' rumbled Kosmin. 'Strange indeed . . . . '

There was another period of silence as the two men reflected. Then Kosmin said, 'Of course, I am not altogether innocent. I conceived that if you ventured into Big Blue against orders you would incur a reprimand. But I propped up no beam.'

'Most peculiar,' said Professor Gench. 'A puzzling situation . . . . A possibility suggests itself —'

'Yes?'

'Why kill us?'

'To the mathematical mind the most elegant solution is the simplest,' reflected Professor Kosmin.

'Factoring out the competition,' mused Professor Gench, 'a cancelling of the unknowns.'

DOVER SPARGILL'S GHASTLY FLOATER

DOVER SPARGILL, aged twenty-one, paced the hearth, slapping his jodhpurs with a riding crop. Hunched in a wingback chair off the side, Attorney James Offbold turned up his eyes as if seeking diving support.

Dover paused in midstride; Attorney Offbold's expression at once became attentive: this insufferable young ass represented thirty thousand dollars a year in fees. Otherwise, Mr. Offbold would have sweated in Guyana before crossing the street at Dover Spargill's bidding.

'That's the whole affair, then?' inquired Dover with a smart slap at his boots.

'That's the entire document, Mr. Spargill, and may I offer my heartfelt congratulations?'

Dover paused in his stride, turned his head in inquiry. 'Congratulations? What for?'

'Now you are of age, you become one of the richest men in the world.'

'Oh, the money.' Dover flicked his riding-crop to the side. Wealth occupied small place in his thoughts, the gesture implied. 'Certainly it's a help; I won't have to worry about making it myself. Although I sometimes think my father was rather unimaginative; time and time again I've pointed out ways of doubling his fortune.'

Offbold coughed, recalling tiger-eyed old Howard Spargill and his canny manipulations. 'Well, I can't quite agree with you, Mr. Spargill; your father was certainly the smartest business man of his day. He started out a prospector and wound up owning Moon Mines, Inc., almost a third of the entire moon.'

Dover shook his head, pursed his lips. 'He also allowed Thornton Bray to organize the other holdings into the Lunar Mineral Cooperative, when he could easily have bought up the claims himself.'

Offbold remarked rather loftily, 'Don't you think that gaining title to a third of the moon is enough? An area larger than all of Europe?'

Dover frowned. ' "Enough" is a word inapplicable in a modern commercial context, as I think you should be the first to acknowledge, Mr. Offbold.'

Offbold made a grumbling noise in his throat, sat staring glumbly into the fire while Dover proceeded to develop the argument, emphasizing salient points with motions of the riding crop. He explained that in the upper financial reaches, the accumulation of wealth was a game requiring little more skill than the manipulation of a pinball machine. Offbold nodded jerkily, finally snapped the lock on his brief-case and rose to his feet.

'Now then, Mr. Spargill, I'll say goodbye; you'll probably have plans for dinner.'

Dover conducted him to the door. Offbold turned for a last set of reminders.

'No doubt, Mr. Spargill, you'll be approached by promoters and confidence men; I scarcely need recommend caution to one of your — ' he winced ' — acumen.'

Dover nodded briskly.

'But in any event, I will perform the formality. The mines are capably managed by the existing staff; the terrestrial interests are under the stewardship of Calmus Associates. I strongly advise against any changes or any new undertakings. If you are approached by anyone wanting money on any pretext whatever — refer him to me, and I will tick him off properly.'

Offbold continued on these lines for a minute or two, while Dover, listening with half-closed eyes, swung his riding crop back and forth.

Offbold finally shook hands and departed. Dover watched him out to his cab.

'Bumbling old idiot . . . . ' He slapped at his boots. 'He means well, no doubt.'

Thornton Bray, chairman of the Board of Directors for Lunar Mines Cooperative, was a large man, florid and moist as sliced watermelon. He had prominent eyes without lashes; his cheeks were smooth and plump as a baby's buttocks. Tucking the signed agreement in his pocket, he shook his head with a rueful smirk.

'Yes sir, a chip off the old block. I'm afraid I overshot myself trying to out-deal you.'

Dover let the smoke of an expensive cigar trickle from the corner of his mouth. He adopted a careless manner, as if to deprecate his victory over Bray and Lunar Mineral Cooperative.

'Yes, sir,' went on Bray, 'you're a big man now. You'll go down in history. First man holding title to an entire world. Think of it! Fifty-nine million square miles! Lord of all you survey!'

Dover glanced to the three-foot globe of the moon on his desk. The surface was divided into irregular areas tined in gray-blue and gray, distinguishing Moon Mines from the Lunar Mineral Cooperative.

'Yes, she'll be all one color now. I wonder . . . . ' He paused. 'I supposed it would hardly be in good taste.'

'What's that?'

'Change the name from "Moon" to "Spargill." '

Bray reflected. 'You'd have your work cut out for you.' He shook hands, with a hearty jerking motion. 'Well, I wish you luck, Mr. Spargill.' He gave his head an admiring shake. 'Not that you need it, with that whipsaw brain of yours.'

Dover gestured affably with his cigar. 'I see a good thing. I go after it, I get it.'

'Good-day then, Mr. Spargill.'

Dover twitched his hand in a jaunty salute, turned back to the globe.

A moment later the videophone buzzed.

Dover spoke over his shoulder. 'Yes?'

'Mr. Offbold, sir,' came the voice of his confidential secretary.

Dover yawned, returned to his desk. 'I'll speak to him.'

The screen revealed a face contorted by anger and desperation. 'Quick,' cried Mr. Offbold, 'you haven't signed any papers, have you?'

Dover put his feet on the desk, flicked the ash from his cigar. 'I've just concluded an advantageous deal, if that's what you mean. Very far-reaching.'

Offbold's face sagged. 'Tell me the worst . . . . '

'Moon Mines, Inc., now is legal owner to 59 million square miles, 42 billion cubic miles, 5×10^{19} tons of satellite. In short, we've bought out the Cooperative. I'm sole owner to the moon.'

Offbold's eyes brimmed with tears. 'Tell me, what did you pay? How much?'

'No small sum,' admitted Dover. 'But I've been to the moon, I've seen the ore reserves on our land and on the Cooperative land and I'll tell you, Offbold, we've come out to the good.'

'How much?'

'Oh – ' Dover puffed hard at his cigar ' – 200 million cash.'

Offbold put his hand to his forehead.

'And the Antarctic Energy interest.'

'*Oh!*'

Dover inquired with asperity. 'What's the matter with you, Offbold?'

Offbold heaved a deep sigh. 'Now you own the moon, what are you going to do with it?'

'Why, continue mining it, naturally.'

'You young fool!' roared Offbold. 'Don't you ever read the papers?'

'Certainly, whenever I have time.'

'Well, take time now!' The screen went dark.

'Miss Foresythe,' called Dover.

'Yes, Mr. Spargill?'

'The afternoon journal, if you please.'

The screen flickered. Dover's eyes went to the lead story.

SCIENCE UNVEILS NEW BOMBSHELL
TRANSMUTATION PROCESS
ANNOUNCED

A method for mass conversion of one element into another has been announced today by Frederick Dexter, chairman of the Applied Research Foundation. Eminent minds claim the discovery will bring about social changes comparable to the Industrial Revolution.

Dexter made the historic announcement at a press conference this morning. 'The device operates on a self-sustaining principle; that is to say, no outside energy is required, provided that a correct internal balancing according to established atomic theory is maintained. A condition equivalent to a temperature of hundreds of millions of degrees is used, but the energy produced — by either fusion or fission — is absorbed by the balancing process, and the cell remains at near-room temperature.'

Dexter revealed that the Foundation itself will manufacture and distribute the transmutation units. Production will begin at once, Dexter announced, in sizes varying from household devices up to monsters capable of gulping many tons a minute.

Dexter was asked as to the technological and economic effects of the discovery. 'It is my opinion,' he said, 'that we are entering a new Golden Age. Platinum will be as cheap as iron; we can now utilize the wastes and slag piles of the already antiquated chemical purification systems to obtain an abundance of pure materials. Mines of course will be — '

Dover said politely, 'You may turn off the screen, Miss Foresythe.'

He walked slowly to the three-foot globe, caused it to spin, and the pocked surface rasped the palm of his hand. '59 million square miles,' mused Dover. '42 billion — '

'Mr. Spargill,' came the voice of his secretary. 'Mr. Offbold is back on the screen.'

'Yes,' said Dover. 'I'll see him.'

Mr. Offbold had himself under restraint; only the swelling

of his neck betrayed the cost at which control had been achieved. He spoke in a labored voice, each word carefully enunciated.

'Mr. Spargill, it is my duty to reveal to you the exact state of your affairs. First, Moon Mine is worth nothing. Nil. Your new acquisition, the Lunar Mineral Cooperative, is likewise valueless.'

'But — I own the whole satellite!' protested Dover.

Mr. Offbold's eyes glittered, his lip curled tartly. 'You could show title to the entire Magellanic Cloud, and it wouldn't affect your bank credit a nickel's worth.'

Dover mulled over the situation.

'You could not sell the entire moon for ten dollars,' barked Offbold. 'No, excuse me, I take that back. No doubt there are spendthrift college boys who would offer you ten, perhaps twenty dollars, if only for the unique distinction of owning the moon. If you receive any such offers, I advise you to close; it is the only way in which the moon has transactional value. So. We write off Moon Mines, Lunar Cooperative, and Antarctic Energy from your assets. Now — 200 million dollars cash.

'There is perhaps 70 or 80 million dollars fluid, in various depreciation, building, amortization funds, etcetera. I have made a rough calculation, and find that when you have sold other holdings sufficient to pay the balance you will have left — ' he paused impressively ' — the South Sahara Pest Control Agency at Timbuctoo, and a considerable acreage in North Arizona, both taken by your father in payment of otherwise uncollectible debts.'

'Sell them both,' Dover directed him. 'Sell everything. Pay all the bills and deposit the balance to my personal account.' He added in a brave voice, 'Everything is turning out very well, just as I planned, in fact . . . . '

'I fail to understand you,' declared Offbold icily.

Dover's voice came hollowly. 'Well, every once in a while a shaking down is good for a great organization. Tones it up, so to speak . . . . '

Offbold lapsed into the vernacular. 'You got shook

down, Mr. Spargill, *you* got shook down.'

Roger Lambro, during a mid-afternoon conversation with Miss Deborah Fowler on the Tivoli Terrace, asked, 'Where in the world is Dover Spargill these days? Haven't seen the chap in ages.'

Miss Fowler absently shook her head. 'He's dropped out of the picture. I've heard rumours . . . . ' She stopped short, unwilling to pass on unpleasant gossip.

Roger Lambro was not quite so delicate. 'Oh?'

She twirled the stem of her Martini glass. 'Well — they say that after he pulled that ghastly floater, he went out to live on his property.' She raised her beautiful eyes to where the moon hung pale as an oyster in the afternoon sky. 'Just think, Roger, perhaps he's up there right now, looking down on us . . . . '

Thornton Bray stood on the marble plaza of his villa at Lake Maggiore, an after-dinner Armagnac in one hand, a Rose Panatela Suprema in the other. He was entertaining a group of business associates with an anecdote of his business career.

' — I might have been more charitable except this young ass, not dry behind the ears, thought all the time he was doing me. *Me*, Thornton Bray!' Bray laughed quietly. 'Thought he was getting something for nothing. So I played him along; after all, business is business. He made the break, I followed through . . . Yes, sir, I wish I could have seen his face when he first felt the clinch.'

'Speaking of the moon,' said one of his friends, 'she certainly looks fine tonight. Can't say as I've ever seen her looking quite so — well, calm, pearly.'

Thornton Bray glanced up to the full moon. 'Yes, she's beautiful. From down here, that is. If you've ever mined up there, you come back to Earth with different ideas. A devilish place, bleak, arid.'

'Funny color to it,' observed another member of the party. 'Green and blue and pink, all at once.'

Bray remonstrated playfully. 'Come now, Jonesy. You've been dipping your beak more than is good for you . . . Have another? By Golly, I think I'll join you.'

Cornelius Armitage, professor of Astronomy at Hale University, muttered waspishly under his breath, wiped the eyepiece of the telescope with a bit of floss.

A teaching assistant sat nearby counting stars in a sky-sample. 'What's the trouble?'

'Steam in the lens, a frightful condition. The moon looks all fuzzy.' He inspected the glass. 'There, that's better.'

He bent once more to his observations.

The teaching assistant looked up at a new sound. Professor Armitage was sitting bolt upright, his eyeglasses on the table, rubbing his eyes, blinking. 'I've been reading far too much; got to take it a little easier.'

'All done for the night?' inquired the teaching assistant.

Professor Armitage nodded wearly. 'I'm just too tired and bleary-eyed.'

Lieutenant MacLeod, overlooking a student's work at the Maritime Institute, shook his head indulgently. 'Those figures would set us three hundred miles inland. You've probably failed to correct for refraction.'

Cadet Glasskamp set his lips rebelliously. The problem was futile in any event; celestial navigation was seldom used in this day of loran and automatic piloting. Lunar occultation of stars to determine Greenwich time was three centuries antiquated; the exercise was no more than drudgery.

Lieutenant MacLeod admitted as much, but he claimed that working the difficult old systems clarified the primary concepts of hour angle, declination, right ascension, local time, and the like, as did none of the modern short-cut methods.

Cadet Glasskamp bent over his problem. Twenty minutes later he looked up. 'I can't find anything wrong here. Might have been an error in the observation.'

'Nonsense,' said the lieutenant. 'I caught the sight myself.' Nevertheless, he checked on Glasskamp's figures, once, twice, a third time, and finally opening the Nautical Almanac, calculated the time of occultation.

He chewed his lip in amazement. 'Twenty-two minutes? I don't believe it. That shot was right on the nose.'

'Perhaps you didn't allow for refraction of the star's light around the moon.'

Lieutenant MacLeod gave Cadet Glasskamp a pitying look. 'Refraction occurs when a light passes through an atmosphere. There's no atmosphere on the moon—although if there were — ' he calculated under his breath ' — the moon moves half a degree an hour, that's thirty minutes. Earth atmosphere refracts a thousand seconds; if there were an atmosphere dense as Earth's on the moon, you'd have to double it, light passing through twice. Two thousand. Say twelve thousand — that's twenty minutes. If so — that would create forty chronological minutes, at half a degree per hour. Apparently,' said the lieutenant jocularly, 'we've discovered that the moon has an atmosphere roughly half as dense as the Earth's.'

Sunday morning breakfast in the home of Sir Brampton Pasmore moved along its usual lazy routine. Sir Brampton read a favorite technical journal with his kippers; Lady Iris scanned the *Times Magazine*.

Lady Iris uttered an amused exclamation. 'Here's something in your field, my dear.' She read. ' "Does the Moon Have an Atmosphere? Strange Signs and Portents." '

'Pooh,' scoffed Sir Brampton. 'I marvel at the *Times* for publishing that yellow sensational balderdash. Expect that stuff from the Americans . . . .'

Lady Iris knitted her brows. 'They seem perfectly serious. They speak of meteor trails appearing.'

'Ridiculous,' said Sir Brampton, returning to his paper. 'It hasn't been ten years since the moon was extensively explored for minerals, before transmuters, of course. There certainly was no atmosphere then; why should there be now?'

Lady Iris shook her head doubtfully. 'Couldn't someone give the moon an atmosphere?'

'Impractical, my dear,' Sir Brampton murmured.

'I don't see why.'

Sir Brampton laid aside his paper. 'It's a scientific matter, dear, that I'm not sure you'd understand.'

Lady Iris bridled sharply. 'Are you by any chance suggesting —'

'No, naturally not,' Sir Brampton said hurriedly. 'What I meant was . . . Oh, well, then it's a matter of escape velocity of a celestial body, and the molecular motion of gases. Lunar gravity is insufficiently powerful to retain an atmosphere, at least for any length of time; the molecules move at sufficient speed to escape into space. Hydrogen would whiff off at once. Oxygen and nitrogen — well, I believe they'd probably last longer, perhaps years, but eventually they'd escape. So you see, an atmosphere on the moon just isn't practical.'

Lady Iris tapped her paper with a stubborn finger. 'It said in the *Times* there's an atmosphere. That means it's there. The *Times* is never wrong. Why doesn't somebody drop by and find out for sure?'

Sir Brampton sighed. 'The moon doesn't interest anyone any more, my dear. Martian ruins are the current excitement. The moon is uncomfortable and dangerous, there's nothing to be learned, and now that transmutation supplies all our mineral wants, there's no reason whatever to visit the moon. . . . Besides, I understand that some crank with legal title discourages trespassing; he has a special patrol that turns back visitors.'

'Well, well, well,' breathed lovely Deborah Fowler Lambro to her husband Roger. 'Remember Dover Spargill? Just look at this!'

She handed across the bulletin from the news-facsimile.

'Moon being readied for habitation, announces Dover Spargill, owner of the moon . . . .'

Lady Iris looked at Sir Brampton with glowing eyes. 'I told

you so,' said she, and Sir Brampton crouched behing the
Report of the Royal Astrophysical Society.

Thornton Bray walked back and forth, hands behind his
back. Was it possible . . . No, of course not. And yet . . .
Dover Spargill had been so innocent a sheep, so succulent
for the plucking.

He reached for the videophone, dialed his attorney.
'Herman, remember when we first organized the Lunar
Cooperative?'

'All of twenty-five years ago,' mused Herman Birth, a tall
lemon-colored man with the flat-topped face of a falcon.

'There was an old duffer, dead now, who refused to sign
up. He only held a few square miles, in Aristillus crater, I
believe. When we sold Lunar Co-op to Spargill, that
particular parcel was not included. I wonder what the status
of that claim is now?'

Birth turned his head, spoke a few words to someone out
of the range of vision, returned to Bray. 'What do you make
of this atmosphere talk?'

Bray curled his lips. 'Eyewash. Where would it come from?
Moon surface is a thirteenth of Earth surface; there'd be
billions and billions of tons.'

'Spargill might be using transmuters.'

'Suppose he is? Do you have any conception of the size
of a project like that? The moon's a big place. The heaviest
transmuter I know of has a capacity of a hundred tons a
minute and that's chicken feed.'

'He might have built special installations.'

'Where would he get the money? I know on reliable
information that he was cleaned out when he took over Lunar
Co-op . . . Just a minute, I'll call the Applied Research
Foundation and make some inquiries.'

He dialled rapidly, and a moment later was looking into
a cautious round face. 'Hello, Sam.'

Sam Abbot nodded. 'What can I do for you, Bray?'

'I want a little confidential information, Sam.'

'What's on your mind?'

'Has Applied Research sold Dover Spargill any transmuters?'

Sam Abbot's face crinkled in a sudden broad grin. 'I'll give you a straight answer, Bray: not a one. Not a single one.'

Bray blinked. 'How do you account for the talk of an atmosphere on the moon?'

Abbot shrugged. 'I don't account for it; that's not my job.'

Bray, muttering in irritation, returned to Herman Birch. Birch nodded a wise head. 'That claim was open. I've just filed in your name.'

Bray clamped his heavy mouth. 'Good. Now I've got a legal right to visit my claim. Rent me a fast ship . . . . '

The radar alarm sounded eighty thousand miles out from the moon. The pilot threw down the switch. A harsh voice said, 'You are approaching my property.'

Bray pulled himself to the speaker. 'I'm going out to my own property, the Niobe claim in Aristillus Crater. If you interfere with me, I'll call the Space Patrol.'

The voice made no answer; Bray visualized the frantic search through block maps and title deeds. Ten minutes passed.

A new voice said, 'Aboard approaching ship: who is claimant to the Niobe claim?'

'Me. Thornton Bray.'

'Oh. Bray,' said the voice in a different tone. 'This is Spargill. Why didn't you say who you were? Drop on down to home camp.'

'Where are you?' inquired Bray cautiously.

'We're in Hesiodus, at the south point of Mare Nubium — beside Pitatus. The old Goldenrod workings.'

The camp in Hesiodus Crater occupied a typical old mining compound: a large dome of plastic anchored into the rock by a web of cables which also served to contain the air-pressure from within. The pilot landed the ship and Bray, already clad in a space suit, jumped out to the surface.

Three men approached; under the faceplate of the first, Bray recognized the face of Dover Spargill.

Dover waved. 'How are you, Bray? Nice of you to drop out . . . What's all this about the Niobe claim?'

Bray explained. ' . . . and since the land was ownerless, I decided I had better snap it up,' he finished.

As he spoke he examined his surroundings. The lunar sky, which he remembered as black, was a deep hyacinth blue. 'Looks like all the talk of a moon atmosphere is true.'

Dover nodded. 'Oh yes . . . Come along over to the dome.' He led Bray across a flat of crushed pumice. A mile behind rose the walls of the crater, tall irregular spires. At the base of the walls Bray discerned a row of black cubes.

'What's the pressure here now, Spargill?'

'Got her up to seven pounds.'

'Barometric? That is to say, against a mercury column?'

'Oh my no. A misleading statement. Seven pounds against a spring scale.'

Bray snorted delicately. 'Tremendous waste of money, Spargill.'

'Do you really think so? I'm sorry to hear you say that; I rather hoped something useful might eventuate . . . . Look there.' He pointed against the wall of the dome. 'Geraniums. Growing outside on the moon. Never thought you'd see a sight like that in the old days, did you, Bray?'

'Mmmph. What good are geraniums? Monumental waste. As fast as you make atmosphere it'll dissipate into space. Not enough travity here.'

Dover closed the outer hatch on Bray and himself. They removed their suits, and Dover conducted Bray to the main lounge, where a dozen men and women sat reading, talking, playing cards, drinking beer.

'You've got quite a colony here,' said Bray in a mystified voice. 'Do they work for nothing?'

Dover laughed shortly. 'Of course not . . . . This is only a small part of our operation. We've got units going at almost all the old mines . . . . Have some coffee?'

Bray declined brusquely. 'Exactly what are your plans, if I may ask?'

Dover leaned back in the chair. 'It's a long story, Bray.

First, I hope you'll let bygones be bygones. I suppose I fleeced you pretty thoroughly when I took Lunar Co-op away from you, eh?'

Bray said in a strangled voice, 'You fleeced *me*? . . . . Well, let it go. I want to hear about this — ' he jerked a thumb toward the sky ' — this mad stunt of yours.'

Dover said soothingly, 'It's probably not so impractical as you think. Consider the future, Bray. Do you see what I see?'

'Forests, meadows, grass-lands. Moon, the green planet! Trees five hundred feet tall! We're filling craters with water right now. Moon, the world of a million lakes! In five more years we'll have thirteen pounds pressure, and we'll be living out-of-doors.'

'Waste, waste, waste,' intoned Bray. 'You'll never get a stable atmosphere.'

Dover scratched his head. 'Well, of course I may be mistaken — '

'Sure you are,' said Bray bluffly. 'I hate to see you making a fool of yourself, Dover. For old time's sake, I'm willing to — '

'My theory,' explained Dover, 'was that the composition of the atmosphere determined how fast it dissipated. Naturally we expect to make adjustments for a long time to come.'

'Well, of course — '

'But actually, we're building a special kind of atmosphere, rather different from Earth's.'

Bray's nostrils flared in interest. 'How so?'

'Well, in the first place, xenon replaces nitrogen. Specific gravity of 4.5, as against 1 for nitrogen. Then we're using the heaviest possible isotopes for oxygen, carbon and nitrogen, and deuterium rather than hydrogen for our water. It all works out to a pretty dense atmosphere — physiologically identical to Earth air, but about three and a half times as dense. So our vapor loss into space will be minimized to almost nothing.'

Bray cracked his knuckles. Something must be wrong.

Dover was saying, 'We could easily make the atmosphere even denser, if we so desire — by substituting radon for the xenon.'

'Radon! My God! — you'd fry!'

Dover smilingly shook his head. 'Radon has many isotopes, not all significantly radioactive. On Earth we're familiar only with the breakdown product of radium, thorium, actinium. But radon's disadvantage is that it's too heavy. A gust of wind would bowl a man off his feet, like hitting him with a sack of sawdust.'

'Hm . . . Interesting,' remarked Bray absently. Some means must be found to repair what he now recognized as an error in judgment: allowing Dover to become sole owner. Bray, as a lunar property holder, was entitled to a certain advisory status. Reason, sweet reason, was the operational phrase.

He explored the ground cautiously. 'What do you propose to do with all this property?' He winked slyly. 'Sell it at a fancy figure?'

Dover made a deprecatory motion. 'I suppose that an unprincipled man, by subdividing and selling, could easily become a multibillionaire . . . Did you say something?'

'No,' said Bray, swallowing hard. 'I just coughed.'

'But I have a different end in view. I want to see the moon become a garden suburb of Earth — a park, a residential area. Certainly I want no cheap box housing projects on the moon, no tourist hotels . . . . '

'Naturally you're using Applied Research transmuters?'

'Of course. Are there any other kind?'

'No, not that I know of.'

'There are special mammoth units built specially for this project. We've got two thousand in operation already. We push them under a mountain, bulldoze rock into the hoppers. Every week two more units go into operation; there's a tremendous amount of material to transmute, and we're on a fifteen-year schedule. That means that we've got to average three billion tons a day, for atmosphere alone; so far, we're up to the mark.'

Bray grimaced, clenched his fist. Observing Dover's questioning look, he blurted, 'Sam Abbot at Applied Research is a damn liar. Said he never sold you any transmuters.'

'But that's correct, we're using them free, on a loan basis.'

'Free!'

Dover turned out his hands in a gesture of frankness. 'That's the only way I could undertake the project. Buying our Lunar Co-op took almost everything I had. But my father originally endowed the Foundation, and there was a certain sense of obligation. In a way, we're partners in the deal.' He nodded towards the other occupants of the lounge. 'All Foundation staff. They're sinking the profits from producing the transmuters into the scheme; of course they'll get it all back ten-fold.'

'But you still retain control?'

'All except the Niobe claim.' Dover laughed jovially. 'You slipped one over on me there. I thought that I was sole owner, and now I fear that . . . Well, no matter.'

Bray cleared his throat. 'As you say, we're the sole owners, you and I. I imagine we should form some kind of supervisory board to protect our interests so to speak.'

Dover seemed surprised. 'Do you think that such a formality is necessary? After all, the Niobe claim — '

Bray said portentously, 'I'm afraid I'll have to insist.'

Dover frowned. 'I don't think the claim will impose as much of a burden on your time as you fear.'

Bray raised his eyebrows. 'How so?'

'Well — ' Dover hesitated ' — you haven't visited your holdings yet?'

'No. All I know that it's a ten-mile square block in the floor of Aristillus.'

Dover got up. 'Perhaps we had better fly up and take a look at it.'

In a small stub-winged flier they rose up out of Hesiodus, flew north along the shore of Mare Nubium.

'All good basalt,' said Dover. 'A few years of weathering should produce a magnificent red soil. We're experimenting with bacteria to hasten the process.'

Sinus Medii passed below, and the eastern littoral of Mare Vaporum. Ahead loomed the great crags of the Appenines, a little to the left was the great crater Eratosthenes.

Bray craned his neck. 'Surely that's not water?'

'Oh yes,' smiled Dover. 'Lake Eratosthenes and one other for primary evaporation points. Water will come rather slower than the air; the moon will be a dry world for quite some time yet.'

Bray said bluffly, 'I believe I'll put up a big resort hotel on my property — amusement park, big casino, dog-racing.' He nudged Dover waggishly. 'Thank God, there's no blue laws out here, eh Dover?'

Dover said stiffly, 'We hope to govern ourselves, with the aid of our native good taste.'

'Well,' said Bray, 'if I had a bit more land, I wouldn't be forced to make do on so little. Personally I don't like the idea, but what'll you have? There's just the Niobe claim, and no more. I hope it doesn't turn out an eyesore . . . Perhaps if you'd make me a good deal for old time's sake, let me buy back a chunk of Lunar Cooperative for, say —'

Dover shook his head. 'I'm afraid that's impossible.'

Bray snapped shut his jaw. 'Then I'll have to do the best I can at Aristillus. A skyscraper, maybe. We'll make it the hot-spot of the moon. Sort of a Latin Quarter, a Barbary Coast.'

'Sounds interesting.'

The Appenines stabbed up at them from below. 'Beautiful mountain scenery,' said Dover. 'Remarkable. Wait twenty or thirty years, and you'll really see something. That's Palus Putredinus below, and ahead, those three craters —'

'Lake Aristillus,' said Dover absently.

Bray froze in his seat. The gleam of water was unmistakable.

'A beautiful crater,' said Dover. 'And it makes a beautiful lake, ten thousand feet deep, I believe.'

The flier circled over the placid blue surface. A small island protruded from the center.

Bray found his voice. 'Do you mean to say,' he demanded, 'that you've submerged my property under ten thousand feet of water?'

Dover nodded. 'See there . . . . ' He pointed to a cascade of water tumbling down the eastern wall. 'Back along that rill sixty units are turning out water and xenon. I'll name the river after you, if you'd like. Bray River . . . . From your point of view, rather a sad coincidence that we decided on Eratosthenes and Aristillus for our first lakes. I didn't have the heart to break the news to you back at the camp.'

Bray roared. 'This is insufferable! You've flooded my property, you've — '

Dover said in a conciliatory voice, 'Naturally we had no idea that the property was not ours; if I had known that you wanted to build a 'hot spot' — as you call it — I'd never have planned the lake.'

'I'll sue, I'll collect damages!'

'Damages?' asked Dover in a pained voice. 'Why surely — '

Bray rolled his eyes in fury. 'I can prove that the property was worth millions, that — '

'Er — how long ago did you come into possession of the Niobe claim?'

Bray subsided suddenly. 'Well, as a matter of fact — It makes no difference! You're guilty of — '

'Surely it's obvious, Mr. Bray, that you filed claim on property already under water.' Dover scratched his head. 'I suppose the claim is legal enough. Can't see what you'll do with your property, though, Mr. Bray. You might try stocking it with trout . . . . '

PHALID'S FATE

1

AFTER TWO MONTHS of unconsciousness, Ryan Wratch opened his eyes. Or more accurately, he folded into tight pleats two hundred tiny shutters of dirty purplish-brown tissue and thereupon looked out on a new world.

For perhaps twenty seconds, Wratch stared at delirium made tangible, madness beyond all expression. He heard a high-pitched staccato, a vague somehow familiar shrillness, then once more lost consciousness.

Dr. Plogetz, who was short and stocky, with a smooth pink face and white hair, straightened up from the thing on the table, put down his lensed instrument.

He turned to the man in the gray-green uniform who wore the three golden sunbursts of a Sector Commander. The Commander was thin, brown and tough, with a rather harsh and humorless expression.

'Organically, everything is in excellent shape,' said the doctor. 'The nerve junctures are healed, the blood adapters function beautifully — '

He broke off as the black alien shape on the table — a thing with a large, insect-looking head, a long black carapace extending over its back like a cloak, oddly jointed legs — stirred one of its arm-members: these, rubbery tentacles with mottled gray undersides, haphazard grayish finger flaps.

Dr. Plogetz picked up his digital enlarger, inspected the organs inside the chitin-plated torso.

'Reflex,' he murmured. 'As I was saying, there's no dout

it's a healthy creature organically. Psychologically —' he pursed his lips '— naturally it's too early to warrant speculation.'

Sector Commander Sandion nodded.

'When will it — or he, I should say — regain consciousness?'

Dr. Plogetz pressed his wrist band. A voice sounded from the tiny speaker.

'Yes, doctor?'

'Bring in a sonfrane hood — let's see — about a number twenty-six.' Then he said to Sandion: 'I'll give him a stimulant — revive him at once. But first —'

A nurse entered — a dark-haired, blue-eyed, very beautiful young lady — bringing the specified hood.

'Now, Miss Elder,' said Dr. Plogetz, 'adjust it completely around the optic slit. Take care not to bind those little gill-flaps at the side of the head.'

Plogetz took a deep breath before continuing with his explanation.

'I want to minimize the shock to his brain,' explained the doctor. 'The visual images will be confusing, to say the least. The Phalid's color spectrum, remember, is twice as long and the field of vision is three or four times as wide as that of the average human. It has two hundred eyes, and the impressions of two hundred separate optic units must be integrated. A human brain accommodates two images, but it's questionable whether it could do the same for two hundred. That's why we've left intact a bit of the creature's former brain — the lobe coordinating the various images.' Here Plogetz paused long enough to give the complex black head an appraising glance.

'Even with this help, Wratch's sight will be a new and fantastic thing,' he mused. 'All pictures seen through Phalid eyes and integrated by that bit of Phalid brain will be something never before envisioned by a human mind.'

'No doubt it will be a tremendous strain on his nerves,' observed Sandion.

The doctor nodded, inspected the blindfold.

'Two cc. of three per cent arthrodine,' he said to the

nurse. Then again to Sandion: 'We've left intact another lobe of the former brain, the speech information and recognition center, a matter probably as essential as his visual organization. It was necessary to excise the rest of the brain tissue — a pity in some ways. The memories and associations would be invaluable to your young man, and the Phalids undoubtedly have special senses I'd be interested in hearing about and researching . . . Ah, yes,' said the doctor as the nurse handed him a hypodermic. 'Peculiar affair. I can graft a human brain into this — creature; whereas if I transferred a brain into another human body, I'd kill that brain.' He gave the empty hypodermic back to the nurse, wiped his hands. 'Strange world we live in, isn't it, Commander?'

Commander Sandion, with a quick sardonic glance, nodded.

'Strange world indeed, Doctor.'

Personality, the sense of his own distinctive ego, drifted up from a murky limbo. For the second time, Ryan Wratch folded the two hundred little screens in the eyeslit that ran more than halfway around what was now *his* head. He saw nothing but blackness, felt an oppression before his vision.

He lay quietly, remembering the crazy welter of light and shape and unknown fragments of color he had seen before, and for the moment was content to lie in the dark.

Gradually he became aware of new sensations in the functioning of his body. He was no longer breathing. Instead, a continuous current of air blew along throbbing conduits and out the gill flaps in his head. At what point he inhaled, he could not determine.

He became conscious of a peculiar tactile sensitivity, an exact perception of texture. The sensitive areas were on the underside and tips of his arm-members, with the rest of his body rather less sensible. In this way he knew the exact quality of the cloth under him, felt the weave, the lay of the threads, the essential, absolute intrinsic nature of the fiber.

He heard strident harsh sounds. Suddenly, and with a feeling of shock, he realized that these were human voices. They were calling his name.

'Wratch! Do you understand me? Move your right arm if you do.'

Wratch moved his right arm-member.

'I understand you very well,' he said. 'Why can't I see?' He spoke instinctively, without thought, not listening to his own voice. Something strange caused him to stop and ponder. The words had coursed smoothly from his brain to the bone at the sounding diaphragm in his chest. When he spoke, the voice sounded natural on the hair tendrils under the carapace at his back — his hearing members. But after an instant's groping, Wratch's brain realized that the voice had not been human. It had been a series of drones and buzzes, very different from the one which had questioned him.

Now he tried to enunciate the language of men, and found it impossible. His speech organ was ill-adapted to sibilants, nasals, dentals, fricatives, explosives — although he could indicate vowels by pitching the tone of his voice. After another moment's effort, he realized his attempts were unintelligible.

'Are you trying to speak English?' came the question. 'Move right arm for yes, left for no.'

Wratch moved his right tentacle. Then deciding he wished to see, felt at the eye-slit to find what was obstructing his vision. A detaining touch restrained him.

'You'd better leave the hood as it is for the present, until you become a little more familiar with the Phalid's senses.'

Wratch, recollecting the dazzle and cacophony that had greeted him on awakening, dropped his tentacle.

'I don't understand how he masters the use of his members so quickly,' said Sandion.

'The Phalid nervous system is somewhat similar to the human,' said Dr. Plogetz. 'Wratch forms a volition in his brain, which passes through adapters to the vertebral cord, and reflexes essentially take care of the rest. If he tried to walk by directing motion of each leg separately, he'd be disjointed and awkward. However if he merely wills the body to walk, it will walk naturally, automatically.'

Plogetz looked back to the creature on the table.

'Are you comfortable? Are your senses clear?'

Wratch jerked his right tentacle.

'Do you feel any influence of the Phalid's will? That is, is there any conflict upon your brain from the body?'

Wratch thought. Apparently there was not. He felt as much Ryan Wratch as he ever had, though there was the sense of being locked up, of an unnatural imprisonment.

He tried to speak once more. Strange, he thought, how easy the Phalid speech came to him, a tongue he had never heard. As before, he failed to arrive at even an approximation to human speech.

'Here's a pencil and a writing board,' said the voice. 'Writing blindfolded might be difficult, but try it.'

Wratch grasped the pencil and fighting an impulse to scribble a line of vibrating angles, wrote:

'Can you read this?'

'Yes,' said the voice.

'Who are you? Dr. Plogetz?'

'Yes.'

'Operation a success?'

'Yes.'

'I seem to know the Phalid language. I speak it automatically. My brain thinks human and the voice comes out in Phalid.'

'That's nothing to wonder at.'

How shrill was Dr. Plogetz' voice! Wratch remembered how it had sounded before the transfer — a normal, pleasant, rather deep baritone.

'We left a segment of the Phalid's brain in the head-case — the focal point of language production and comprehension. An ignorance of the Phalid tongue would be very inconvenient for you. We've also left the node which coordinates the images of the two hundred eyes — there'd be only a blur otherwise. Even as it is, I imagine you'll notice considerable distortion.'

Considerable distortion! thought Wratch. Ha! if Dr. Plogetz could only look at a color photograph of what he'd seen.

Another voice addressed him, a voice even shriller, with a flat rasp that grated upon Wratch's new nerves.

'Hello, Wratch. It's Sandion — Commander Sandion.'

Wratch remembered him well enough, a thin brown man, very bitter and intense, who carried much of the responsibility in the campaign against the mysterious Phalids. It was Sandion who had questioned him after the incident out by Kordecker Three-forty-three near Sagittarius, where the Phalids' sudden attack had killed Wratch's two brothers and left Wratch dying.

'Hello Commander,' wrote Wratch. 'How long have I been unconscious?'

'Nearly two months.'

Wratch buzzed surprise.

'What has been happening?'

'They've attacked fifteen more ships — fifteen at least. Ships destroyed, crews and passengers dead or missing. They waylaid three cruisers separately — one in Hercules, one again in Andromeda, and another not three light years from Procyon.'

'Getting bolder!' Wratch wrote.

'They can afford to,' said Sandion bitterly. 'They've reduced our fleet by a third already. They've got too damn much mobility. We're like a blind man trying to fight twenty midgets with long knives. And without knowing the location of their home planet, we're helpless.'

'That's my job,' wrote Wratch. 'Don't forget I owe them something myself. My two brothers.'

'*Um*,' Sandion grunted, and said gruffly: 'Your job — and your suicide.'

Wratch nodded his body. His head, mounted on the horny collar which topped the black carapace, could not be nodded.

'When Plogetz got to me I was dying — ninety-nine percent dead. What could I lose?'

Sandion grunted again. 'Well, I've got to run along. Take it easy and rest.'

He grinned sardonically at Miss Elder. 'Lucky dog that you are, with a beautiful nurse and all.'

Lot of good that does me, thought Ryan Wratch.

Sector Commander Sandion went to the port, whose faintly grayed crystal transmitted a view of a dozen glistening towers set in parks and lakes, meshes of slender skyways, swarming air-traffic. Sandion's flier hung outside Dr. Plogetz' office. He climbed in, and the car darted off.

Dr. Plogetz turned back to Wratch.

'Now,' he said, 'I'm going to take away the hood. Don't worry about the visual confusion. Just relax and slowly open your eyes . . . .'

2

Two weeks later Wratch was able to move around his suite of rooms without falling over the furtniture. That is not to say he was seeing things as he saw them before. It was like learning to see all over again, in a world four times as complex. Even so, if Wratch's future had held the slightest hope for anything other than a desperate struggle, and a dreary death, he might have enjoyed the experience.

Now, in spite of all, he was constantly amazed and charmed by the colors, the tones and shades — ardent, cool, gloomy, fiery, mystic. These imparted to everything he saw a vibrant semblance at once new and wonderfully strange.

The human eye sees red, orange, yellow, green, blue, violet. Wratch had seven more colors — three below red, three above violet. And there was another wave-length to which his two hundred eyes were sensitive — a color far up on the spectrum, a glorious, misty color. All this he determined with the aid of a small spectroscope Dr. Plogetz gave him.

He described the single high band of color to a very interested Dr. Plogetz, who suggested that Wratch call this color 'kalychrome', a word, according to Dr. Plogetz, derived from the Greek. Wratch was willing, inasmuch as the Phalid word for the color was phonetically 'zz-za-mmm', more or less — a rather awkward term to be writing on the blackboard Dr. Plogetz had brought him. The other colors were delineated as sub-red 1, sub-red 2, sub-red 3, super-violet 1, super-violet 2, super-violet 3.

It fascinated Wratch merely to look out across the city, to watch the changing colors of the sky — which was no longer blue, but a tint of blue and super-violets 1 and 2. The towers were no longer towers. Distorted by the Phalid's visual node, they appeared to Wratch as ugly spindles, and the tapered little fliers which before he had thought sleek and beautiful seemed squat and misshapen. Nothing, in fact, appeared as before. The Phalid eyes and the Phalid brain segment altered the aspect of everything once familiar.

Men and women had ceased to be human beings. They had become scurrying little leprous things, flat-faced, with moist unpleasant features.

But in compensation for his loss of some human faculties, Wratch discovered within himself a power which may or may not have been previously latent within his own brain. Lacking normal perception of the people around him, unable to interpret facial expression, tone of voice, and the hundred little social mannerisms, Wratch gradually discovered that in any event he was aware of their inward emotions. Perhaps it was a universal faculty, perhaps an attribute locked into the two little Phalid brain-nodes.

In this way Wratch learned that the beautiful Miss Elder was sickened and frightened when her duties brought her near him; that Dr. Plogetz considered him with little feeling other than intense interest.

It rather puzzled Wratch to find that Miss Elder no longer seemed beautiful. He remembered her as a gorgeous creature with lustrous dark hair, large tender eyes, a body supple as a weeping willow. To his two hundred eyes now, Miss Elder was a pallid biped with a face like a deep-sea globefish, a complexion no more pleasant than a slab of raw liver.

And when he looked at himself in a mirror — ah! What an infinitely superior creature, said his eyes — tall, stately, graceful! What a glossy carapace, what supple arm tentacles! A noble countenance, with keen horizon-scanning eyes, an alert beak, and what symmetrical black whisker-sponges! Almost regal in appearance.

And Ryan Wratch grew somewhat uneasy to find how completely he was forced to accept the Phalid's version of outward events, and he put himself on continual guard against the subtle influence of his alien senses.

Several days later, Sector Commander Sandion came back to assess Wratch's progress.

'I understand you're adapting very well,' said Sandion.

Wratch still found it impossible to talk the language of men. He went to the blackboard.

'When do I start?' he wrote.

'You can start tomorrow, if you're ready,' Sandion said.

'!!!' wrote Wratch; then: 'Brief me on the current situation.'

'In the last week, two patrol corvettes and two liners have been destroyed, out near Canopus,' said Sandion. 'Crews and passengers, those not killed, were taken away. The Phalids are apparently maintaining a strong force somewhere near. They've got scouts all through this area. We've seen and destroyed three or four no bigger than a flier. Well, tomorrow you leave for Canopus in another corvette. You'll patrol slowly until attacked. Then the crew will leave in skimmers, taking their chances on making Lojuk by Fitzsimmon's Star where we've got a station.

'Thereupon you will follow the procedure we've already discussed.'

'I'm ready,' wrote Ryan Wratch.

'Well, *damn*it,' said Captain Dick Humber, and he threw his helmet onto the seat. 'We can't do anything more except send out printed invitations. Nine damn days and we haven't seen a trace of them.'

'Perhaps we *won't* see anything,' said Cabron, the navigator. 'Perhaps there'll be a flash and we'll be dead.'

Humber glanced at the long black form gazing out the port.

'Well, you've got more to look forward to than Wratch,' he said mildly. 'Wratch begins his job where you leave off.'

A black tentacle twitched.

'So far Wratch has done pretty well for himself,' grumbled Cabron. 'I don't know how many hands he can look into with all those damn eyes, but I know he's eight hundred ahead in the poker game.'

Wratch inwardly grinned. It was so easy reading joy, doubt, dismay in an opponent's mind, and as he had no intention of collecting, winning seemed a harmless pastime and the first real test of his new senses.

A shrill alarm sounded. A second of frozen inaction.

'Hit the ships,' cried Captain Dick Humber. 'This is it!'

A well disciplined rush, ports opening, slamming, dogging down.

'So long, Wratch! Good luck!' Captain Humber squeezed the black tentacle. He climbed through the opening, the vent that led to safety at Lojuk. Wratch restrained the small impulse to follow, saw the escape-skimmer's port blink shut an instant before the hull port snapped back.

The hiss of opening airlocks, four slight shocks as the skimmers were kicked from their cradles. Silence.

This was it, thought Wratch. Up to now, it had all been speculation. *If* the Phalids contacted them, *if* the men got away, *if* . . . .

According to the schedule, Wratch slipped his arm-members into a manacle, clicked it shut, waited for his seeming compatriots to release him. All, so far, according to plan.

But the minutes passed and still no glowing force-spheres — the Phalid weapon fields which dissolved matter to loose atoms.

A great shape floated across the viewports — a tremendous bulk larger than Earth's greatest passenger liners.

After some time, there came a scrape against the hull, as a shuttle from the war ship shackled on.

The port swung open. Wratch glimpsed the approach of dark, quick bodies . . . a swimming vision of Kordecker 343, his two dead brothers — horribly burned — and the stunned Phalid abandoned by the alien swarm . . . the remnants of whose body Ryan Wratch now wore as his own.

Three Phalids entered, the arm-tentacles grasping queerly-fashioned weapons: alien mysterious creatures, whom only one man — Ryan Wratch — had ever seen and lived.

They saw him, hesitated. How noble were the figures to Ryan Wratch's Phalid eyes, how stately the stride! Wratch felt with his brain for the emotions he had been able to detect in men, but drew blank. Were emotions, then, a human attribute?

Uncertain that the Phalids possessed the faculty, Wratch tried to achieve a state of pleasure and welcome.

But the Phalids seemed quickly to become indifferent to him. They reconnoitered the ship and finding nothing, returned. To Wratch's surprise, they ignored him, and began to leave the ship.

'A moment,' he called in the Phalid's buzzing language. 'Release your brother from these cursed metal bonds.'

They halted and peered at him, taken somewhat aback, so it seemed to Wratch.

'Impossible,' said one. 'You well know the *Bza* — ' the word they used was untranslatable, but meant 'custom, order, regulation, usual practice' — 'which makes necessary the prime report to Zau-amuz,' or so the name, or title, sounded to Wratch.

'I weaken, I am faint,' complained Wratch.

'Patience!' buzzed the Phalid sharply; and with a tinge of doubt, 'Where is your forbearance, your stoicism?'

Wratch became aware that his conduct was at odds with established code and quickly lapsed to passivity.

Ten minutes later the three returned, gathered up the

ship's log, and one or two instruments which excited their interest. Almost as an afterthought one stepped over to Wratch.

'The key is on that shelf,' buzzed Wratch.

He was released, and forced an emotion of relief and thankfulness through his mind. He followed them into the small boxlike ship, marveling at the casualness with which they accepted him.

He stood quietly in a corner of the ship as they flew to the great hulk which now floated ten miles distant, and the Phalids were equally silent. Had they no curiosity?

How beautiful the great Phalid ship, hanging dull-gleaming in black space, seemed to Wratch's Phalid eyes, how much more graceful and powerful-seeming than the squat stubby vessels of the scurrying little Earthmen!

Such was the message of Wratch's eyes. But his brain was tense and wary. He was afraid, too, but fear had so long been a minor consideration that he was barely aware of it. Wratch had reconciled himself to death, but torture would be unwelcome. He repressed a human impulse to shrug. His own body was dead, burnt now to a handful of ash, and he knew that never again would he see the planet of his birth. But if by some fantastic chance he completed his present mission, countless lives would be made secure.

Wratch watched closely to discover the plotting controls of the ship and discern their functions, on the slim chance he might have need of the knowledge. They were comparatively simple, he discovered, arrayed in a system which seemed universal and standard.

They drew close to the Phalid ship, a dark cylinder flat at top and bottom, with longitudinal driving bands of sub-red metal.

The shuttle drew close, slowed, poised, fitted itself into a recess in the side of the mother-ship, and the ports snapped open.

Wratch followed the Phalids out into a passageway. Here, to his amazement, they abandoned him, stalked away in different directions, leaving him standing nonplussed in the corridor, unattended, unquestioned, apparently left entirely to his own devices.

How different from the discipline of an Earth ship! The rescued man would have been hustled off in a flurry of excitement to the Commander's office. Questions would have been barked at him, his memory searched for any detail of enemy arrangements he conceivably might have noted.

Wratch stood bewildered in the corridor as Phalids of the ship, intent on their duties, pushed past him. He tried to reason out the situation. Perhaps he had been detected and they were testing his intentions? Somehow he could not believe this. The attitude of those who had brought him aboard seemed too casual for such craftiness.

But perhaps there was no trickery or subterfuge here. Wratch reminded himself that an alien race could not be judged entirely by human standards.

On none of the Phalids could he observe badges or marks of rank. Each seemed programmed to some special duty — like extremely intelligent ants, thought Wratch.

In that case, when he was brought aboard, there would be no need to take him for questioning; it would be assumed that his own instincts and training would lead him to his duty automatically. This hypothesis might explain the delay in releasing him earlier. A race of individuals — like the Earthmen — would have been impelled by surprise, curiosity, sympathy, to free a prisoner before they made another move.

Wratch wandered down the passageway, peering into the chambers opening to either side. He marveled, yet could not be sure of what he saw because of his deceitful Phalid vision.

At the far end he found configurations his intelligence told him must be propulsion units. Noting the location, he turned and started back.

3

From appearances, the plan of the ship was basically that of longitudinal corridors at opposite sides of the ship, with — as in Earth ships — the controls forward, the driving engines aft. Design, engineering, mechanics — all were universal concepts, thought Wratch. Here the problem was to find the most expedient way of crossing space. The solution, a space ship not greatly differentiated in basic design from those of Earth.

In spite of his seeming liberty, Wratch was uneasy. He had been expecting suspicion, intense scrutiny, perhaps quick exposure for what he was. It was disquieting to be so completely ignored.

Suddenly his uncertainty was dispelled. A great buzzing voice permeated the ship.

'Where is he who was found on the ship of the insect-men? He has not yet come before Zau-amuz.' The voice carried puzzled rather than suspicious overtones.

Where, who, is Zau-amuz? Wratch wondered. Where would he go to find him? On an Earth ship, the command center would be forward and high over the bow. He hastened his steps in this direction, watching through each portal for any hint or sign of impending trouble.

He caught a glimpse through a barred door of two or three dozen humans, whether men or women his Phalid vision could not tell. He hesitated an instant to look. No, they could wait. For now, he was anxious to find Zau-amuz before a search or an inquiry be made.

In a chamber below the pilot house Wratch saw one he recognized as the master of the ship. The chamber itself was decorated in a style that charmed his Phalid senses — a soft rug of two super-violet tones, walls of blue tint covered with fantastically rich fret-work, low furniture of pink and white plastic, inset with medallions of that high spectrum color which Dr. Plogetz had named 'kalychrome'.

Zau-amuz was an impressive Phalid, twice Wratch's size. Its carapace was enameled a shade of super-violet. Its legs seemed underdeveloped, too weak to support its weight for any length of time. It reclined on a long pallet.

Entirely ignorant of correct procedures, but hoping that formal courtesy and rigid rules of ceremony were not customs practiced by the Phalids, Wratch advanced slowly.

'Revered one, I am he who was removed from the ship of the insect-men,' said Wratch.

'You are dilatory,' said the great Phalid. 'Also, where is your sense of Bza?' — the untranslatable word meaning 'custom, regulation, ancient manners'.

'Your pardon, intelligence. As a prisoner of the insect-men, I have seen such unpleasantness that my senses have temporarily lost their fullest efficiency.'

'Ah, yes,' admitted the Phalid lord. 'Such events are not unheard of. How did you chance to fall into the hands of the insect-things?'

Wratch related the incidents of the attack and his subsequent incapacitation and capture.

'Situation understood,' said Zau-amuz. None of the brusqueness, the sharpness that Wratch associated with Earth discipline was evident. Instead, the Phalid seemed to take for granted the loyalty and industry of his fellows. 'Have you any significant observations to report?'

'None, grandeur, except that the insect-men were so terrified at the approach of this ship that they fled in the wildest panic.'

'We have already observed that,' said Zau-amuz, with the faintest hint of boredom. 'Go. Perform some needful duty. If your senses do not adjust themselves with promptitude, throw yourself into space.'

'I go, magnificence.'

Wratch withdrew, well-pleased with the course of the interview. He was affirmed an accredited member of the ship's company. The inquisition had been simpler than any he could have imagined. Now if only the ship would return to the Phalid home-planet, and if he were allowed a few moments aground by himself, all might yet be well.

He wandered about the ship and presently came to a dark hall evidently intended for the absorption of nourishment. Here were twenty or thirty Phalids, ladling brown porridge into the stomach sac in their chest, champing on stalks of a celery-like growth, plucking segments from clusters like bunches of grapes and consuming these with undisguised relish. These grape bunches seemed to be the most appetizing. In fact Wratch became aware of a great hunger in his body for these grape-things, a need not unlike a thirsty man longing for water.

He entered, and as unobtrusively as possible, took a bunch from a tub and let his body feed itself. To his surprise, he discovered the little objects were alive, that they squirmed and writhed in his finger flaps, and pulsed frantically in his stomach sac. But they were delicious; and they filled him with a sense of wonderful well-being. He wanted very much to take a second bunch, but possibly, he thought, it was not correct etiquette. So he waited till he saw one of the other Phalids reach for a second clump, and then did likewise.

After his meal, he went to the security area containing the humans he'd seen earlier. The door was inset with a heavy transparent plate and was barred with a simple exterior bar. Inside he noted two Phalids moving around among the Earthmen, feeling them, scrutinizing their skin and eyes, like veterinarians inspecting cattle.

Wratch became slightly nauseated. Poor devils, he thought, and pitied them. He, at least, had a duty to spur him, but the captives were like sheep being taken to slaughter, bewildered, frightened, innocent.

A sudden project formed itself in his mind. Perhaps, with no risk to himself, he could manage one additional undertaking.

He searched back along the passageway, counted about thirty paces from the containment cell to the entrance port of the ship's launch. It was large enough, Wratch thought, to accommodate, with some crowding, all of the detained humans. He had noticed emergency canisters of water in the launch, and presumably there would be food. In any event, it was a better prospect than being taken as prisoners to the Phalid home-planet.

The passageway was temporarily clear. Wratch quickly made sure that the port was free to be opened, returned to the cell.

The two Phalids within were at the point of leaving, conducting one of the captives — who hung back and cried in terror — out into the corridor. Wratch waited till they had stalked out of sight; then he lifted the bar, entered the cell.

The prisoners looked at him apathetically. Wratch, consciously noting such features as longer hair, lesser stature, saw that about half of the prisoners were women, evidently taken from a passenger ship destroyed by the Phalids.

Wratch extracted a pen and paper, quickly wrote:

'I am not a true Phalid. I will help you escape. Tell your comrades. You may speak to me in English. I understand.'

He handed the message to the man nearest him.

The man read, looked at Wratch astounded.

'Hey, Wright, Chapman, look here!' he cried, and passed the note to two others. In a moment the note had been read by everyone.

They were displaying too much excitement. Wratch feared a passing Phalid might be warned by the unusual activity. He wrote again:

'Act more naturally. I will stand outside the door. When I signal, come out quickly, turn to the right, enter the second port to your left, about thirty yards down the passage. Inside is a ship, with simple controls. This must be done *fast*.' He underlined the word 'fast'. 'Once you are in the ship, you are on your own.'

They read this.

'How do we know it's not a trick?' came one voice.

'Trick or not, it's a chance,' said the first man. 'Go ahead,' he told Wratch. 'We'll wait for your sign.'

Wratch waved his tentacle in what he hoped was a reassuring sign, left the door unbarred. The passageway was empty. Listening carefully, he detected no sound of approaching footsteps, the slow *clack — clack — clack* made by the horn rim around the spongy center of a Phalid's foot against the polished composition deck.

He flung open the door, gestured to the tense Earthlings; then quickly loped down the passageway, to be as far as possible from the scene of the escape.

But from a side corridor he met the two Phalids who had come from the prison, returning the one they had taken away. Wratch now saw this to be a woman. It would be difficult to delay them, although as a last resort there was always his little emergency case, strapped high and inconspicuous up and under his carapace, for the eventuality of an outright attack.

But that was to be used only as the last resort. He stationed himself in the passageway.

'What are your conclusions as to the intelligence of this race?' he asked.

They paused, scrutinized him.

'They have a queer and whimsical sense of values,' said one of the Phalids, after a moment. 'Their actions are governed not by *Bza*, the ordained way, but rather by individual volition.'

'What a strange madhouse their home-world must be!' exclaimed Wratch.

'Undoubtedly,' said the second Phalid, who was showing signs of impatience.

'But are these beings sufficiently amenable for our purposes?'

'Probably,' was the answer. 'Thievery is a task peculiarly adapted to their unpredictable guile.'

Thievery? Were humans being captured and transported across light-years of space by some cosmic crime syndicate? But the two Phalids impatiently pushed past Wratch. Anxiously he hurried behind them, dreading that he find the Earthmen still in the passageway. If they had been quick, they would already be clear of the ship. And given ten or fifteen minutes' start, it would be a difficult job finding them again.

The Phalids reached the prison cell, opened the portal, shoved the lone prisoner inside. Then they stood transfixed by surprise: empty!

Buzzing sharply, they hurried excitedly away.

Presently the ship quivered and slowed, presumably while the Phalids searched the void for their stolen craft.

After a few moments the Phalid ship again resumed its speed. Wratch guessed the prisoners had made good their escape. Relieved, he wandered for a time about the ship, watching, listening, but overhearing little of importance. The Phalids communicated rarely among themselves.

Wratch found only one view-screen on the entire ship — above the bow, just over Zau-amuz's chamber. Here Wratch lingered, half expecting to be questioned or ejected, but neither of the two Phalids at the controls took the slightest notice of him.

Wratch scanned the void for familiar star-patterns, and for the first time regretted the seven new colors in his spectrum: the stars were entirely different in guise.

Wratch felt completely lost. He made a stealthy search for star-charts, but none were in evidence.

Restless, he found himself wandering back toward the security cell. The truth was, Wratch had been perplexed about the one prisoner left behind. How great must be her misery, he thought.

He peered through the panel. A single human crouched in a far corner. Wratch had known it was a woman solely by the length of her hair; otherwise his Phalid eyes gave him no hint as to her appearance.

4

On impulse, Wratch unbarred the door and let himself into the cell, though later, he cursed himself for taking such a risk. Suppose his interest in the prisoner should excite suspicion? Suppose he should be taken before Zau-amuz and this time questioned more closely?

As he approached, the woman looked up, and Wratch felt her brain undergoing a change from apathy to dull horror and hate. He sensed a stange vitality, though to his eyes she seemed an unpleasant white moist thing, with head surmounted by a fibrous matted mass of hair.

'The others have escaped and I think they are safe,' he

wrote. 'I helped them. I am sorry you were out of the cell at the time. Keep your spirits up. You have a friend aboard.'

Amazement seeped into her brain, followed by doubtful tendrils of hope.

'Who are you?' came her voice, halting, puzzled.

'I am human,' wrote Wratch. 'There's a man's brain inside this ugly skull-case.'

She looked at him, and he felt the sudden warm glow of her admiration.

'You are very brave,' she said.

'So are you,' he wrote; then on an impulse: 'Don't feel desperate. I'll try my best to help you!'

'I don't mind so much — now,' she said. 'It's just knowing there's someone nearby. I hated being entirely alone.'

'I've got to go,' wrote Wratch. 'It wouldn't do to be caught here. I'll be back as soon as it's safe.'

As he stalked out the door, his brain caught her wonder and thankfulness, and a hint of a pleasant, warm friendliness.

The interview with the woman cheered Wratch. Alien and disassociated from humanity as he had become, his brain had gradually been changing to a cold and mechanical thing, a thinking device. And, thought Wratch with a sudden twinge of bitterness, actually he was little more than that — a mechanism with a certain function to perform before it submitted to destruction.

Once he activated the device that would consummate his mission, if he ever got that far, his life would be no more than a mote of dust.

Somehow, seeing the woman prisoner, whose predicament was in some ways worse than his own, feeling the warmness emanating from her brain, had created within him an impulse to live again as a human being. Which was impossible. His own body was dead, and according to Dr. Plogetz, his brain would not possibly survive another neural transplant.

Time passed. Days? Weeks? Several times he paid fleeting

visits to the prisoner. She was a young woman, he decided, taking for evidence the clean contour of her chin and jaw, the even color of her facial features.

The visits always cheered him, and conversely left him with a sense of dissatisfaction with what life had left him. There had been so much that Ryan Wratch had missed, though he had experienced much that would never be given to more careful men: the solemnity of plunging through an endless black void alone, the thrill of landfall on a strange planet, the companionship of two brothers in the rude pleasures of space outposts, the fascination of sighting uncharted planets out on the border between known and unknown, worlds which might show him some new and wondrous beauty or civilization, rare new metal or jewels, fabulous ruins of a cosmic antiquity.

There was a wonderful fascination to freelance exploration, and Wratch knew that even if he were given a new lease on life, never again could he reconcile himself to a quiet retiring existence on Earth.

Wratch thought of the things life had witheld from him. The color, the brilliant gaiety of Earth's cosmopolitan cities during the most spectacular and prosperous period in world history; the music, the spectacles, the resort towns, almost feverish in their pleasures; the society of civilized women, laughter, beauty, youth.

Angrily, Wratch thrust these thoughts from his mind. He was a — how had he put it? — a mechanism with a certain function to perform before it could permit itself to be destroyed.

Time passed, light-years dwindled behind the Phalid space-vessel. But whether they traveled away from Sol or toward it, Wratch had no idea. He paced the corridors, rested in the dark soft-floored room set aside for this use, gave his stomach sac brown porridge and the dark red celery growth.

None of the other Phalids bothered or questioned him, none seemed to notice his lack of occupation. Each Phalid had a job to do, performed it with a maximum of plodding efficiency. Wratch did not doubt, however, that in an emergency, a Phalid could act with some initiative; but constitutionally it was built to follow routine — *Bza* — blindly, to let responsibility rest on the horny black shoulders of those such as Zau-amuz.

Then one day, Wratch, strolling dully through the engine room, noted an unusual alertness and scurry. He hurried up to the pilot area, and from the view-screen saw a great gray world below. Off to the side hung a dim greenish star.

This was the Phalid home-world whose position was a shrouded secret to those of the Tellurian Space Navy. This was Wratch's goal.

Wratch scanned the star field, but try as he might, he could recognize no familiar constellations.

He watched the face of the planet draw near, discerned misty continents, brackish-looking seas.

He became aware that the pilots were regarding him with puzzled attention from their wide optic slits.

'We make port, brother,' one of the pilots said finally. 'How is it you are not at your duty?'

'My duty is here,' said Wratch, thinking quickly, hoping he had not chosen the wrong reply. 'I observe cloud-shapes as we land.'

'Is that the will of Zau-amuz?' persisted the Phalid. 'It is strange, for it is not *Bza*. There is some mistake. I will ask the Named One.' He took a communication device, pressed it to his chest diaphragm.

'Where is the duty of the one who is expected to note cloud-shapes?' he buzzed. And the answer came back.

'There is none such. Send him to me.'

'Through that passage,' said the Phalid, passive and dull now that the matter had passed beyond his hands. 'Zau-amuz will correct your orders.'

Wratch could do nothing but obey. There was no possible means of evasion. The passage led to only one place — the chamber of Zau-amuz.

Wratch reached a tentacle into the emergency case strapped high up under his carapace, brought forth a small metal object. It was a pity for him to be apprehended now, with his goal so close.

He stepped forth to find Zau-amuz regarding him with an intense scrutiny.

'Strange things have been happening aboard,' buzzed the Named One. 'Earth prisoners escape, leaving behind no clue as to the manner of their going. A brother Phalid wastes much time wandering through the corridors and in the pilot house, watching the stars, when *Bza* requires him to be at his duties around the ship. Another brother — or possibly the same — goes on non-existent orders to study cloud patterns as we approach Mother-world. And these phenomena occur only after a brother is rescued from a vessel of the insect-people, who in this case do not put up their usual frantic resistance, but flee with strange cowardice. Now — ' and Zau-amuz' tones became sharp and shrill ' —these matters point to an inescapable conclusion.'

'They do,' said Wratch. 'Death.'

He leveled his handweapon at the enormous Phalid. A sharp flash, and the Named One's great head split and curled to a tiny black crisp. Fetor and reek filled the chamber.

Zau-amuz slumped over, quivered, and was still.

Down the passage ran one of the pilots. Seeing the prone body, the creature threw his tall black body into a contorted posture, vented a scream of such hideous anguish that Wratch's brain sang and hummed with a tale of a thousand horrors, outrage beyond a man's comprehension — massacre, torture, perversion, betrayal of a world's trust.

Wratch promptly killed the pilot, then ran back to the control center, pausing at the entryway.

'Boldness!' he said to himself. 'No backing down now!'

He went slowly into the room, watching the remaining Phalid pilot with desperate intentness, trying to read the hidden brain. He attempted a fantastic deceit.

Every Phalid looked exactly like the next, so far as he knew. At least no physical differentiations were evident to his perceptions.

He slipped into the position so recently occupied by the dead Phalid pilot.

'What was the confusion?'

'Za-amuz gave new directions,' said Wratch. 'We are to land the ship far out in the wilderness.'

The pilot gave a sharp buzz.

'A strange contradiction to his recent orders. Did he specify exactly at what coordinates?'

'He gave us authority to use our own judgment,' said Wratch, with the feeling that he was treading on the brink of something unprecedented. 'We are merely to select an uninhabited, isolated area and land.'

'Strange, strange!' buzzed the pilot. 'How many peculiar events in the last few periods! Perhaps we had better confirm with Zau-amuz.'

'No!' said Wratch imperatively. 'He is busily engaged at the moment.'

The pilot made adjustments on the complicated panel. Wratch, completely ignorant of what his duties consisted, sat back warily.

'Attention to your work!' barked the pilot suddenly. 'Compensate for radial torque!'

'I am ill,' said Wratch. 'My vision dims. Compensate the torque yourself.'

'What manner of fantasy is this?' cried the pilot in wild impatience. 'Since when do a Phalid's eyes dim at his duty? It is not *Bza*!'

'Nevertheless, that is how it must be,' said Wratch. 'You will have to land the ship alone.'

And for lack of an alternative, the pilot, buzzing an undertone of nervous excitement and bewildered indignation, set himself to the task.

The planet grew large. Wratch found it within himself to be amused at the pilot's frantic efforts.

5

Into view came a city, a beautiful place to Wratch's Phalid eyes, with low domed buildings of a dark glistening substance, a number of pentagon-shaped squares, dark-brown and inset with vast formal mosaics of two shades of sub-red, one tall pylon-shaped tower, terminating in a sphere from which protruded two slender opposing truncated cones, the whole of which slowly revolved against the sallow olive-green sky.

The city crouched over murky and flat rolling land. A sluggish river ran by at a distance, and then a marsh. Even though accustomed now to the shades and values of the thirteen Phalid colors, Wratch could not but marvel at the bizarre effects the dim green sun wrought upon the landscape.

They passed over the city, and presently over what appeared to be an industrial district. Wratch saw vast flaring pits, gaunt black frameworks on the sky, slag-wastes, cranes startlingly like those of Earth.

The city vanished beyond the horizon. Below was wilderness.

'Land by that high hill,' said Wratch. 'Close to the edge of the forest.'

'I understood that your eyes were weakened,' said the pilot, not angrily or suspiciously — such emotions seemed foreign to their nature — but merely surprised.

'They see well for distance,' explained Wratch.

'A strange, strange voyage!' buzzed the Phalid.

Bringing the great ship down on an even keel was a racking task for a single pilot and Wratch was compelled to admire the deftness with which the Phalid met the problem. A race at a high level of adaptability, he thought, when the problem before them was clear and compelling. Guileless and innocent, almost, when a situation could be met by *Bza*.

The ship sank low toward the soft dark turf, hesitated, grounded, settled its great weight, was still.

'Now, the orders of Zau-amuz are that you await his call here, while I perform a duty elsewhere,' said Wratch.

He stood erect, a tall black creature, horny of body and carapace, with jointed legs, mottled arm-tentacles, a complex insectoid head. But inside the head pulsed an Earthman's brain, and this brain was yelling, 'Now! The signalling device . . . .'

Taut with excitement, he strode down the passge to the containment cell, unbarred the door, beckoned urgently to the woman.

She hesitated, not recognizing him, and he sensed her fright. Nevertheless she faced him defiantly. He gestured more urgently. There was no time to write. He pointed to himself, then to her. She suddenly understood, came forward. He motioned her to be cautious and led her out into the passageway.

An agonized outcry was heard. The Phalids had found Zau-amuz. Now openly hurrying, Wratch took the girl toward the exit port. The tale of assassination traveled fast, each Phalid they passed seemed paralyzed, bereft of reason and will.

The exit port was an intricate device, beyond his understanding.

'Open the port,' Wratch commanded a Phalid standing nearby. 'It was Zau-amuz' last order.'

The Phalid obeyed, dazedly.

Wratch and the woman tumbled out on the strange sward of the Phalid world. As they did so, from within came the vast droning of the ship's speaker system.

'Terrible treachery! Unthinkable deeds! Capture the two who have left the ship!'

Wratch broke into a shambling run, fumbling meanwhile in the emergency case under his carapace. In the case was a device in three parts — a tiny atomic power cell, a rugged, craftily constructed converter, a collapsible transmission grid. Wratch brought these forth as he ran, but had no time to pause and assemble them. Already Phalids were streaming from the ship, bounding over the murky sward in ungainly leaps.

The woman was no hindrance. She easily kept pace with his swiftly shambling Phalid body. It became evident to Wratch's mind that she must be young and strong to run so well. Inconsequentially, he wished he could see her as she really was — or rather, as human eyes would see her. To his present vision she was pallid, moist and reptilian.

The rocky barren hill he had noted was to the left, while ahead and to the right stretched a forest of a vegetation which — though his eyes found it familiar, intimately, terribly familiar — his Earth brain apprehended it as the strangest growth he'd seen in his lifetime.

The trees were huge, thick-boled like mushrooms, with fluffy tendriled foliage shaped and textured like giant sea-anemones. They were bright in all the colors of Earth, in the seven neighboring Phalid colors, and in every conceivable tone, combination and gradation. The heart-cavity at the top of each glimmered in beautiful kalychrome.

The colors were as clear and bright as sunlight through stained glass and the forest was as vivid as the wan green sunlight would allow. It seemed especially gorgeous beside the dark rolling hills and the dank green swamps covered with low rushes. And though the trees, if trees they were, were strangely beautiful, the trunks and limbs had a perturbingly plump, meaty look.

Wratch needed perhaps three minutes to do what was necessary, and the forest seemed to be the only sanctuary available, the sole possibility for a moment's concealment.

Wratch fleetingly wondered about the dampening familiarity of the forest. Was it an intuition, an aura from the Phalids themselves? Yet how could it be? Wratch's long wobbly strides faltered, but only for a moment. The forest was ahead and the Phalids were behind.

He drove his shambling body hard for the purple-shadowed aisles. Suddenly he found it was his Phalid *body*, not his brain, that feared the colored forest. Each cell tingled with a deep-grained fear, an instinct that thrilled the fibers of his being. The gay streamered growths seemed grostesque monsters, the dark shaded depths forbidding as death itself.

A flash from a Phalid weapon passed beside them. The forest was at hand. Wratch did not hesitate. Every nerve quivering, he plunged within, the human girl close behind.

They ran on, changing course to confuse the pursuers. The girl was becoming tired, and her steps were obviously lagging. Wratch looked behind, saw nothing but the thick boles, a hundred fantastic colors.

It was a forest of death. He passed several dull husks of long dead Phalids, black dry carapaces like wing-cases discarded by gigantic beetles, and with a shock of horror he saw a human skeleton, pale, decayed, and looking inexpressibly forlorn in this alien jungle.

Presently he stopped, listened, every hearing-hair tense in the sounding chamber under his carapace.

Silence. No crashing steps. Had they shaken off pursuit?

The dread felt throughout his body slowly began to invest Wratch's brain. He looked high, low, but saw nothing other than slowly stirring foliage, thick boles, red, green, yellow, orange, blue, the seven Phalid colors, the infinite combinations. Nevertheless Wratch seemed to feel intelligence near, seemed to hear malevolent voices talking above his head, gloating in a frightening anticipation.

Sprouting from the bole of a nearby tree he saw a clump of the delicious grape-things he had eaten aboard the ship. He was tired, he needed refreshment. He almost reached to pluck them but, he thought, he had no time for food. Or perhaps some instinct had warned him? He drew back his arm-tentacle, turned away. His first concern was to assemble the signal transmitter.

He laid the parts on the dank ground, set to work. Overhead three Phalid air-ships whistled down the green-brown sky, searching. He noticed the spongy foliage above. Had it settled closer, lower than before? The thought sent sympathetic spasms through his body.

Resolutely he ignored the terror-reflex, fitted the three pieces of equipment into the device whose successful functioning was being awaited by a planet.

He was nearly finished; one final connection and his signal

would sweep out into space to a thousand ships of Earth's fleet.

Then a shrill grinding scream. The girl! He whirled, saw her struggling with three of four glistening stalks sprouting from the ground. They seemed fantastically mobile, as they wrapped around her, twined her close.

Wratch felt a cool smooth fumbling at his back. At the touch his shiny black body went limp and relaxed, to a flood of singing peace. He was merged with the eternal, immersed in a blissful consummation of life beyond his experience or comprehension.

Wratch's Earth brain protested, struggled in frantic alarm, sent commands down unwilling nerves. He kicked out. His heretofore lax limbs snapped the brittle stalk. Some measure of volition returned to his body. He tore at the root-things that pressed around the girl. She screamed and gasped, her agony pierced Wratch's brain.

He stamped, beat, crushed the flexible stalks — drew the girl aside. Blood was seeping from her knee. She shuddered, pressed close against him, and he sensed a throat-catching relief in her brain, to be free, to be beside him. And Wratch, remembering Miss Elder's disgust and nausea, felt greatly surprised.

After another moment Wratch brought out a small laser and laid a smoking waste around them. Now he thought he knew why the Phalids had relinquished the chase at the forest's verge, why his Phalid instincts had cried out at the thought of the strange-hued aisles. Apparently the Phalids used the forest to perform executions.

More roots broke the surface, this time strangely hesitant, as if directed by an injured intelligence. A great buzzing voice sounded out of the foliage overhead. Wratch held his weapon ready.

'Brother, little brother, are you abnormal of mind?' said the voice in gentle, surprised tones. 'You burn the arms that fold you to eternity? Did not *Bza* bring you to your Father?'

Wratch looked all about for the Phalid who spoke, saw no one. 'No,' he said, 'I came for another reason. Come out, wherever you are, or I'll burn down every tree in sight.'

A pause. Wratch felt an intelligence, a monstrous alien intelligence, touch his brain.

It recoiled.

'Small wonder you kill the arms of the Father! Your body is that of the children, but your brain is a hideous thing, a guileful vacillating power, and you know nothing of *Bza*.'

'True,' said Wratch, holding his laser. 'I am of the planet Earth, who those of this planet have attacked. Who are you? Where are you?'

'I am all about you,' said the voice. 'I am the forest — the Father.'

For a moment Wratch's brain was staggered. Then he regained mental balance. Very interesting, but time was wasting. He backed slowly to where he had dropped the transmitter.

It was gone.

6

Rigid with anxiety, Wratch whirled around. He saw the transmitter high overhead, held in one of the coiling white shoots.

'Drop that!' he buzzed urgently.

'Calmness, brother, calmness and quiet in the Father-forest. That is *Bza*.'

Wratch beat at the base of the stalk. It snapped, toppled. In an instant the transmitter dropped free. A stalk quickly wound around him from behind and pinned him down. The transmitter was torn from his grip, Wratch was helpless. The girl ran over, tore at the stalk, but it was sheathed with a leathery pliable skin.

Wratch buzzed frantically at her. If only she could talk, if only she could understand!

He wrenched the transmitter loose from the twisting coils, threw it into an open space.

'Zz — zz — zz-zz!' he said peremptorily, gesturing urgently. Why couldn't she understand.

She slowly stood erect, looked at Wratch doubtfully, then looked at the transmitter. She picked it up.

'Is this what you want?'

'Zz — zz — zz!' buzzed Wratch.

'Once for no, twice for yes,' she said, dodging from a creeping white arm. 'Do you want me to do something with it?'

'Zz — zz!' and Wratch tried to nod his stiff neck.

She put her hand on the switch. 'Turn this?'

'Zz — zz!'

She snapped it on. It hummed, sang, vibrated. The grid grew white, swam with a hundred colors, and threw a tremendous signal out through subspace, a beacon summoning Earth's warships to the Father-forest, to the planet of the Phalids. In five minutes every alarm panel in the fleet would be flashing. A thousand warships would follow the beam down.

Ryan Wratch relaxed. They could kill him now. His mission was done. He had kept faith with his brothers. The Father-forest was going to kill him. He knew it, felt the certainty of his death and the benign motive behind it. The white shoots tightened, began to send out eagerly exploring tendrils through the cracks and chinks in his chitin.

Wratch looked at the girl. He felt her fear. It was not fear for herself! It was fear and wild pity for him!

Suddenly, Ryan Wratch wanted to live.

'Release me!' he called to the forest. 'I will talk with you!'

'Why seek to evade *Bza*?' asked a gentle voice. 'Your brain is an alien thing and you may burn some more of our white arms.'

'Not unless they fasten on me again. Release me! If you don't, my companion will burn a great circle through the forest.'

The arms fell loose. Wratch stepped clear. The girl ran to him, exhausted and at a loss. Wratch stroked her shoulder with an arm-member.

He looked carefully around for stealthy white shoots; there were none. He detected a sense of watchful caution in the forest, but also a slow withdrawal of its menace.

He looked back down at the girl, feeling strangely protective.

He scratched on the turf. 'Thanks. We won!'

'Won't the Phalids come for us?' asked the girl.

'Phalids are afraid of the forest. We can hold out till our ships come,' wrote Wratch in the dark loam. And he felt a hope, a warm happiness in her brain.

'Will we get back to Earth?'

Something stiffened inside him. Quick thoughts like a spray of icy water. Earth? What was there for him on Earth? His body was dead. No one had expected him to survive his mission.

Slowly, he wrote, 'I don't know.'

Then he glanced at the grid, still sending its message and felt the grim satisfaction of a desperate job completed.

He looked around. There was no sign of life, just the sense of brooding, watching forest, petulant and savage.

A sudden intuition came to him. In curiosity he buzzed the Phalid attention-signal loud into the air.

'What is your wish?' came the answer from the many-colored foliage.

'Why do you call yourself the Father?'

'From the forest comes the Fruit of Life,' said the voice. 'He who eats it is impregnated with a second life. Presently the light of the green sun brings another of the Children.'

Faintness. Nausea. Wratch shuddered. He remembered his avid eating of the fruit aboard the Phalid ship.

Wratch sprawled his shiny black body awkwardly in the saloon of the fleet flagship — the *Canadian Might*. Human furniture would never fit his gaunt frame. Even the special chair built in the ship's machine shop was not entirely comfortable.

Beside him sat the girl. Wratch now knew that her name

was Constance. Commander Sandion had just left the saloon for his office on the bridge deck. Except for Constance Averill, who sat quietly nearby, the room was empty.

Wratch sighed inwardly, mentally. His body, actually, could not sigh. Air pumped itself through a thousand conduits inside his shell as automatically as a human heart beats.

Wratch glanced around the room without moving his head, such was the virtue of his optic slit and two hundred eyes. He knew it was pleasant, knew that Earthmen had planned this room to be warm and livable, out here in the cold black void. But to Wratch it seemed stark, barren, and unfamiliar.

Earth lay a week ahead. Two weeks astern, insignificant in Lyra, hung the dark and murky planet of the Phalids, occupied now by an Earth garrison, guarded by two impregnable satellites in an orbit a thousand miles above.

The door opened. The staff anthropologist entered, sat down, began to speak excitedly. He was a fussy, harmless little man with a high bald dome, a gingery mustache, quick brown eyes.

For two weeeks he had been bothering Wratch, night and day. Wratch, who was absorbed in his own dark thoughts, cared little for talk. Except with Constance Averill, and she spoke very little now.

'From what you've told me,' said the anthropologist, 'I've arrived at a tentative theory. It implies a peculiar set of conditions, but probably no stranger than analogous circumstances would appear to the Phalids.

'They are a divided race. Instead of male and female, they differentiate, roughly, as plant and animal. The fruit of the plant fertilizes the animal. The animal, driven by hunger or perhaps *Bza*, comes to steal the fruit. The forest traps it, consumes it, and is stimulated to produce more fruit.'

The anthropologist regarded them in triumph, as if his minor researches had won the war.

An assistant entered, leaned deferentially over the anthropologist. 'Details of the treaty have just arrived.'

The anthropologist was plainly interested and rather pleased. 'I wonder, what social effect this will have on the Phalids?' he said. 'What will become of their *Bza*, their homogeneity, their culture patterns? Excuse me,' he said to Wratch and Constance Averill. 'I really must apply McDougall's Theorem to this whole situation.'

He trotted away. Wratch and Constance Averill were alone.

Wratch looked wearily around the room. It was low, ill-proportioned; the colors were harsh and discordant. The men of the crew, the anthropologists, Constance Averill — they were ugly alien things. Their voices rasped on his membranes, their movements offended him.

He became aware of Constance Averill's flow of thoughts. There was warmth and eagerness and good humour. And now she was wistful and oddly timid.

'You're not happy, are you?'

He wrote: 'I was able to finish the job. I'm glad of that. Now I'm a museum piece. A freak.'

'Don't *say* that!' Wratch sensed her pity. 'You're the bravest man we have!'

'I'm not a man. I'm stuck. Nothing looks the same through these Phalid eyes.'

'What do I look like?' she asked with interest.

'Half jellyfish, half-witch,' he wrote.

Wratch felt her recoil in feminine alarm.

'I'm really not bad looking,' she assured him.

There was a pause.

'You need someone to look after you,' she finally said. 'And I'm going to do it.'

Wratch was genuinely surprised. His finger-flaps twitched as he wrote:

'No! I'm going out in space and live the rest of my life alone. I don't need anyone.'

She stood up. She was crying.

'Don't! Don't talk like that! It's horrible — what they've done to you!' She wiped her eyes furiously with her hand.

'All right!' she said angrily. 'I'm crazy. I'm insane. I think you're the most wonderful man I know. I love you. I don't care what you look like. So you've got me — and I'm going to make sure that I —'

The ship's third officer entered, hesitated.

'A message for you, Mr. Wratch. Just arrived.'

Wratch clumsily opened the envelope. The note read:

> Dear Mr. Wratch: Good news for you — and you deserve it. We've got your body patched up and waiting. It was a hard fight.
>
> I didn't want to raise false hopes — it's been touch and go. As soon as your brain left its body, the best doctors and surgeons in the world worked night and day and the transplants were successful!
>
> You'll be feeling more cheeful now, no doubt! I'll be seeing you within a week.
>
> Dr. Plogetz

Wratch handed the note to Constance Averill.

The two hundred Phalid eyes would not cry, but Constance took care of that for both of them.

It was the waiting room of the Atlantic Combine, the largest hospital on Earth. Half a hundred people sat in the lobby, waiting for friends and relatives discharged from the wards in the towers above.

A slender girl with lustrous dark red hair, a clear face delicate and lovely as a flower but with underlying strength, sat in the waiting room. She watched the elevator, intently eyeing the men as they emerged and came to seek familiar faces in the waiting room. Once or twice she looked closely, then relaxed in her seat.

The minutes passed. The doors slid back once more, the discharged patients stepped out.

One of these was a young man, thin but well-muscled. He had a wide good-humored mouth, a long chin with a scar running up his cheek.

The girl stared hopefully, uncertainly — slowly stood up, took a few hesitant steps forward. The young man had paused, was looking through the crowd. She stood still. Was she mistaken? No, she couldn't be wrong. She stepped forward. He saw her, examined her intently. Suddenly he smiled, reached out, took both of ther hands.

'Constance.' It was a declaration, not a question. For almost a minute they stared at each other — remembering.

He held her arm very close as they left the hospital together.

DP

The world had grown accustomed to the televised, newsreeled sight of stolid refugees plodding hopelessly away from calamity, belongings piled on their back. The slaughter in which people had indulged with periodic regularity had blunted the fine edge of their humanity, made them less sensitive to the sufferings of others.

Anyhow, they told themselves, these *displaced persons were* different . . . .

AN OLD WOODCUTTER WOMAN, hunting mushrooms up the north fork of the Kreuzberg, raised her eyes and saw the strangers. They came step by step through the ferns, arms extended, milk-blue eyes blank as clam shells. When they chanced into patches of sunlight, they cried out in hurt voices and clutched at their naked scalps, which were as white as ivory, and netted with pale blue veins.

The old woman stood like a stump, the breath scraping in her throat. She stumbled back, almost falling at each step, her legs moving back to support her at the last critical instant. The strange people came to a wavering halt, peering through sunlight and dark-green shadow. The woman took an hysterical breath, turned, and put her gnarled old legs to flight.

A hundred yards downhill she broke out on a trail; here she found her voice. She ran, uttering cracked screams and hoarse cries, lurching from side to side. She ran till she came to a wayside shrine, where she flung herself into a heap to gasp out prayer and frantic supplication.

Two woodsmen, in leather breeches and rusty black coats,

coming up the path from Tedratz, stared at her in curiosity and amusement. She struggled to her knees, pointed up the trail. 'Fiends from the pit! Walking in all their evil; with my two eyes I've seen them!'

'Come now,' the older woodsman said indulgently. 'You've had a drop or two, and it's not reverent to talk so at a holy place.'

'I saw them,' bellowed the old woman. 'Naked as eggs and white as lard; they came running at me waving their arms, crying out for my very soul!'

'They had horns and tails?' the younger man asked jocularly. 'They prodded you with their forks, switched you with their whips?'

'Ach, you blackguards! You laugh, you mock; go up the slope, see for yourself . . . . Only five hundred meters, and then perhaps you'll mock!'

'Come along,' said the first. 'Perhaps someone's been plaguing the old woman; if so, we'll put him right.'

They sauntered on, disappeared through the firs. The old woman rose to her feet, hobbled as rapidly as she could toward the village.

Five quiet minutes passed. She heard a clatter; the two woodsmen came running at breakneck speed down the path. 'What now?' she quavered, but they pushed past her and ran shouting into Tedratz.

Half an hour later fifty men armed with rifles and shotguns stalked cautiously back up the trail, their dogs on leash. They passed the shrine; the dogs began to strain and growl.

'Up through here,' whispered the older of the two woodsmen. They climbed the bank, threaded the firs, crossed sun-flooded meadows and balsam-scented shade.

From a rocky ravine, tinkling and chiming with a stream of glacier water, came the strange, sad voices.

The dogs snarled and moaned; the men edged forward, peered into the meadow. The strangers were clustered under an overhanging ledge, clawing feebly into the dirt.

'Horrible things!' hissed the foremost man. 'Like great

potato-bugs!' He aimed his gun, but another struck up the barrel. 'Not yet! Don't waste good powder; let the dogs hunt them down. If fiends they be, their spite will find none of us!'

The idea had merit; the dogs were loosed. They bounded forward, full of hate. The shadows boiled with fur and fangs and jerking white flesh.

One of the men jumped forward, his voice thick with rage. 'Look, they've killed Tupp, my good old Tupp!' He raised his gun and fired, an act which became the signal for further shooting. And presently, all the strangers had been done to death, by one means or another.

Breathing hard, the men pulled off the dogs and stood looking down at the bodies. 'A good job, whatever they are — man, beast, or fiend,' said Johann Kirchner, the inkeeper. 'But there's the point! What are they? When have such creatures been seen before?'

'Strange happenings for this earth; strange events for Austria!'

The men stared at the white tangle of bodies, none pressing too close, and now with the waning of urgency their mood became uneasy. Old Alois, the baker, crossed himself and, furtively examining the sky, muttered about the Apocalypse. Franz, the village atheist, had his reputation to maintain. 'Demons,' he asserted, 'presumably would not succumb so easily to dog-bite and bullet; these must be refugees from the Russian zone, victims of torture and experimentation.' Heinrich, the village Communist, angrily pointed out how much closer lay the big American Laager near Innsbruck; this was the effect of capitalist Coca-Cola and comic books upon decent Austrians.

'Nonsense,' snapped another. 'Never an Austrian born of woman had such heads, such eyes, such skin. These things are something else. Salamanders!'

'Zombies,' muttered another. 'Corpses, raised from the dead.'

Alois held up his hand. 'Hist!'

Into the ravine came the pad and rustle of aimless steps, the forlorn cries of the troglodytes.

The men crouched back into the shadows; along the ridge appeared silhouettes, crooked, lumpy shapes feeling their way forward, recoiling from the shafts of sunlight.

Guns cracked and spat; once more the dogs were loosed. they bounded up the side of the ravine and disappeared.

Panting up the slope, the men came to the base of a great overhanging cliff, and here they stopped short. The base of the cliff was broken open. Vague pale-eyed shapes wadded the gap, swaying, shuddering, resisting, moving forward inch by inch, step by step.

'Dynamite!' cried the men. 'Dynamite, gasoline, fire!'

These measures were never put into effect. The commandant of the French occupation garrison arrived with three platoons. He contemplated the fissure, the oyster-pale faces, the oyster-shell eyes and threw up his hands. He dictated a rapid message for the Innsbruck headquarters, then required the villagers to put away their guns and depart the scene.

The villagers sullenly retired; the French soldiers, brave in their sky-blue shorts, gingerly took up positions; and with a hasty enclosure of barbed wire and rails restrained the troglodytes to an area immediately in front of the fissure.

The April 18 edition of the *Innsbruck Kurier* included a skeptical paragraph: 'A strange tribe of mountainside hermits, living in a Kreuzberg cave near Tedratz, was reported today. Local inhabitants are mystified. The Tedratz constabulary, assisted by units of the French garrison, is investigating.'

A rather less cautious account found its way into the channels of the wire services: 'Innsbruck, April 19. A strange tribe has appeared from the recesses of the Kreuzberg near Innsbruck, in the Tyrol. They are said to be hairless, blind, and to speak an incomprehensible language.

'According to unconfirmed reports, the troglodytes were attacked by terrified inhabitants of nearby Tedratz, and after bitter resistance were driven back into their caves.

'French occupation troops have sealed off the entire Kreuzertal. A spokesman for Colonel Courtin, the local Commandant, refuses either to confirm or deny that these "troglodytes" have even appeared.'

Bureau chiefs at the wire services looked long and carefully at the story. Why should French occupation troops interfere in what appeared on the face a purely civil disturbance? A secret colony of war criminals? Unlikely. What then? Mysterious race of troglodytes? Clearly hokum. What then? The story might develop, or it might go limp. In any case, on the late afternoon of April 19, a convoy of four cars started up the Kreuzertal, carrying reporters, photographers and a member of the U.N. Minorities Commission, who by chance happened to be billeted in Innsbruck.

The road to Tedratz wound among grassy meadows, dark story-book forests, in and out of little Alpine villages, with the massive snow-capped knob of the Kreuzberg gradually pushing higher into the sky.

At Tedratz, the party alighted and started up the now notorious trail, to be brought short almost at once at a barricade manned by French soldiers. Upon display of credentials, the reporters and photographers were allowed to pass. The U.N. commissioner had nothing to show, and the NCO in charge of the barricade politely turned him back.

'But I am an official of the United Nations!' cried the outraged commissioner.

'That may well be,' assented the NCO. 'However, you are not a journalist, and my orders are uncompromising.' And the angry commissioner was asked to wait in Tedratz until word could be taken to Colonel Courtin at the camp.

The commissioner seized on the word. ' "Camp"? How is this? I thought there was only a cave, a hole in the mountainside?'

The NCO shrugged. 'Monsieur le Commissionaire is free to conjecture as he sees best.'

A private was taken on as a guide; the reporters and photographers started up the trail, with the long, yellow afternoon light slanting down through the firs.

It was a jocular group; repartee and wisecracks were freely exchanged. Presently the party became winded, as the trail was steep and they were all out of condition. They stopped by a wayside shrine to rest. 'How much farther?' asked a photographer.

'Only a little bit; then you shall see.'

Once more they set out and almost immediately passed a platoon of soldiers stringing barbed wire from tree to tree.

'This will be the third extension,' remarked their guide over his shoulder. 'Every day they come pushing up out of the rock. It is' — he selected a word — 'formidable'.

The jocularity and wisecracks died; the journalists peered through the firs, aware of the sudden coolness of the evening.

They came to the camp, and were taken to Colonel Courtin, a small man full of excitable motion. He swung his arm. 'There, my friends, is what you came to see; look your fill, since it is through your eyes that the world must see.'

For three minutes they stared, muttering to one another, while Courtin teetered on his toes.

'How many are there?' came an awed question.

'Twenty thousand by the latest estimate, and they issue even faster. All from that little hole.' He jumped up on tiptoe, and pointed. 'It is incredible. And still they come, like the objects a magician removes from his hat.'

'But — do they eat?'

Courtin held out his hands. 'Is it for me to ask? I furnish no food; I have none: my budget will not allow it. I am a man of compassion. If you will observe, I have hung the tarpaulins to prevent the sunlight.'

'With that skin, they'd be pretty sensitive, eh?'

'Sensitive!' Courtin rolled up his eyes. 'The sunlight burns them like fire.'

'Funny that they're not more interested in what goes on around them.'

'They are dazed, my friend. Dazed and blinded and completely confused.'

'But — what are they?'

'That, my friend, is a question I am without resource to answer.'

The journalists regained a measure of composure, and swept the enclosure with studiously impassive glances calculated to suggest, *we have seen so many strange sights that now nothing can surprise us.* 'I suppose they're men . . . of sorts,' said one.

'But of course. What else?'

'What else indeed? But where do they come from? Lost Atlantis? The land of Oz?'

'Now then,' said Colonel Courtin, 'you make jokes. It is a serious business, my friends; where will it end?'

'That's the big question, Colonel. Whose baby is it?'

'I do not understand.'

'Who takes responsibility for them? France?'

'No, no,' cried Colonel Courtin. 'You must not credit me with such a statement.'

'Austria, then?'

Colonel Courtin shrugged. 'The Austrians are a poor people. Perhaps — of course I speculate — your great country will once again share of its plenitude.'

'Perhaps, perhaps not. The one man of the crowd who might have had something to say is down in Tedratz — the chap from the Minorities Commission.'

The story pushed everything from the front pages, and grew bigger day by day.

From the U.P. wire:

Innsbruck, April 23 (UP): The Kreuzberg miracle continues to confound the world. Today a record number of troglodytes pushed through the gap, bringing the total surface population up to forty-six thousand . . . .

From the syndicated column, *Science Today* by Ralph V. Dunstaple, for April 28:

The scientific world seethes with the troglodyte controversy. According to the theory most frequently voiced, the 'trogs' are descended from cavemen of the glacial eras, driven underground by the advancing walls of ice. Other conjectures, more or less scientific, refer to the lost tribes of Israel, the fourth dimension, Armageddon, the Nazi experiments.

Linguistic experts meanwhile report progress in their efforts to understand the language of the trogs. Dr. Allen K. Mendelson of the Princeton Institute of Advanced Research, spokesman for the group, classifies the trog speech as 'one of the agglutinatives, with the slightest possible kinship to the Basque tongue — so faint as to be highly speculative, and it is only fair to say that there is considerable disagreement among us on this point. The trogs, incidentally, have no words for "sun", "moon", "fight", "bird", "animal", and a host of other concepts we take for granted. "Food" and "fungus", however, are the same word.'

From the *New York Herald Tribune*:

TROGS HUMAN, CLAIM SAVANTS;
INTERBREEDING POSSIBLE
by Mollie Lemmon
Milan, April 30: Trogs are physiologically identical with surface humanity, and sexual intercourse between man and trog might well be fertile. Such was the opinion of a group of doctors and geneticists at an informal poll conducted yesterday at the Milan Genetical Clinic, where a group of trogs are undergoing examination.'

From *The Trog Story*, a daily syndicated feature by Harlan B. Temple, April 31:

Today I saw the hundred thousandth trog push his way up out of the bowels of the Alps; everywhere in the world people are asking, where will it stop? I certainly have no answer. This tremendous migration, unparalleled since the days of Alaric the Goth, seems only just now shifting into high gear. Two new rifts have opened into the Kreuzberg; the trogs come shoving out in close ranks, faces blank as custard, and only God knows what is in their minds.

The camps — there are now six, interconnected like knots on a rope — extend down the hillside and into the Kreuzertal. Tarpaulins over the treetops give the mountainside, seen from a distance, the look of a lawn with handkerchiefs spread out flat to dry.

The food situation has improved considerably over the past three days, thanks to the efforts of the Red Cross, CARE, and FAO. The basic ration is a mush of rice, wheat, millet or other cereal, mixed with carrots, greens, dried eggs, and reinforced with vitamins; the trogs appear to thrive on it.

I cannot say that the trogs are a noble, enlightened, or even ingratiating race. Their cultural level is abysmally low; they possess no tools, they wear neither clothing nor ornaments. To their credit, it must be said that they are utterly inoffensive and mild; I have never witnessed a quarrel or seen a trog exhibit anything but passive obedience.

Still they rise in the hundreds and thousands. What brings them forth? Do they flee a subterranean Attila, some pandemonic Stalin? The linguists who have been studying the trog speech are close-mouthed, but I have it from a highly informed source that a report will be published within the next day or so . . . .

Report to the Assembly of the U.N., May 4, by V.G. Hendlemann, Co-ordinator for the Committee of Associated Anthropologists:

'I will state the tentative conclusions at which this committee has arrived. The processes and inductions which have led to these conclusions are outlined in the appendix to this report.

'Our preliminary survey of the troglodyte language has convinced a majority of us that the trogs are probably the descendants of a group of European cave-dwellers who either by choice or by necessity took up underground residence at least fifty thousand, at most two hundred thousand years ago.

'The trog which we see today is a result of evolution and mutation, and represents adaptation to the special conditions under which the trogs have existed. He is quite definitely of the species *homo spaiens*, with a cranial capacity roughly identical to that of surface man.

'In our conversations with the trogs we have endeavored to

ascertain the cause of the migration. Not one of the trogs makes himself completely clear on the subject, but we have been given to understand that the great caves which the race inhabited have been stricken by a volcanic convulsion and are being gradually filled with lava. If this be the case the trogs are seen to become literally "displaced persons."

'In their former home the trogs subsisted on fungus grown in shallow "paddies", fertilized by their own wastes, finely pulverized coal, and warmed by volcanic heat.

'They have no grasp of "time" as we understand the word. They have only the sparest traditions of the past and are unable to conceive of a future further removed than a few minutes. Since they exist in the present, they neither expect, hope, dread, nor otherwise take congnizance of what possibly may befall them.

'In spite of their deficiencies of cultural background, the trogs appear to have a not discreditable native intelligence. The committee agrees that a troglodyte child reared in ordinary surface surroundings, and given a typical education, might well become a valuable citizen, indistinguishable from any other human being except by his appearance.'

Excerpt from a speech by Porfirio Hernandez, Mexican delegate to the U.N. Assembly, on May 17:

'. . . We have ignored this matter too long. Far from being a scientific curiosity or a freak, this is a very human problem, one of the most pressing problems of our day and we must handle it as such. The trogs are issuing from the ground at an ever-increasing rate; the Kreuzertal, or Kreuzer Valley, is inundated with trogs as if by a flood. We have heard reports, we have deliberated, we have made solemn noises, but the fact remains that every one of us is sitting on his hands. These people — we must call them people — must be settled somewhere permanently; they must be made self-supporting. This hot iron must be grasped; we fail in our responsibilities otherwise . . . .'

Excerpt from a speech, May 19, by Sir Lyandras Chandryasam, delegate from India:

'. . . My esteemed colleague from Mexico has used brave words; he exhibits a humanitarianism that is unquestionably praiseworthy. But he puts forward no positive program. May I ask how many trogs have come to the surface, thus to be cared for? Is not the latest figure somewhere short of a million? I would like to point out that in India alone, five million people yearly die of malnutrition or preventable disease; but no one jumps up here in the Assembly to cry for a crusade to help these unfortunate victims of nature. No, it is this strange race, with no claim upon anyone, which has contributed nothing to the civilization of the world, which now we feel has first call upon our hearts and purse-strings. I say, is not this a paradoxical circumstance . . . .'

From a speech, May 20, by Dr. Karl Byrnisted, delegate from Iceland:

'. . . Sir Lyandras Chandryasam's emotion is understandable, but I would like to remind him that the streets of India swarm with millions upon millions of so-called sacred cattle and apes, who eat what and where they wish, very possibly the food to keep five million persons alive. The recurrent famines in India could be relieved, I believe, by a rationalistic dealing with these parasites, and by steps to make the new birth-control clinics popular, such as a tax on babies. In this way, the Indian government, by vigorous methods, may cope with its terrible problem. These trogs, on the other hand, are completely unable to help themselves; they are like babies flung fresh into a world where even the genial sunlight kills them . . . .'

From a speech, May 21, by Porfirio Hernandez, delegate from Mexico:

'I have been challenged to propose a positive program for dealing with the trogs . . . . I feel that as an activating principle, each member of the U.N. agree to accept a number of trogs proportionate to its national wealth, resources, and density of population . . . . Obviously the exact percentages will have to thrashed out elsewhere . . . . I hereby move the President of the Assembly appoint such a committee, and instruct them to prepare such a recommendation, said committee to report within two weeks.'

(Motion defeated, 20 to 35)

The Trog Story, June 2, by Harlan B. Temple:

'No matter how many times I walk through Trog Valley, the former Kreuzertal, I never escape a feeling of the profoundest bewilderment and awe. The trogs number now well over a million; yesterday they chiseled open four new openings into the outside world, and they are pouring out at the rate of thousands every hour. And everywhere is heard the question, where will it stop? Suppose the earth is a honeycomb, a hive with more trogs than surface men?

'Sooner or later our organization will break down; more trogs will come up than it is within our power to feed. Organization already has failed to some extent. All the trogs are getting at least one meal a day, but not enough clothes, not enough shelter is being provided. Every day hundreds die from sunburn. I understand that the Old-Clothes-for-Trogs drive has nowhere hit its quota; I find it hard to comprehend. Is there no feeling of concern or sympathy for these people, merely because they do not look like so many chorus boys and screen starlets?'

From the *Christian Science Monitor*:

CONTROVERSIAL TROG BILL
PASSES U.N. ASSEMBLY
New York, June 4: By a 35 to 20 vote — exactly reversing its first tally on the measure — the U.N. Assembly yesterday accepted the motion of Mexico's Ambassador Hernandez to set up a committee for the purpose of recommending a demographic distribution of trogs among member states.

Tabulation of voting on the measure found the Soviet block lined up with the United States and the British Commonwealth in opposition to the measure — presumably the countries which would be awarded the larger numbers of trogs.

Handbill passed out at rally of the Socialist Reich (Neo-Nazi) party at Bremen, West Germany, June 10:

A NEW THREAT
COMRADES! It took a war to clean Germany of the Jews; must we now submit to an invasion of troglodyte filth? All Germany cries *no*! All Germany cries: hold our borders firm

against these cretin moles! Send them to Russia; send them to the Arctic wastes! Let them return to their burrows; let them perish! But guard the Fatherland; guard the sacred German Soil!

(Rally broken up by police, handbills seized.)

Letter to the *London Times*, June 18:

To the Editor:

I speak for a large number of my acquaintances when I say that the prospect of taking to ourselves a large colony of 'troglodytes' awakens in me no feeling of enthusiasm. Surely England has troubles more than enough of its own, without the added imposition of an unassimilable and non-productive minority to eat our already meager rations and raise our already sky-high taxes.

> Yours, etc.,
> Sir Clayman Winifred, Bart.
> Lower Ditchley, Hants.

Letter to the *London Times*, June 21:

To the Editor:

Noting Sir Clayman Winifred's letter of June 18, I took a quick check-up of my friends and was dumbfounded to find out how closely they hew to Sir Clayman's line. Surely this isn't our tradition, not to get under the load and help life with everything we've got? The troglodytes are human beings, victims of a disaster we have no means of appreciating. They must be cared for, and if a qualified committee of experts sets us a quota, I say, let's bite the bullet and do our part.

The Ameriphobe section of our press takes great delight in baiting our cousins across the sea for the alleged denial of civil rights to their Blacks — which, may I add, is present in its most violent and virulent form in a country of the British Commonwealth: the Union of South Africa. What do these journalists say to evidences of the same unworthy emotion here in England?

> Yours, etc.,
> J.C.T. Harrodsmere
> Tisley-on-Thames, Berkshire.

Headline in the *New York Herald Tribune*, June 22:

FOUR NEW TROG CAMPS OPENED; POPULATION AT
TWO MILLION

Letter to the *London Times*, June 24:

To the Editor:
   I read the letter of J.C.T. Harrodsmere in connection with
the trog controversy with great interest. I think that in his
praiseworthy efforts to have England do its bit, he is overlooking
an important fact: namely, we of England are a close-knit
people, of clear clean vigorous blood, and admixture of any
nature could only be for the worse. I know Mr. Harrodsmere
will be quick to say, no admixture is intended. But mistakes
occur, and as I understand a man-trog union to be theoretically
fertile, in due course there would be a number of little half-
breeds scampering like rats around our gutters, a bad show all
around. There are countries where this type of mongrelization
is accepted: the United States, for instance, boasts that it is the
world's 'melting pot'. Why not send the trogs to the wide open
spaces of the U.S. where there is room and to spare, and where
they can 'melt' to their heart's content?
                                 Yours, etc.,
                                 Col. G.P. Barstaple (ret.), Queens Own Hussars,
                                 Mide Hill, Warwickshire.

Letter to the *London Times*, June 28:

To the Editor:
   Contrasting the bank accounts, the general air of aliveness
of mongrel U.S.A. and non-mongrel England, I say maybe it
might do us good to trade off a few retired colonels for a few
trogs extra to our quota. Here's to more and better
mongrelization!
                                 Yours, etc.,
                                 (Miss) Elizabeth Darrow Brown
                                 London, S.W.

The Trog Story, June 30, by Harlan B. Temple:

'Will it come as a surprise to my readers if I say the trog situation is getting out of hand? They are coming not slower but faster; every day we have more trogs and every day we have more at a greater rate than the day before. If the sentence sounds confused, it only reflects my state of mind and the local conditions.

'Something has got to be done.

'Nothing is being done.

'The wrangling that is going on is a matter of public record. Each country is liberal with advice, but with little else. Sweden says, send them to the center of Australia; Australia points to Greenland; Denmark would prefer the Ethiopian uplands; Ethiopia politely indicates Mexico; Mexico says, much more room in Arizona; and at Washington, senators from below the Mason-Dixon Line threaten to filibuster from now till Kingdom Come rather than admit a single trog to the continental limits of the U.S. Thank the Lord for an efficient food administration! The U.N. and the world at large can be proud of the organization by which the trogs are being fed.

'Incidental Notes: trog babies are being born — over fifty yesterday.'

From the *San Franciso Chronicle*:

REDS OFFER HAVEN TO TROGS
PROPOSAL STIRS WORLD
New York. July 3: Ivan Pudestov, the USSR's chief delegate to the U.N. Assembly, today blew the trog question wide open with a proposal to take complete responsibility for the trogs.

The offer startled the U.N. and took the world completely by surprise, since heretofore the Soviet delegation has held itself aloof from the bitter trog controversy, apparently in hopes that the free world would split itself apart on the problem . . . .

Editorial in the *Milwaukee Journal*, July 5, headed 'A Question of Integrity':

At first blush, the Russian offer to take the trogs appears to ease our shoulders of a great weight. Here is exactly what we have been grasping for, a solution without sacrifice, a sop to our consciences, a convenient carpet to sweep our dirt under.

The man in the street, and the responsible official, suddenly are telling each other that perhaps the Russians aren't so bad after all, that there's a great deal of room in Siberia, that the Russians and the trogs are both barbarians and really not so much different, that the trogs were probably Russian to begin with, etc.

Let's break the bubble of illusion, once and for all. We can't go on forever holding our Christian integrity in one hand and our inclinations in the other . . . . Doesn't it seem an odd coincidence that while the Russians are desperately short of uranium miners at the murderous East German and Ural pits, the trogs, accustomed to life underground, might be expected to make a good labor force? . . . In effect, we would be turning over to Russia millions of slaves to be worked to death. We have rejected forced repatriation in West Europe and Korea, let's reject forced patriation and enslavement of the trogs.

Headline in the *New York Times*, July 20:

REDS BAN U.N. SUPERVISION OF TROG COMMUNITIES
SOVEREIGNTY ENDANGERED, SAYS PUDESTOV
ANGRILY WITHDRAWS TROG OFFER

Headline in the *New York Daily News*, July 26:

BELGIUM OFFERS CONGO FOR TROG HABITATION
ASKS FUNDS TO RECLAIM JUNGLE
U.N. GIVES QUALIFIED NOD

From *The Trog Story*, July 28, by Harlan B. Temple:

'Four million (give or take a hundred thousand) trogs now breathe surface air. The Kreuzertal camps now constitute one of the world's largest cities, ranking behind only New York, London, Tokyo. The formerly peaceful Tyrolean valley is now a vast array of tarpaulins, circus tents, quonset huts, water tanks, and general disorder. Trog City doesn't smell too good either.

'Today might well mark the high tide in what the Austrians are calling "the invasion from hell". Trogs still push through a dozen gaps ten abreast, but the pressure doesn't seem so intense. Every once in a while a space appears in the ranks, where formerly they came packed like asparagus in crates. Another difference: the first trogs were meaty and fairly well nourished. These late arrivals are thin and ravenous. Whatever strange subterranean economy they practiced, it seems to have broken down completely . . . .'

From *The Trog Story*, August 1, by Harlan B. Temple:

'Something horrible is going on under the surface of the earth. Trogs are staggering forth with raw stumps for arms, with great wounds . . . .'

From *The Trog Story*, August 8, by Harlan B. Temple:

'Operation Exodus got underway today. One thousand trogs departed the Kreuzertal bound for their new home near Cabinda, at the mouth of the Congo River. Trucks and buses took them to Innsbruck, where they will board special trains to Venice and Trieste. Here, ships supplied by the U.S. Maritime Commission will take them to their new home.

'As one thousand trogs departed Trog City, twenty thousand pushed up from their underground homeland, and camp officials are privately expressing concern over conditions. Trog City has expanded double, triple, ten times over the original estimates. The machinery of supply, sanitation and housing is breaking down. From now on, any attempts to remedy the situation are at best stopgaps, like adhesive tape on a rotten hose, when what is needed is a new hose or, rather, a four-inch pipe.

'Even to maintain equilibrium, thirty thousand trogs per day will have to be siphoned out of the Kreuzertal camps, an obvious impossibility under present budgets and efforts . . . .'

From *Newsweek*, August 14:

Camp Hope, in the bush near Cabinda, last week took on the semblance of the Guadalcanal army base during World War II. There was the old familiar sense of massive confusion, the grind of bulldozers, sweating white, beet-red, brown and black skins, the raw earth dumped against primeval vegetation, bugs, salt tablets, Atabrine . . . .

From the U.P. wire:

Cabinda, Belgian Congo, August 20 (UP): The first contingent of trogs landed last night under shelter of dark, and marched to temporary quarters, under the command of specially trained group captains.

Liaison officers state that the trogs are overjoyed at the prospect of a permanent home, and show an eagerness to get to work. According to present plans, they will till collective farms, and continuously clear the jungle for additional settlers.

On the other side of the ledger, it is rumored that the native tribesmen are showing unrest. Agitators, said to be Communist-inspired, are preying on the superstitious fears of a people themselves not far removed from savagery . . .

Headline in the *New York Times*, August 22:

CONGO WARRIORS RUN AMOK AT CAMP HOPE
KILL 800 TROG SETTLERS IN SINGLE HOUR
Military Law Established
Belgian Governor Protests: Says Congo Unsuitable

From the U.P. Wire:

Trieste, August 23 (UP): Three shiploads of trogs bound for Trogland in the Congo, today marked a record number of embarkations. The total number of trogs to sail from European ports now stands at 24,965.

Cabinda, August 23 (UP): The warlike Matemba Confederation is practically in a state of revolt against further trog immigration, while President-General Bernard Cassou professes grave pessimism over eventualities.

Mont Blanc, August 24 (UP): Ten trogs today took up experimental residence in a ski-hut to see how well trogs can cope with the rigors of cold weather.

Announcement of this experiment confirms a rumor that Denmark has offered Greenland to the trogs, if it is found that they are able to survive Arctic conditions.

Cabinda, August 28 (UP): The Congo, home of witch-doctors, tribal dances, cannibalism and Tarzan, seethes with native unrest. Sullen anger smolders in the villages, riots are frequent and dozens of native workmen at Camp Hope have been killed or hospitalized.

Needless to say, the trogs, whose advent precipitated the crisis, are segregated from contact with natives, to avoid a repetition of the bloodbath of August 22 . . . .

Cabinda, August 29 (UP): President-General Bernard Cassou today refused to allow debarkation of trogs from four ships standing off Cabinda roadstead.

Mont Blanc, September 2 (UP): The veil of secrecy at the experimental trog home was lifted a significant crack this morning, when the bodies of two trogs were taken down to Chamonix via the ski-lift . . . .

From *The Trog Story*, September 10, by Harlan B. Temple:

'It is one a.m.; I've just come down from Camp No. 4. The trog columns have dwindled to a straggle of old, crippled, diseased. The stench is frightful . . . . But why go on? Frankly, I'm heartsick. I wish I had never taken on this assignment. It's doing something terrible to my soul; my hair is literally turning gray. I pause a moment, the noise of my typewriter stops, I listen to the vast murmur through the Kreuzertal; despondency, futility, despair come at me in a wave. Most of us here at Trog City, I think, feel the same.

'There are now five or six million trogs in the camp; no one knows the exact count; no one even cares. The situation has passed that point. The flow has dwindled, one merciful dispensation — in fact, at Camp No. 4, you can hear the rumble of the lava rising into the trog caverns.

'Morale is going from bad to worse here at Trog City. Every day a dozen of the unpaid volunteers throw up their hands, and go home. I can't say as I blame them. Lord knows they've given the best they have, and no one backs them up. Everywhere in the world it's the same story, with everyone pointing at someone else. It's enough to make a man sick. In fact it has. I'm sick — desperately sick.

'But you don't read *The Trog Story* to hear me gripe. You want factual reporting. Very well, here it is. Big news today was that movement of trogs out of the camp to Trieste has been held up pending clarification of the Congo situation. Otherwise, everything's the same here — hunger, smell, careless trogs dying of sunburn . . . .'

Headline in the *New York Times*, September 20:

TROG QUOTA PROBLEM RETURNED TO
STUDY GROUP FOR ADJUSTMENT

From the U.P. Wire:

Cabinda, September 25 (UP): Eight ships, loaded with 9,462 trog refugees, still wait at anchor, as native chieftains reiterated their opposition to trog immigration . . . .

Trog City, October 8 (UP): The trog migration is at its end. Yesterday for the first time no new trogs came up from below, leaving the estimated population of Trog City at six million.

New York, October 13 (UP): Deadlock still grips the Trog Resettlement Committee, with the original positions, for the most part, unchanged. Densely populated countries claim they have no room and no jobs; the underdeveloped states insist that they have not enough money to feed their own mouths. The U.S., with both room and money, already has serious minority headaches and doesn't want new ones . . . .

Chamonix, France, October 18 (UP): The Trog Experimental Station closed its doors yesterday, with one survivor of the original ten trogs riding the ski-lift back down the slopes of Mont Blanc.

Dr. Sven Emeldson, director of the station, released the following statement: 'Our work proves that the trogs, even if provided shelter adequate for a European, cannot stand the rigors of the North; they seem especially sensitive to pulmonary ailments . . . .'

New York, October 26 (UP): After weeks of acrimony, a revised set of trog immigration quotas was released for action by the U.N. Assembly. Typical figures are: USA 31%, USSR 16%, Canada 8%, Australia 8%, France 6%, Mexico 6%.

New York, October 30 (UP): Senator Bullrod of Mississippi today promised to talk till his 'lungs came out at the elbows' before he would allow the Trog Resettlement Bill to come to a vote before the Senate. An informal check revealed insufficient strength to impose closure . . . .

St. Arlberg, Austria, November 5 (UP): First snow of the season fell last night . . . .

Trog City, November 10 (UP): Last night, frost lay a sparkling sheath across the valley . . . .

Trog City, November 15(UP): Trog sufferers from influenza have been isolated in a special section . . . .

Buenos Aires, November 23 (UP): Dictator Peron today flatly refused to meet the Argentine quota of relief supplies to Trog City until some definite commitment has been made by the U.N. . . .

Trog City, December 2 (UP): Influenza, following the snow and rain of last week, has made a new onslaught on the trogs; camp authorities are desperately trying to cope with the epidemic . . . .

Trog City, December 8 (UP): Two crematoriums, fired by fuel oil, are roaring full time in an effort to keep ahead of the mounting influenza casualties . . . .

From *The Trog Story*, December 13, by Harlan B. Temple:

'This is it . . . .'

From the U.P. Wire:

Los Angeles, December 14 (UP): The Christmas buying rush got under way early this year, in spite of unseasonably bad weather . . . .

Trog City, December 15 (UP): A desperate appeal for penicillin, sulfa, blankets, kerosene heaters, and trained personnel was sounded today by Camp Commandant Howard Kerkovits. He admitted that disease among the trogs was completely out of control, beyond all human power to cope with . . . .

From *The Trog Story*, December 23, by Harlan B. Temple:

'I don't know why I should be sitting here writing this, because — since there are no more trogs — there is no more trog story.'

THE PHANTOM MILKMAN

I'VE HAD ALL I CAN STAND. I've got to get out, away from the walls, the glass, the white stone, the black asphalt. All of a sudden I see the city for the terrible place that it is. Lights burn my eyes, voices crawl on my skin like sticky insects, and I notice that the people look like insects too. Burly brown beetles, wispy mosquito-men in tight black trousers, sour sow-bug women, mantids and scorpions, fat little dung-beetles, wasp-girls gliding with poisonous nicety, children like loathsome little flies. . . . This isn't a pleasant thought; I must not think of people so; the image could linger to haunt me. I think I'm a hundred times more sensitive than anyone else in the world, and I'm given to very strange fancies. I could list some that would startle you, and it's just as well that I don't. But I do have this frantic urge to flee the city. It's settled; I'm going.

I consult my maps — there's the Andes, the Atlas, the Altai; Mt. Godwin-Austin, Mt. Kilimanjaro; Stromboli and Etna. I compare Siberia above Baikal Nor with the Pacific between Antofagasta and Easter Island. Arabia is hot; Greenland is cold. Tristan da Cunha is very remote; Bouvet even more so. There's Timbuktu, Zanzibar, Bali, the Great Australian Bight.

I am definitely leaving the city. I have found a cabin in Maple Valley, four miles west of Sunbury. It stands a hundred feet back from Maple Valley Road, under two tall trees. It has three rooms and a porch, a fireplace, a good roof, a good well and a windmill.

Mrs. Lipscomb is skeptical, even a little shocked. 'A good-looking girl like you shouldn't go off by yourself; time to hide away when you're old and nobody wants you.' She predicts hair-raising adventures, but I don't care. I was married to Poole for six weeks; nothing could happen that would be any worse.

I'm in my new house. There's lots of work ahead of me: scrubbing, chopping wood. I'll probably bulge with muscles before the winter's over.

My cats are delighted. They are Homer and Moses. Homer is yellow; Moses is black and white. Which reminds me: milk. I saw a Sunbury Dairy delivery truck on the highway. I'll write them an order now.

Sunbury Dairy   November 14
Sunbury
Dear Sirs:
   Please leave me a quart of milk three times a week on whatever days are convenient. Please bill me.

                                        Isabel Durbrow
                                        RFD Route 2, Box 82
                                        Sunbury

My mailbox is battered and dusty; one day I'll paint it: red, white and blue, to cheer the mailman. He delivers at ten in the morning, in an old blue panel truck.

When I mail the letter, I see that there's already one in the box. It's for me — forwarded by Mrs. Lipscomb. I take it slowly. I don't want it; I recognize the handwriting: it's from Poole, the dark-visaged brute I woke up from childhood to find myself married to. I tear it in pieces: I'm not even curious. I'm still young and very pretty, but right now there's no one I want, Poole least of all. I shall wear blue jeans and write by the fireplace all winter; and in the spring, who knows?

During the night the wind comes up; the windmill cries from the cold. I lie in bed, with Homer and Moses at my feet. The coals in the fireplace flicker. . . . Tomorrow I'll write Mrs. Lipscomb; by no means must she give Poole my address.

I have written the letter. I run down the slope to the mailbox. It's a glorious late autumn day. The wind is crisp, the hills are like an ocean of gold with scarlet and yellow trees for surf.

I pull open the mailbox. . . .Now, this is odd! My letter to Sunbury Dairy — gone. Perhaps the carrier came early? But it's only nine o'clock. I put in the letter to Mrs. Lipscomb and look all around. . . .Nothing. Who would want my letter? My cats stand with tails erect, looking keenly up the road, first in one direction then the other, like surveyors planning a new highway. Well, come kittens, you'll drink canned milk today.

At ten o'clock the carrier passes, driving his dusty blue panel truck. He did not come early. That means — somone took my letter.

It's all clear; I understand everything. I'm really rather angry. This morning I found milk on my porch — a quart — bottled by the Maple Valley Dairy — a competitor? I don't know, but they have no right to go through my mailbox; they thought I'd never notice. . . .I won't use the milk; it can sit and go sour; I'll report them to the Sunbury Dairy and the post office besides. . . .

I've worked quite hard. I'm not really an athletic woman, much as I'd like to be. The pile of wood that I've chopped and sawed is quite disproportionate to the time I've spent. Homer and Moses help me not at all. They sit on the logs, wind in and out underfoot. It's time for their noon meal. I'll give them canned milk, which they detest.

I pour milk into a bowl; the cats strop their ribs on my shins.

I guess they're not hungry. Homer takes five or six laps, then draws back, making a waggish face. Moses glances up to see if I'm joking. I know my cats very well; to some extent I can understand their language. It's not all in the 'meows' and 'maroos'; there's the slope of the whiskers and set of the ear. Naturally they understand each other better than I do, but I generally get the gist.

Neither one likes the milk.

'Very well,' I say severely, 'you're not going to waste good milk; you won't get any more.'

They saunter across the room and sit down. Perhaps the milk is sour; if so, that's the last straw. I smell the milk, like hay and pasturage. Surely this isn't pasteurized milk! And I look at the cap. It says. 'Maple Valley Dairy. Fresh milk. Sweet and clean from careless cows.'

I presume that 'carelss' is understood in the sense of 'free from care', rather than 'slovenly'.

Well, careless cows or not, Homer and Moses have turned up their noses. What a wonderful poem I could write, in the Edwardian manner.

Homer and Moses have turned up their noses;
They're quite disappointed with tea.
Their scones are like stones, the fish is all bones;
The milk that they've tasted; it's certainly wasted,
But they're getting no other from me.

They'll just learn to like fresh milk or do without, ungrateful little scamps.

I have been scrubbing floors and whitewashing the kitchen. No more chopping and sawing. I've ordered wood from the farmer down the road. The cabin is looking very cheerful. I have curtains at the windows, books on the mantel, sprays of autumn leaves in a big blue bottle I found in the shed.

Speaking of bottles: tomorrow morning the milk is delivered. I must put out the bottle.

Homer and Moses still won't drink Maple Valley Dairy milk. . . .They look at me so wistfully when I pour it out, I suppose I'll have to give in and get something else. It's lovely milk; I'd drink it myself if I liked milk.

Today I drove into Sunbury, and just for a test I brought home a bottle of Sunbury Dairy milk. Now we'll see. . .I fill a bowl. Homer and Moses are wondering almost audibly if this is the same distasteful stuff I've been serving the last week. I put down the bowl; they fall to with such gusto that milk splashes onto their whiskers and drips all over the floor. That settles it. Tonight I'll put a note in the bottle, stopping delivery from Maple Valley Dairy.

I don't understand! I wrote very clearly. 'Please deliver no more milk.' Lo and behold, the driver has the gall to leave me two bottles. I certainly won't pay for it. The ineffable, unutterable nerve of the man!

Sunbury Dairy doesn't deliver up Maple Valley. I'll just buy milk with my groceries. And tonight I'll write a firm note to Maple Valley Dairy.

November 21

Dear Sirs:
   Leave no more milk! I don't want it. My cats won't drink it. Here is fifty cents for the two bottles I have used.
   Isabel Durbrow.

I am perplexed and angry. The insolence of the people is incredible. They took the two bottles back, then left me another. And a note. It's on rough gray paper, and it reads:
   'You asked for it; you are going to get it'.
   The note has a rather unpleasant ring to it. It certainly couldn't be a threat. . . .I don't think I like these people. . . .They must deliver very early; I've never heard so much as a step.
   The farmer down the road is delivering my wood. I say to him, 'Mr. Gable, this Maple Valley Dairy, they have a very odd way of doing business.'
   'Maple Valley Dairy?' Mr. Gable looks blank. 'I don't think I know them.'
   'Oh,' I ask him, 'don't you buy their milk?'

'I've got four cows of my own for milk.'

'Maple Valley Dairy must be further up the road.'

'I hardly think so,' says Mr. Gable. 'I've never heard of them.'

I show him the bottle; he looks surprised, and shrugs.

Many of these country people don't travel more than a mile or two from home the whole of their lives.

Tomorrow is milk day; I believe I'll get up early and tell the driver just what I think of the situation.

It is six o'clock; very gray and cold. The milk is already on the porch. What time do they deliver, in Heaven's name?

Tomorrow is milk day again. This time I'll get up at four o'clock and wait till he arrives.

The alarm goes off. It startles me. The room is still dark. I'm warm and drowsy. For a moment I can't remember why I should get up. . . . The milk, the insufferable Maple Valley Dairy. Perhaps I'll let it go till next time. . . . I hear a thump on the porch. There he is now: I jump up, struggle into a bathrobe, run across the room.

I open the door. The milk is on the porch. I don't see the milkman. I don't see the truck. I don't hear anything. How could he get away so fast? It's incredible. I find this whole matter very disturbing.

To make matters worse, there's another letter from Poole in the mail. This one I read, and am sorry that I bothered. He is planning to fight the divorce. He wants to come back and live with me. He explains at great length the effect I have on him; it's conceited and parts are rather disgusting. Where have I disappeared to? He's sick of this stalling around. The letter is typical of Poole, miserable soul in a large flamboyant body. I was never a person to him; I was an ornamental vessel into which he could spend his passion — a lump of thera-peutic clay he could knead and pound and twist. He is a very ugly man; I was his wife all of six weeks. . . . I'd hate to have him find me out here. But Mrs. Lipscomb won't tell . . . .

Farmer Gable brought me another load of wood. He says he smells winter in the air. I suppose it'll snow before long. Then won't the fire feel good!

The alarm goes off. Three-thirty. I'm going to catch that milkman if it's the last thing I do.

I crawl out on the cold floor. Homer and Moses wonder what the hell's going on. I find my slippers, my bathrobe. I go to the porch.

No milk yet. Good. I'm in time. So I wait. The east is only tinged with gray; a pale moon shines on the porch. The hill across the road is tarnished silver, the trees black.

I wait. . . .It is four o'clock. The moon is setting.

I wait. . . .It is four thirty.

Then five.

No milkman.

I am cold and still. My joints ache. I cross the room and light a fire in the wood stove. I see Homer looking at the door. I run to the window. The milk is in its usual place.

There is something very wrong here. I look up the valley, down the valley. The sky is wide and dreary. The trees stand on top of the hills like people looking out to sea. I can't believe that anyone is playing a joke on me. . . .Today I'll go looking for the Maple Valley Dairy.

I haven't found it. I've driven the valley one end to the other. No one's heard of it.

I stopped the Sunbury Dairy delivery truck. He never heard of it, either.

The telephone book doesn't list it.

No one knows them at the post office. . .or the police station. . .or the feed store.

It would almost seem that there is no Maple Valley Dairy. Except for the milk they leave on my porch three times a week.

I can't think of anything to do — except ignore them. . . .It would be interesting if it weren't so frightening. . . .I won't move; I won't return to the city . . . .

Tonight it's snowing. The flakes drift past the window, the fire roars up the flue. I've made myself a wonderful hot buttered rum. Homer and Moses sit purring. It's very cozy — except I keep looking at the window, wondering what's watching me.

Tomorrow there'll be more milk. They can't be doing this for nothing! Could it be that — no . . . for a moment I felt a throb. Poole. . . . He's cruel enough, and he's sneaky enough, but I don't see how he could have done it.

I'm lying awake. It's early morning. I don't think the milk has come; I've heard nothing.

It's stopped snowing; there's a wonderful hush outside.

A faint thud. The milk. I'm out of bed, but now I'm terribly frightened. I force myself to the window. I've no idea what I'll see.

The milk is there; the bottle shining, white. . . . Nothing else. I turn away. Back to bed. Homer and Moses look bored.

I swing back in sudden excitement; my flashlight, where is it? There'll be tracks.

I open the door. The snow is an even white blanket everywhere — shimmering. glimmering, pale and clear. No tracks. . . . Not a mark!

If I have any sense, I'll leave Maple Valley, I'll never come back. . . .

Around the neck of the bottle hangs a printed form. I reach out into the cold.

> Dear Customer:
> Does our service satisfy you?
> Have you any complaints?
> Can we leave you any other commodities?
> Just let us know; we will deliver and you will be billed.

I write on the card:

My cats don't like your milk and I don't like you. The only

thing I want you to leave is your footprints, going away. No more milk! I won't pay for it!

Isabel Durbrow.

I can't get my car started; the battery's dead. It's snowing again. I'll wait till it stops, then hike up to my neighbor, Mr. Gable's, for a push.

It's still snowing. Tomorrow the milk. I've asked for his footprints. Tomorrow morning. . . .

I haven't slept. I'm still awake, listening. There are noises off in the woods, and windmill creaks and groans, a dismal sound.

Three o'clock. Homer and Moses jump down to the floor — two soft thuds. They pad back and forth, then jump back up on the bed. They're restless tonight. Homer is telling Moses, 'I don't like this stuff at all. We never saw stuff like this going on in the city.'

Moses agrees without reservation.

I lie quiet, huddled under the blankets, listening. The snow crunches a little. Homer and Moses turn to look.

A thud. I am out of bed; I run to the door.

The milk.

I run out in my slippers.

The footprints.

There are two of them in the snow just under the milk bottle. Two foot-prints, the mark of two feet. Bare feet!

I yell. 'You cowards! You miserable sneaks! I'm not afraid of you!'

I am though. It's easy to yell when you know that no one will answer . . . but I'm not sure. . . . Suppose they do?

There is a note on the bottle. It reads:

'You ordered milk; you'll be billed. You ordered footprints; you'll be billed. On the first of the month all accounts are due and payable.'

I sit in the chair by the fire.

I don't know what to do. I'm terribly scared. I don't dare

to look at the window for fear of seeing a face. I don't dare to wander up into the woods.

I know I should leave. But I hate to let anyone or anything drive me away. Someone *must* be playing a joke on me . . . but they're not. . . . I wonder how they expect me to pay; in what coin?. . . What is the value of a footprint? Of six quarts of goblin milk the cats won't drink? Today is the 30th of November.

Tomorrow is the first.

At ten o'clock the mailman drives past. I run down and beg him to help me start my car. It takes only a minute; the motor catches at once.

I drive into Sunbury and put in a long distance call, to Howard Mansfield. He's a young engineer I knew before I was married. I tell him everything in a rush. He sounds concerned but he takes the practical viewpoint. He says he'll come tomorrow and check the situation. I think he's more interested in checking me. I don't mind; he'll behave himself if I tell him to. And I do want someone here the next time the milk comes . . . Which should be the morning of the day after tomorrow.

It's clear and cool. I've recharged the battery; I've bought groceries; I drive home. The fire in the stove has gone down; I build it up and make another in the fireplace.

I fry two lamb chops and make a salad. I feed Homer and Moses and eat my dinner.

Now it's very quiet. The cold makes small creaking noises outside; about ten o'clock the wind starts to come up. I'm tired, but I'm too nervous to go to sleep. These are the last hours of November 30th, they're running out. . . .

I hear a soft sound outside, a tap at the door. The knob turns, but the door is bolted. For some reason I look at the clock. Eleven-thirty. Not yet the first. Howard has arrived?

I slowly go to the door. I wish I had a gun.

'Who's there?' My voice sounds strange.

'It's me.' I recognize the voice. Poole!

'Go away!'

'Open up. Or I'll bust in.'

'Go away.' I'm suddenly very frightened. It's so dark and everyone so far away; how could he have found me? Mrs. Lipscomb? Or through Howard?

'I'm coming in, Isabel. Open up, or I'll tear a hole in the wall!'

'I'll shoot you. . . .'

He laughs. 'You wouldn't shoot me. . . I'm your husband.'

The door creaks as he puts his shoulder to it. The screws pull out of old wood; the bolt snaps loose, the door bursts open.

He poses for a moment, half-smiling. He has very black hair, a sharp thin nose, pale skin. His cheeks are red with the cold. He has the look of a decadent young Roman senator, and I know he's capable of anything queer or cruel.

'Hello, honey. I've come to take you back.'

I know I'm in for a long hard pull. Telling him to get out, to go away, is a waste of breath.

'Shut the door.' I go back to the fire. I won't give him the satisfaction of seeing that I'm frightened.

He comes slowly across the room. Homer and Moses crouch on the bed hoping he won't notice them.

'You're pretty well hid out.'

'I'm not hiding.' And I wonder again if, after all, he's behind the Maple Valley Dairy. He *must* be.

'Have you come to collect for the milk, Poole?' I try to speak softly, as if I've known all the time.

He looks at me, half-smiling. I see he's puzzled. He pretends that he understands. 'Yeah. I've been missing my cream.'

I sit looking at him, trying to convey my contempt. He wants me to fear him. He knows I don't love him. Fear or love — one suits him as well as the other. Indifference he won't take.

His mouth starts to twist. It looks as if he's thinking wistful thoughts, but I know he is becoming angry.

I don't want him angry. I say, 'It's almost my bed-time, Poole.'

He nods. 'That's a good idea.'

I say nothing.

He swings a chair around, straddles it with his arms along the back, his chin on his arms. The firelight glows on his face.

'You're pretty cool, Isabel.'

'I've no reason to be otherwise.'

'You're my wife.'

'No.'

He jumps up, grabs my wrist, looks down into my eyes. He's playing with me. We both know what he's planning; he advances to it by easy stages.

'Poole,' I say in a cold voice, 'you make me sick.'

He slaps my face. Not hard. Just enough to indicate that he's the master. I stare at him; I don't intend to lose control. He can kill me; I won't show fear; nothing but contempt.

He reads my mind, he takes it as a challenge; his lips slowly curl. He drops my arms, sits down, grins at me. Whatever he felt when he came here, now it's hate. Because I see through his poses, past his good looks, his black, white and rose beauty.

'The way I see it,' says Poole, 'you're up here playing around with two or three other men.'

I blush; I can't help it. 'Think what you like.'

'Maybe it's just one man.'

'If he finds you here — he'll give you a beating.'

He looks at me interestedly; then laughs, stretches his magnificent arms, writhes his shoulder muscles. He is proud of his physique.

'It's a good bluff, Isabel. But knowing you, your virginal mind. . . .'

The clock strikes twelve. Someone taps at the door. Poole jerks around, looks at the door, then at me.

I jump to my feet. I stare at the door.

'Who's that?' demands Poole.

'I — really don't — know.' I'm not sure. But it's twelve o'clock; it's December first. Who else could it be? 'It's — it's the milkman.' I start for the door — slowly. Of course I don't intend to open it.

'Milkman, eh? At midnight?' He jumps up, catches my arm. 'Come to collect the milk bill, I suppose.'

'That's quite right.' My voice sounds strained and dry.

'Maybe he'd like to collect from me.'

'I'll take care of him, Poole.' I try to pull away, knowing that whatever I seem to want, he won't allow. 'Let me go.'

'I'll pay your milk bill. . . . After all, dear,' he says silkily, 'I'm your husband.'

He shoves me across the room, goes to the door. I bury my face in my arms.

The door swings wide. 'So you're the milkman,' he says. his voice trails away. I hear a sudden gasp. I don't look.

Poole is paying the milk bill.

The door creaks slowly shut. A quick shuffle of steps on the porch, a crunching of snow.

After a while I get up, prop a chair under the door knob, build up the fire. I sit looking at the flames. I don't go near the window.

The cold yellow dawn-sun is shining through the window. the room is cold. I build a roaring fire, put on the coffee, look around the cabin. I've put in lots of work, but I don't have much to pack. Howard is coming today. He can help me.

The sun shines bright through the window. At last — I open the door, step out on the porch. The sun is dazzling on the snow. Poole's convertible is parked by the roadside, empty. There's a shuffle of prints around the door, but away from the porch the snow is pure and clean.

A bill is stuck in the milk bottle and it's marked, 'Paid in full.'

I go inside the house, where I drink coffee, pet Homer and Moses, and try to stop my hands from shaking.

ALFRED'S ARK

BEN HIXEY, EDITOR of the Marketville, Iowa, *Weekly Courier*, leaned back in his chair, lit the stub of a dead cigar, inspected his visitor through the smoke. 'Alfred, you look the picture of deep despair. Why the long face?'

Alfred Johnson, the local feed-and-grain merchant, made no immediate reply. He looked out of the window, at his boots, at Ben, at his own thick hands. He rubbed his stiff brown hair, releasing a faint haze of dust and chaff. He said finally, 'I don't hardly know how to tell you, Ben, without causing a lot of excitement.'

'Begin at the beginning,' said Ben. 'I'm a hard man to excite. You're not getting married again?'

Alfred shook his head, grinning the painful grin of a man who has learned the hard way. 'Twice was enough.'

'Well, give. Let's hear the excitement.'

'Do you read your Bible, Ben?'

'Bible?' Ben clapped his hand down on the latest issue of *Editor and Publisher*. 'Here's my Bible.'

'Seriously, now.'

'No,' said Ben, blowing a plume of smoke toward the ceiling. 'I can't say as I'm a real deep-dyed student in such matters.'

'You don't need the Bible to tell you there's wickedness in the world,' Alfred said. 'Lots of it.'

Ben agreed. 'I'd never vote for it, but it sure helps circulation.'

'Six thousand years ago the world was like it is today — full of sin. You remember what happened?'

'Off-hand, no.'

'The Lord sent a great flood. He washed the world clean of wickedness. Ben, there's going to be another flood.'

'Now Alfred,' said Ben briskly, 'are you pulling my leg?'

'No, sir. You study your Bible, you'll see for yourself. The day is coming and it's coming soon!'

Ben rearranged the papers on his desk. 'I suppose you want me to print big headlines about this flood?'

Alfred hitched himself forward, struck the desk earnestly with his fist. 'Here's my plan, Ben. I want the good citizens of this town to get together. I want us to build an ark, to put aboard two beasts of every kind, plenty of food and drink, a selection of good literature, and make ourselves ready. Don't laugh at me, Ben. It's coming.'

'Just when is the big day?'

'June 20th. That gives us less than a year. Not much time, but enough.'

'Alfred — are you serious?'

'I most surely am, Ben.'

'I always took you for a sensible man, Alfred. You can't believe something so fantastic as all this.'

Alfred smiled. 'I never expected you to take it on my say-so. I'm going to prove it to you.' He took a Bible from his pocket, walked around the desk, held it in front of Ben's restless gaze. 'Look here . . .'

For half an hour he argued his case, pointing out the significant pasages, explaining implications which Ben might otherwise have missed. 'Now,' he said, 'now do you believe me?'

Ben leaned back in his chair. 'Alfred, you want my advice?'

'I'd like your *help*, Ben. I'd like you and your family aboard this ark I'm fixing to build.'

'I'll give you my advice. Get yourself married again. It's the lesser of the evils, and it'll take your mind off this flood proposition.'

Alfred rose to his feet. 'I guess you won't run an announcement in the paper?'

'No, sir. And do you know why? Because I don't want

to make you the laughing-stock of the county. You go home and clean up, take a run into Davenport, get good and drunk, and forget all this stuff.

Alfred waved his hand in resignation, departed.

Ben Hixey sighed, shook his head, returned to work.

Alfred returned a moment or two later. 'Here's something you can do for me, Ben. I want to put my business up for sale. I want to run a big ad on your front page. At the bottom I want you to print: 'Flood coming, June 20th. Help and funds needed to build an ark.' Will you do that?'

'It's your advertisement,' said Ben.

Two weeks later on a vacant lot next to his house, Alfred Johnson began construction of an ark. He had sold his business for a price his friends considered outrageous. 'He stole it from you, Alfred!' Alfred shook his head. 'I stole from him. In a year that business will be washed clean out of sight. I only took his money because in a year his money won't be any good either.'

'Alfred,' his friends told him in disgust, 'you're making a fool of yourself!'

'Maybe so,' said Alfred. 'And maybe while you're swimming I'll be standing. Ever think of that?'

'You're really in earnest, Alfred?'

'Of course I'm in earnest. You ever hear of divine revelation? That's what I had. Now if you've only come to jaw, excuse me, I gotta get to work.

The ark took shape: a barge fifty feet long, thirty feet wide, ten feet deep. Alfred became something of a local celebrity, and the townspeople made it a practice to come past and check on progress. Alfred received a great deal of jocular advice.

'That barge sure ain't big enough, Alfred,' called Bill Olafson. 'Not when you consider the elephants and rhinoceroses and giraffes and lions and tigers and hippos and grizzly bears.'

'I'm not taking savage beasts,' said Alfred. 'Just a few pedigreed cattle, cows, horses and sheep, nothing but good stock. If the Lord wanted the others saved he'd have sent me more money. I got just enough for what you see.'

'What about a woman, Alfred? You ain't married. You planning to repopulate the world by this here immaculate conception idea?'

'If the right woman don't come along,' said Alfred, 'I'll just up and hire a woman for the day. When she sees I'm the only man left alive, she'll marry me quick enough.'

The fall passed into winter; spring came, and the ark was complete. Alfred began loading aboard stores of all kinds.

Ben Hixey came out to see him one day. 'Well, Alfred, I must say you got the courage of your conviction.'

'It's not courage, Ben. It's cowardice. I don't want to drown. I'm sorry some of you other folks ain't cowards along with me.'

'I'm more worried about the H-bomb, Alfred. That's what I'd like to build an ark against.'

'In just about a month there won't be any H-bomb left, Ben. There won't be bombs of any kind, never again, if I got anything to say about it — and I guess I will, the way things look.'

Ben surveyed the ark with wondering eyes. 'You're really convinced of this business, aren't you, Alfred?'

'I sure am, Ben. There's a lot of good folk I'll hate to see go — but I gave you all warning. I wrote the President and the Governor and the head of *Reader's Digest*.'

'Yeah? What did they say?'

'They wrote back thanks for my suggestions. But I could see they didn't believe me.'

Ben Hixey smiled. 'I don't either, Alfred.'

'You'll see, Ben.'

June arrived in a spell of wonderful summer weather. Never had the countryside looked so fresh and beautiful. Alfred bought his livestock, and on June 15 herded them aboard the ark. His friends and neighbors took photographs, and made a ceremonial presentation of a glass cage containing two fleas. The problem of securing a woman to become progenetrix of the future race solved itself: a press agent announced that his client, the beautiful movie starlet Maida Brent had volunteered her services, and would be aboard the ark on the morning of June 20th.

'No,' said Alfred Johnson. 'June 20th begins at midnight. She's got to be aboard on the night of June 19th.'

The press agent, after consultation with Miss Brent, agreed.

June 18th dawned bright and sunny, although radio and TV weather reports mentioned peculiar kinks in the jet stream.

On the morning of June 19th, Alfred Johnson, wearing new shoes and a new suit, called in on Ben Hixey. 'Last time around, Ben.'

Ben looked up from an AP dispatch, grinning rather ruefully. 'I've been reading the weather report.'

Alfred nodded. 'I know. Rain.' He held out his hand. 'Goodbye, Ben.'

At noon on June 19th, deep dull clouds began rolling in from the north. Miss Maida Brent arrived at seven o'clock in her Cadillac convertible, and amid the mingled flickers of lightning and flashbulbs went aboard the ark. The press agent attempted to come aboard also, but Alfred barred the way. 'Sorry. Crew is complete now.'

'But Miss Brent can't stay aboard all night, Mr. Johnson.'

'She'll be aboard for forty days and forty nights. She might as well get used to it. Now scram.'

The press agent shrugged, went to wait in the car. Miss Maida Brent would no doubt leave the ark when she was ready.

The rain began to fall during the evening, and at ten o'clock was coming down heavily. At eleven, the press agent sloshed over to the ark. 'Maida! Hey Maida!'

Maida Brent appeared in the doorway of the cabin. 'Well?'

'Let's go! We've got all the stuff we need.'

Maida Brent sniffed, looked toward the massive black sky. 'What's the weather report say?'

'Rain.'

'Alfred and I are playing checkers. We're quite cozy. You go on. Bye.'

The press agent turned up the collar to his coat, hopped stiff-legged back to the car, where he morosely tried to catnap. The thudding of the rain kept him awake.

Dawn failed to reveal itself. At nine o'clock, a wan wet gloom showed gutters ankle deep in water. The rain pelted down ever harder. Along the streets, cars driven by the curious began to appear, their radios turned to the weather report. Puzzled forecasters spoke of stationary cold fronts, occluded lows, cyclones and anti-cyclones. The forecast: rain.

The street became crowded. News came in that the Perry River Bridge had washed out, that Pewter Creek was in flood. Flood? Yes, flood!

Bill Olafson came splashing through the mud. 'Hey Alfred! Where are you?'

Alfred looked calmly out of the cabin. 'Hello, Bill.'

'My wife and kids want to take a look at your ark. Okay if I bring 'em aboard for a spell?'

'Sorry, Bill. No can do.'

Bill walked uncertainly back to the car. There was a tremendous rumble of thunder — he looked skyward in apprehension.

Alfred heard a sound from the rear of the ark. He pulled on his slicker, his boots, trudged back to find two teenaged boys and their girl friends mounting a ladder.

Alfred dislodged the ladder. 'Keep clear, boys. Git away now. I don't wanta speak to you again.'

'Alfred!' Maida's voice came thinly through the thrash of rain. 'There's people coming aboard!'

Alfred ran back to meet a score of his friends and neighbors led by Bill Olafson carrying suitcases into the cabin. 'Get off this ark, friends,' said Alfred in a kindly voice. 'There's not room aboard.'

'We came to see how things were,' said Bill.

'They're fine. Now git.'

'I don't think so, Alfred.' He reached over the side.
'Okay Mama, pass up Joanne and the puppy. Quick.
Before those others get here.'

'If you don't go,' said Alfred, 'I'll have to make you git.'

'Just don't try no funny stuff, Alfred.'

Alfred stepped forward; Bill hit him in the nose. Others
of Alfred's friends and neighbors lifted him, carried him
kicking and cursing to the rail, threw him off the ark and
into the mud.

From the street scores of people came running: men,
women, children. They flung themselves up the rail,
clambered aboard the ark. The cabin was crowded, the rails
were thronged.

There was a clap of thunder; the rain lessened. Overhead
appeared a thin spot in the clouds. The sun burst through.
The rain stopped.

Alfred's friends and neighbors, crowded along the rail,
looked down at Alfred. Alfred, still sitting in the mud,
looked steadily back. Around them the sun glistened on
the wet buildings, the flowing streets.

A PRACTICAL MAN'S GUIDE

RALPH BANKS, EDITOR of *Popular Crafts Monthly*, was a short stocky man with a round pink face, a crisp crew-cut, an intensely energetic manner. He wore gabardine suits and bow ties; he lived in Westchester with a wife, three children, an Irish Setter, a pair of Siamese cats. He was respected by his subordinates; liked, but not quite to the same extent.

The essence of Ralph Banks was practicality — an unerring discrimination between sound and sham, feasible and foolish. The faculty was essential to his job; and in its absence he could not have functioned a day. Across his desk flowed a tide of articles, ideas, sketches, photographs, working models, each of which he must evaluate at a glance. Looking at blueprints for houses, garages, barbecue pits, orchidariums, off-shore cruisers, sailplanes and catamarans, he saw the completed project, functional or not, as the case might be — a feat which he similarly performed with technical drawings for gasoline turbines, hydraulic rams, amateur telescopes, magnetic clutches, monorail systems and one-man submarines. Given a formula for week-killer, anti-freeze compound, invisible ink, fine-grain developer, synthetic cattle-fodder, stoneware glaze or rubber-base paint, he could predict its efficacy. At his fingertips were specifications and performance data for Stutz Bearcat, Mercer, S.G.V., Doble and Stanley Steamer; also Bugatti, Jaguar, Porsche, Nash-Healy and Pegasco; not to mention Ford, Chevrolet, Cadillac, and Chrysler. He could build lawn furniture, hammer copper, polish agate, weave Harris tweed, repair watches, photograph amoebae, lithograph, dye *batik*, etch glass, detect forgeries with infra-red light, and seriously disable a heavier opponent. True, Banks farmed out much of his work to experts and department editors, but final responisibility was his. Blunders evoked quiet ridicule from the competitors and sardonic letters from the readers; Banks made few blunders. For twelve years he had ridden the tiger, and in the process had developed a head for his job which amounted to second-sight; by now he was able to relax, enjoy his work, and indulge himself in his hobby, which was the collecting of freakish inventions.

Every morning his secretary sifted the mail, and when Ralph Banks arrived he would find the material arranged by categories. A special large basket was labelled SCREWBALL ALLEY — and here Editor Banks found the rarest gems of his collection.

The morning of Tuesday, October 27, was like any other. Ralph Banks came to his office, hung up his hat and coat, seated himself, hitched up his chair, loosened his belt, put a wintergreen Lifesaver into his mouth. He consulted his appointments: at 10, Seth R. Framus, a highly-placed consultant to the AEC who had agreed to write an article on nuclear power-plants. Framus had obtained a special clearance and proposed to hint at some new and rather startling developments — something in the nature of a planned news leak. The article would enhance *Popular Crafts'* prestige, and put a handsome feather in Editor Banks' cap.

Banks pressed the intercom key.

'Lorraine.'

'Yes, Mr. Banks.'

'Seth R. Framus is calling this morning at ten. I'll see him as soon as he gets here.'

'Very well.'

Banks turned to his mail. First he checked SCREWBALL ALLEY. Nothing very much this morning. A perpetual-motion device, but he was tired of these, his stockpile long since replete . . . This was better. A timepiece for blind invalids, to be strapped against the temple. Needle pricks notified of the passing quarter-hours, while a small hammer tapped strokes of the hour against the skull . . . Next there was a plan to irrigate Death Valley by installing cloud-condensing equipment along the ridge of the Panamint Mountains . . . Next — a manuscript on pebbled beige paper, entitled, 'Behind the Masque: A Practical Man's Guide'.

Ralph Banks raised his eyebrows, glanced at the note clipped to the title-page.

Dear Sir:

I have learned in the course of a long life that exaggerated modesty brings few rewards. Hence I will put on no face of humility — I will not 'pull my punches' as the expression goes. The following document is a tremendous contribution to human knowledge. In fact it knocks the props from under the entire basis of our existence, the foundation of our moral order. The implications — indeed the bald facts — will come as a shock supreme in its devastation to all but a few. You will observe, and I need hardly emphasize, that this is a field *not to be pursued lightly!* I have therefore prefaced description of techniques with a brief account of my own findings in order to warn any who seek to satisfy a dilettante's curiosity. You will wonder why I have chosen your periodical as an outlet for my work. I will be frank. Yours is a practical magazine; you are a practical man — and I submit the following as a practical guide. I may add, that certain other journals, edited by men less able than yourself, have returned my work with polite but obtuse notes.

Yours sincerely,
Angus McIlwaine
c/o Archives, Smithsonian Institution
Washington, D.C.

An interesting letter, thought Banks. The work of a crackpot — but it gave off an interesting flavor . . . He glanced at the manuscript, thumbed through the pages. McIlwaine's typography made a pretty show. The margins allowed two inches of pebbled beige space at either side. Passages in red interspersed the black paragraphs, and some of these were underlined in purple ink. Small green stars appeared in the left-hand margin from time to time, indicating further emphasis. The effect was colorful and dramatic.

He turned pages, reading sentences, paragraphs.

'I have had serious misgivings (read Banks) but I cannot countenance cowardice or retreat. It is no argument to say that Masquerayne is unrelieved evil. Masquerayne is knowledge and men must never shrink from knowledge. And who knoes, it may lead to ultimate good. Fire has done more good than harm for mankind; so have explosives, and so ultimately, we may hope, will atomic energy. Therefore, as Einstein steeled himself against his qualms to write the equation $E = mc^2$, so I will record my findings.'

Banks grinned. A bona fide crack-pot, straight from the nuthatch. He frowned. 'c/o Archives, Smithsonian Institution.' An incongruity . . . He read on, skimming down the paragraphs, assimilating a line here, a sentence there.

' — a process of looking in, in, still further in; straining, forcing; then at the limits turning, as if in one's tracks, and looking out . . .'

Banks looked up suddenly; the intercom buzzer. He pressed the key.

'Mr. Seth R. Framus is here, Mr. Banks,' came Lorraine's voice.

'Ask him to have a seat, please,' said Banks. 'I'll be with him in just one minute.'

Lorraine, who had, 'Please go right in, Mr. Framus,' formed on her lips, was startled. Mr. Framus himself looked a little surprised; neverthless he took a seat with good grace, tapping at his knee with a folded newspaper.

Banks returned to the manuscript.

'Sometimes it is very quiet (he read) but only when the Ego can dodge behind these viscous milky pillars I have mentioned. It is easily possible to become lost here, in a very arcane manner. What could be more ludicrous, more tragic? A prisoner of self, so to speak!'

Banks called through the intercom to Lorraine, 'Get me the Smithsonian Institution.'

'Yes, Mr. Banks,' said Lorraine, glancing to see if Seth R. Framus had heard. He had, and the tempo at which he tapped his knee with the newspaper increased.

Banks leafed on through the pages.

'Naturally this never halted me. I steeled myself; I composed my nerves, my stomach. I continued. And here, as a footnote, may I mention that it is quite possible to come and go, returning with several of the red devices, many of them still warm.'

The telephone startled Banks. He answered with a trace of irritation: 'Yes, Lorraine?'

'The Smithsonian Institution, Mr. Banks.'

'Oh . . . Hello? I'd like to speak to someone in the Department of Archives. Er — perhaps Mr. McIlwaine?'

'Just a minute,' replied a female voice, 'I'll give you Mr. Crispin.'

Mr. Crispin came on the line; Banks introduced himself. Mr. Crispin inquired how he could be of service.

'I'd like to speak to Mr. McIlwaine,' said Banks.

Crispin asked in a puzzled voice, 'McIlwaine? In what department?'

'Archives, I believe.'

'That's odd . . . Of course we have a number of special projects going on — research teams and the like.'

'Could you possibly make a check for me?'

'Well, certainly, Mr. Banks, if it's necessary.'

'Will you do that please, and call me back collect? Or perhaps I can just hold the line.'

'It'll take five or ten minutes, at least.'

'That's perfectly all right.'

Banks turned the key on the intercom. 'Keep an ear on

the line, Lorraine, let me know when Crispin gets back on.'

Lorraine glanced sideways at Seth R. Framus, whose mouth was showing taut lines of petulance. 'Very well, Mr. Banks,'

Seth R. Framus spoke in a polite voice, 'What's Mr. Banks have going with the Smithsonian, if I may ask?'

Lorraine said helplessly, 'I'm really not sure, Mr. Framus . . . I guess it's something pretty important; he gave me orders to show you right in.'

'Mumph.' Mr. Framus opened his newspaper.

Banks was now skimming the final pages:

'And now — the inescapable conclusion. It is very simple; it can be seen that we are all victims of a gruesome joke — '

He turned to the last page:

'To demonstrate for yourself — '

Lorraine buzzed him on the intercom. 'Mr. Crispin is back on the line; and I think Mr. Framus is in a hurry, Mr. Banks.'

'I'll be right with Mr. Framus,' said Banks. 'Ask him to be good enough to wait just a moment.' He spoke into the telephone: 'Hello, Mr. Crispin?'

'Yes . . . I'm sorry, Mr. Banks; we just don't have an Angus McIlwaine with us.'

Banks thoughtfully scratched his head. 'There's the possibility he's using a pseudonym for his correspondence.'

'In that case, I assume he wishes to preserve his anonymity,' Crispin responded politely.

'Tell me this: suppose I wrote to Angus McIlwaine, care of the Archives, Smithsonian Institution. Who would get the letter?'

Crispin laughed. 'No one, Mr. Banks! You'd just get it back! Because we just don't have any McIlwaines. Unless, of course, whoever it is has made special arrangments . . . No just a minute; maybe I do know your man. That is, if it's really a pseudonym.' . . .

'Fine. Will you connect me?'

'Well, Mr. Banks, I think I'd better check first . . . Perhaps — well, after all, perhaps he wants to retain his anonymity.'

'Would you be good enought to see if Angus McIlwaine is his pseudonym; and if so, have him call me collect?'

'Yes. I can do that, Mr. Banks.'

'Thank you very much.'

Banks hesitated by the intercom. He really should see Mr. Framus . . . but there wasn't much left to the manuscript; he might as well skim through it . . . McIlwaine, whoever he was, was ripe for the funny-farm — but he had a flair; a compelling, urgent style. Banks had read a little — a very little — of abnormal psychology; he knew that hallucinations generated a frightening reality. McIlwaine doubtless had a dose of everything in fhe book . . . Well, thought Banks, just for fun, let's see how he recommends unmasking this 'grisly joke on humanity'; let's check the directions for exploring Masquerayne . . .

'To demonstrate the whole shoddy terrible trick is the task of few minutes — simple and certain. If you are daring — let us say, reckless — if you would tear the silken tissue that binds your eyes, do then as I say.

'First, obtain the following: a basin or carafe of clear water; six tumblers; six pins; a steel knitting needle; a four-foot square of dull black cardboard — '

Lorraine called in through the intercom. 'Mr. Banks, Mr. Framus says — '

'Ask him to wait,' said Banks rapidly. 'Take a list, Lorraine. I want a quart of water in a glass jug — six glasses — a steel knitting needle — a sheet of black cardboard; get this from Art, dull, not gloss — a piece of white chalk — a can of ether — '

'Did you say *ether*, Mr. Banks?'

'Yes, I said *ether*.'

Lorraine made a hasty notation; Banks continued down

the list of his needs. 'I need some red oil and some yellow oil. Get these from Art too. A dozen new nails; big ones. A bottle of perfume, good and strong. And a pound of rice. Got that?'

'A pound of rice, yes sir.'

'What in thunder does he want with all that junk now?' growled Framus.

'I'm sure I don't know,' said Lorraine a little breathlessly. 'Will you excuse me, Mr. Framus? I've got to get this stuff.'

She ran out of the room. Framus half-rose to his feet, undecided whether to stay or whether to stalk from the office. He slowly settled back, now slapping his knee with measured resonant blows. Fifteen more minutes!

In the inner office, Banks came to the final sentence.

'Following these instructions will take you past the barriers of Sight, Direction, Confusion, and the Fallacy of Pain. You will find twin channels — advisedly, I call them arteries — and either one will bring you safely inside the Cordon, and here you can watch the progressions, these events that fill you with disgust at the thought of returning, but from which you'll recoil in worse disgust.'

That was all. Finish. The rest of the page was blank.

Lorraine came in with the equipment. A boy from the Art Department assisted her.

'Mr. Banks,' said Lorraine, 'maybe I shouldn't mention this, but Mr. Framus is acting awful impatient.'

'I'll see him in just a minute,' muttered Banks. 'One minute.'

Lorraine returned to the outer office. Looking over her shoulder on the way out the door, she saw Banks pouring water into each of the glasses.

Precisely fifteen minutes had passed. Seth R. Framus rose to his feet. 'I'm sorry, Miss — I simply can't wait any longer.'

'Mr. Banks said he'd only be a minute, Mr. Framus,' said Lorraine anxiously. 'I think it's some kind of demon-stration . . .'

Framus said with quiet force, 'I'll wait exactly one more

minute.' He took his place, and sat gripping the paper.

One minute passed, then another.

'There's a funny smell in here,' said Seth R. Framus.

Lorraine sniffed the air, and looked embarrassed. 'It must be something on the wind — from the river . . .'

'What's that noise?' asked Framus, staring at Banks' door.

'I don't know,' said Lorraine. 'It doesn't sound like Mr. Banks.'

'Whatever it is,' said Framus, 'I can't wait.' He clapped his hat on his head. 'Mr. Banks can call me when he's free.'

He left the office.

Lorraine sat listening to the sounds from Banks' office: a gurgling of water, mingled with a hissing, frying sound. Then came Banks' voice, subdued and muffled; then a vague roaring sound, as if someone momentarily had opened the door into the engine room of a ship.

Then a murmur, then quiet.

The telephone rang. 'Mr. Banks' office,' said Lorraine.

Mr. Crispin spoke. 'Hello, please put Mr. Banks on the line. I've got the man he was looking for.'

Lorraine buzzed Mr. Banks.

'Hello, Mr. Banks?' a voice from Crispin's end, the deepest, most melancholy voice Lorraine had ever heard.

'He's not on the line yet,' said Lorraine.

'Tell him it's Angus McIlwaine Hunter speaking.'

'I will, Mr. Hunter, as soon as he comes on.' She buzzed again. 'He doesn't answer . . . I guess he's stepped out for a minute.'

'Well, it's not too important. I wonder if he's read my manuscript.'

'I believe so, Mr. Hunter. He seemed fascinated with it.'

'Good. Will you tell him that the last two pages will be along tomorrow? I foolishly omitted them, and they're very important to the article — crucial if I may say so . . . In the nature of an *antidote* . . .'

'I'll tell him, Mr. Hunter.'

'Thank you very much.'

Lorraine once more buzzed Mr. Banks' office, then went

to the door, knocked, looked in. The stuff Mr. Banks had ordered was scattered around in an awful mess. Mr. Banks was gone. Probably stepped out for a cup of coffee.

Lorraine went back to her desk, and sat waiting. After a while she brought out a file and began to work on her nails.

FIRST STAR I SEE TONIGHT

I STOOD IN THE DARK in front of the observatory, watching the quick fiery meteor trails streaking down from Perseus. My plans were completed. I had been meticulous, systematic.

The night was remarkable; clear and limpid . . . a perfect night for what we had arranged, the cosmos and I. And here came Dr. Patcher — old 'Dog' Patcher, as the students called him — the lights of his staid sedan sniffing out the road up the hill. I looked at my watch; ten-fifteen. The old rascal was late, probably had spent an extra three minutes shining his high-top shoes, or punctiliously brushing the coarse white plume of his hair.

The car nosed up over the hill, the head-lights sent scurrying yellow shapes and shadows past my feet. I heard the motor thankfully gasp and die, and after a sedate moment, the slam of the door, the crush-crush of Dr. Patcher's feet across the gravel. He seemed surprised to see me standing in the doorway, and looked at me sharply, as much as to say, 'Nothing better to do, Sisley?'

'Good evening, Dr. Patcher,' I said smoothly. 'It's a lovely night. The Perseids are showing very well . . . Ah! There's one now.' I pointed at one of the instant white meteor streaks.

Dr. Patcher shook his head with that mulish precision, that officious, precarious nicety which has infuriated me from the moment I first laid eyes on him. 'Sorry, Sisley, I can't waste a moment of this wonderful seeing.' He pushed past me, remarking over his shoulder, 'I hope that everything is in order.'

I remained silent. I could hardly say 'no'; if I said 'yes', he would pry and poke until he found something — anything — at which he could raise his eyebrows: a smudge of oil, the roof opening not precisely symetrical to the telescope, a cigarette butt on the floor. Anything. Then I would hear a snort of disparagement; a quick gleam of a glance would flick in my direction; the deficiency would be ostentatiously remedied. And at last he would get busy with his work — if work it could be called. Myself, I considered it trivial, a piddling waste of time, a repetition of what better men at better instruments had already accomplished. Dr. Patcher was seeking comets. He would not be satisfied until a comet bore his name — 'Patcher's Comet'. And night after night, when the seeing was best, Dr. Patcher had crowded me away from the telescope, I who had research that was significant and important. Tonight I would show Dr. Patcher a comet indeed.

He was inside now, rustling and probing; tonight he would find nothing a millimeter out of place. I was wrong. 'Oh, Sisley,' came his silky voice, 'are you busy?'

I hurried inside. Patcher was standing by the senior faculty closet with his old tweed coat already carefully arranged on a hanger. Instantly I knew his complaint. Patcher affected a white laboratory coat, which he called his 'duster'. About twice a month the janitor, in cleaning out the senior faculty closet, would remove the duster and replace it in the junior closet — whether as an act of crafty malice or sheer wool-gathering I had never made up my mind. In any event the ritual ran its course predictably, 'Have you seen my duster, Sisley? It's not in the clothes closet where it should be.'

It was on the tip of my tongue to retort, 'Dr. Patcher, I am a professor of astronomy, not your valet.' To which he would make the carping correction, '*Assistant* professor, my dear Sisley,' thus enraging me. But tonight of all nights a state of normality must be assured, since what was to happen would be so curious and unique that only a framework of absolute humdrum routine would make the circumstances convincing.

So I swallowed my temper and, opening the junior closet, handed Patcher his duster. 'Well, well,' said Patcher as usual, 'what on earth is it doing in there?'

'I suppose the janitor has been careless.'

'We'll have to bring him up short,' said Patcher. 'One place where carelessness can never be tolerated is an observatory.'

'I agree whole-heartedly,' I said, as indeed I did. I am a systematic man, with every aspect of my life conducted along lines of the most rigorous efficiency.

Buttoning his duster, Dr. Patcher looked me up and down. 'You seem restless tonight, Sisley.'

'I? Certainly not. Perhaps a little tired, a little fatigued. I was prospecting up Mount Tinsley today and found several excellent specimens of sphalerite.' Perhaps I should mention that my hobby is mineralogy, that I am an assiduous 'rock-hound', and devote a good deal of time to my collection of rocks, minerals, and crystals.

Dr. Patcher shook his head a little. 'I personally could not afford to dilute my energy to such an extent. I feel that every ounce of my attention belongs to my work.'

This was a provocative misstatement. Dr. Patcher was an ardent horticulturalist and had gone so far as to plant a border of roses around the observatory.

'Well, well,' I said, perhaps a trifle heavily, 'I suppose each of us must go his own way.' I glanced at my watch. twenty-five minutes. 'I'll leave the place in your hands, Doctor. If the visibility is good I'll be here about three — '

'I'm afraid I'll be using the instrument,' said Patcher. 'This is a perfect night in spite of the breeze — '

I thought; it is a perfect night *because* of the breeze.

' — I can't afford to waste a minute.'

I nodded, 'Very well; you can telephone me if you change your mind.'

He looked at me queerly; I seldom showed such good grace. 'Good-night, Sisley.'

'Good-night, Dr. Patcher. Perhaps I'll watch the Perseids for a bit.'

He made no reply. I went outside, strolled around the observatory, re-entered. I cried, 'Dr. Patcher, Dr. Patcher!'

'Yes, yes, what is it?'

'Most extraordinary! Of course I'm no gardener, but I've never seen anything like it before, a luminescent rose!'

'What's that?'

'One of the rose bushes seems to be bearing luminescent blossoms.'

'Oh, nonsense,' muttered Dr. Patcher. 'It's a trick of the vision.'

'A remarkable illusion, if so.'

'Never heard of such a thing,' said Dr. Patcher. 'I can't see how it's possible. Where is this "Luminescent rose-bush"?'

'It's right around here,' I said. 'I could hardly believe my eyes.'

I led him a few feet around the observatory, to where the bed of roses rustled and swayed in the breeze. 'Just in there.'

Dr. Patcher spoke the last words of his existence on earth. 'I don't see any — '

I hurried to my car, which I had parked headed downslope. I started the motor, roared down the hill as fast as the road and my excellent reflexes allowed. Three days ago I had timed myself: six minutes from the observatory to the outskirts of town. Tonight I made it in five.

Slowing to my usual pace, I rounded the last turn and pulled into Sam's Service Station, stopping the car at a spot which I had calculated to a nicety several weeks earlier. And now I had a stroke of rather good luck. Pulled up in the inside lane was a white police car, with a trooper leaning against the fender.

'Hello, Mr. Sisley,' said Sam. 'How's all the stars in their courses tonight?'

At any other time I might have treated the pleasantry to the cool rejoinder it deserved. Sam, a burly young man with a perpetual smudge on his nose, was a typical layman, a total fog concerning the exacting and important work that we do at the observatory. Tonight, however, I welcomed his remark. 'The stars are about as usual, Sam, but if you keep your eyes open, you'll see any number of shooting stars tonight.'

'Honest to Pete?' Sam glanced politely around the sky.

'Yes.' I looked at my watch. 'Astronomers call them the Perseids. Every year about this time we run into a meteoric shower which seems to come from the constellation of Perseus — right up there. A little later in the year come the Leonids, from Leo.'

'Leo, you say,' said Sam, 'that's the sign I was born under.'

'The constellation of Leo is quite low at the moment, but you can see Denebola, the lion's tail — right there.'

Sam shook his head admiringly. 'My mother's nuts on that stuff, but I didn't know she got it from you guys.' He turned to the trooper. 'How about that? All the time I thought these guys up at the observatory was — well, kinda passing the time, but now Professor Sisley tells me that they put out these Sign of the Zodiac books — you know, don't- invest-money-with-a-blonde-woman-today- stuff. Real practical dope.'

The trooper said, 'What do you know? I always figured that stuff for so much hogwash.'

'Of course it is,' I said heatedly. 'All foolishness. I said that was the constellation Leo up there, not the "sign of Leo"!' I checked the time. About thirty seconds. 'I'll have five gallons of ethyl, Sam.'

'Right,' said Sam. 'Can you back up a bit? Wait! I guess the hose will reach . . .' he stood facing the direction I wished him to face.

Glare lit the sky; a flaming gout of white fire plunged down from the heavens, followed an instant later by a flat orange smear of light.

'Good heavens!' cried Sam, standing with his mouth open and the hose in his hand, 'What was that?'

'A meteor,' I said. 'A shooting star.'

'That was a humdinger,' the trooper said. 'You don't see many that close!'

Out of the sky came a sharp report, an explosion.

Sam shook his head and numbly continued to valve gas into the tank. 'Looked like that one struck ground right up close to the observatory too.'

'Yes,' I said, 'it certainly did. I think I'll telephone Dr. Patcher and ask if he noticed it.'

'Notice it!' said Sam. 'He's lucky if he got out of the way!'

Privately elated, I went inside the station, dropped a dime into the box, called the observatory.

'Sorry,' the operator said a moment later. 'There's no reply.'

I returned outside. 'He doesn't answer. He's probably up in the cage and can't be bothered.'

'Cantankerous old devil,' said Sam. 'But then — excuse me, Professor — all you astronomers act a little bit odd, one way or another. I don't mean screwy or anything like that — but just, well, odd. Absent-minded like.'

'Ha, ha,' I said, 'that's where you're mistaken. I imagine that very few people are as methodical and systematic as I am.'

Sam shrugged. 'I can't argue with you, Doc.'

I got into my car and drove through town toward the University; I parked in front of the Faculty Club, walked into the lounge, and ordered a pot of tea.

John Dalrymple of the English Department joined me. 'I say, Sisley, something in your line — saw a whacking great fire-ball a moment or two ago. Lit up the entire sky, marvellous thing.'

'Yes, I saw it at the service station. It apparently struck ground somewhere up near the observatory. This is the time of year for them, you know.'

Dalrymple rubbed his chin. 'Seems to me I see them all the time.'

'Oh indeed! But these are the Perseids, a special belt of meteorites, or perhaps, a small comet traversing a regular orbit. The earth, entering this orbit, collides with the rocks and pebbles that make up the comet. When we watch, it seems as if the meteors are coming from the constellation of Perseus — hence we call them Perseids.'

Dalrymple rose to his feet. 'Well put, old man, awfully interesting and all that, but I've got something to say to Benjamin. See you again.'

'Good evening, Dalrymple.'

I read a magazine, played a game of chess with Hodges of the Economics Department, and discovered out loud it was twelve-thirty. I rose to my feet. 'Excuse me; Dr. Patcher's alone at the observatory. I think I'll call and find out how long he's going to be.'

I called the observatory once more, and was told, 'Sorry, sir, no answer.'

'He's probably up in the cage,' I told Hodges. 'If he gets too involved, he refuses to budge from his instruments.'

'Rather crusty old bird, isn't he?'

'Not the easiest person in the world to work with. No doubt he has his good points, but . . . . Well, good-night, Hodges; thanks for the game. I think I'll snooze a bit in the lounge before heading back up the hill. I'm due at three, or thereabouts.'

At two o'clock Jake the night janitor aroused me. 'Everybody's gone home, sir, and the heat's been turned off. Don't know as you'd want to catch your death of cold sitting here.'

'No, by all means. Thank you, Jake.' I looked at my watch and announced its findings. 'I must be off to work.'

'You and me,' said Jake, 'we keep strange hours.'

'The best time of the day is night,' I said. 'By day, of course, I mean the sidereal day.'

'Oh, I understand you, sir. I'm used to hearing all manner of strange talk, and I understand lots better than some of 'em think.'

'I'm sure you do, Jake.'

'The things I've heard, Mr. Sisley.'

'Yes, interesting indeed. Well, good-night, Jake. I must be off to work.'

'Getcher coat, Mr. Sisley?'

'Yes, please. Do you have the exact time?'

The night was glorious beyond description. Stars, stars, stars — magnificent flowers of heaven, spurting pips of various lights down from their appointed places. I know the night skies as I know my own face; I know all the lore, the fable, the mystery. I know where to expect Arcturus, in one corner of the Great Diamond, with Denebola to the side, Spica below, Cor Caroli above; I know Argo Navis and the Northern Cross, sometimes called Cygnus, and the little rocking-horse of Lyra, with Vega at the head. I know how to sight down the three stars in Aquila, with Altair at the center, to find Fomalhaut, when it comes peering briefly over the southern horizon. I know the Lair of the Howling Dog, with Vindemiatrix close by; I can find Algol the demon star and Mira the wonderful on the spine of Cetus the whale. I know Orion and his wonderful upraised arm, with the river Eridanus winding across twenty million lightyears of desolation. Ah, the stars! Poetry the poor day-dweller never dreams of! Poetry in the star names: Alpheta, Achernar, Alpheratz; Canopus, Antares, Markab; Sirius, Rigel, Bellatrix, Aldebran, Betelgeuse, Fomalhaut, Alphard, Spica, Procyon, Deneb Kaitos, Alpha Centauri: rolling magnificent sounds, each a king of myriad worlds. And now, with old Dog Patcher gone to his reward, the heavens were mine, to explore at my leisure; possibly with the help of young Katkus, who would eventually be promoted to my place . . . when *I* became head of the department.

I drove up the familiar road, winding among aromatic eucalyptus, and breasted over the edge of the observatory parking area.

It was as I had left it, with Patcher's shiny old sedan pressed close the the wall, much more lonesome and pathetic than ever Patcher's body would look, at least to my eyes.

But I must not cry out the alarm too quickly; first I had one or two matters to take care of.

I found my flashlight and walked out on the slope behind the observatory. I knew approximately where to look and exactly what I was looking for — and there it was, a bit of cardboard, a scrap of red paper, a length of stick. Everything was proceeding as I had planned, and after all, why should it not? It is very easy to kill a man, so I have found. I had chosen merely one of many ways, perhaps a trifle more elaborate than necessary, but it seemed such a fitting end for old Dog Patcher. I could have arranged for his car to have left the road; there would have been precedent in the death of Professor Harlow T. Kane, Patcher's predecessor as Senior Astronomer, who had lost his life in just such a manner . . . So the thoughts ran through my head as I burned the stick and cardboard and paper and scattered the ashes.

I returned to the observatory, sauntered inside, looked over the big reflector with a sense of proprietorship . . . about time now to sound the alarm.

I wandered outside, turned my flashlight on the body. Everything is just so. I ran back in, telephoned the sheriff's office, since the observatory is outside the city limits. 'Sheriff?'

A sleepy voice grumbled, 'What in Sam Hill's the idea, waking me up this time of night?'

'This is Professor Sisley up at the observatory. Something terrible has happened! I've just discovered the body of Dr. Patcher!'

The sheriff was a fat and amiable man, much more concerned with his take from slot machines and poker rooms than the prevention of crime. He arrived at the observatory with a doctor. They stood looking down at the body, the sheriff holding a flashlight, neither one showing zest or enthusiasm.

'Looks like he's been beaned with a rock,' said the sheriff. 'Find out how long he's been dead, will you, Doc?'

The sheriff turned to me. 'Just what happened, Professor?'

'It looks to me,' I said, 'as if he's been struck by a meteorite.'

'A meteorite, hey?' He pulled at his chin doubtfully, 'Ain't that a little far-fetched? One chance in a thousand, you might say?'

'I can't be sure, naturally. You'll have to get an expert to check on that piece of metal or rock, whatever it is.'

The sheriff was still rubbing his chin.

'When I left him at about ten-thirty,' I said, 'he said he was going out to watch the meteors — we're passing through the Perseids, you know — and shortly after — I was in town by then, at Sam's Service Station — we saw a very large shooting-star, meteor, fire-ball, whatever you want to call it, come down from the sky. Sam saw it, the state tropper saw it — '

'Yeah,' said the sheriff, 'I saw it myself. Monstrous thing . . .' He bent over Dr. Patcher's dead body. 'You think this might be a meteorite, hey?'

'I certainly couldn't say at a glance, but Professor Doheny, of the Geology Department at the university would tell you in jig-time.'

'Humph,' said the sheriff. To the doctor, 'Any idea when he died, Doc?'

'Oh, roughly five or six hours ago.'

'Humph. That's ten-thirty to eleven-thirty . . . That meteor came down at, let's see — '

'At exactly twelve minutes to eleven.'

'Well, well,' said the sheriff, looking at me with mild speculation. After this, I told myself, I would volunteer no more information. But no matter, no harm done.

'I suppose,' said the sheriff, 'we'd better wait till it's light, and then we can look around a little more.'

'If you will come into the observatory,' I said, 'I'll brew up a pot of coffee. This night air is a trifle brisk.'

Dawn came; the sheriff called his office; an ambulance climbed the hill. I was asked a few more questions, photographs were taken, and Patcher's body was finally removed.

Newspapers from coast to coast featured accounts of the 'freak accident'. The 'man bites dog' angle was played up heavily; the astronomer who made a career of hunting down comets had gotten a taste of his own medicine. Of course a meteor is by no means a comet, but in the general hullabaloo no one cared very much, and I suppose that insofar as the public is concerned it is all one and the same.

The president of the University telephoned his sympathy. 'You'll take Patcher's place, of course; I hope you won't refuse out of any misplaced feelings of delicacy. I've approached young Katkus, and he'll move up to your previous position.'

'Thank you, sir,' said I, 'I'll do my best. With your encouragement and the help of young Katkus I'll see that Patcher's work goes on; indeed, I think it would be a fitting memorial if the first comet we found were to be named for poor old Patcher.'

'Excellent idea,' said the president. 'I'll put through your appointment at once.'

So events proceeded in their course. I cleaned Patcher's notes and books out of the study and moved my own in. Young Katkus made his appearance, and I was pleased by the modest manner in which he accepted his good fortune.

A week passed and the sheriff called at my apartment. 'Come in, sheriff, come in. Glad to see you. Here' — I moved some journals — 'have a chair.'

'Thanks, thanks very much.' He eased his fat little body gingerly into the seat.

I had not quite finished my breakfast. 'Will you have a cup of coffee?'

He hesitated. 'No, think I'd better not. Not today.'

'What's on your mind, sheriff?'

He put his hands on his knees. 'Well, Professor, it's that Patcher accident. I'd like to talk it over with you.'

'Why certainly, if you wish . . . but I thought that was all water under the bridge.'

'Well — not entirely. We've been lying low, you might say. Maybe it's an accident — and again, maybe it's not.'

I said with great interest, 'What do you mean, sheriff? Surely . . . ?'

As I have mentioned, the sheriff is a mild man, and looks more like an insurance salesman than a law-enforcement officer. But at this moment, a rather dogged and unpleasant expression stiffened his features.

'I've been doing a bit of investigating, and a bit of thinking. And I've got to admit I'm puzzled.'

'How so?'

'Well, there's no question but what Dr. Patcher was killed with a meteorite. That chunk of rock was a funny kind of nickel-iron mixture, and showed a peculiar set of marks under the microscope. Professor Doheny said meteorite it was, and no doubt about it.'

'Oh?' I said, sipping my coffee.

'There's no question that a streak of fire was seen shooting down out of the sky at about the time Dr. Patcher was killed.'

'Yes, I believe so. In fact, I saw it myself. Quite an impressive phenomenon.'

'I thought at first that a meteorite would be hot, and I wondered why Patcher's hair wasn't singed, but I find that when a meteor comes down, only a little bit of the surface heats up and glows off, but the rest, the inside, stays icy-cold.'

'Right,' I said cordially. 'Exactly right.'

'But let's suppose,' said the sheriff, looking at me sidewise with an expression I can only call crafty, 'let's suppose that someone wanted to kill poor old Dr. Patcher — '

I shook my head doubtfully. 'Far-fetched.'

' — and wanted to fake the murder so that it looked like an accident, how would he go about it?'

'But — who would want to do away with Patcher?'

The sheriff laughed uneasily. 'That's what's got us stumped. There's no one with a speck of motive — except, possibly, yourself.'

'That's ridiculous.'

'Of course, of course. But we were just — '

'Why should I want to kill Dr. Patcher?'

'I hear,' said the sheriff, watching me sidelong, 'that he was a hard man to get along with.'

'Not when you understood his foibles.'

'I hear that you and he had a few bust-ups over the work up at the observatory?'

'Now that,' I said with feeling, 'is pure rubbish. Naturally, we had our differences. I felt, as many of my colleagues did, that Patcher was entering upon his dotage, and it had begun to show in the rather trivial nature of the work he was doing.'

'Exactly what was the work, Professor; in words of one syllable?'

'Well,' and I laughed, 'he was actually going over the sky with a fine-tooth comb, looking for comets, and I'll admit that occasionally it was a vexation, when I had important work to do —'

'Er, what is your work, Professor?'

'I am conducting a statistical count of the Cepheid variables in the Great Nebula of Andromeda.'

'Ah, I see,' said the sheriff. 'Pretty tough job, sounds like.'

'The work is progressing now, of course. But certainly you don't think — you can't assume —'

The sheriff waved his hand. 'We don't assume nothing. We just, well, call it figure a little.'

'How could I, how could anyone, control what might literally be called a bolt from the blue?'

'Ah, now we're getting down to brass tacks. How could you, indeed? I admit I racked my brains, and I think I've got it puzzled out.'

'My dear sheriff, are you accusing —'

'No, no, sit still. We're just talking things over. I was telling you how you could — if you wanted, mind you, *if* you wanted — fake a meteor.'

'Well,' I asked in fine scorn, 'how could I fake a meteor?'

'You'd need something to make a good streak of light. You'd need something to get it up there. You'd need a way of setting it off at the right time.'

'How?'

'Well, the first could be a good strong old-fashioned sky-rocket.'

'Why — theoretically, I suppose so. But — '

'I thought of all kinds of things,' said the sheriff. 'Airplanes, balloons, birds — everything except flying fish. The answer has to be one thing: a kite. A big box-kite.'

'I admire your ingenuity, sheriff. But — '

'Then you'd need some way to send this thing off, and aim it right. Now I may be all wet on this — but I imagine that you had the rocket fixed with a couple of wire loops over the string, so that it would follow the string to the ground.'

'Sheriff, I — '

'Now as for setting it off — why that's a simple matter. I could probably rig up something of the sort myself. A wrist-watch with the glass off, a flashlight battery, a contact stuck on the dial, insulated from the rest of the watch, so that when the minute hand met it, the circuit would open. Then you'd use magnesium floss and magnesium tape to start the fuse of your rocket, and that's practically the whole of it.'

'My dear sheriff,' I said with all my dignity, 'if I were guilty of such a preposterous offense, how in the world would I dispose of the kite?'

'Well,' said the sheriff, scratching his chin, 'I hadn't thought of that. I suppose you could haul it down and burn it, together with the string.'

I was taken aback. Actually, I hadn't thought of anything so simple. The kite I had blown up with half a stick of dynamite, fused to explode after the rocket had started down; the string I had soaked in a solution of potassium chlorate; it had burned to dust like a train of gunpowder. 'Humph. Well, if you are accusing me of this crime you have conceived — '

'No, no, no!' cried the sheriff. 'I ain't accusing nobody. We're just siting here chewing this thing over. But I admit I am wondering why you bought all of that kite-string from Fuller's Hardware about three weeks ago.'

I stared at him indignantly. 'Kite-string? Nonsense. I bought that string at the request of Dr. Patcher himself, with which to tie up his sweet peas, and if you check at his home they'll tell you the same story.'

The sheriff nodded. 'I see. Well, just a point I'm glad to have cleared up. I understand you're an amateur rock-hunter?'

'That's perfectly true,' I said. 'I have a small but not unrepresentative collection.'

'Any meteorite in the bunch?' the sheriff asked carelessly.

Just as carelessly I replied. 'Why I believe so. One or two.'

'I wonder if I could see them.'

'Certainly, if you wish. I keep my collection out there in the back rooms. I'm very methodical about all this; I don't let the rocks intrude into the astronomy, or vice versa.'

'That's how hobbies should be,' said the sheriff.

We went out to the back porch, which I have converted to a display room. On all sides are chests of narrow drawers, glass-topped tables where my choicest pieces are on view, geological charts, and the like. At the far end is my little laboratory, with my reagents, scales, and furnace. Midway is the file cabinet where I have indexed and catalogued each piece in my collection.

The sheriff glanced with an unconvincing show of interest along the trays and shelves. 'Now, let's see them meteorites.'

Although I knew their respective whereabouts to the inch, I made a move of indecision. 'I'll have to check in the catalogue; I'm afraid it's slipped my mind.'

I pulled open the filing cabinet, flipped the dividers to M. 'Meteorites — RG-17. Ah yes, right on here, sheriff. Case R, tray G, space 17. As you see, I'm nothing if not systematic . . .'

'What's the matter?' asked the sheriff.

I suppose I was staring at the sheet of paper. It read:

RG-17-A — Meteorite — Nickel-iron
Weight — 171 grams
Origin — Burnt Rock Ranch, Arizona

RG-17-B — Meteorite — Granite stone

Weight — 216 grams
Origin — Kelsey, Nevada

RG-17-C — Meteorite — Nickel-iron
Weight — 1,842 grams
Origin — Kilgore, Mojave Desert

Meticulously, systematically, I had typed in red against RG-17-C: 'Removed from collection, August 9.' Three days before Patcher's death.

'What's the matter?' asked the sheriff. 'Ain't feeling so good?'

'The meteorites,' I croaked, 'are over here.'

'Lemme see that sheet of paper.'

'No — it's just a memorandum.'

'Sure — but I want to see it.'

'I'll show you the meteorites.'

'Show me that paper.'

'Go to blazes.'

'Professor Sisley — '

I went to the tray, pulled it open. 'Here, the meteorites. Look at them!'

The sheriff stepped over, bent his head. 'Hm. Yeah. Just rocks.' He cocked an eye at the sheet of paper I gripped in my hand. 'Are you going to show me that paper of not?'

'No. It's got nothing to do with this business. It's a record of where I obtained these rocks. They're valuable, and I promised not to reveal the source.'

'Well, well.' The sheriff turned away. I walked quickly to the toilet, locked the door, quickly tore the paper to shreds, flushed it down the drain.

'There,' I said, emerging, 'the paper is gone. If it was evidence, that's gone too.'

The sheriff shook his head a little mournfully. 'I should have known better than to come calling so friendly-like. I should have had a search-warrant and my two big deputies. But now — ' he paused, chewed thoughtfully at something inside his mouth.

'Well,' I asked impatiently, 'are you going to arrest me or not?'

'Arrest you? No, Professor Sisley. We know what we know, you and I, but how will we get a jury to see it? You claim a meteorite killed Dr. Patcher, and a thousand people saw a meteor head toward him. I'll say, Professor Sisley was mad at Dr. Patcher; Professor Sisley could have whopped Dr. Patcher with a rock, then fired his sky-rocket down from a kite. You'll say, prove it. And I'll say, Professor Sisley flushed a piece of paper down the toilet. And then the judge will give me a hard look, bang his gavel a couple times and that's all there is to it. No, Professor, I'm not going to arrest you. My job wouldn't be worth a plugged nickel. But I'll tell you what I'm going to do — just like I told Doc Patcher when the head man before him died so sudden, year before last.'

'Well, go ahead, say it! What are you going to do?'

'It's really not a great lot,' the sheriff said modestly. 'I'm just going to let events take their course.'

'I can't say I understand your meaning.'

But the sheriff had gone. I blew my nose, mopped my brow, and considered the file which had so nearly betrayed me. Even at this juncture, I took a measure of satisfaction in the fact that it was system and method which had come so close to undoing me, and not the absent-mindedness which an ignorant public ascribes to men of learning.

I am senior astronomer at the observatory. My work is progressing. I have control of the telescope. I have the vastness of the universe under my fingertips.

Young Katkus is developing well, although he currently displays a particularly irritating waywardness and independence. The young idiot thinks he is hot on the track of an undiscovered planet beyond Pluto, and if I gave him his head, he'd waste every minute of good seeing peering back and forth along the ecliptic. He sulks now and again, but he'll have to wait his chance, as I did, as Dr. Patcher did before me, and, presumably, Dr. Kane before him.

Dr. Kane — I have not thought of him since the day his car went out of control and took him over the cliff. I must learn who preceded him as senior astronomer. A telephone call to Nolbert at Administration Hall will do the trick . . . I find that Dr. Kane succeeded a Professor Maddov, who drowned when a boat he and Dr. Kane were paddling capsized on Lake Niblis. Nolbert says the tragedy weighed on Dr. Kane to the day of his death, which came as an equally violent shock to the department. He had been computing the magnetic orientation of globular clusters, a profoundly interesting topic, although it was no secret that Dr. Patcher considered the work fruitless and didactic. It is sometimes tempting to speculate — but no, they all are decently in their graves and I have more serious demands upon my attention. Such as Katkus, who comes demanding the telescope at the very moment when air and sky are at their best. I tell him quite decisively that off-train investigations such as his must be conducted when the telescope is otherwise idle. He goes off sulking. I can feel no deep concern for his hurt feelings; he must learn to fit himself to the schedule of research as mapped out by the senior astronomer, that is, at last, myself.

I saw the sheriff today; he nodded quite politely. I'm still wondering what he meant by letting events take their course? Cryptic and not comfortable; it has put me quite out of sorts. Perhaps, after all, I was overly sharp with Katkus. He is sitting at his desk, pretending to check the new plates into the glossary, watching me from the corner of his eye.

I wonder what is passing through his mind.

THE TEMPLE OF HAN

IN THE NIP-AND-TUCK BUSINESS of keeping himself alive, Briar Kelly had not yet been able to shed his disguise. The adventure had turned a little sour; he had not bargained for so much turmoil.

Up to the moment he had entered the queer dark temple at North City, the disguise had served him well. He had melded with the Han; no one had looked at him twice. Once inside the temple he was alone and disguise was unnecessary.

It was an oddly impressive place. A Gothic web of trusses supported the ceiling; alcoves along the wall were crammed with statuary. Red and green lamps cast an illumination which was absorbed by thick black drapes.

Walking slowly down the central nave, every nerve tingling, Kelly had approached the tall black mirror at the far end. He watched his own looming reflection with hypnotic fascination. There were limpid depths beyond, and Kelly would have looked more closely had he not seen the jewel: a ball of cool green fire resting on a black velvet cushion.

With marvelling fingers Kelly had lifted it, turned it over — then tumult had broken loose. Red and green lights flickered; an alarm horn brayed like a crazy bull. Vengeful priests appeared in the alcoves and the disguise had become a liability. The tubular black cloak constricted his legs as he ran along the aisle, down the shabby steps, through the foul back alleys to his flier. Now as he crouched low over the controls sweat beaded up under the white grease-paint and his skin itched and crawled.

Ten feet below, the salt-crusted mudflats fell swiftly astern. Dirty yellow rushes whipped the hull. Pressing an elbow to his hip, Kelly felt the hard shape of the jewel. The sensation aroused mixed feelings, apprehension predominating. He dropped the flier even closer to the ground. 'Five minutes of this, I'll be out of detection range,' thought Kelly. 'Back at Bucktown, I'm just one among fifty thousand. They can't very well locate me, unless Herli talks, or Mapes . . . .'

He hazarded a glance at the rear-vision plate. North City could still be seen, an exaggerated Mont St. Michel jutting up from the dreary salt marsh. Misty exhalations blurred the detail; it faded into the sky, finally droped below the horizon. Kelly eased up the nose of the flier, rose tangentially from the surface, aiming into Magra Taratempos, the hot white sun.

The atmosphere thinned, the sky deepened to black, stars came out. There in the distance was old Sol, a yellow star hanging between Sadal Suud and Sadal Melik in Aquarius — only thirty light years to home —

Kelly heard a faint swishing sound. The light changed, shifting white to red. He blinked, looked around in bewilderment.

Magra Taratempos had disappeared. Low to the left a giant red sun hulked above the horizon; below, the salt marshes swam in a new claret glow.

In amazement Kelly gazed from red sun to planet, back up across the heavens where Magra Taratempos had hung only a moment before.

'I've gone crazy,' said Kelly. 'Unless . . . .'

Two or three months before, a peculiar rumor had circulated Bucktown. For lack of better entertainment, the sophisticates of the city had made a joke of the story, until it finally grew stale and was no more heard.

Kelly, who worked as computer switchman at the astrogation station, was well acquainted with the rumor. It went to the effect that a Han priest, dour and intense under his black cloak, had been tripped into the marsh by a drunken pollen collector. Like a turtle the priest had shoved his white face out from under the hood of his cloak, and rasped in the pidgin of the planet: 'You abuse the priest of Han; you mock us and the name of the Great God. Time is short. The Seventh year is at hand, and you godless Earth-things will seek to flee, but there will be nowhere for you to go.'

Such had been the tale. Kelly remembered the pleased excitement which had fluttered from tongue to tongue. He grimaced, examined the sky in new apprehension.

The facts were before his eyes, undeniable. Magra Tara-tempos had vanished. In a different quarter of the sky a new sun had appeared.

Careless of radar tracing, he nosed up and broke entirely clear of the atmosphere. The stellar patterns had changed. Blackness curtained half the sky, here and there shone a lone spark of a star or the wisp of a far galaxy. To the other quarter a vast blot of light stretched across the sky, a narrow elongated luminosity with a central swelling, the whole peppered with a million tiny points of light.

Kelly cut the power from his engine; the flier drifted. Unquestionably the luminous blot was a galaxy seen from one of its outer fringes. In ever-growing bewilderment, Kelly looked back at the planet below. To the south he could see the triangular plateau shouldering up from the swamp, and Lake Lenore near Bucktown. Below was the salt marsh, and far to the north, the rugged pile where the Han had their city.

'Let's face it,' said Kelly. 'Unless I'm out of my mind — and I don't think I am — the entire planet has been picked up and taken to a new sun . . . I've heard of strange things, but this . . . .'

He felt the weight of the jewel in his pocket, and with it a new thrill of apprehension. To the best of his knowledge, the Han priest could not identify him. At Bucktown it had been Herli and Mapes who had urged him into the escapade, but they would hold their tongues. Ostensibly he had flown to his cabin along the lakeshore, and there was no one to know of his comings and goings . . . . He turned the flier down toward Bucktown, and a half-hour later landed at his cabin beside Lake Lenore. He had scraped the grease-paint from his face; the cloak he had jettisoned over the swamp;

and the jewel still weighed heavy in his pocket.

The cabin, a low flat-roofed building with aluminum walls and a glass front, appeared strange and unfamiliar in the new light. Kelly walked warily to the door. He looked right and left. No one, nothing was visible. He put his ear to the panel of the door. No sound.

He slid back the panel, stepped inside, swept the interior with a swift glance. Everything appeared as he had left it.

He started toward the video screen, then halted.

The jewel.

He took it from his packet, examined it closely for the first time. It was a sphere the size of a golf-ball. The center shone with a sharp green fire, decrasing toward the outer surface. He hefted it. It was unnaturally heavy. Strangely fascinating, altogether lovely. Think of it around the neck of Lynette Mason . . . .

Not now. Kelly wrapped it in paper, tucked it into an empty pint jar. Behind the cabin, an old shag-bark slanted up out of the black humus and overhung the roof like a gray and tattered beach-umbrella. Kelly dug a hole under one of the arched roots, buried the jewel.

Returning to the cabin, he walked to the screen, reached out to call the station. The buzzer sounded . . . Kelly drew his band back.

Better not to answer.

The buzzer sounded again — again. Kelly stood holding his breath, looking at the black face of the screen.

Silence.

He washed the last of the grease-paint from his face, changed his clothes, ran outside, jumped into his flier and took off for Bucktown.

He landed on the roof of the station, noting that Herli's car was parked in its wonted slot. Suddenly he felt less puzzled and forlorn. The station, with its machinery and solid Earth-style regulations, projected reassurance, a sense of normality. Somehow the ingenuity and aggressive attack which had taken men to the stars would solve the present enigma.

Or would it? Ingenuity could take men through space, but

ingenuity would find itself strained locating a speck of a planet a hundred thousand light-years in an unknown direction. And Kelly still had his own problem: the jewel. Into his mind's-eye came a picture: the cabin by the lake, the dilapidated gray parasol of the shag-bark, and glowing under the root, the green eye of the sacred jewel. In the vision he saw the black-robed figure of a Han priest moving across the open space before the cabin, and he saw the flash of the dough-white face.

Kelly turned a troubled glance up at the big red sun, entered the station.

The administration section was vacant; Kelly climbed the stair to the operations department.

He stopped in the doorway, surveyed the room. It covered the entire square of the upper floor. Work-benches made a circuit of the room, with windows above. A polished cylinder came down through the ceiling, and below was the screen to catch the projection.

Four men stood by the star-index, running a tape. Herli glanced up briefly, turned back to the clicking mechanism.

Strange. Herli should have been interested, should at least have said hello.

Kelly self-consciously crossed the room. He cleared his throat. 'Well — I made it. I'm back.'

'So I see,' said Herli.

Kelly fell silent. He glanced up through the window at the red sun. 'What do you make of it?'

'Not the least idea. We're running the tapes on the off chance it's been registered — a last-gasp kind of hope.'

There was more silence. They had been talking before he had entered the room; Kelly sensed this from their posture.

At last Mapes said with a forced casualness, 'Seen the news?'

'No,' said Kelly. 'No, I haven't.' There was more in Mapes' voice, something more personal than the shift of the planet. After a moment's hesitation he went to the screen, pushed the code for news.

The screen lit, showed a view of the swamp. Kelly leaned

forward. Buried up to their necks were a dozen boys and girls from the Bucktown High School. Crawling eagerly over them were the small three-legged salt-crabs; others popped up out of the slime, or tunnelled under towards the squirming bodies.

Kelly could not stand the screams. He reached forward —

Herli said shaply, 'Leave it on!' — harder than Kelly had ever heard him speak. 'The announcement is due pretty soon.'

The announcement came, in the rasping toneless pidgin of the Han priests.

'Among the outsiders is a wicked thief. He has despoiled us of the Seven-year Eye. Let him come forward for his due. Until the thief has brought the Seven-year Eye in his own hand to the sacred temple of Han, every hour one of the outsiders will be buried in the crab-warren. If the thief hangs back, all will be so dealt with, and there will be an end to the Earth-things.'

Mapes said in a tight voice. 'Did you take their Seven-year Eye?'

Kelly nodded numbly. Yes.'

Herli made a sharp sound in his throat, turned away.

Kelly said miserably, 'I don't know what came over me. There it was — glowing like a little green moon . . . . I took it.'

Herli said gutturally, 'Don't just stand there.'

Kelly reached out, pushed buttons. The screen changed, a Han priest stared forth into Kelly's face.

Kelly said, 'I stole your jewel . . . . Don't kill any more people. I'll bring it back to you.

The priest said, 'Every hour until you arrive one of the Earth-things dies painfully.'

Kelly leaned forward, slammed off the screen with a sudden furious sweep of his hand. He turned in anger.

'Don't stand there glaring at me! You, Herli, you told me I wouldn't even make it into the temple! And if any of you guys had been where I was and saw that jewel like I saw it, you'd have taken it too.'

Mapes growled under his breath. Herli's shoulders seemed to sag; he looked away. 'Maybe you're right, Briar.'

Kelly said, 'Are we helpless? Why didn't we fight when they took those twelve kids? There's maybe a million Han, but there's fifty thousand of us — and they have no weapons that I know of.'

'They've seized the power station,' said Herli. 'Without power we can't distill water, we can't radiate our hydroponics. We're in a tough situation.'

Kelly turned away. 'So long, fellows.'

No one answered him. He walked down the stairs, across the parking strip to his flier. He was conscious of their eyes watching from the window.

In, up, away. First to his cabin by the lake, under the shagbark for the Seven-year Eye, then an arcing flight over the planet, south to north, to the gray fortress of North Settlement, and the dark temple in its center.

Kelly dropped the flier directly in front of the temple. No reason now for stealth.

He climbed to the ground, looked about through the strange purple twilight which had come to the ramshackle city. A few Han moved past, and Kelly saw the flash of their faces.

He walked slowly up the steps to the temple, paused indecisively in the doorway. There was no point in adding further provocation to his offenses. No doubt they planned to kill him; he might as well make it as easy as possible.

'Hello,' he called into the dark interior, in a voice he tried to keep firm. 'Anyone in there? Priests! I've brought back the jewel . . . .'

There was no response. Listening intently, he could hear a distant murmur. He took a few steps into the temple, peered up the nave. The muffled red and green illumination confused rather than aided his vision. He noticed a curious irregularity to the floor. He took a step forward — another — another — he stepped on something soft. There was the flash of white below him. The floor was covered by the black-robed priests, lying flat on their faces.

The priest he had trod on made no sound. Kelly hesitated. Time was passing . . . . He crammed all his doubts, fears, vacillations into a corner of his mind, strode forward, careless of where he stepped.

Down the center of the nave he walked, holding the green jewel in his hand. Ahead he saw the sheen of the tall black mirror, and there on the black cushion was a second jewel identical to the one he carried. A Han priest stood like a ghost in a black robe, he watched Kelly approach without movement. Kelly laid the jewel on the cushion beside its twin.

'There it is. I've brought it back. I'm sorry I took it. I — well, I acted on a wild impulse.'

The priest picked up the jewel, held it under his chin as if feeling the warmth from the green fire.

'Your impulse has cost fifteen Earth lives.'

'Fifteen?' faltered Kelly. 'There were but twelve — '

'Two hours delay has sent two to the crab-warren,' said the Han. 'And yourself. Fifteen.'

Kelly said with a shaky bravado, 'You're taking a lot on yourself — these murders — '

'I am not acquainted with your idiom,' said the priest, 'but it seems as if you convey a foolish note of menace. What can you few Earth-things do against Great God Han, who has just now taken our planet across the galaxy?'

Kelly said stupidly, 'Your god Han — moved the planet?'

'Certainly. He has taken us far and forever distant from Earth to this mellow sun; such is his gratitude for our prayers and for the tribute of the Eye.'

Kelly said with studied carelessness, 'You have your jewel back; I don't see why you're so indignant — '

The priest said, 'Look here.' Kelly followed his gesture, saw a square black hole edged with a coping of polished stone. 'This shaft is eighteen miles deep. Every priest of Han descends to the coomb once a week and carries back to the surface a basket of crystallized stellite. On rare occasions the matrix of the eye is found, and then there is great gratification in the city . . . . Such a jewel did you steal.'

Kelly took his eyes away from the shaft. Eighteen miles. . . .

'I naturally wasn't aware of the — '

'No matter; the deed is done. Now the planet has moved and Earth's power cannot prevent such punishments as we intend to visit upon you.'

Kelly tried to keep his voice steady. 'Punish? What do you mean?'

Behind him he heard a rustling, the shuffle of movement. He looked over his shoulder. The black cloaks merged with the drapes of the temple, and the Han faces floated in mid-air.

'You will be killed,' said the priest. Kelly stared into the white face. 'If the manner of your going is of any interest to you — 'The priest conveyed details which froze Kelly's flesh, clabbered the moisture in his mouth. 'Your death will thereby deter other Earth-things from like crimes.'

Kelly protested in spite of himself. 'You have your jewel; there it is . . . . If you insist on killing me — kill me, but — '

'Strange,' said the Han priest. 'You Earth-things fear pain more than anything else you can conceive. This fear is your deadliest enemy. We Han fear nothing — ' he looked up at the tall black mirror, bowed slightly ' — nothing but our Great God Han.'

Kelly stared at the shimmering black surface. 'What's that mirror to do with your God Han?'

'That is no mirror; that is the portal to the place of the Gods, and every seven years a priest must go through to convey the consecrated Eye to Han.'

Kelly tried to plumb the dark depths of the mirror. 'What lies beyond? What kind of land?'

The priest made no answer.

Kelly laughed in a shrill voice he did not recognize. He lurched forward, threw up his fist in a blow which carried every ounce of his strength and weight. He struck the priest at a point where a man's jaw would be, felt a brittle crunch. The priest spun around, fell in the tangle of his cloak.

Kelly turned on the priests in the nave, and they rose in fury. Kelly was desperate, fearless now. He laughed again, reached down, scooped both jewels from the cushion. 'Great God Han lives behind the mirror, and moves planets for jewels. I have two jewels; maybe Han will move a planet for me. . . .'

He jumped close to the black mirror. He put out his hand and felt a soft surface like a curtain of air. He paused in sudden trepidation. Beyond was the unknown. . . .

Pushing at him came the first rank of the Han priests.

Kelly could not delay. If he died passing through the black curtain, if he suffocated in airless space — it would be clean and fast.

He leaned forward, closed his eyes, held his breath, stepped through. . . .

Kelly had come a tremendous distance, not to be reckoned in miles or hours, but in quantities like abstract, irrational ideas.

He opened his eyes. They functioned. He was not dead. . . . Or was he? . . . He took a step forward, sensed solidity under his feet. He looked down, saw a glassy black floor where small sparks burst, flickered, died. Constellations? Universes? Or merely — sparks?

He took another step. It might have been a yard, a mile, a light-year; he moved with the floating ease of a man walking in a dream.

He stood on the lip of an amphitheater, a bowl like a lunar crater. He took another step. He stood in the center of the bowl. He halted, fought to convince himself of his consciousness. Blood made a rushing sound as it flowed through his veins. He swayed, might have fallen if gravity had existed to pull him down. But there was no gravity. His feet clung to the surface by some mysterious adhesion beyond his experience. The blood-sound rose and pulsed in his ears. He was alive.

He looked in back of him, and in the blurring of his eyes could not distinguish what he saw. He turned, took a step forward —

He was intruding. He felt the sudden irritated attention of gigantic, overwhelming personalities.

He gazed about the glassy floor, and the faintest of watery gray lights seeping down from above collected in the concavity where he stood. Space was vast, interminable, without perspective.

Kelly saw the beings he had disturbed — *felt* rather than saw them: a dozen giant shapes looming indistinctly above.

One of these shapes formed a thought, and a surge of meaning permeated space, impinged on Kelly's mind, translating itself into words:

'What is this thing? From whose world did it come?'

'From mine.' Kelly looked from shape to shape, to determine which god might be Han.

'Remove it quickly — ' and to Kelly's mind came a jumble of impressions he had no words to express. 'We must deal with the matter of . . . .' Again a quick listing of ideas which refused to translate in Kelly's mind. He felt Han's attention focusing on him. He stood transfixed, waiting for the obliteration he knew to be imminent.

But he held the jewels, and their green glow shone up through his fingers. He cried out, 'Wait, I came here for a purpose; I want a planet back where it belongs, and I have jewels to pay — '

He felt the baleful pressure of Han's will on his mind — increasing, increasing; he groaned in helpless anguish.

'Wait,' came a calm thought, transcendently clear and serene.

'I must destroy it,' Han protested. 'It is the enemy of my jewel-senders.'

'Wait,' came from yet another of the shades, and Kelly caught a nuance of antagonism to Han. 'We must act judicially.'

'Why are you here?' came the query of the Leader.

Kelly said, 'The Han priests are murdering people of my race.'

'Ah!' came a thought like an exclamation, from the Antagonist. 'Han's jewel-senders do evil and unnatural deeds.'

'A minor matter,' came the restless thought of still another shape. 'Han must protect his jewel-senders.'

And Kelly caught the implication that the jewel-sending

was of cardinal importance; that the jewels were vital to the gods.

The Antagonist chose to make an issue of the matter. 'The condition of injustice which Han has effected must be abated.'

The Leader meditated. And now came a sly thought to Kelly, which he sensed had been channelled from the Antagonist. 'Challenge Han to a . . .' The thought could only be translated as duel. 'I will aid you. Relax your mind.' Kelly gradually relaxed his state of mind and felt something like a damp shadow entering his brain, absorbing, recording . . . . All in an instant. Then the contact vanished.

Kelly felt the Leader's mind wavering in favor of Han. He said hurriedly, improvising as best he could: 'Leader, in one of the legends of Earth, a man journeyed to the land of the giants. As they came to kill him, he challenged the foremost to a duel, with his life as the stake.' '*Of three trials*,' came a thought. 'Of three trials,' added Kelly. 'In the story, the man won and was permitted to return to his native land. After this fashion, let me duel in three trials with Han.'

A surge of thoughts thickened the air — rancorous contempt from Han, subtle encouragement from the Antagonist, amusement from the Leader.

'You invoke a barbaric principle,' said the Leader. 'But by a simple logic, it is a just device, and shall be honored. You shall duel Han in three trials.'

'Why waste time?' inquired Han. 'I can powder him to less than the strings of atoms.'

'No.' said the Leader. 'The trial may not be on a basis of sheer potential. You and this man are at odds over an issue which has no fundamental right or wrong. It is the welfare of his people, opposed to the welfare of your jewel-senders. Since the issues are equal, there would be no justice in an unequal duel. The trial must be on a basis which will not unwontedly handicap either party.'

'Let a problem be stated,' suggested the Antogonist. 'He who first arrives at a solution wins the trial.'

Han was scornfully silent. So the Leader formulated a

problem — a grandiloquent statement in terms of multiple dimensions and quasi-time and a dozen concepts which Kelly's brain could in no way grasp.

'That is hardly a fair problem,' the Antagonist intervened, 'lying as it does entirely out of the man's experience. Let me formulate a problem.' And he stated a situation which at first startled Kelly, and then brought him hope.

The problem was one he had encountered a year previously at the station. A system to integrate twenty-five different communication bands into one channel was under consideration, and it was necessary to thrust a beam of protons past a bank of twenty-five mutually interacting magnets and hit a pin-point filter at the far end of its vector casing. The solution was simple enough — a statement of the initial vector in terms of a coordinate equation and a voltage potential — yet the solution had occupied the station computers for two months. Kelly knew this solution as he knew his own name.

'Hurry!' came the Antagonist's secret thought, focused to him alone.

Kelly blurted out the answer.

There was a wave of astonishment through the group, and he felt their suspicious inspection.

'You are quick indeed,' said the Leader, non-plussed.

'Another problem,' called the Antagonist. Once more he brought a question from Kelly's experience, this concerning the behavior of positrons in the secondary layer of a star in a cluster of six, all at specified temperatures and masses. And this time Kelly's mind worked even faster. He immediately stated the answer. Still he anticipated Han by mere seconds.

Han protested. 'How could this small pink brain move faster than my cosmic consciousness?'

'How is this?' asked the Leader. 'How do you calculate so swiftly?'

Kelly fumbled for ideas, finally strung together a lame statement: 'I do not calculate. In my brain is a mass of cells whose molecules form themselves into models of the problem. They move in an instant, the problem is solved, and the solution comes to fruition.'

Anxiously he waited, but the reply seemed to satisfy the group. These creatures — or gods, if such they were — were they so naive? Only the Antagonist suggested complex motives. Han, Kelly sensed, was old, of great force, of a hard and inflexible nature. The Leader was venerable beyond thought, calm and untroubled as space itself.

'What now?' came from the Antagonist. 'Shall there be another problem? Or shall the man be declared the victor?'

Kelly would have been well pleased to let well enough alone, but this evidently did not suit the purposes of the Antagonist.

'No!' The thoughts of Han roared forth almost like sound. 'Because of a ridiculous freak in this creature's brain, must I admit him my superior? I can fling him through a thousand dimensions with a thought, snap him out of existence, out of memory — '

'Perhaps because you are an Entity,' came the Antagonist's taunt, 'and of pure — ' another confusing concept, a mixture of energy, divinity, force, intelligence. 'The man is but a combination of atoms, and moves through the oxidation of carbon and hydrogen. Perhaps if you were as he, he might face you on more equal terms, hand to hand.'

A curious tenseness stiffened the mental atmosphere. Han's thoughts came sluggishly, tinged for the first time with doubt.

'Let that be the third trial,' said the Leader composedly. Han gave a mental shrug. One of the towering shadows shrunk, condensed, swirled to a man-like shape, solidified further, and at last stood facing Kelly, a thing like a man, glowing with a green phosphorescence like the heart of the Seven-year Eye.

The Antagonist's secret thought came to Kelly: 'Seize the jewel at the back of the neck.'

Kelly scanned the slowly advancing figure. It was exactly his height and heft, naked, but radiating an inhuman confidence. The face was blurred, fuzzy, and Kelly could never afterward describe the countenance. He tore his gaze away.

'How do we fight?' he demanded, beads of sweat dripping from his body. 'Do we set any rules — or no holds barred?'

'Tooth and nail,' came the calm thoughts of the Leader. 'Han now has organic sensibilities like yours. If you kill this body, or render it unconscious, you win. If you lose this trial, then we shall decide.'

'Suppose he kills me?' objected Kelly, but no one seemed to hear.

Eyes glaring, Han rushed at him. Kelly took a step backward, jabbed tentatively with his left fist. Han rushed forward. Kelly punched furiously, kneed the onrushing body, heard it grunt and fall, to leap erect instantly. A tingle of joy ran down Kelly's spine, and more confidently he stepped forward, lashing out with rights and lefts. Han leapt close and clinched his arms around Kelly's body. Now he began to squeeze, and Kelly felt a power greater than any man's in those green-glowing arms.

'The jewel,' came a sly thought. Sparks were exploding in Kelly's eyes; his ribs creaked. He swung a frenzied hand, clawing at Han's neck. He felt a hard protuberance, he dug his nails under, tore the jewel free.

A shrill cry of utmost pain and horror — and the god-man puffed away into black smoke which babbled in a frenzy back and forth through the darkness. It surged around Kelly, and little tendrils of the smoke seemed to pluck at the jewel clenched in his hand. But they had no great force, and Kelly found he could repel the wisps with the power of his own brain.

He suddenly understood the function of the jewel. It was the focus for the god. It centralized the myriad forces. The jewel gone, the god was a welter of conflicting volitions, vagrant impulses, insubstantial.

Kelly felt the Antagonist's triumphant thoughts. And he himself felt an elation he had never known. The Leader's cool comment brought him back to himself:

'You seem to have won the contest.' There was a pause. 'In the absence of opposition we will render any requests you may make.' There was no concern in his thoughts for the decentralized Han. The black smoke was dissipating, Han was no more than a memory. 'Already you have delayed us long. We have the problem of — ' the now familiar confusion of ideas, which Kelly vaguely understood. It seemed there was a vortex of universes which possessed consciousness, as mighty or mightier than these entitities, on tangental courses which allowed interpenetration.

'Well,' said Kelly, 'I'd like you to move the planet I just came from back to its old orbit around Magra Taratempos.'

The Leader made a small exertion. 'The world you mention now moves in its previous position.'

'Suppose the Han priests come through and request it altered once again?'

'The portal no longer exists. It was held extant by Han; when Han dissolved, the portal closed . . . . Is that the total of your desires?'

Kelly's mind raced, became a turmoil. This was his chance. Wealth, longevity, power, knowledge . . . . Somehow thoughts would not form themselves — there were curses attached to unnatural gifts —

'I'd like to get back to Bucktown safely . . . .'

Abruptly, Kelly found himself in the glare of the outer world. He stood on the hill above Bucktown, and he breathed the salt air of the marshes. Above hung a hot white sun — Magra Taratempos.

He became aware of an object clenched in his hand, the jewel he had torn out of Han's neck. There were two others in his pocket.

Across the city, he saw the light blue steel box of the station. What should he tell Herli and Mapes? Would they believe the truth? He looked at the three jewels. Two he could sell for a fortune on Earth. But one shone brilliantly in the bright sunlight and that was for Lynette Mason's tan and graceful neck.

THE HOUSE LORDS

THE TWO MEN, with not a word spoken, had become very agitated. Caffridge, the host, rose to his feet, took quick steps back and forth across the room. He went to the window, looked into the sky toward the distant star BGD 1169. The guest, Richard Emerson, was affected to an even greater degree. He sat back in his chair, face white, mouth loose, eyes wide and glistening.

Nothing had been said and there was nothing visible to explain their emotion. They sat in an ordinary suburban living room, notable only for a profusion of curios, oddities and surreal trinkets hanging on the walls.

At a scratching sound, Caffridge turned from the window. He called sharply, 'Sarvis!'

The black and white cat, sharpening its claws on a carved column of exotic wood, laid its ears back, but continued to scratch unconcernedly.

'You rascal!' Caffridge picked up the cat, hustled him outside through the animal's special door. He returned to Emerson. 'We seem to be thinking the same thought.'

Emerson was gripping the arms of his chair. 'How did I miss it before?' he muttered.

'It's a strange business,' said Caffridge. 'I don't know what we should do.'

'It's out of my hands now, thank heaven!' said Emerson.

Caffridge picked up the small white box which contained Emerson's report. 'Do you want to come along with me?'

Emerson shook his head. 'I've nothing more to say. I don't want to see that again.' He nodded toward the box.

'Very well,' said Caffridge gloomily. 'I'll show this to the Board tonight. After that . . . . '

Emerson smiled, weary and skeptical. 'After that, what?'

The Astrographical Society functioned as a nonprofit organization, devoted to extraterrestrial research and exploration. The dues paid in by a million active members were augmented by revenue from special patents and grants, licenses and counseling fees, with the result that over the years the Society had become very wealthy. A dozen spaceships carried the blue and green Astrographical chevron to remote places; the monthly publication was studied by school children and savants alike; the Astrographical Museum housed a wonderful melange of objects gathered across the universe.

In a specially equipped cupola on the roof of the museum, the Board of Directors met once a month to transact business and to watch and hear visualized reports from research teams. Theodore Caffridge, Chairman of the Board, arriving at the meeting, dropped the box containing Team Commander Richard Emerson's report into the projective mechanism. He stood silently, a tall somber figure, waiting while conversation around the table died.

'Gentlemen,' said Caffridge in a dull monotone, 'I have already examined this report. It is the strangest of my experience. I am seriously disturbed, and I should remark that Commander Emerson shares my feeling.'

He paused. The Directors looked at him curiously.

'Come, Caffridge, don't be mysterious!'

'Let's hear it, Theodore!'

Caffridge smiled the faintest, most remote smile imaginable. 'The report is here; you can see for yourselves.'

He touched a switch; the walls of the room dissolved into gray mist; colors swirled and cleared. The Board of Directors became a cluster of invisible eyes and ears, projected into the cabin of the spaceship *Gaea*. Their vantage point was the recording globe at the peak of Emerson's helmet. They saw what he saw, heard what he heard.

Emerson's voice came from a speaker. 'We are in orbit over planet Two of star BGD one-one-six-nine, in Argo Navis Four. We were attracted here by a series of pulses radiating in the C-three phase. These would seem to indicate a highly organized technical civilization, so naturally we stopped to investigate.'

The images around the walls of the room shifted as Emerson stepped up to the controls. Through the observation port the Directors could see a world swinging below, in the full illumination of an unseen sun.

Emerson detailed the physical characteristics of the world, which resembled those of Earth. 'The atmosphere seems breathable; there is vegetation roughly comparable to our own.'

Emerson approached the ship's telescreen; again the images around the walls shifted. 'The signals had led us to expect some sort of intelligent occupancy. We were not disappointed. The autochthons live, not in organized settlements, but in isolated dwellings. For lack of a better word, we've been calling them palaces.' Emerson adjusted a dial on the console; the view on the telescreen expanded enormously and the Directors were looking into a forest as dense as a jungle. The view shifted across the treetops to a clearing about a mile in diameter. The 'palace' occupied the center of the clearing — a dozen tall walls, steep and high as cliffs, joined apparently at random. They were constructed of some shimmering metalloid substance, and open to the sky. No portals or apertures were visible.

'That's about all the detail I can pick up from this altitude,' came Emerson's voice. 'Notice the absence of roof, the apparent lack of interior furnishing. It hardly seems a dwelling. Notice also how the clearing is landscaped — like a formal garden.'

He backed away from the telescreen; the Directors once more sat in the cabinet of the *Gaea*. 'We have been broadcasting international symbols on all bands,' said Emerson. 'So far there has been no response. I think that we will set down in that clearing. There is an element of risk attached, but I believe that a race apparently so sophisticated will neither be surprised nor shocked by the appearance of a strange spaceship.'

The *Gaea* settled into an atmosphere of BGD 1169-2, and the hull shivered to the slur of the thin gas whipping past.

Emerson spoke into the pickup, noting that the ship hovered above the area previously observed and was about to land.

The ship struck solid ground. There was a momentary fluctuation as the stabilizers took hold; then a sense of anchorage. Switches cut impulsion; the half-heard whine died down the scale into silence. The crew stood at the observation posts, staring out over the clearing.

At the center rose the palace — tall planes of glistening metalloid. Even from this close view, no openings, no windows, no doors or vents could be seen.

The grounds surrounding the palace were carefully tended. Avenues of white-trunked trees held square black leaves, large as trays, turned up to the sun. There were irregular beds of black moss, feathery maroon ferns, fluffy pink and white growths like cotton candy. In the background rose the forest; a tangle of blue-green trees and broad-leaved shrubs, red, black, gray, and yellow.

Inside the *Gaea* the crew stood ready to depart at any sign of hostility.

The palace remained quiet.

Half an hour passed. A small shape appeared briefly outside the wall of the palace. Cope, the young third officer, saw it first and called to Emerson. 'Look there!'

Emerson focused the magnifier. 'It's a child — a *human* child!'

The crew came to stare. Intelligent life among the stars was a rarity; to find such life in the human mold was cause for astonishment.

Emerson increased magnification.

'It's a boy, about seven or eight years of age,' he said. 'He's looking directly at us, but he doesn't seem particularly interested.'

The child turned back to the palace, and disappeared. Emerson uttered a soft ejaculation. 'Did you see that?'

'What happened?' asked Wilhelm, the big blond second officer.

'He walked through the weall! As if it were air!'

Time passed; there was no further show of life. The crew fidgeted. 'Why don't they show some interest?' complained Swett, the steward.

Emerson shook his head in puzzlement. 'Spaceships certainly don't drop down every day.'

Wilhelm suddenly called out, 'There's more of them — two, three, six — a whole damn tribe!'

They came from the forest, quietly, almost stealthily, singly and in pairs, men and women, until a dozen stood near the ship. They wore woven smocks of coarse fiber, crude leather shoes with flaring tops. At their belts hung daggers of several sizes and complicated little devices that looked to be built of wood and twisted gut. They were a hard-bitten lot, with heavy-boned faces and glinting eyes. They walked with a careful bend to the knee, which gave them a furtive aspect. They kept the ship between themselves and the palace at all times, as if anxious to escape observation.

Emerson said, 'I can't understand it. These aren't just humanoid types; they're human in every respect!' He looked across to where Boyd, the biologist, was finishing his tests. 'What's the story?'

'Clean bill of health,' said Boyd. 'No dangerous pollen, no air-borne proteides, nothing remarkable in any way.'

'I'm going outside,' said Emerson.

Wilhelm protested, 'They look unpredictable and they're armed.'

'I'll take a chance,' said Emerson. 'If they were hostile, I don't think they'd expose themselves.'

Wilhelm was not convinced. 'You never can tell what a strange race has in mind.'

'Nevertheless,' said Emerson, 'I'm going out. You fellows cover me. Also stand by, in case we want to leave in a hurry.'

'Are you going out alone?' Wilhelm asked dubiously. 'There's no point in risking two lives.'

Wilhelm's square raw-boned face took on a mulish set. 'I'll go with you. Two eyes see better than one.'

Emerson laughed. 'I've already got two eyes. Besides, you're second in command; your place is here in the ship.'

Cope, the young third officer, slender and dark, hardly out of his teens, spoke. 'I'd like to go out with you.'

'Very well, Cope,' said Emerson. 'Let's go!'

Ten minutes later the two men stepped out of the ship, descended the ramp, stood on the soil of BGD 1169-2. The men and women from the forest still stood behind the ship, peering from time to time toward the palace. When Emerson and Cope appeared, they drew together, ready for attack, defense or flight. Two of them fingered wooden contrivances at their belts, which Emerson saw to be dart catapults. But otherwise there was no motion, friendly or otherwise.

Emerson halted twenty feet distant, raised his hand, smiled in what he hoped to be a friendly manner. 'Hello.'

They stared at him, then began muttering among themselves. Emerson and Cope moved a step or two closer; the voices became audible. A lank, gray-haired man, who seemed to wield a degree of authority, spoke with peevish energy, as if refuting nonsense. 'No, no — impossible for them to be Freemen!'

The gnarled, beady-eyed man to whom he spoke retorted, 'Impossible? What do you take them for, then, if not Freemen?'

Emerson and Cope stared in amazement. These men spoke English!

Someone else remarked, 'They're not House Lords! Who ever saw House Lords like these!'

A fourth voice was equally definite. 'And it's a certainty that they're not servants.'

'All of you talk in circles,' snapped one of the women. 'Why don't you ask them and be done with it?'

English! The accent was blurred, the intonation unusual, but the language, nonetheless, was their own! Emerson and

Cope came a step closer; the forest people fell silent, and shifted their feet nervously.

Emerson spoke. 'I am Richard Emerson,' he said. 'This is Howard Cope. Who are you people?'

The gray-haired chief surveyed them with crafty impudence. 'Who are we? We're Freemen, as you must know very well. What do you here? What House are you from?'

Emerson said, 'We're from Earth.'

'Earth?'

Emerson looked around the blank faces. 'You don't know of Earth?'

'No.'

'But you speak an Earth language!'

The chief grinned. 'How else can men speak?'

Emerson laughed weakly. 'There are a number of other languages.'

The chief shook his head skeptically. 'I can't believe that.'

Emerson and Cope exchanged glances of bewildered amusement. 'Who lives in the palace?' Emerson asked.

The chief seemed incredulous at Emerson's ignorance. 'The House Lords, naturally. Genarro, Hesphor and the rest.'

Emerson considered the tall walls, which seemed, on the whole, ill-adapted to human requirements. 'They are men, like ourselves?'

The chief laughed jeeringly. 'If you would call such luxurious creatures men! We tolerate them only for their females.' From the men of the group came a lascivious murmur. 'The soft, sweet House Lord girls!'

The forest women hissed in anger. 'They're as worthless as the men!' exclaimed one leathery old creature.

There was a sudden nervous motion at the outskirts of the group. 'Here they come! The House Lords!'

Quickly, with long, bent-kneed strides, the savages retreated, and were gone into the forest.

Emerson and Cope walked around the ship. Crossing the clearing in leisurely fashion were a young man, a young woman, a girl and the boy they had seen before. They were the most handsome beings the Earthmen had ever seen. The young man wore a skintight garment of emerald-green sequins, a complicated headdress of silver spines; the boy wore red trousers, a dark blue jacket and a long-billed blue cap. The young woman and the girl wore simple sheaths of white and blue, stretching with easy elasticity as they walked. They were bareheaded and their pale hair fell flowing to their shoulders.

They halted a few yards from the ship, considered the spacemen with sober curiosity. Their expressions were intent and intelligent, with an underlying hauteur. The young man glanced casually toward the forest, held up a small rod. A puff of darkness came forth and a black bubble wafted toward the forest, expanding enormously as it went.

From the forest came yelps of fear, the stumble of racing feet. The black bubble exploded among the trees, scattering hundreds of smaller black bubbles, which grew and exploded in their turn.

The sound of flight diminished in the distance. The four young House Lords, smiling a little, returned their attention to Emerson and Cope.

'And who may you be? Surely not Wild men?'

'No, we're not Wild men,' said Emerson.

The boy said, 'But you're not House Lords.'

'And certainly you're not servants,' said the girl, who was several years older than the boy, perhaps fourteen or fifteen.

Emerson explained patiently, 'We are scientists, from Earth.'

Like the forest people, the House Lords were puzzled. 'Earth?'

'My God!' exclaimed Emerson. 'Surely you know of Earth!'

They slowly shook their heads.

'But you're human beings — Earth people!'

'No,' said the young man, 'we are House Lords. "Earth" is nothing to us.'

'But you speak our language — an Earth language!'

They shrugged and smiled. 'There are a hundred ways in which your people might have learned our speech.'

The matter seemed to interest them very little. The young woman looked toward the forest. 'Best be careful of the Wild Men; they'll do you harm if they can.' She turned. 'Come, let us go back.'

'Wait!' cried Emerson.

They observed him with austere politeness. 'Yes?'

'Aren't you curious about us, or interested in where we came from?'

The young man smilingly shook his head, and the silver spines of his headgear chimed like bells. 'Why should we be interested?'

Emerson laughed in mingled astonishment and irritation.

'We're strangers from space — from Earth, which you claim you never heard of.'

'Exactly. If we have never heard of you, how can we be interested?'

Emerson threw up his hands. 'Suit yourself. However, we're interested in you.'

The young man nodded, accepting this as a matter of course. The boy and girl were already walking away; the young woman had half-turned and was waiting. 'Come, Hesphor,' she called softly.

'I'd like to talk to you,' Emerson said. 'There's a mystery here — something we should straighten out.'

'No mystery. We are House Lords, and this our House.'

'May we come into your house?'

The young man hesitated, glanced at the young woman. She pursed her lips, shook her head. 'Lord Genarro.'

The young man made a small grimace. 'The servants are gone; Genarro sleeps. They may come for a short time.'

The young woman shrugged. 'If Genarro wakes, he will not be pleased.'

'Ah, but Genarro —'

'But Genarro,' the woman interrupted quickly, 'is the First Lord of the House!'

Hesphor seemed momentarily sulky. 'Genarro sleeps,

and the servants are gone. These wild things may enter.'

He signaled to Cope and Emerson. 'Come.'

The House Lords strolled back through the garden, talking quietly together. Emerson and Cope followed, half angry, half sheepish. 'This is fantastic,' Emerson muttered. 'Snubbed by the aristocracy half an hour after we arrive.'

'I guess we'll have to put up with it,' said Cope. 'They know things we've never even thought of. That black bubble, for instance.'

The boy and girl reached the wall of the palace. Without hesitation they walked through the glistening surface. The young man and woman followed. When Emerson and Cope reached the wall, it was solid, supernormally cold. They felt along the smooth surface, pushing, groping in exasperation.

The boy came back through the wall. 'Are you coming in?'

'We'd like to,' said Emerson.

'That's solid there.' The boy watched them in amusement. 'Can't you tell where it's permeable?'

'No,' said Emerson.

'Neither can the Wild Men,' said the boy. He pointed. 'Go through there.'

Emerson and Cope passed through, and the wall felt like a thin film of cool water.

They stood on a dull blue floor, with silver filaments tracing a looped pattern. The walls rose high all around them. A hundred feet above, bars of a black substance protruded from shallow ledges, and the air seemed to quiver, like the air over a hot road.

There was no furniture in the room, no trace of human habitation.

'Come,' said the boy. He crossed the room, walked through the wall opposite. Emerson and Cope followed. 'I hope we can find our way out,' said Cope. 'I wouldn't want to climb these walls.'

They stood in a hall similar to the first, but with a floor of a resilient white material. Their bodies felt light, their steps took them farther than they expected. The young man and woman were waiting for them. The boy had stepped back through the wall; the girl was nowhere in sight.

'We can stay with you a moment or two,' said the young man. 'Our servants are gone; the house is quiet. Perhaps you'd care to eat?' Without waiting for response he reached forward. His hands disappeared into nothingness. He drew them back, pulling forth a rack supporting trays and bowls of foodstuffs — wedges of red jelly, tall white cones, black wafers, small green globular fruits, flagons containing liquids of various colors.

'You may eat,' said the young woman, motioning with her hand.

'Thank you,' said Emerson. He and Cope gingerly sampled the food. It was strange and rich, and tingled in the mouth like carbonated water.

'Where does this food come from?' asked Emerson. 'How can you pull it out of the air like that?'

The young man shrugged. 'Why should we trouble ourselves, as long as it's there?'

Cope asked quizzically, 'What would you do if your servants left you?'

'Such a thing could never happen.'

'I'd like to see your servants,' said Emerson.

'They're not here now.' The young man removed his headgear, tucked it into an invisible niche. 'Tell us about this "Earth" of yours.'

'It's a planet like this one,' said Emerson, 'although men and women live much differently.'

'Do you have servants?'

'None of us have servants now.'

'Mmph,' said the young woman scornfully. 'Like the Wild Men.'

Cope asked, 'How long have you lived here?'

The question seemed to puzzle the House Lords. 'How long? What do you mean?'

'How many years?'

'What is a "year"?'

'A unit of time — the interval a planet takes to make a

revolution around its sun. Just as a day is the time a planet takes to rotate on its axis.'

The House Lords were amused. 'That's a queer thought . . . magnificently arbitrary. What possible use is such an idea?'

Emerson said dryly, 'We find time measurements useful.'

The House Lords smiled at each other. 'That well may be,' Hesphor remarked.

'Who are the Wild Men?' asked Cope.

'Just riffraff,' said the young woman with a shudder. 'Outcasts from Houses where there is no room.'

'They harass us; they try to steal our women,' said the young man. He held up his hand. 'Listen.' He and the young woman looked at each other.

Emerson and Cope could hear nothing.

'Lord Genarro,' said the young woman. 'He comes.'

Hesphor looked uneasily at the wall, glanced at Emerson and Cope, then planted himself obstinately in the middle of the hall.

There was a slight sound. A tall man dressed in shining black strode through the wall. His hair was copper-gold, his eyes frost-blue. He saw Emerson and Cope; he took a great stride forward. 'What are these wild things doing here! Are you all mad? Out, out with them!'

Hesphor interposed. 'They are strangers from another world. They mean no harm.'

'Out with them! Eating our food! Ogling the Lady Faelm!' He advanced menacingly; Emerson and Cope stepped back. 'Wild things, go!'

'Just as you llike,' said Emerson. 'Show us the way out.'

'One moment!' said Hesphor. 'I invited them here; they are my charges.'

Genarro turned his displeasure against the young House Lord. 'Do you wish to join the Wild Men?'

Hesphor stared at him; their eyes locked. Hesphor wilted and turned away.

'Very well,' he muttered. 'They shall leave.' He whistled;

through the wall came the boy. 'Take the strangers to their ship.'

'Quickly!' roared Genarro. 'The air reeks; they are covered with filth!'

'This way!' The boy scampered through the wall; Emerson and Cope followed with alacrity.

Through two walls they passed and once more stood in the open air. Cope heaved a deep sigh. 'Genarro's hospitality leaves much to be desired.'

The girl came out of the palace and joined the boy.

'Come,' said the boy. 'We'll take you to your ship. You'd best be away before the servants return.'

Emerson looked back toward the palace, shrugged. 'Let's go.'

They followed the boy and girl through the formal garden, past the white-trunked trees, the beds of black moss, the pink and white candy floss. The *Gaea*, at the far end of the clearing, seemed familiar and homelike; Emerson and Cope hurried their steps.

They passed a clump of gray-stalked bamboo; there was a rustle of movement, a quick rush and they were surrounded by Wild Men. Hands gripped Emerson and Cope, their weapons were snatched.

The boy and girl, struggling, kicking, screaming, were seized; nooses were dropped around their bodies and they were tugged toward the jungle.

'Loose us!' yelled the boy. 'The servants will pulverize you.'

'The servants are gone,' cried the Wild Men's chief happily. 'And I've got what I've wanted for many years — a fresh, beautiful House Lord girl.'

The girl sobbed and screamed and tore at her bonds; the boy struggled and kicked. 'Easy, boy,' the chief warned. 'We're close enough to cutting your throat as it is.'

'Why are you taking *us*?' panted Emerson. 'We're no good to you.'

'Only in what your friends will give to have you back.' The chief grinned knowingly over his shoulder. 'Weapons, good cloth, good shoes.'

'We don't carry such things with us!'

'You'll suffer till we get them!' the chief promised.

The forest was only fifty yards away. The boy flung himself flat on the ground, the girl did likewise. Emerson felt the grasp on his arms relax; he broke loose, swinging his fists. He struck a Wild Man, who fell to the ground. The chief snatched out his catapult, aimed it. 'One move —you're dead!'

Emerson stood rigid. The Wild Men seized the boy and girl; the party moved ahead.

But now the raid had been noticed at the palace; the air throbbed to a weird high whistle. A peculiar field of energy seemed to pulse above the walls. The Wild Men increased their pace.

From the palace came a fan of black energy, shearing down like a great dark vane, striking the ground at the forest's edge.

The Wild Men stopped short. Escape was blocked at this point. They released their hostages, turned, and ran parallel to the edge of the clearing.

Out of the palace came Genarro and Hesphor, and behind them, Faelm and another woman. Across the clearing came the sound of Genarro's voice, full of threat and passion.

Emerson and Cope ran like men in a nightmare. The *Gaea* loomed before them; they pounded up the ramp, plunged into the open hatch.

Inside, the crew waited white-faced and anxious. The door slid shut, power roared through the ship and the *Gaea* rose from the clearing.

Soon the *Gaea* was in space, far from any star. Without comment, Emerson set a course for Earth.

The images vanished. The Directors of the Astrographical Society sat stiff in their seats.

Theodor Caffridge spoke. His voice sounded flat and prosaic.

'As you have seen, Commander Emerson and crew underwent a most peculiar experience.'

'Peculiar!' Ben Haynault whistled. 'That's an understatement if there ever was one!'

'But what does it mean?' demanded Pritchard. 'Those people speaking English!'

'And knowing nothing of Earth!'

Caffridge said in his flat voice, 'Emerson and I have formed a tentative hypothesis. Like you, we were mystified. Who were these House Lords? How could they speak an Earth language, but still know nothing of Earth? How did the House Lords control their servants, these tremendous creatures which were never really seen, except perhaps as flickers of light and shadow?'

Caffridge paused. No one spoke; he went on. 'Commander Emerson had no answer to these questions. Neither did I. Then something very ordinary occurred, an event quite insignificant in itself. But it set off a charge in both our minds.

'What happened was that my cat Sarvis came into the house. He used his special little swinging door. My small House Lord, Sarvis. He came into his palace, he went to his dish and looked for his dinner.'

There was frozen silence in the Board room, the arrestment in time which comes of surprise and shock.

Then someone coughed; there was the hiss of breath, a bit of nervous laughter, general uneasy motion.

'Theodore,' Ben Haynault asked in a husky voice, 'what are you implying?'

'I've given you the facts. You must draw your own inferences.'

Paul Pritchard muttered, 'It was a hoax, surely. There's no other explanation. A society of crackpots . . . escapists. . . . '

Caffridge smiled. 'You might discuss that theory with Emerson.'

Pritchard fell silent.

'Emerson considers himself lucky,' Caffridge went on reflectively. 'I'm inclined to agree. If some wild thing came into my house and disrupted Sarvis, I'd consider it a

domestic disturbance of the highest order. I might not have
been quite so forbearing.'

'What can we do?' asked Haynault quietly.

Caffridge went to the window and stood looked up into
the southern sky. 'We can hope that they already have all
the House Lords they want.'

PLANET OF THE BLACK DUST

ABOUT THE MIDDLE of the dog watch, Captain Creed came up on the bridge of the freighter *Perseus*. He walked to the forward port and stood gazing at the blood-red star which lay directly ahead.

It was a nameless little sun in the tail of the Serpens group, isolated from the usual commercial routes. The Earth-Rasalague route ran far to one side, the Delta Aquila ran far to the other and the Delta Aquila-Sabik inter-sector service was yet a half light-year further out.

Captain Creed stood watching the small red star, deep in tought — a large man, with a paunch, a bland white face, a careful coal-black beard. His heavy black eyes, underhung with dark circles, were without expression or life. He wore a neat black suit, his boots shone with a high polish, his hands were white and immaculately kept.

Captain Creed was more than mere master of the *Perseus*. In partnership with his brother, he owned the European-Arcturus Line — a syndicate impressive in name only.

The Home Office, however, was one dingy room in the old Co-Martian Tower in Tran, and the firm's sole assets consisted, first, of the *Perseus* itself, and second, of the profit anticipated from a cargo of aromatic oils which Captain Creed had taken on consignment from McVann's Star in Ophiuchus.

The *Perseus* could not be considered the more valuable of the two items. It was outdated and slow, pitted by meteors and burned by many atmospheres, of little more than 6000 tons capacity.

The cargo was another matter — flask upon flask of rare

aromatics, essence of syrang blooms, oil of star-poppies, attar of green orchids, musk of rushed mian flies, distillation of McVann's blue bush — exotic liquids brought in by the bulb-men of McVann's Star a half ounce at a time. And Captain Creed was highly annoyed when the insurance evaluator permitted but an eighty-million-dollar policy; he had argued vehemently to have the figure moved closer to the cargo's true value.

Now, as he stood on the bridge smoking his cigar, he was joined by the first mate, Blaine, who was tall and thin and, except for a single scrub of black hair, egg-bald. Blaine had a long knife-nose, a mouth twisted to a perpetual snarl. He had a quick restless way of talking that sometimes disconcerted the Captain's careful nature.

'They're all fixed,' he announced. 'They'll go in about ten minutes — ' Captain Creed quelled him with a frown and a quick motion of the head, and Blaine saw that they were not alone. Holderlin, second mate and quartermaster, a young man of hard face and cruel blue eyes, stood forward at the helm.

Holderlin wore only loose tattered trousers, and the scarlet glare from the star ahead gave a devilish red glow to his body, put a lurid cast on his face. Like two hawks they watched him, and his expression did not entirely reassure them.

After a moment Captain Creed spoke smoothly. 'I doubt if you are right, Mr. Blaine. The period of that type of variable star is slower and more even, as I think you'll find if you check your observations.'

Blaine shot another quick look at Holderlin, then, mumbling indistinguishably, left for the engine room.

Creed presently stepped across the bridge.

'Take her five degrees closer to the star, Mr. Holderlin. We're somewhat off course, and the gravity will swing us back around.'

Holderlin gave him one look of surprise, then silently obeyed. What nonsense was this? Already the ship was gripped hard by gravity. Did they still hope to beguile him with such slim pretexts? If so, they must think him stupid indeed.

Even a child would by now have been warned by the happenings aboard the *Perseus*. First at Porphyry, the port on McVann's Star, Captain Creed had discharged his communicator and his two mechanics for reasons unexplained.

Not an unusual circumstance in itself, but Captain Creed had hired no replacements, leaving Farjoram, a half-mad Callistonian cook, the only other man aboard.

On several occasions, after Porphyry had been cleared, Holderlin had surprised Blaine and Creed intent at the radio. Later, when he inspected the frequency log he found no record of transmission.

And four or five days ago, while off watch and supposedly asleep, he had noticed that the entrance port to the starboard lifeboat was ajar. He had said nothing, but later, when Blaine and Captain Creed were both asleep, he inspected the lifeboats, port and starboard. The fuel in the starboard had been drained except for the slightest trickle and the radio transmitter had been tampered with.

The port flier was well fueled and provisioned. So Holderlin quietly refueled the starboard flier and cautiously stowed away spare fuel.

Now came Blaine's unwary statement to Captain Creed, and Creed's peculiar orders to steer toward the star. Holderlin's tough brown face was unexpressive as he watched Creed's great bulk by the port, blotting out the sun ahead. But his brain searched through every angle of the situation. For fourteen of his thirty-three years he had roamed space and of necessity had learned how best to look out for Robert Holderlin.

A slight shock shook the hull. Captain Creed turned his head negligently, then once again looked out on space. Holderlin said nothing, but his eyes were very alert.

A few minutes passed, and Blaine came back to the bridge. Holderlin sensed, but did not see, the look which passed between Creed and the gaunt first mate.

'Ah,' said Captain Creed, 'we seem to be close enough. Starboard ten degrees and set her on automatic.'

Holderlin adjusted the controls. He could feel the surge of power, but the ship did not respond.

'She doesn't answer, sir,' he said.

'What's this!' cried Captain Creed. 'Mr. Blaine! Check navigation circuits! The ship is not responding!'

Creed must dislike overt action, thought Holderlin, to insist on such elaborate circumstances — or they knew he carried a gun. Blaine ran off, and returned in a very short time, a wolfish grin on his lips.

'Steering is fused, Captain. That lining they put in at Aureolis has given out.'

Captain Creed looked from the small furious sun ahead to Blaine and Holderlin. With his entire fortune at stake, he seemed strangely unperturbed by the prospect of disaster. But then Captain Creed's white face was always controlled. He gave the order that Holderlin had been expecting.

'Abandon ship!' he said. 'Mr. Blaine, despatch the distress signal! Mr. Holderlin, find Farjoram and stand by the starboard flier!'

Holderlin left to find the cook. But he noted as he passed that Blaine, at the transmitter, had not yet activated the big red 'Emergency' relay.

Presently Captain Creed and Blaine joined Holderlin and the cook on the back walk.

'Shall I accompany your flier, Captain, or Mr. Blaine's?' asked Holderlin, as if he had not understood Captain Creed's previous order, or was challenging it. Blaine looked in sudden alarm at the captain.

'You will take charge of the starboard boat, Mr. Holderlin,' replied the Captain silkily. 'I wish Mr. Blaine to accompany me.' He turned to enter the port flier. But Holderlin stepped forward and produced a sheet of paper he had been carrying for several days.

'A moment, if you please, sir. If I am to be in charge of the starboard flier, for the protection of myself and the cook — in the event your flier is lost — will you sign this certification of shipwreck?'

'Neither of us will be lost, Mr. Holderlin,' replied Captain

Creed, smoothing his black beard. 'Mr. Blaine contacted a patrol cruiser not far away.'

'Nevertheless, sir, I believe the Code requires such a document.'

Blaine nudged the captain slyly.

'Well certainly, Mr. Holderlin, we must observe the law,' said Captain Creed, and he signed the certification. Then he and Blaine entered their shuttle.

'Take off, Mr. Holderlin!' Captain Creed ordered through the port. 'We will wait till you clear.'

Holderlin turned. The cook had disappeared.

'Farjoram!' he cried. '*Farjoram*!'

Holderlin ran to find him and discovered the fuzzy-skinned little Callistonian huddled in his cabin, red eyes bulging in terror. There was foam at his mouth.

'Come on!' said Holderlin gruffly.

The Callistonian babbled in frenzy.

'No, no! Get away, you go!'

Holderlin remembered a story about how this Farjoram and eight others had drifted in a lifeboat for four months through the Phenesian Blackness. When at last they had been picked up, only Farjoram remained alive among the picked bones of his fellows. Holderlin shuddered a little.

'Hurry!' came Captain Creed's call. 'We're out of time.'

'Come!' said Holderlin roughly. 'They'll kill you if you don't.'

As if in answer, the wild-eyed Callistonian drew a long knife from his pocket and in one sudden motion pushed it upward into his throat. He fell jerking at Holderlin's feet. Holderlin returned alone.

'Where's Farjoram?' queried Creed sharply.

'He killed himself, sir. With a knife.'

'What the hell!' murmured Creed, 'take off alone then. The rendezvous is at a hundred million miles on the line between this star and Delta Aquila.'

'Right, sir,' said Holderlin. Without further words he sealed himself in and eased away.

The sun was close, but not too close. It would have pulled

a small unfueled flier to doom, but it was not so near as to prevent another ship from approaching the *Perseus*, shackling into her fore and aft chocks and towing her off to safety.

Holderlin used his blasts for a few seconds, then cut them, as if his fuel were exhausted. Presented, as he drifted away from the *Perseus*, apparently helpless in the red star's gravity, he saw the port flier break clear and head out, not toward Delta Aquila, but back the way they had come.

Holderlin drifted quietly a few minutes, in the event that Captain Creed or Blaine were watching. But there was little time to waste. The other ship that he suspected had been following must now lie astern and would presently draw alongside the *Perseus*. After the precious cargo was transferred, the *Perseus* would hurtle into the scarlet sun.

Holderlin had different plans. He tucked away the certificate signed by Captain Creed, then steered his little ship back to the *Perseus*.

He brought the bow of the flier against the *Perseus'* forward hitch, then slipped into his suit, clambered out into space and shackled the two together. Once back inside he eased open the throttle and nudged the bow of the *Perseus* to a proximate position.

He pushed himself across the emptiness, this time to the *Perseus'* entrance port and, shedding his suit, ran up to the bridge. He sent out a detector wave and the almost instant alarm told him Creed's other ship stood close — too close for a possible escape to the only refuge he could think of — the lone planet of the red star.

He picked up the other ship on his screen, a long black vessel with high-straked bow and a bridge built into the hull. Holderlin instantly recognized the type, a class of fast heavily-armed ships designed for the frontier run.

Two years before he had shipped aboard one of the same class, now he recalled an incident of that voyage. Out past Fomalhaut, they'd engaged in a running battle with a pirate of the Clantilian system, and one well-placed shot had put them out of action. Holderlin remembered the exact details.

With a little luck and steady aim he might duplicate that shot.

So Holderin watched and waited as the sleek black vessel drew close. The shuttle dangling against the *Perseus'* bow was turned partly away in the shadow and was, he hoped, inconspicuous.

But the ship came easing up with an insolent leisure, there seemed to be no suspicion aboard. Holderlin's hard face creased in a grin as he sighted along the *Perseus'* ancient needle beam.

Like an immense black shark, the ship drifted over him. He fired, then laughed aloud as a great hold opened behind the bridge. The lights died, the driving beams cut off and the black ship rolled sluggishly in recoil, a great helpless hulk.

Holderlin ran to the bank of controls. He could consider himself safe for a few hours, and by then he would be well concealed. And if those aboard were not able to rig up auxiliary power quickly, they might even be forced to take to their lifeboats — for the red star glowed close ahead.

The *Perseus* heaved into life and, with the lifeboat dragging crazily from the bow, blasted away toward the lone planet beyond the scarlet sun.

An hour later he entered its green-tinted atmosphere. In order to avoid any sighting by the raider, he circled to the far side.

The planet appeared to be a world of about half Earth's size, scarred with gorges and precipitous crags, interspersed with plains. These escarpments brimmed with a black froth, which the screen presently revealed to be thick, fronded vegetation.

The chartreuse atmosphere supported great fleecy clouds, glowing in the lurid sunlight in shades of orange, gold, reds and yellow.

Holderlin let the *Perseus* fall toward the base of a great black peak where dense forest offered good concealment. For two tense hours he crouched in the lifeboat, jockeying the nose of the *Perseus* back and forth as it settled on its landing thrusters through a green murk. Finally the *Perseus* crashed down through the black trees onto solid soil. Holderlin fell limply back in his seat.

After some time he stirred himself. The green atmosphere did not look healthy, he returned to the *Perseus* in his suit.

The soft black fronds had closed over the ship. The *Perseus* was well concealed. Holderlin rigged a detector-alarm and went to sleep.

When he awoke he retested the atmosphere, which, as he suspected, showed poison. But it was warm enough, there was a sufficiency of oxygen and no tissue-irritant gasses were evident.

So he fitted a respirator with appropriate filters and jumped out to inspect *Perseus'* steerage. He sank immediately to his ankles in an impalpable black dust like soot; passing puffs of air blew whirls of black smoke around him.

Every step stirred up clouds which settled on his clothes and into his boots. Holderlin cursed and plodded around to the steering units.

The situation was both better and worse than he had expected. The linings were split and broken, and fragments had wedged inside. The filaments were destroyed but the backplates were still whole and in place; apparently the field coils were not burnt out.

He couldn't recall seeing any spare linings aboard, but to make sure he ransacked the ship — to no avail. However, a supply of flux was in its place as provided by the Code, from the early days of space-flight when the more durable linings were unknown.

Long ago, every ship carried dozens of spares — yet often as not these would burn out or split in the heat and pressure, and the ship would be forced to land on a convenient planet and mold another supply. Now Holderlin's concern was to find a bed of clean clay to accomplish that effect.

The ground at his feet was covered by the black dust. Perhaps, if he dug through the topsoil . . . .

Holderlin heard a heavy shuffling tread through the forest.

Alarmed, he ran back to the entrance port.

A thin shambling creature fifteen feet high, vaguely manlike, with a spider's gaunt construction, passed close beside the ship. Its skin was green, the face peculiarly long and vacant. A fierce shock of reddish hair splayed out from the back of its head. Its eyes were bulging milky orbs, ears wide and extended. It passed the *Perseus* with hardly a glance and showed neither awe nor interest.

'Hey!' cried Holderlin, jumping to the ground. '*Come back here*!'

The thing paused a moment to regard him dully through the greenish-red light, then slowly shambled off, stirring up thick black clouds of dust. It disappeared into the feathery black jungle.

Holderlin returned to the problem of repairing the *Perseus*. He required clay enough to mold four new linings — three or four hundred pounds. He brought a spade from the ship and dug into the surface.

He worked half an hour and turned up nothing but hot black humus. And the deeper he dug, the thicker and tougher grew the roots of the fungus trees. Soon he gave up in disgust.

As he climbed, sweating and dusty, from his hole, a little breeze raced along the top of the jungle fronds, and in the black fog which floated down Holderlin discovered the origin of the black powder at his feet. Spores, shedding from the trees.

He needed clay, not tree-spawn, clean yellow clay and the nearer the better. He did not fancy carrying a weight on his shoulder any great distance. He looked to where the lifeboat dangled from the bow of the *Perseus*. An idea formed.

The shackle, with the entire weight of the flier hanging on it, was locked. Holderlin scratched his head. He would have to balance the boat on the gravity units, releasing the shackle from all strain, to remove it.

But, when he finally poised the flier in mid-air and climbed out on the nose, his shift of position weighted the bow; now if he unscrewed the shackle, the boat very likely would nose down and throw him to the ground.

Cursing both shackle and lifeboat, Holderlin let the boat hang against the hull as before and made his way to the ground. He entered the ship and outfitted himself with a sack, a light spade, a canteen of water and spare charges for his respirator. The ship's receivers crackled.

'Aboard the *Perseus*! Aboard the *Perseus*! Respond, *Perseus*!'

Holderlin chuckled grimly and sat down.

'Aboard the *Perseus*!' came the call again. 'This is Captin Creed speaking. If you are listening, respond immediately. You have bested us fair and square, and we hold no grudge. But no matter how you reached this planet you cannot go farther.

'A detector screen surrounds you, and we will heterodyne any distress call you broadcast.'

Evidently Captain Creed had not yet surmised who had run off with his ship, or how it had been accomplished. Another voice broke in, harder and sharper.

'Respond immediately,' said the new voice, 'giving your position, and you will receive a share in the venture. If you do not, we will find you if it means searching the planet foot by foot!'

During this pronouncement, the strength of the radio carrier wave had increased, and now Holderlin heard a low mutter, rapidly waxing to a roar. Running to the port, he spied the black pirate ship sweeping toward him across the green sky, just under the canopy of many-colored clouds.

Almost overhead, the brake blasts spewed and the approaching ship slowed in its course. Trapped, thought Holderlin. With racing pulse he leapt for the flier. He'd blast the shackle loose!

But the black ship passed across the mountain, where it slowly sank from sight, sunlight glinting from its sides. Holderlin breathed easily again. This world was small, and the mountain made a prominent landmark. The same reasons that brought him here to hide had led them here to seek him.

At least he knew where his enemies were stationed, a matter

of some advantage. How to escape them, he as yet had no notion. With a fast well-armed ship they seemed invulnerable.

Holderlin shrugged. First he must accomplish repair. Then he would try to win clear. And if he could bring that scented cargo only as far as Laroknik on Gavnad, the sixth of Delta Aquila, his fortune would be made.

Holderlin put aside his dreaming. He took his sack and plodded off through the black dust in the direction of the mountain. A half mile from the ship, the feathery black canopy overhead thinned, and he entered a clearing.

Within moved a score of the tall manlike creatures. They appeared to be working with an enormous beast, evidently domesticated.

It had a gigantic round body, supported on a circle of wide arching legs. With two long tentacles it stuffed black tree-fronds into a maw on top of its hulk.

Holderlin passed uneasily through the clearing. Beyond a few dull glances, they took no heed of him. Continuing on a mile or so, he came to the edge of the forest and the steep rises of the mountains.

Almost at his feet he found what he sought. In the diminished gravity he loaded into his sack a great deal more than he might have carried on Earth — perhaps a half of his needs — and set out in return.

But as he began wading through the black dust the sack grew heavy, and by the time he reached the clearing where the natives tended their beast, his arms and his back ached in a dull agony.

He stood resting, watching the placid natives at their work. It occurred that possibly one of them might be induced to serve him.

'Hey — *you*!' he called to the nearest, as best he could through the respirator. 'Come here!'

It looked at Holderlin without interest.

'Come over here!' he called again, although plainly the creature could not understand him. 'I need some help. I'll give you — ' he fumbled in his pockets and pulled out a small signal mirror — 'this.'

He displayed it, and presently the native shambled across the glade to him. It stooped to take the mirror, and a hint of interest came over the long doleful face.

'Now take this,' said Holderlin, giving over the sack of clay. 'Follow me.'

At last the creature understood what was required of him, and with neither zeal nor reluctance, took the bag in its rickety arms and shuffled along behind Holderlin and on to the ship. When they arrived, Holderlin went within and brought out a length of shiny chain. He showed it to his helper.

'One more trip, understand? One more trip. Let's go.' The creature obediently followed him.

Holderlin dug the clay, loaded the bag into the native's arms.

Above them came the sound of voices, footsteps, scuffling and grating on the rock. Holderlin crept for cover. The natire stood stupidly, holding the sack of clay.

Three figures came into sight, two of them panting through respirators — Blaine and a tall man whose pointed ears and high-arched eyebrows proclaimed Trankli blood. The third was a native with a red mop of hair.

'What's this?' cried the Trankli half-breed, spying Holderlin's helper. 'That sack is — '

They were the last words he spoke. An energy beam cut him down. Blaine whirled about, grabbing for his weapon. A voice brought him up short.

'Freeze, Blaine! You're as good as dead!'

Blaine slowly dropped his hands to his sides, glaring madly in the direction of the voice, his malformed lip twitching. Holderlin stepped from the shadow into the scarlet sunlight and his face was ruthless.

'Looking for me?'

He walked over and took Blaine's needle-beam. He noted the native's reddish mop of hair. This one had passed him in the woods, was evidently in league with his enemies. He pointed his weapon, fired. The tall black body crumpled like a broken straw. Holderlin's worker watched impassively.

'Can't have any tale-bearers,' said Holderlin, turning his ice-blue eyes on Blaine.

'Why don't you give it up, Holderlin?' snarled Blaine. 'You can't get away alive.'

'Do you think you'll outlive me?' mocked Holderlin. 'I'll take your communicator.' He did so. 'The native was taking you to the *Perseus*, and you were going to signal its position. Right?'

'That's right,' admitted Blaine sourly.

Holderlin mused.

'What ship are you in?'

'The *Maetho* — Killer Donahue's. You can't get away, Holderlin. Not with Donahue after you.'

'We'll see,' said Holderlin shortly.

So it was Killer Donahue's *Maetho*! Holderlin had heard of Donahue — a slight man of forty years, with dark hair and a pair of black eyes which saw around corners and into men's minds. He recalled stories of a droll clown's face, out of place on a murderer and pirate.

Holderlin thought a moment, staring at the flaccid Blaine. The surviving native stood disinterestedly holding the clay.

'Well, you wanted to see the *Perseus*,' Holderlin said at last. 'Start moving.' He gestured with his gun.

Blaint went slowly, sullenly.

'Do you want to die here and now?' inquired Holderlin.

'You got the gun,' growled Blaine. 'I got no say at all.'

'Good,' said Holderlin. 'Then move faster. And tonight we'll cook.' He motioned to the waiting native. With Blaine ahead, they plodded off toward the ship.

'What's over the mountain? Donahue's hideout?' Holderlin asked.

Blaine nodded sourly, then decided he had nothing to lose by truckling to Holderlin.

'He gets thame powder here, sells it on Fan.'

Thame was an aphrodisiac.

'The natives collect it, bring it in little pots. He gives them salt for it. They love salt.'

Holderlin was silent, saving his energy for plowing through the black dust.

'Suppose you did get away,' Blaine presently put forward, 'you couldn't sell those oils. One whiff of sorang and you'd have the Tellurian Corps on your neck.'

'I'm not selling them,' said Holderlin. 'What do you think I got that certification of shipwreck for? I'm going to claim salvage. That's ninety percent of the value of ship and cargo, by law.'

Blaine was silent.

When at last they arrived, weary and begrimed with black dust, the native dropped the sack and held out a gangling arm.

'*Fawp, fawp*,' it said.

Holderlin looked at him in puzzlement.

'It wants salt,' said Blaine, still intent on ingratiating Holderlin. 'They do anything for salt.'

'Is that so?' said Holderlin. 'Well, we'll go in the galley and find some salt.'

Holderlin gave the native the bit of chain and a handful of salt and dismissed it. He turned back to Blaine and gave him the communicator.

'Call up Creed or Donahue and tell them that the native says you won't reach the ship till tomorrow night — it's that far off.'

Blaine hesitated only an instant, long enough for Holderlin to lay a hand on his weapon. He called Creed, and Creed seemed satisfied with the information.

'Tell him you won't call again till tomorrow night,' said Holderlin. 'Say that's because Holderlin might catch an echo of the beam from the mountain.'

Blaine did so.

'Good,' said Holderlin. 'Blaine, we're going to get along very well. Maybe I won't have to kill you when I'm done here.'

Blaine swallowed nervously. He disliked this kind of talk. Holderlin stretched his arms.

'Now we'll make linings. And because you ruined them,

you'll do most of the work.'

All night they baked linings in the surface; Blaine, as Holderlin had promised, working the hardest. His bald head glistened in the glow from the heat.

As soon as the linings were finished — no longer clay, but heavy metallic tubes — Holderlin clamped them in place. When the angry little sun came over the horizon, the *Perseus* was once more in condition to travel.

With Blaine's help, Holderlin unshackled the flier from the hull and brought it to the ground beside the *Perseus*. Then Holderlin locked Blaine in a storage locker.

'You're lucky,' he observed. 'You can sleep. I have to work.' Holderlin had seen a container of vanzitrol in the *Perseus* armory. He ladled about a pound into a sack, enough to blast the *Perseus* clear through the planet.

He found a detonator and lifted off with the flier. Feeling safe from observation, he skimmed low over the black jungle until, about thirty miles from the *Perseus*, he found a suitable clearing.

He landed, buried the vanzitrol and set the detonator. Then he returned to the *Perseus* and slept for five hours.

When he awoke, he aroused Blaine and they flew to the mined clearing. Holderlin set the flier down some distance away, concealed by the dense, intervening jungle.

'Now Blaine,' he said, 'call Creed and tell him you've found the *Perseus*. Tell him to take a bearing and come at once. Tell him there's an adjacent clearing to land in.'

'Then what?' asked Blaine doubtfully.

'Then you'll wait in the clearing until the *Maetho* is about to set down. After that I'll give you a choice. If you want to return aboard the *Maetho*, you can stay where you are. If you want to stay with me, you'll run like hell for the flier. Suit yourself.'

Blaine did not answer. An odd, hard look crept into his eyes.

'Send the message,' said Holderlin.

Blaine did so. They had cornered Holderlin in the *Perseus*, said Blaine, and Mordang, the Trankli half-breed, was holding him in a locked storeroom while Blaine signaled.

'Very good, Blaine!' came back Creed's voice. Then Donahue asked a few sharp questions. Had the *Perseus* crashed? No, replied Blaine, she was sound. Could the *Perseus* bring her weapons to bear on the clearing? No, the clearing was quite safe, a half mile astern of the *Perseus*. Donahue ordered Blaine to wait for the ship.

Twenty minutes later Holderlin, hidden in the jungle, and Blaine standing nervously in the clearing, saw the hulk of the *Maetho* come drifting overhead.

It hovered about five hundred yards above. Blaine waved an arm to the ship at Holderlin's brittle command.

There was a long pause. The cautious Donahue was inspecting the situation.

Presently Holderlin, waiting tensely at the edge of the forest, saw a small scout boat leave the *Maetho*, drift down toward the clearing. His mouth tightened. He cursed.

This meant Creed or Donahue had sensed a trap. He'd have to move quickly to escape with his skin. Blaine also saw the scheme had failed, and fidgeted uncertainly.

He decided Holderlin offered the least immediate danger and casually began to leave the clearing. At once Donahue's voice crackled in the air.

'Blaine! Stay where you are!'

Blaine broke into a run, but the black dust hampered him. From the *Maetho* came a stab of raw energy and amid a great puff of black dust Blaine exploded to component atoms.

Holderlin was already to his flier. A slim chance remained that the scout boat landing would miss the mine and the *Maetho* would set down and be blown to scrap. But the detonator was sensitive, the clearing small.

A blast rent the air. The ground swayed and a hail of earth, rocks, bits of trees spattered far out over the jungle. The *Maetho* was tossed upward. A choking pall of black dust thickened the sky.

Holderlin jerked his flier into the air and dashed away, low to the ground through the trees. He flew for his life, threading the heavy foliage as best he could, crashing through those he could not dodge.

Nor was he too soon, for the *Maetho's* armament had opened a savage fire on the jungle. Twice, terrible explosions narrowly missed him.

He gained clear of the area, slowed his flight, and wove a careful course through the trees.

When the *Maetho* was finished firing, the jungle lay torn into craters and tangled, smoking ruin. Holderlin gingerly peered through the tree-tops and saw the warship flying back across the mountain to its base.

He returned to the *Perseus* and sat brooding in his quarters. It would only be a matter of hours before Creed and Donahue found another native to guide them to his ship.

He sprawled on his bunk, hands behind his head. An isolated bit of information Blaine had given him suddenly blossomed — a plan of action. He got up carefully, spooned out some more vanzitrol, gathered up a few sacks of salt from the galley, took off in the flier.

Hours later, with night fast falling across the black forest, he returned. He went into the *Perseus* and sent out a call.

'Aboard the *Maetho*! *Maetho*, come in!' The screen flickered to life. There was Donahue's droll face and behind him the black-bearded Captain Creed.

'Well,' said Donahue crisply. 'What do you want?' His dark eyes glittered.

Holderlin grinned. 'Nothing. In two minutes I'm destroying your ship. If you enjoy life, you'll get clear.'

'What's that?' Donahue's voice snapped like breaking wood. 'Do you take us for fools?'

'You'll know in a minute,' responded Holderlin. 'Three of the pots of thame you took aboard today are loaded with explosives. I've got a remote detonator you can't jam. *Now*! You've got two minutes to get clear.'

Donahue whirled, cut in the ship's loud speaker. 'Abandon ship! All hands! *Get clear*!'

Then he whirled about. Holderlin watched in interest. Creed was striding for the door. He met Donahue's eyes and

saw murder. He stopped in his tracks, slowly turned to face
Donahue.

Obscenities poured from Donahue's lips.

'You white-faced dog, you've ruined me!' Donahue
screamed in a high-pitched crazy voice. His thin body shook
like an epileptic's.

'Let's leave this ship and argue later,' Creed suggested
coolly.

'I'm leaving, but you'll stay here, you swine!' cried
Donahue in a rage, pointing his gun.

A sharp beam flashed from Creed's sleeve. Donahue fell
screaming to the ground, his shoulder burned raw.

He fired from the floor, missing Creed. Creed crouched
behind a locker, unable to gain the door. Another shot from
Donahue smashed the power cables, the screen went dark.

Holderlin sat looking at his watch. He held one hand
poised over a small black key.

Twenty seconds, ten seconds, eight seconds, seven, six,
five, four, three, two — 'I'll give them ten seconds more,'
he told himself. He waited another moment, then closed the
key, listening for the shock from across the mountain.

Whoom!

Holderlin stood up with a grin on his face. He sealed the
ports and sat back in the *Perseus'* controls. A busy week
lay ahead of him.

ULTIMATE QUEST

CHIRAM CAME INTO THE ROOM, walked with short, firm steps to the podium. Only then did he appear to notice the two dozen men and women seated on neat rows of folding chairs.

'I can give you about twenty minutes,' said Chiram. 'Exactly what do you want?'

'How about a short statement?' suggested Ed Jeff, of All-planet News-Fax. 'Then perhaps you'd answer a few questions.'

Chiram leaned back, a stocky middle-aged man with an air of decision. He had a leonine ruff of hair the color and texture of steel wool, eyes sharp and monitory, a heavy well-shaped mouth. His clothes were gray and dark blue — conservative but informal, as if Chiram dressed by habit, uninfluenced by either vanity or ostentation.

'My associates and I', he said, 'financed by Jay Banners, have embarked on a program of research which will ultimately lead to an attempted circumnavigation of the universe.' He stopped; the reporters waited. Chiram said dryly, 'That is the statement.'

Voices collided and tumbled getting to Chiram's ears. He held up his hand. 'One at a time . . . . You, sir — what was your question?'

'You said a circumnavigation of the universe? Not merely the galaxy?'

Chiram nodded. 'The universe.'

'How do you know it's spherical?'

'We don't,' said Chiram, smiling grimly. 'There is no first-hand evidence, very little mathematical indication, one way or another. It's an assumption on which we're staking our lives.'

The reporters made respectful sounds. Chiram relaxed a trifle. 'Estimates of the circumference run in the neighbourhood of ten to a hundred billion light years. We plan to set out from Earth, assume a course — almost any course. After a sufficient period of travel, at a sufficiently high speed, we hope to return from the opposite direction.'

'What's the chance of hitting Earth on the way back?'

Chiram compressed his lips; the question had been put in what he considered a glib tone.

'In theory,' he replied stiffly, 'if we steer a sufficiently exact course we will return automatically. Our research program is concentrating on the mechanics of straight flight. A hundredth of a second error at a hundred billion light years means three hundred thousand light years. If we missed the home galaxy by that margin we'd be lost forever. Our first problem is to guarantee ourselves a mathematically straight course.'

'Can't you line up on stars ahead or behind?'

Chiram shook his head. 'The light from behind can't catch up with us; in fact, we'll overtake it and add the images of the stars behind to those of the stars ahead.' He clasped his blunt hands on the desk. 'That is our second problem: seeing. Our speed will approximate instantaneity. Assuming ninety percent efficiency in our destriation field, an average speed of six or seven thousand light years a second will take us a hundred billion light years in six months. The impact of radiation on an unshielded object at this speed would be cataclysmic. The weakest infra-red light would be compacted, by a kind of Doppler effect, to cosmic rays; ordinary visible light would become a thousand times harder, more energetic, and cosmic rays would strike at a frequency of approximately ten to the thirty-first power. I can't imagine the effect of radiation like that, but it could be disastrous. We are trying to develop a system of vision that can function under this tremendous impact. Longitudinal sight will be normal, of course, withlight striking the side of our ship at normal frequencies.

'How long will it take to resolve these problems?'

Chiram said in a measured voice, 'We are making satisfactory progress.'

'How will you know for sure when you've returned? One galaxy must look a lot like another . . . . '

Chiram drummed his fingers on the table. 'That's a good question. I'm sorry to say I have no precise answer. We will trust to alertness and careful examination of any galaxy in our path which shows the proper size and configuration. The fact that our galaxy is roughly double the average size will help us. We shall have to trust a good deal to luck.'

'Suppose the universe isn't spherical, but infinite?'

Chiram fixed the man with a contemptuous stare. 'You're talking foolishness. How can I answer that question?'

The reporter hurriedly corrected himself. 'What I meant was, will you set a limit to the time before you turn around and come back?'

'We believe the universe is spherical,' said Chiram coolly. 'In a fourth-dimensional sense, of course. We will remain under constant acceleration and our speed will increase constantly. If the universe is spherical, we will return; if it is infinite, we will fly on forever.'

Two ships landed, a slender cylinder and a peculiar impractical-looking hull roughly the shape of a doughnut. Chiram stepped out of the cylinder, marched up the concrete ramp to the glass-walled office.

Jay Banners, who was putting up the money, and a lank young man were waiting for him. Banners resembled Chiram in outward proportion, but his hair was sparse, the lines of his face were softer. He looked easy, amiable; there was nothing of the spartan or the ascetic in Jay Banners.

Chiram was associated with the discovery of striatics,

the gravitron and the subsequent inertia-negative destriation fields; he had been a member of the original Centauri expedition. Banners had never been into space, but he held majority stock in Star Island Development, and he was director of half a dozen other corporations.

He waved a pudgy hand at Chiram. 'Herb, meet my son, Jay Junior. And now I'll give you a surprise. Jay wants to go along on the trip. So I told him we'd see what we could do.' He glanced at Chiram expectantly.

Chiram pulled up the corners of his mouth, squinted as if he were eating an unexpectedly sour pickle. 'Well, now, Banners . . . I don't know if it's advisable . . . Inexperienced member,' he muttered. 'Got our crew pretty well lined out . . . .'

'Oh, come now,' said Banners bluffly. 'It isn't as if Jay was a rank amateur. He's just out of engineering school; studied astrogation and all that stuff, hey, Jay?'

'That's right,' said Jay languidly.

Chiram turned chilly eyes to Jay Banners Jr. — a loose-limbed young man with oily black hair worn over-long for Chiram's taste. He said, 'It's a pretty tough grind, young fellow. Strict discipline. We're cooped up in a little cabin with no amusements, a very serious proposition. And about one chance in ten of geting back . . . . An old man like me can afford to throw his life away. A lad like you has that all before him.'

Jay shrugged carelessly, and the older Banners said, 'I've told him all this, Herb, and he insists that he wants to go. And then I figured that maybe it would be a good thing to have a Banners aboard. Make it the Chiram-Banners Expedition for a fact, eh, Herb?'

Chiram drummed his fingers savagely on the desk, at a loss for words.

Jay said, 'We've learned a lot of new methods at school. Might help you out once in a while if you get stumped.'

Chiram became red in the face, turned away.

'Now, Jay,' said Banners, 'take it easy on an old man. I know you're up to date on all the latest ideas, but don't forget that men like Herb Chiram pioneered the whole business.'

Jay shrugged again, smoking moodily.

'It's settled, then,' said Banners jovially. 'And look here, Herb, don't hold back on him on my account. Treat him like a hired hand. He's tough — just like his old man. He can stand it. If he gets out of line, give it to him good.'

Chiram walked to a window, stood looking out.

Banners said, 'We saw you bringing down the ships. How did the test turn out?'

'Very well,' said Chiram. 'From Earth to Pluto we deviated nineteen degrees of arc from the true line. That's on the order of ten to the minus eighth or ninth part of an arc. Maybe closer. I haven't figured it out yet. It's close enough.'

Jay flicked ashes to the floor with his little finger. 'Probably be best to install navigational computers just to be on the safe side.'

Chiram said in a keen, cold, voice, 'Computers are grossly inaccurate compared to the sleeve and piston principle.'

'Explain to Jay how it works,' said Banners. 'I never could quite get it. I know that it has to do with the leaders alternating.'

Chiram spoke in a heavy impatient voice. 'An object in free flight moves in a true course, when it's insulated from gravity — as inside a destriation shell. Our problem was to combine free-flight accuracy with acceleration. We decided to use two ships, Nip and Tuck, alternately accelerating and flying free — the ship in free flight correcting the course of the ship under acceleration.

'Assume one component, flying free — say Nip, the cylinder. Tuck, the tube, is ten thousand miles astern. Tuck accelerates; the application of power may or may not cause a slight deviation. As soon as the destriation shells meet, sensor beams make contact and any slight deviation in course is corrected. Tuck slides over Nip, the power is shut off, it flies free on ahead. . hen it has taken a ten-thousand-mile lead, Nip accelerates, plunges through the hole in Tuck.

The process is automatic, very rapid, very accurate.'

'Aren't the constant acceleration changes rather jarring?' Banners asked skeptically.

Jay looped a leg over the desk. 'Nope. Don't forget, pop, we've integrated inertia completely with the ship since your day. Don't feel a thing any more, except the ship-generated gravity.'

Banners laughed indulgently, clapped Chiram's stiff shoulder. 'Don't say I didn't warn you, Herb. This lad here is pretty far ahead of us old-timers . . . . That's how it goes — out with the old, in with the new.'

Jay blew a complacent gust of smoke across the room. Chiram stared at him for several seconds, two short paces up the room, two back.

'Banners,' he said crisply, 'everything considered, I don't think it wise for your son to make the trip.'

Jay raised his eyebrows; his mouth sagged. Banners stared; then his face relaxed. 'Now, Herb, I know it's dangerous; I know you don't like the responsibility. But Jay's got his mind made up. Some girl's been after him, I expect. And I'd like to see the lad make the trip. In fact, I've been thinking I might even go myself . . . . '

Chiram said hastily, 'Very well, very well . . . . I warn you, young fellow, it's a tough grind. It's snap to orders and no back-talk. If that's understood — I guess I have nothing further to say.'

'You'll get along,' exclaimed Banners. 'With your experience, Herb, and your training, Jay — I can't see how the trip won't be a great success. Think of it, Herb! The Chiram-Banners Expedition — Commander, Herb Chiram; Navigator, Jay Banners, Jr.! Doesn't that sound good, now?'

'It makes my head swim,' said Chiram.

Jay dropped his cigarette butt to the floor, said thoughtfully. 'You know, that Nip and Tuck idea may be sound — but I'd trust more to a good navcom . . . . At least we ought to ship a couple for the corroboratic index.'

Chiram frowned. ' "Corroboratic index"? ' hat's that?' he asked contemptuously.

Jay said, 'A rather new concept. One of these days, I'll explain it to you. In rough terms, it's the average area of the integral under a series of probability curves, each given the proper weighting.'

Banners nodded heavily. 'Young fellow's got a sound head on him, Herb. Maybe we'd better install a couple. No harm playing safe.'

Chiram bowed slightly to Jay. 'The computers are in your charge. See that they do not exceed two cubic feet in volume.'

Jay nodded. 'Fine. I can cut it smaller than that. Instruments have become more compact and precise since your time, Mr. Chiram.' He rubbed his upper lip. 'In fact — if you like — I'll take the navigation chores off your hands. I'm pretty good at it — made an A in navigation all during school.'

Chiram snorted. 'You'll do no such thing, young fellow. And you'll understand right now, before the day's a minute older, that you'll do what you're told, you'll obey orders, and you'll keep your schoolbook ideas to yourself unless they're asked for!'

Jay stared in astonishment; he turned and looked at his father, who wagged his head solemnly. 'That's the way it goes, Jay. Old Herb here is a tough one. You've picked a hard rock when you try to put it over Herb. What he says, goes; remember it.'

Chiram, Jay Banners Jr., a taciturn technician named Bob Galt, and Julius Johnson, the cook, a taffy-colored, smiling man with a flat face and flat head, together made up the crew of Nip the cylinder. Two old-time spacemen, Art Henry and Joe Lavindar, were stationed aboard Tuck the tube.

The takeoff was recorded by cameras, television, and witnessed by a crowd of four million. The two ships rose separately and left for rendezvous a million miles past the Moon. Here they would orient themselves and set out toward Deneb in Cygnus, slightly off from the prime plane of the Milky Way.

Chiram called his crew together in the small salon below

the bridge deck, which would serve as mess hall and recreation room. Bob Galt sat at one end of the bench, a stooped, small-boned man, completely self-possessed and self-sufficient, with a face like an angry parrot's. Beside him sat Julius, the cook, his wide mouth curved in a perpetual grin. Jay slouched back at the end of the bench with legs crossed, eyes half-closed.

Chiram faced them, stocky, erect, his ruff of iron-gray hair freshly trimmed.

'Now men, as you know, we have a stiff grind ahead of us. If we return, we're heroes. The chances are we'll never get back. If space is infinite we'll fly forever. If our course deviates from a straight line, we're just as bad off. Then, of course, you've all read the fantastic speculations on the possibility of attack by aliens. I do not need to label this as nonsense.

'Our greatest danger is ourselves. Boredom, petty irritations — these are our worse enemies. We're crowded together. I can think of no situation so calculated to bring out the best or worst in a man. Now you, Bob, and you, Julius — I've shipped with you many a time; I know you well. Jay, you represent your father, and I'm sure that, like the rest of us, you're determined to make the trip as easy on all our nerves as possible.

'There's not much work to do. I wish there were more. Julius, of course, is in charge of the galley.' His voice took on a sardonic edge. 'Jay has his computers to attend to, and I understand he's keeping a detailed record . . . . Well, every man to his own poison.'

'I'll take the first watch, Jay the second, Bob the third. Our main duties will be to chart what we can see on the view screens and keep the destriation field within normal limits. Each of us will be responsible for the cleanliness of himself, his clothes, his bunk. Everyone must be neat. Nothing is as demoralizing as slovenliness. Shaving and clean clothes are mandatory . . . . That's all for now.'

He turned, swung himself up onto the bridge deck.

*

The moon was a great silver melon spattered with black frost; it hulked below and off to the left. Directly ahead floated Tuck, the tube, with a cluster of stars shining through the hole.

Chiram nosed the cylinder into the opening, activated a control; the cylinder shivered, jerked as the guide beams excited relays, pulled the ships into rigid alignment.

Dead ahead was Deneb, guideline of their course around the universe.

Chiram called by radio to Tuck. 'Everything all right in there?'

'Ready to go,' came back Henry's voice.

Chiram said, 'Throw in your field.' He engaged another control; the gravity unit buzzed, rattled, settled into a drone; the crew was tied to the ship, and, like the ship, free of inertia.

Chiram spun a polished wheel, and the voyage had begun.

An instant passed. Then a flicker at the side port was Tuck, racing ahead. Another flicker was Nip threading Tuck. The flickers became swifter, became a continuous quiver, vanished.

Stars began to move, slide past each other, like shining motes in a drift of sunlit air. They streamed past — now bunched, now sparse, clusters, swarms, flaring clouds of gas, which vanished as they passed aft of amidships they, their light lagging behind the thistledown rush of Nip and Tuck.

Flame, dazzle, flicker — stars in pairs, trios, quartets, stars in hurrying multitudinous companies. Stars in rivers and stars like isolated beacons. Stars approached from far ahead, passing over, around, under, like wind-blown sparks. And presently the stars vanished in front and to the side, and Nip and Tuck were in intergalactic space.

Speed added to speed, built up in constant increments. Ship threaded ship like a needle in a shuttle, each guiding the other down a geometrically straight line. So straight that in a million light years the error might be a hundred miles — an error which might or might not average out over long distances.

Jay computed the course twice. 'Right on,' he announced. 'We're right on course.'

'Glad to hear it,' said Chiram sardonically. 'Watch it close now.'

The great nebula in Andromeda passed under them, a whirling pancake of cold fire. It passed behind out of sight.

Speed, speed, speed. Acceleration as fast as the relays could shuttle ship back and forth through ship. Speed building up toward instantaneity.

Watches passed, days passed. The galaxies flitted by like luminous bats — straggling watch-springs, hot puddles of gas. At the start and close of every watch, Jay checked his computer, then spent two or three hours writing in his journal — minutiae of the voyage, vignettes of personal philosophy, observations on the personalities of his shipmates.

Julius and Bob played cards and chess; occasionally Chiram joined them. Jay played a few games of chess — long enough to find that Julius could beat him as often as he set his mind to it — then gave up. Julius grinned his grin, spoke little; Bob wore his angry parrot's face, spoke not at all. Chiram kept himself aloof, watched every detail of the voyage with a careful, humorless eye, gave what orders were necessary in a carefully modulated voice. And Jay, after a few futile attempts to argue navigational techniques with Chiram, became as taciturn as the others.

The galaxies slid backward. One day — or its ship-board equivalent — Jay called Chiram over.

'We're off course. Look — there's no doubt about it. A whole degree. I've suspected it for several days.'

Chiram frowned, shook his head, half-turned away. 'You've got an error of precession somewhere.'

Jay sniffed. 'More likely the sensors are malfunctioning.'

Chiram glanced at the small navigational computers, said stonily, 'Hardly possible. Our sensors detect and compensate automatically. Two separate programs are involved, working independently — one correcting on a basis of wave interference, the other by correlation of angle and beam strength. They're perfectly synchronized and integrated, otherwise the alarm would sound. Your calculations are off somewhere.'

Grumbling, Jay turned to look at the dial. 'One degree,' he mumbled. 'That's a million light years — a hundred million light years — ' But Chiram had walked away.

Jay seated himself beside the navcom console, watched the screen intently. If it told the truth they were irretrievably lost. Jay slouched to the table where Bob and Julius played chess, stood looking down with hands clasped behind his back. They took no heed of his presence.

'Well,' said Jay, looking across the room toward the computers, 'we're goners. We're done for.'

'Yeah? How's that?' asked Julius, moving a pawn.

'The navcom doesn't lie,' said Jay. 'We're a full degree off course.'

Bob Galt darted an unemotional glance up at Jay, returned to the board.

'I told the old man,' Jay said bitterly. 'I told him before we took off that his rig was too damn complicated to work.'

'We all got to die sometime, kid,' said Julius. 'It might as well be out here . . . . I'm not worryin'. We're eatin' good; my chess game's got old Galt here on the run . . . .' The grin widened.

Bob sneered. 'The hell you say.' He moved a knight to threaten the pawn. 'Try that one on.'

Julius bent his heavy head over the board. 'Relax, kid, watch the scenery . . . . '

Jay hesitated, then turned away, crossed the room, flung himself on his bunk, mouthing silent curses. He lay quiet for twenty minutes, staring up at the hull. A degree off course . . . .

He rose on his elbow, watched the galaxies flitting past the view screen. Stars — millions, billions of stars, curdled into luminous whorls. Out here these were nameless, unknown to the astronomers on that far atom, Earth. . . . He considered Earth, so far distant as to be unknowable. Presumably if they returned to the home galaxy Earth could be found. But now — a degree off course! And no one aboard seemed concerned either way. . . . Well, by God, thought Jay furiously, these full animals might not care for their lives, but he was Jay Banners Jr. and he had his whole life to live! . . . Now then, if he returned the ship to its course, there would still be a chance of hitting the galaxy on the way back. They would thank him for it, Chiram and Bob Galt and Julius, when he finally told them; there would be jocular comment, chaffing — and, of course, that bull-headed Chiram would walk around with his neck stiff. Nevertheless he'd have Jay to thank for bringing them home; he'd have to back down, admit himself wrong. . . . And if the story happened to leak out — Jay's vision soared. Newspapers, television, cheers from crowded streets. . . .

Jay rose to his feet. Chiram lay in his bunk asleep, his feet in clean white socks neatly placed one on the other.

Jay glanced across the cabin. It was nominally Galt's watch; he sat absorbed in his game, with one hand crooked over his queen. Julius, his brow furrowed, was wiping at his mouth with a big yellow hand.

Jay glanced across the room, climbed the three steps to the bridge, nonchalantly leaned across the console table, watching the view on the forward screen. Black space, the galaxies like luminous jellyfish in a midnight ocean. They floated in from far ahead, drifted effortlessly past, the near ones sliding over the far ones in an impossible shift of perspective.

The sight was soothing, hypnotic, dreamlike in its silent majesty. . . . Behind him Julius laughed. Jay blinked, straightened, came back to himself. He looked cautiously toward the controls to his right. Only Chiram was supposed to enter the cubicle. He peered out the side panel. Tuck, the partnership, was naturally invisible, flitting back and forth across Nip in constant acceleration. Jay glanced downward for their speed: already the parsec-units were registering as exponentials and still the rate of acceleration increased. He turned his attention back to the controls. There it was: a mere touch, and the sensor beams would weaken infinitesimally on one side, to twist the axis on which the two ships rode.

He took a casual step toward the controls, darted out his arm . . . a great blow fell on his shoulder. He reeled back, sank to the deck. He became aware of three pairs of legs, heard a harsh unsympathetic voice: 'I've been waiting for a trick like this.'

'He's just an addled kid,' came Julius' voice, light, careless.

Bob Galt's feet moved abruptly, turned half away.

Chiram said in the same harsh voice. 'Pick him up, take him to his bunk, chain his ankle to the stanchion. . . . Can't trust a lunatic like that at large.'

Jay had little to complain about. He was fed from a tray, and released to use the latrine. These were the only attentions he received. What sluggish life there was in the ship flowed on and past him. His presence was ignored; he spoke to no one.

From his bunk he could see the length of the ship and all that happened aboard: Julius and Bob Galt at their interminable chess; Julius facing him, rubbing his big flat face with a hand when puzzled or preoccupied, Galt sitting crouched over the board with only the hard angles of his profile showing. Chiram played no more cards or chess; his sole diversion was a slow pacing up and down the cabin with half an hour's work at an exerciser morning and night.

The routine became utterly familiar to Jay. The same colors, the same pattern of shadows, the same pragmatic thud to Chiram's tread, the same grin on Julius' face, the same slope to Galt's shoulders.

The ship plunged into darkness. There were no more

galaxies, no more nebulae. 'We've evidently passed the outer fringe of the exploding universe,' Jay heard Chiram say ruefully. Jay asked himself, what now? Infinity? He had understood the exploding universe was like a balloon being inflated, time and space together — not just the blast of a trillion stars into nothingness . . . .

The ports showed dead black outside, without spark or flash. They were still accelerating.

Jay turned his back to the cabin, wrote in his journal — pages of introspection, fragments of quick-scribbled poetry, which he often returned to, recopied, revised. He kept statistical charts: the detailed study of Chiram's pacing, his average number of steps per foot of deck, the pattern behind Julius' menus. He carefully noted his dreams and spent hours trying to trace their genesis from his past. He wrote careful and elaborate excoriations of Chiram — 'for the record' he told himself — and equally cogent self-justifications. He made interminable lists — places he had visited, girlfriends, books, colors, songs. He sketched Chiram, Julius, Bob Galt, time and time again.

Hours, days, weeks. Conversation dwindled, died. Julius and Bob played chess, and when Bob was at his watch duties Julius played solitaire — unhurriedly, carefully, glancing at each card as in surprise.

Darkness outside the port . . . . Were they actually moving? Or was motion a peculiarity of the home space, where there were objects by which to measure it? Eternal darkness outside the port. Suppose one were on foot, walking out there . . . .

Jay put down his journal, stared. His eyes bulged. A sound scraped up his throat. Chiram paused in his pacing, turned his head. Jay pointed a long trembling arm toward the port.

'It was a face! I saw it looking in the port!'

Chiram turned startled eyes to the portal screen. Galt, asleep, grumbled, grunted. Julius, playing solitaire, shuffled the cards with imperturbable movements of smooth yellow arms. Chiram looked skeptically back at Jay.

Jay cried, 'I saw it plain as day, I tell you! I'm not crazy! It was a whitish figure, and it came flitting up and then the face looked in through the port . . . . '

Julius stopped shuffling, Galt was leaning out of his bunk. Chiram strode across the floor, peered out briefly. He turned back to Jay, said in a brusque voice, 'You've had a bad dream.'

Jay laid his head on his arm, blinked back tears. So far, far from home. . . . Ghosts peering in from space. . . . Was this where souls came when they died? Out here to wander the void, so completely forlorn and lonesome. . . .

'I saw it,' he said. 'I saw it, I tell you. I saw it!'

'Relax, kid, relax,' said Julius. 'You'll give us all the willies.'

Jay lay on his side, staring at the port. He gave a great gasp. 'I saw it again! It's a face, I tell you!' He rose up from his bunk, his lank black hair dangling past his forehead. His mouth wobbled, glistened wetly.

Chiram went to the medicine chest, loaded a hypospray. He motioned; Galt and Julius held Jay's arms and legs; the opiate seeped through Jay's pale skin, into his blood, into his brain. . . .

When he awoke, Galt and Julius were playing chess, and Chiram was asleep. He looked fearfully to the port. Darkness. Blackness. Lightlessness.

He sighed, moaned. Julius flashed him a glance, returned to the chessboard. Jay sighed, reached for his journal.

Weeks, months. Fantastic speed toward — what? One day Jay called Chiram from his pacing.

'Well?' asked Chiram crisply.

'If you'll let me loose,' muttered Jay, 'I'd like to take up my duties again.'

Chiram said in a carefully passionless voice, 'I'm sorry that you've had to be confined. It was necessary, not for punishment, but for the safety of the expedition. Because you are irresponsible. Because I can't trust you.'

Jay said, 'I promise you that I'll act — well — responsibly. I've learned my lesson. . . . Suppose we go on forever like this? Into nothing? Do you intend to keep me chained the rest of my life?'

Chiram stared at him thoughtfully, trying to fathom the ultimate justice of the situation.

Galt called down from the bridge deck. 'Hey, Cap! There's a glow ahead! *Light*!'

Three bounds took Chiram to the port. Jay rose up on his elbow.

Far ahead hung an amorphous ball of glowing fog.

Chiram said in a hushed voice, 'That's what a universe of billions of galaxies would look like — from a great distance.'

'Have we made it around, Cap?' Galt asked, his voice sharp.

Chiram said slowly, 'I don't know, Bob. . . . We've come so far — so much farther than anyone had predicted. . . . It might be our universe, or it might be another. I'm as much in the dark as you are.'

'If it is our universe, Cap, what are the chances of hitting home?'

There was a pause. Chiram said, 'Darned if I know, Bob. I'm hoping.'

'Think we better slow down? We're hitting an awful clip.'

'Twenty-two thousand light years a second. We can slow down a lot faster than we pick up, just by slacking off the field.'

There was silence. Then Galt said, 'She's expanding mighty fast. . . . '

Chiram said in an even voice, 'It's no universe. It's a cloud of gas. I'm going to get a spectral reading on it.'

The glowing fog grew large, flooded under the ship, was gone. Ahead was blackness. Chiram came down from the bridge-deck, took up his pacing, head bent.

He looked up and his eyes met Jay's. Jay was still propped up on his arms, still looking out ahead into the void.

Chiram said, 'Very well. I'll take a chance on you.'

Jay slowly sank back on the bunk, lay lax and loose. Chiram said, 'These are your orders. You are forbidden to set foot on the bridge. Next time, I'll have to kill you.'

Jay nodded wordlessly. His eyes glistened under the long lank hair. Chiram pulled a key from his pocket, unlocked the shackles, and without a word resumed his pacing.

For five minutes Jay lay unmoving on his bunk. Julius said from the galley, 'Come and get it.'

Jay saw four places had been set at the table.

Jay washed, shaved. Freedom was a luxury. This was living again — even if it were nothing but eat, sleep, stare out into darkness. This was life: it would be like this the rest of his life. . . . Curious existence. It seemed natural, sensible. Earth was a trifling recollection, a scene remembered from childhood.

The navigation computers. . . . Yes, what would they tell him now? They had been far from his mind; perhaps he had banned them from his consciousness as a symbol of his disgrace. . . . Still, what did they say?

He went to the corner, stared for a minute at the visuals.

'Well, kid, how's it look?' Julius asked him lightly. 'Are we on course?'

Jay slowly said, 'The last time I looked we were one degree off to the right. Now we're eighty-five degrees off — to the left!'

Julius shook his head in genial perplexity, grinning. 'Looks mighty bad from here.'

Jay chewed at his lip. 'Something damn strange. . . .'

Galt yelled loudly. 'Hey, Cap! There's more light ahead — and this time it's stars for sure!'

They came on the universe like an island rising from the sea — first a blur without detail, then larger, clearer, and finally great masses dwarfed the ship. Galaxies pelted on them, flats of wild light rushing past.

Chiram stood like a man of marble on the bridge, one hand on the control of the destriation field. Galt stood beside him, head hunched down into his shoulders.

They passed flat over a great whirlpool galaxy, and the individual stars glinted and glanced and promised wonderful bright planets.

Galt said, 'That sort of looks like home, Cap.'

Chiram shook his head. 'Not large enough. Don't forget we've got a markedly large galaxy — several times average. Of course,' and his voice blurred, 'this may not even be our home universe. It might be a different set entirely. There's no way of knowing. . . . If we run directly into an exceptionally large galaxy, with approximately the right configuration — we'll stop.'

'Look,' said Bob, 'there's a big one out there, see it? That looks about like ours, too.' His voice rose. 'That's it, Cap!'

Chiram said irresolutely, 'Well, Bob, I don't know. She's a long way to the side. Of course, we've come a long way, but if we once turn off our course, and we've made a mistake — then we're lost for sure.'

'We're lost if we pass it by,' said Galt.

Chiram wavered in a hell of indecision. Jay saw his mouth twitch. He reached, took a firm grip on the field control.

Jay said suddenly, 'That's not it: this isn't even the right universe.'

Galt turned an angry red face down. 'Shut up!'

Chiram paid no heed. His hand tightened on the field cut-off.

Jay said, 'Captain, I can prove it. Listen!'

Chiram turned his head. 'How can you prove it?'

'The computer keeps a steady axis. When we were a few weeks out, I saw a degree of deflection. I misinterpreted the reading. I thought it indicated an error in course. I was wrong; it was showing how far around we had traveled. One three hundred and sixtieth. I just looked at it again. It read eight-five degrees to the other side — or two eighty-five degrees around. In other words, we've come more than three-quarters of the way. And when the read-out is back at zero again we'll know we're home.'

Chiram narrowed his eyes, surveyed Jay — looked at him, through him, beyond. Galt's angry mouth pushed out doubtfully, his color faded. He glanced to the big galaxy, now passing close by amidships.

Chiram asked, 'What's the reading now?'

Jay ran, raised the dust lid. 'Two eighty-six.'

Chiram said, 'We'll go on. Dead ahead.'

'Dead ahead,' said Galt.

Chiram smiled grimly. 'I hope you don't mean that.'

They passed the 'universe', and were off into a new ocean of blackness. It was the old routine — except now there was a restlessness aboard. Chiram watched Jay's calculations carefully. Slowly the angle of degree increased; 290 — 300 — 310 — 320.

Galt spent his time on the bridge watching ahead, hardly coming down to eat. No more chess — Julius played solitaire, slowly, with careful attention to each card.

330, and Chiram joined Galt's restless watch.

340. 'We should be getting close,' said Galt, staring into the bottomless blackness.

Chiram said, 'We'll be there when and if we get there.'

350. Galt bent forward, hands pressed to the chart table, head on a level with his elbows.

'It's light! Light!'

Chiram came to stare at the pale flow straight ahead.

'There it is.' He cut acceleration; they plunged free at constant speed. For the first time since the start of the voyage their partner ship Tuck appeared; they had almost forgotten its existence.

At 335 galaxies swept past like the first suburbs of a city.

At 357 they felt as if they were riding down familiar streets.

358: they scanned back and forth expectantly. There was quick movement of feet on the deck, the restless movement of heads. Chiram kept saying, 'Too soon, too soon. . . . There's a long way to go yet. . . .'

359: Chiram had tacitly relaxed his orders to Jay, all four stood on the bridge together pointing.

360: 'There! The big one!'

Ahead lay the great wheeling spiral galaxy. Huge arms of glowing stars spread open to embrace the ship. Chiram relaxed the field, the ship slowed like a bullet shot into water.

They coasted into the outer lanes of stars, across the far-flung tendrils, past the globular clusters, across the central knot.

Ahead, like magic, the sky suddenly showed full of familiar patterns.

'Dead ahead!' cried Chiram. 'See — that's Cygnus; that's where we started for. . . . And there — that small yellow star. . . .'

PARAPSYCHE

1

JEAN MARSILE, fifteen years old, blonde and pretty, jumped at the chair where her father sat. 'Boo!'

Art Marsile turned his head with provoking calmness. 'I thought you were going out on a date.'

Jean tugged at her blue jeans, smoothed the seams of her pale blue sweater. 'I am.'

'Where are you going?'

'Out on a weenie-roast. We're going to the haunted house. Because it's Hallowe'en,' she added.

From across the room came a snort of derision and contempt. Jean ignored the sound.

Art Marsile, tall, tough as harness-leather, parched and coffee-brown from years of California sun, looked Jean up and down with unconvincing sternness. 'What haunted house is this?' he asked curiously while Jean finished getting ready.

'The old Freelock house. There's a ghost living there — that's what everybody says. Ever since Benjamin Freelock killed his wife.'

'What everybody *says*, eh? Has anyone seen anything?'

Jean nodded. 'Lots of people. The Mexicans who live down the hill. They say there's lights and noises.'

From across the room came a mocking bray of laughter. 'Stupid bunch of wetbacks.'

Art Marsile turned a brief glance toward his son Hugh, the child of his first wife, then looked back to Jean. 'You're not scared?'

Jean calmly shook her head. 'I don't believe any of it.'

'I see.' Art Marsile nodded thoughtfully. 'Who's going with you?'

'Don Berwick. And —' Jean named others of the party.

Hugh spoke from across the room, his voice rich with disgust. 'They call it a weenie-roast. All they do is go up there and neck.'

Jean performed an impudent dance-step. 'We've got to neck somewhere.'

Art Marsile grunted. 'Just don't get in trouble.'

'Father!'

'You're human, aren't you?'

'Yes, but I'm — well . . . . '

Hugh said, 'They go out in the country and drink beer.'

'I don't either!'

'The guys do.'

'I know they do,' growled Art Marsile. 'And you know how I know? Because I used to do the same thing. And I'd do it again if I could get some pretty young girl to go with me.'

'Father!' cried Jean. 'You're *bad*!'

'Probably no worse than Don Berwick. So you be careful.'

'Yes, Father!'

The door-bell rang; Don Berwick, a stocky square-shouldered lad of seventeen, entered, spent a few minutes in civil small-talk with Art Marsile and Hugh; then he and Jean went to the door. Art followed them out on to the porch. 'Look here, Don. I don't want any boozing. Not when you're driving a car with Jean inside. Understand?'

'Yes, sir.'

'Okay. Have yourself a good time.' He went back inside the house. Hugh was standing near the door, at eighteen already taller than his father. He was big-jointed and thin, his long bony face sour and mulish. 'I don't see why you let her get away with it.'

'She's only young once,' said Art Marsile evenly. 'Let her have her fun . . . You should be out yourself, instead of staying home complaining about other people.'

'I'm not complaining. I'm saying what ought to be said.'

'What "ought" she be doing?' asked Art in a dry voice.

'There's schoolwork.'

'She can't do much better than straight A's, Hugh.'

'There's the revival meeting, tonight.'

'That's where you're going?'

'Yes. It's Walter Mott preaching. He's a great inspiration.'

Art Marsile turned back to his magazine. 'Walter Mott the Devil-Buster.'

'That's what they call him.'

'If you get a kick out of hell-fire and damnation,' said Art Marsile, 'that's your business. I wouldn't go, I wouldn't make Jean go.'

'If I had anything to say, she'd go and like it. It would do her good.'

Art Marsile looked at Hugh in a wonder which had grown rather than lessened over the years. 'It would do you good to drink some beer and kiss a few girls yourself. But I wouldn't make you do it. I'm damned if I'll make anybody do anything for their own good.'

Hugh left the room, presently reappearing wearing limp gray slacks and a black sweater with the block letter he had won at basketball. 'I'm going,' he said.

Art Marsile nodded, Hugh departed. Art read his magazine, switched on television, watched a late movie, his mind on his children. Hugh might or might not be his own flesh and blood; Jean was the child of his second wife. His first wife had run off with a hillbilly musician shortly after Hugh's birth. Hugh resembled the musician more than Art. Art knew nothing for certain, but tried to give Hugh the benefit of the doubt. The second wife had died in an automobile collision, returning from the New Year's Day Rose Parade in Pasadena. If Art felt grief, no one knew it. He worked his orange grove with all-consuming intensity; he prospered; he bought new land, he made money which he showed no disposition to spend. Jean and Hugh grew into adolescence, treated with as much fairness as Art was capable of. Since Art could not bring himself to show affection to Hugh, he tried to conceal his love for Jean. But Jean would not be fooled. She hugged and kissed Art, rumpled his hair, and had no secrets from her father.

Hugh lived in a different world. Hugh played basketball with tremendous zeal, joined all the school's organizations, soon became an officer in most of them. He bought a manual of parliamentary procedure, studied it with much more thoroughness than his mathematics texts. At sixteen Hugh had gone to an open-air evangelist rally, and from this time forward, whatever faint linkage existed between his mind and Art Marsile's was dissolved.

Hugh worked summers in the orange grove. Art Marsile paid him scale for whatever he did, and got his money's worth: Hugh was a hard and tireless worker. With his wages he bought a car, and then a hand megaphone.

'What on Earth do you want that thing for?' asked Art. Hugh had already made a list of the uses to which the instrument could be put: messages across the orange grove, emergencies and rescues, announcements at basketball games, talking to people in general. Art made the request that the implement should not be employed to address him, nor used at the dinner table to say grace — an innovation which Hugh recently had introduced into the household, and which Art tolerated with noncommittal patience. Jean was less complacent and teased Hugh unmercifully, until Art quieted her. 'If he feels he wants to say grace, it's his business.'

'Why can't he say it to himself then? God doesn't need to be thanked every time we eat a meal.'

'That's irreverent,' Hugh remarked.

'It's not either. It's good sense. If God hadn't arranged that we become hungry, we wouldn't have to eat. Why should we give thanks for doing something we have to do to stay alive? You don't say grace every time you breathe.'

Art let them wrangle: why stop a good argument? It's something everybody's got to work out for himself, he thought. The argument had continued sporadically, Hugh's growing evangelism colliding with Jean's skepticism. Art kept his views to himself, intervening only when the argument became name-calling. And tonight, Hallowe'en, Hugh was off to a revival meeting and Jean to a hot dog roast at a haunted house.

Art expected Jean home at around midnight, but at eleven she burst in the door, eyes glowing in excitement. 'Father! We saw the ghost!'

Art rose to his feet, turned off the television.

'You think I'm fooling! We saw it! We really did! As close as from here to you!'

Don Berwick came in. 'It's true, Mr. Marsile!'

'You kids been drinnking?' Art inquired suspiciously.

'No, sir!' said Don. 'I promised you I wouldn't.'

'Well, what happened?'

Jean reported. They had driven up Indian Hill to the Freelock house, a desolate weather-beaten hulk, shrouded among cypress and ragged cedar, the doors hanging on their hinges, the windows broken. The original plan had been to build a fire in the fireplace, but the inside of the house was so dirty and unpleasant that the girls objected. The fire was built in the backyard, on a patch of gravel still bare of weeds. The supplies were unloaded, the girls spread blankets; the normal processes of a barbecue got under weay.

Jean reminded Art of the Freelock murder: beyond question, a horrible affair. Benjamin Freelock, a crabbed old man of sixty, suspected his young wife, twenty-eight years old, of carrying on with his nephew. He gagged her, hung her by her wrists from a beam in the living room, presently brought in the corpse of the nephew, which he hung by the wrists six feet in front of her. He stripped both bodies, the living and the dead, of their clothes, then went about his normal business as a real-estate agent. Two days later he revived the barely-conscious wife, inquired if she were ready to confess. She was unable to speak coherently. He poured kerosene over her, set her afire, and departed the house.

The house smouldered and smoked but failed to catch fire.

A Mexican living in a shack a hundred yards down the road called the fire department. Freelock, apprehended, made a sober and detailed confession and later died at a home for the criminally insane.

The affair had occurred five years previously. The house was abandoned and — perhaps inevitably — There was talk of haunting. Jean explicitly corroborated these reports. The group had been jocular, skylarking, inviting ghosts to the feast: all ostensibly casual and careless, but all inwardly thrilling to the spooky look of the house, and the memory of the macabre killing. Jean had noticed a flickering of red light at the window of the living room. She had assumed it to be a reflection of the fire, then had looked again. There was no glass in the window. Others noticed; there were squeals and squeaks from the girls. All rose to their feet. Inside the living room, clearly visible, hung a body, twisting and writhing, clothed in flames. And from within came a series of agonized throat-wrenching sobs.

At this point Art snorted. 'Somebody was playing a trick.'

'No, no!' Jean and Don both protested.

'We're not that dumb,' said Jean indignantly. 'Okay, Betty Hall and Peggy were hysterical and Johnny Palgrave wasn't any better. But, the rest of us were perfectly sensible!'

Don laughed; Jean turned an indignant look on him. 'We were excited,' she explained. 'Of course! Who wouldn't be? But it didn't interfere with our eyesight. Not mine! Anyway, that's not all. Don went *inside*.'

'What?' Art was truly surprised. 'You went inside? What for?'

'To investigate.'

'You thought it was a trick, eh?'

'No. It couldn't have been a trick. All of us knew that. It wasn't only the flames and the groans — they were real but not *quite* real. It was a feeling. A kind of — well, I can't describe it. But it must have been what that woman felt while she was hanging. That place is *haunted* Mr. Marsile!'

'So you went inside. Wasn't that kinda rash?'

'Maybe . . . But all my life I've told myself if I ever saw

a ghost, I was going to walk right up to him. Tonight I got the opportunity.' Don grinned. 'It was like jumping into cold water.'

'What did you see? You kids keep a man in suspense!'

'Well, we'd run back a ways, and were standing by the car. These two girls were still yelling, and Johnny Palgrave had left. I finally went to the front door. I was scared. So bad I could hardly move my legs — but it seemed as if most of it was outside of me. The atmosphere of the place. I went up the front door, and told Jean to wait —'

'Oh,' said Art. 'You were there too.'

'Certainly. I wanted to know too.'

'Go on.'

'We looked through the door. It wasn't quite as bright as it had seemed through the window. A double-exposure sort of thing. But the fire was bright enough to see the other body hanging there.'

'He was naked,' said Jean primly, as if the apparition should have exhibited a greater sense of propriety.

'We stood watching. Nothing happened. I went inside, picked up a stick, tried to touch the hanging thing. The stick went right through.'

'And then,' said Jean, 'everything faded. The groans and the fire. Everything.'

'Huh. You're telling me the truth? You're not pulling your old dad's leg?'

'No, Father! My word of honor!'

'Huh . . . Then what did you do? High-tail it for home?'

'Are you kidding? We hadn't eaten yet. We went back to the fire, and ate, and then we came home. Don's going back tomorrow night with a camera.'

Art looked at Don speculatively. He cleared his throat, then said gruffly. 'Mind if I come along?'

'No, Mr. Marsile. Of course not.'

'You want to go back right now?'

'Sure, if you like.'

'Can I come, Father?'

Art nodded. 'You got clear once. I guess whatever's there ain't gonna hurt you.'

2

They stopped by Don's house for his camera, then drove south into the country, through sweet smelling orange groves, past dim white houses. At the edge of the desert, they turned up Indian Hill. The road twisted and wound, through sagebrush, half-wild oleander, scrub-oak. Ahead, in the light of a late-rising moon, stood the Freelock house.

'It's spooky enough,' said Art.

He turned into the overgrown driveway. 'There's where we parked,' said Jean. 'There's where we had our fire.' The headlights picked out the circle of dead gray ash. Art stopped the car, set the brakes, took his flashlight from the glove-compartment.

They sat in the dark a few moments, watching and listening. Cricket sounds came out of the night; the half moon rode pale and lonely through the ragged black trees. Art opened the door, got out. Don and Jean followed. They went to the patch of gravel, wan and gray in the moonlight. The rocks crunched under their feet. They halted, disinclined to make sounds so incongruous and intrusive.

'We were right here,' Jean whispered. 'See that window there? That's the living room.'

They stood staring at the dark old house. Far away a dog barked, lonesome and melancholy. Art muttered. 'I've always heard that if you come out looking for these things, they never happen. It's only when you don't expect them . . . I'm gonna take a look inside.'

He went around to the front porch. The yard was a waste of dead milk-weed stalks and feathery fox-tail, bone color in the moonlight. Jean and Don came behind. Art mounted the steps, paused.

Jean and Don stopped. After a moment Don asked, 'Do you feel it, Mr. Marsile? Something cold and . . . lonely?'

'Yeah. Something like that.'

Art continued more slowly. The feeling of grief, of desolation, of precious remembrance lost and gone, grew stronger.

They entered the house. The room was dark. Was that a glow? A flicker of red? A whimper, a sob? If so, it came and went; the woe vanished abruptly. Art drew a deep breath. 'That's how it was before,' whispered Jean. 'Only worse.'

Art flicked on his flashlight. Don pointed. 'That's the stick I used. That's where the thing hung.'

Outside a car turned into the driveway: the State Highway Patrol. A searchlight swept up the steps, picked up Art Marsile on the porch with Don and Jean close behind him.

A trooper got out of the car. 'Hello Art . . . What's going on?'

'I'm trying to find out.'

'We got a report of a disturbance up here, thought we'd take a look.'

'I thought I'd look too.'

'See anything?'

'Nothing I'd swear to. It's quiet now, that's for sure.'

'Yeah. Well, sergeant told me to check.' The trooper climbed the steps, flashed his light around the room. He turned back to Jean and Don. 'You kids were in the bunch up here tonight?'

'Yes.'

'You saw those ghosts?'

Don told him what they'd seen. The trooper listened without comment, flashed his light around the room once again. He shook his head. 'Looks to me like somebody was playing a trick.' He went to the patrol car, spoke into the microphone, made his report. 'Well, I checked. I'll be on my way.'

The patrol car backed out, drove away. Art, Jean and Don went to their own car, followed. They drove down the hill in silence.

'What do you think, Dad?' Jean asked presently.

Art made a non-committal sound. 'Lots of funny things happen in the world. I guess this is another of 'em.'

'But you believe us, don't you?'

'I believe you, all right.'

'But *why*? asked Don. 'Why *should* there be ghosts?'

Art shook his head. 'Nobody knows, nobody seems to care. It's not fashionable to believe in ghosts. Let alone *see* them.'

'I know what I saw,' said Don. 'It was *there*.'

'But what was it?' asked Jean. 'A spirit? A ghost? A memory? Some kind of trick?'

'It's just one of the things nobody knows the answers to.'

'I want to know,' said Don. 'There's got to be a reason. Nothing happens without a reason. *Some* kind of reason.'

Art agreed. 'That's what we're brought up to believe. But whenever there's something out of the ordinary, people shrug their shoulders and pretend it didn't happen. Miracles, things being thrown around a house, ghosts, poltergeists, apparitions, spirit messages — you read about 'em all the time. People just go back about their business. I don't understand it. There's a big field of knowledge here — as big as all of science, maybe bigger. And nobody dares to look into it. There's thousands of people digging for pots in Egypt and counting the field-mice in Pakistan . . . . Why don't a few look into this stuff? Because it's too big, too scary, too hard to prove? Maybe they're afraid to be laughed at. I don't know.'

'I never knew you thought like this, Daddy,' said Jean.

'Like what?' asked Art. 'I'm just a hard-head working-man. When I see something I want to know why. And when something funny happens, I don't try to kid myself it doesn't exist . . . I'll tell you kids something I never told no one else. I don't want you spreading it either, you hear?'

'I won't say anything.'

'I won't either.'

'Well, you know what a dowser is? Some people call 'em water-witches.'

'Sure,' said Don. 'They find water with a forked stick.'

'Yeah. Well, I own quite a bit of land. Some good citrus land, some not so good. There's one tract I got out at the edge of the desert, about four hundred acres, dry as ashes. If I could get water, I might grow something, but it's outside the irrigation district. One day I heard of this dowser and hired him to walk over the four hundred acres. He walked back and forth while his stick jumped He was kinda puzzled at first, then he said, 'Mr. Marsile, you drill here. You'll get water. It's about two hundred feet down, you should be able to draw about twenty gallons a minute.' Then he said, 'Over here, if you drill, you'll hit oil. It's deep, it'll cost you money to reach it, but it's there. Lots of it.'

'Daddy — you never told me this!'

'I didn't intend to. Not just yet. Anyway I went down for the water, I hit her on the nose at two hundred feet. I pump just about twenty gallons a minute. As for the oil, I've had three geologists to check the ground. They all say the same. Nothing. Wrong formation, wrong lay of the land, the wind even blows the wrong way. I don't know. I can't get it out of my mind. It'll cost twenty or thirty thousand — maybe more — to run a test-hold . . . I could swing it, but I'd have to go into debt. I don't like to do that.'

Jean and Don were silent. They passed through the main part of Orange City, crossed the Los Angeles freeway, and returned to Art Marsile's house, under the four big pepper trees.

'Come on in,' Art told Don. 'Jean can make us some hot chocolate. It's too late for coffee.'

Hugh was sitting in the living room, reading. His feet, in black socks, were long and limp as dead salmon. 'Where you all been?'

'We saw the ghost, Hugh!' Jean called out triumphantly.

Hugh laughed unroariously.

'It's true!' cried Jean.

'Of all the silly tripe!'

'Don't believe me then.' Jean went haughtily into the kitchen to make hot chocolate.

Hugh, still grinning, looked at Art. 'What're they trying to cook up?'

'They sure saw something, Hugh.'

Hugh sat up straight in astonishment. '*You* don't believe in ghosts?'

Art said evenly, 'I have an open mind. They saw something, that's for sure. Ghosts, spooks — what difference does it make what you call 'em? Nobody knows anything about the subject. The field's wide open.'

Don said, 'I wonder if there's anyplace you could go to learn about these things?'

'Certainly not at any of the universities. None that I ever heard of, anyway. Anyway, what could they teach? Ghost-hunting? Mind-reading? There's not even a name for the subject.'

Hugh laughed derisively. 'Who'd want to take such ridiculous courses?'

'I would,' said Don. 'I never thought about it before, but it's like Mr. Marsile says; nobody knows anything about these things — and they're all around us. Suppose the government spent a hundred million dollars on research, like they did on the atom bomb? Who knows what they'd turn up?'

'It's not a proper field for investigation,' said Hugh after a minute. 'It conflicts with what the Scriptures tell us.'

'It wasn't considered proper to teach evolution either,' said Art. 'I see now where the ministers are swingin' around to sayin' it's right after all.'

'Not the real four-square preachers!' cried Hugh indignantly. 'Nobody'll ever convince me I was descended from a monkey! And nobody'll ever convince me there's ghosts because the Bible's against it.'

Jean brought in the chocolate. 'I wish for once, Hugh, that every time we're trying to talk, you wouldn't bring the Bible into it. I know what I saw tonight, whether it's in the Bible or whether it isn't.'

'Well, all this to the side,' said Art, 'it's an interesting subject. Everybody's interested in it. But everybody's afraid to look into it scientifically.'

'I wouldn't be,' said Don. 'I'd really like to.'

Art shook his head. 'You'd find the going mighty tough, Don. You'd need money, nobody'd give you any. People would laugh at you. You'd be starting cold, from scratch. You'd hardly know where to begin. Does dowsing for water have any connection to ghosts? How does this telepathy business work? Can anybody read the future? Are ghosts alive? Can they think? Are they spirits or just imprints, like footsteps? If they're alive, where do they live? What's it like where they live? If they give off light, where do they draw the power? There's thousands of questions.'

Don sat silently, his chocolate forgotten.

Hugh said huskily. 'Those are things we were never meant to know.'

'I can't believe that, Hugh,' said Art. 'Anything our mind is able to understand we got a right to know.' He put down his cup. 'Well, I'm gonna turn in. Don't you kids set up till all hours. Good night.' He left the room.

'Golly,' said Don, in an awed voice. 'When you think of it, it almost — this is a whole area that nobody knows anything about.'

Jean said, 'There must be *somebody* studying it. After all, we're not the only people in the world with ideas.'

'Seems to me I've read of a group in England,' said Don grudgingly. 'A society for psychic research. Tomorrow let's go to the library and find out.'

'Okay. We'll start the Orange City Society for Psychic Research.'

Hugh said coldly. 'You ought to know better than to talk like that. It's sacrilegious.'

'Don't talk nonsense,' said Jean crossly. 'Why on earth is it sacrilegious?'

'Because there's one authority on right and wrong — the Bible. If you sin and go to Hell, you suffer the torments of the damned. If you live a Christian life, you go to Heaven. That's the Gospel. There's nothing about spirits, or ghosts, or any of that other stuff.'

'The Bible isn't necessarily right,' said Don.

Hugh was astounded. 'Of course it's right! Every word of it is right!'

Don shrugged. 'Anyway, I'm going to check on this psychic research. I'm going to find out what ghosts are, what they're made of, what makes them tick. Nothing happens without a reason; that's common sense. I'm going to find out that reason.'

'I am too,' said Jean. 'I'm just as interested as you are.'

'It's evil knowledge,' intoned Hugh. 'You'll go to Hell. You'll live in eternal torment.'

'How come you're such an authority on Hell and torment?' Don asked.

'I made my choice tonight,' said Hugh. 'I gave myself to Christ. I promised to preach the Holy gospel, to fight the Devil and all his works.'

Don rose to his feet. 'Well, that answered my question. Good night, Jean.'

Jean went with him out to the car; when she came back Hugh was waiting for her. 'Good night, Hugh,' she said, and slipped past him. 'Just a minute,' he said.

'What for?'

'I want to warn you about what you're doing.' His voice took on volume. 'There's enough wickedness in the world without inventing more. Don Berwick is going to Hell. You don't want to join him there, do you?'

'I don't believe in Hell,' said Jean sweetly.

'It's in the Bible, it's the Holy Word. They that sin shall suffer fire and pain without end, the furnaces shall open for them, they'll be doomed forever. That's the Christian gospel.'

'It's no such thing,' said Jean. 'I know this much: Christ was kind and gentle. He tried to get people to be decent to each other. All this talk about fire and torment is nonsense. And I'm going to bed.'

3

The school year came to an end; both Don and Hugh graduated. The Korean War had started; both Don and Hugh received greetings from the President. Hugh won a medical exemption by reason of his pitifully flat feet and his extreme height — he now stood almost seven feet tall. Don was drafted and assigned to a paratroop battalion. Ten months passed, and Don's mother received news that Don was 'missing in action' and presumed dead.

The years passed. Art Marsile prospered, but his mode of life varied little. Hugh studied at the Athbill School of Divinity at Lawrence, Kansas; Jean enrolled at UCLA.

Three years after Don's disappearance, Don's mother received an official letter from the State Department in Washington notifying her that Sergeant Donald Berwick was not dead, as had been assumed, and shortly would be arriving home.

Two weeks later, Don Berwick returned to Orange City. He was reticent about his war experience, but it became known that he had been an undeclared prisoner-of-war, that he had escaped from a Manchurian labor camp and had made his way to Japan. He looked considerably older than his twenty-three years; he walked with a faint hitch in his stride, and his face was much more firmly modeled than anyone in Orange City had remembered it: the forehead low and wide, the nose straight and blunt, the cheekbones and jaw pronounced, the cheeks hollow.

On his second day in Orange City he went to see Art Marsile, whom he found a trifle thinner, a trifle more leathery. Art brought out beer from the refrigerator, told him what news there was: that Jean was making good grades; that Hugh had become an evangelist, and had changed his name, now calling himself Hugh Bronny — his mother's maiden-name. 'And what do you plan to do, Don!'

Don settled himself back into the couch. 'You remember the night we went up to the Freelock house, Art?'

'Yep.'

'I've never forgotten that night. Afterwards I did a lot of reading — all the books I could find on the subject. In Manchuria I had time to do a lot of thinking. I still want to be a scientist, Art — a new kind of scientist. I'm going to the University. I'm going to learn as much mathematics, psychology, biology and physics as possible. Then I'm going to apply scientific techniques to the so-called supernatural.'

Art nodded. 'I'm glad to hear that, Don. I'm going to ask you a personal question. How are you fixed for money?'

'Pretty good, Art. I got an awful whack of cumulative back pay. I'll go to school on the GI Bill.'

'Good enough. If you run short, I've got quite a bit. Whatever you need, it's yours.'

'Thanks, Art. I'll sure call on you if I need help. But I think I'll make out pretty well.' He rose to his feet and shuffled uneasily.

Art said gruffly, 'Why don't you stay to dinner? I telephoned Jean you were here; she's due home in a few minutes.'

Don sat down, a queer hard pounding under his ribs. Outside a car door slammed. Feet came running up the walk, the front door opened. 'Don!'

'Seems like absence does make the heart grow fonder,' observed Art Marsile, grinning.

'Father, don't you look while I'm kissing Don!'

'Okay. Just let me know when you're done.'

Don applied for admission at Caltech, and was accepted. A year later he and Jean were married.

There was news from Hugh meanwhile. He had established himself in Kansas, and held weekly revival meetings in various parts of Texas, Kansas, Oklahoma and Arkansas. Occasionally he sent home hand-bills: 'Huge Rally. Fighting Hugh Bronny, Leader of the Christian Crusade.'

On Easter of the year Don was to take his BS degree, Art drove out to Don and Jean's apartment in Westwood. 'I'm gonna make the jump,' he announced as he came through the door. 'In fact, I already made it.'

'What jump, Father?'

'Remember my telling you about the dowser, how he told me there was oil?'

'Yes.'

'Well, I'm going to do some wild-catting. I had a good year, I can blow whatever it's gonna take. If I hit it, fine. If I don't it's out of my system.'

Don laughed. 'Either way, it'll be interesting.'

'That's how I figure,' said Art. 'The geologists say no, the dowser says yes. We'll see who's right.'

'How long before you know for sure?'

Art shook his head. 'They start down next month. They drill till they hit oil — or until I run out of money. Whichever comes first.'

'Here's hoping,' said Don. 'If hope will do you any good.'

'We'll all hope. We'll drink a toast,' said Jean. 'If Hugh were here we'd ask him to pray.'

'Hugh *will* be here,' said Art. 'That's another thing.'

Jean made a face. 'I thought he was established in Kansas.'

'Well, he's coming west,' said Art in the level voice he always used in connection with Hugh. 'Seems to be a pretty big man in his field now. They've got him booked for meetings all over Southern California. He's going to make his headquarters in Orange City.'

'Father! Surely he's not going to move in with you!'

'It's his privilege, if he wants to, Jean. It's his home.'

'I suppose so. But I thought that later, after Don got his degree, we'd move back to Orange City.'

Art grinned. 'When Don gets his degree, you two are going to the Hawaiian Islands. It's a present from me. By the time you come back — then we'll see. Things may be cleared up. Maybe Hugh's got other plans in mind.'

But Hugh had no other plans in mind. He arrived in Orange City the next week, tall, gaunt and solemn, wearing a pale blue suit, a Panama hat on his craggy forehead. Art received him with decent cordiality, and Hugh took up residence in his old home.

The drilling on 'Marsile No. 1' began. Don finished his undergraduate studies and received his BS; he and Jean flew to Honolulu for the month's vacation which had been Art's present to them.

During their absence they received two short letters from Art: the drilling was proceeding slowly and expensively. Nothing at five hundred feet; in the second letter, nothing at twelve hundred feet, with the drills scratching slowly through hard metamorphic rock. He made a dry comment that Hugh disapproved of the venture, on the basis that money being wasted on the drilling could be put to better use; namely, the Christian Crusade, an evangelistic movement which Hugh had founded.

The month passsed; Don and Jean returned to Orange City. Art met them at the airport. His face was dour and drawn: Marsile No. 1 was still dry. 'We're down to eighteen hundred,' said Art glumly. 'The rock gets harder and meaner every foot. And I'm running low on money.'

Jean hugged him. 'That's nothing to fret about. It was just a gamble — just a game.'

'Damn expensive game. And I like to win my games, you know.'

They drove to the old house under the pepper trees, walked up the iris-bordered gravel path, entered the house.

'Good heavens!' cried Jean in wonder. 'What's all this?'

'Some of Hugh's publicity,' said Art dryly.

Wordlessly, Jean and Don examined the placards thumbtacked to the wall. Most conspicuous was a large photograph of Hugh Bronny speaking into a microphone, fist poised in grim exultation. Four placards bore a picture of Hugh with scarehead printing: 'March in the Christian Crusade with Hugh Bronny!' 'Hugh Bronny, the Devil's enemy!' 'Sweep America clean with Fighting Hugh Bronny!' A cartoon showed Hugh Bronny depicted as a muscular giant. He carried a broom labelled, 'The Fighting Gospel,' with which he dispersed a rabble of half-human vermin. Some wore horns and bat-wings; others were characterized by bald heads, large hooked noses, heavy-lidded eyes; others were marked with the hammer-and-sickle. 'Clean out the atheists, the communists, the deniers of Christ!' 'Keep America pure!' cried another card. 'Hear Fighting Hugh Bronny at the old-fashioned fundamental go-for-broke revival! Bring the children. Free soft drinks.'

Jean finally turned back to Art; she opened her mouth, then closed it again.

'I know,' said Art. 'It's kinda crude. But — well, it's Hugh's business. This is his home, he's got a right to hang up what he wants.'

'But you live here too, Father!'

Art nodded. 'I can stand it. I don't like the things, but what's the good of making Hugh take them down? That don't change Hugh, it only makes things tougher.'

'Sometimes I think you carry tolerance too far, Dad.'

'Now I don't know about that. Here comes Hugh now. I guess he's been asleep.'

A door closed, slow steps sounded along the hall.

'He's changed a bit,' said Art in an undertone.

Hugh came into the room. He wore an unpressed black suit, a blue shirt, a long gray necktie, long-toed black shoes. He seemed enormously tall, almost seven feet; his head seemed larger and craggier than ever; his eyes flamed blue from cavernous sockets. He had gained force since Don had seen him last — force and poise and intensity, and absolute assurance.

Hugh did not offer to shake hands. 'Hello, Jean. Hello, Don. You both look well.'

'We should,' said Jean with a nervous laugh, 'we've done nothing but lie in the sun and sleep for a month.'

Hugh nodded somberly, as if frivolity and self-indulgence were all very nice, but he didn't have the time.

'I'm glad you're here. I want to talk about this oil well business. Do you know how much money has gone into it?'

'No,' said Jean. 'I don't care.'

'But there's no oil out there on the desert. That money could be put to a worthy Christian use. I could do wonderful things with it.'

'No, you couldn't,' said Art. 'I told you once before, Hugh, I'm not putting any money into your Christian Crusade.'

'Just what is a Christian Crusade?' asked Jean.

Hugh bent his head forward and swung his arms. 'The Christian Crusade is a great and growing cause. The Christian Crusade aims to bring the power of the Bible against the evils of this earthly sphere. The Christian Crusade aims to make the United States of America a Christian God-fearing community; we believe in America for the Americans, Russia for the communists, Africa for the Negroes, Israel for the Jews and Hell for the atheists!'

'I don't plan to finance it,' said Art with a feeble grin.

Jean turned to Don, made a small helpless gesture. Don shrugged.

Hugh looked from one to the other. 'I hear you've just graduated from college,' he said to Don.

'Yes, that's right.'

'And now you're a scientist?'

'Not quite. I've acquired some of the necessary background.'

'So now what will you do?'

Jean said, 'Father, take us out to the oil well.'

'Don't call it an oil well yet,' said Art. 'It's dry as last week's biscuits. Around Orange City they call it "Marsile's Folly." '

Hugh made an unverbalized rumble of disgust.

'If I strike there'll be lots of foolish people around here. Because I quietly bought up mineral rights everywhere in sight. Coming, Hugh?'

'No. I'm working on my sermons.'

They drove east from Orange City. The dark green foliage of the citrus groves came to an abrupt halt, with dun hills and the parched vegetation of the desert beyond.

They turned off at a side road, wound between balls of dry tumbleweed and gray-brown boulders, then suddenly came on another dark-green orange grove. Art stopped the car, pointed. 'See that tank and the windmill? That's where the dowser told me to get my water. I got enough to irrigate that whole grove. Now look — ' he started forward ' — just around this little hill . . . . There was the derrick, the drill-rig, drill crew in sweat-stained shirts and hard hats. Art called to the foreman. 'I don't see no gusher, Chet.'

'We're down to shale again, Art. Better going than the schist. But not a whiff of oil. You know what I think?'

'Yeah. I know what you think. You think I'm pouring money down a gopher hole. Maybe I am. I got another four thousand dollars to blow. When that's gone — we quit.'

'Four thousand won't take us much farther. 'Specially if we hit any more of that schist, or that black trap.'

'Well, keep biting at her, and when she blows, cap her quick; I don't want to lose a gallon.'

Chet grinned. 'All the oil you'll get out of that hole won't come to more'n a gallon.'

4

They returned to Orange City, tired and disappointed.

Jean said grimly, 'I know we're going to argue with Hugh the whole time we're here. Damn it, Dad, he's a fascist! Where did he ever learn such things? Not from you!'

Art sighed. 'I guess it's just Hugh. He's got a good mind, but — well, maybe it's his funny looks that he couldn't apply himself normally. And now he's found a place where his looks help him out . . . And it don't do no good arguing with him, because he doesn't listen.'

'I'll try to behave myself.'

But at dinner the argument started. Hugh insisted on knowing what field of investigation Don proposed to enter. Don told him, matter-of-factly. 'I plan to study para-psychological phenomena — psychic research, some people call it.'

Hugh frowned his great eyebrow-buckling frown. 'I'm not sure as I understand. Does this mean you study black-magic, witchcraft, the occult?'

'In a certain sense, yes.'

'It's charlatanry!' said Hugh in disgust.

Don nodded. 'Ninety-five percent of it is, unfortunately.
. . . It's the remaining five percent I'm interested in.
Especially the so-called spiritualistic phenomena.'

Hugh leaned forward. 'Surely you consider that sort of
study irreverent? Are the souls of the dead any concern
of man?'

'I don't recognize any limitation to human knowledge,
Hugh. If souls exist, they're made of some sort of substance.
Perhaps not molecules — but something. I'm curious what
that *something* is.'

Hugh shook his head. 'And how do you go about investigating the after-life?'

'The same way you investigate anything else. Isolate facts,
check, reject. If there is life after death, it exists. Somewhere.
If something exists somewhere, it can be examined,
measured, perhaps even seen or visited — providing we find
the proper tools.'

'It's sacrilege,' croaked Hugh.

Don laughed. 'Calm down, Hugh. Let's talk without
getting excited. You asked me what I was interested in.
I'm telling you . . . If it's any comfort to you, I'm not
at all sure there is an after-life.'

Hugh glared from his cavernous eye-sockets. 'Are you
admitting to atheism?'

'If you want to put it that way,' said Don. 'I don't see
why you make it out a bad word. Atheism is the assertion
of human self-reliance, dignity and individuality.'

'You are forever damned,' said Hugh in a hushed sibilant
voice.

'I don't think so,' said Don reasonably. 'Of course I
don't know anything for sure. No one knows the basic
answers. Why is everything? Why is *anything*? Why is the
universe? These are tremendous questions. They aren't
answered by replying. 'Because the creator so willed.' The
same mystery applies to the Creator. And if there is a
Creator, I'm sure he's not angry when I use the brain and

the curiosity He endowed me with,' said Don smiling.

Hugh rose to his feet, nodded stiffly. 'Good night.' He left the room.

Jean broke the silence. 'Well, that's that.'

'I'm sorry if I caused any family trouble,' said Don.

'Nonsense,' said Art. 'I've always liked a good argument. Hugh's got no call to get his feelings hurt. You didn't call him names.'

'Hugh forgets that the constitution guarantees freedom of religion,' said Jean indignantly.

Art chuckled, looked at the posters on the wall. 'If this Christian Crusade really takes hold, Hugh'll change the constitution.'

'He shouldn't use the word "Christian",' Jean said indignantly. 'Christianity stands for gentleness and kindness, and Hugh is a bigot.'

Art drew a deep breath. 'I'm not proud of Hugh . . . I'm not proud of myself, because I raised him.'

'Hush Father, don't be foolish. Let's talk of more interesting things. Like how we're going to spend our first million when Marsile No. 1 comes in.'

Art laughed. 'You and Don can go about your ghost-hunting. Me, I'm going to buy some nice pasture-land and raise race-horses.'

A week passed, two weeks. Marsile No. 1 remained dry, and Art Marsile reached the end of his bank-roll. He returned to the house, grim and dusty. 'Well, that's it,' he said. 'I paid off the rig. I blew what loose money I had and I'm not going into debt.'

Jean soothed him. 'You're perfectly right, Dad, and now we'll forget all about it.'

Art looked around the living room. 'Why the suitcases?'

'You know we planned to leave today.'

'You don't need to go anywhere. Your home is here, as long as you like living here.'

'We do like it, but we've got to get to work. And we can't commute to Los Angeles every day.'

'And how are you going to set about going to work?'

'First,' said Don, 'I've got to raise money. I'll apply for a Guggenheim Fellowship. I'll make contacts at the Society for Psychical Research, and see if I can sell some ideas to the Finance Committee. Perhaps one of the universities will set up a study group, like the ESP section at Duke. There's a number of possibilities.'

Art shook his head in gruff vexation. 'If Marsile No. 1 came through, you wouldn't have needed to worry.'

'I know, Art. I was pulling for it as hard as you were.'

They took their luggage to the car. Hugh came to the doorway, and stood watching. Jean kissed Art, waved to Hugh. 'We'll be out next weekend, Daddy. Now you forget Marsile No. 1 and get back to oranges.'

They drove to Los Angeles in a driving rainstorm, returned to their apartment in Westwood. Jean ran up the steps, opened the door; Don struggled up with the suitcases. He found Jean standing rigidly in the middle of the floor. 'What's the trouble?' he asked, putting down the suitcases.

Jean made no answer. Don went to her. 'What's wrong, Jean?'

'Don,' she whispered, 'something terrible's happened. To Art.'

Don stared at her. 'Surely not. We just left him, not an hour ago . . . .'

Jean rushed to the telephone, called Orange City. The bell rang and rang. No one answered. Jean put down the receiver, stood up. Don put his arms around her.

'I feel it, Don,' she whispered. 'I know something's happened.'

Half an hour later the telephone rang. Hugh spoke in a harsh babble. 'Jean? Is this you? Jean?'

'Hugh! Father —'

'He's dead. A truck skidded into him — on the way out to the crazy oil well —'

'We'll be right out, Hugh.'

Jean hung up listlessly. She turned. Don read the news in her face. He kissed her, patted her head. 'I'm going to make you a cup of coffee.'

Jean came out in the kitchen with him. 'Don.'

'Yes?'

'Let's go see Ivalee.'

He stood looking at her, coffee-pot in his hand. 'You're sure you want to?'

'Yes.'

'All right.'

'Right now.'

Don put down the coffee-pot. 'I'll telephone to make sure she's not busy.' He went to the phone, made the call. 'It's all right. Let's go.'

Half an hour later they rang the bell of a neat white house in Long Beach. Ivalee Trembath opened the door, a slender woman of forty-five with steady gray eyes and silky white hair. She greeted them quietly, with simple friendliness, led them into the living room. If she noticed Jean's drawn face and over-bright eyes, she made no comment. Don said, 'Iva, we need help — do you feel up to a seance?'

Ivalee looked from Don to Jean, then seated herself slowly in an arm-chair. 'Sit down.' Don and Jean seated themselves. 'Do you want to speak to Molly?'

'Yes, please.'

Ivalee lowered her head, looked at her hands. She began to breathe in long slow breaths. 'Molly. Molly. Are you there?' There was silence. Outside a car whirred past over the wet asphalt. 'Molly?' Ivalee's head sank, her shoulders sagged.

'Hello, Iva,' said a clear bright voice from Ivalee's mouth. 'Hello, folks.'

'Hello, Molly,' said Don. 'How are you?'

'Fine as rain. I see you got a little rain down below too. We sure could have used it in 1906. What a sight that was, dear old Frisco! Reeking up in flames like rags in a bonfire. Well, well. I've seen lots in my day.' Molly's voice faded a little; there was a murmur, then another voice said harshly, 'Come, come, enough of this nonsense! We're not having anymore of this peeking and prying.'

Ivalee Trembath whimpered like a sleeping puppy, rocked back and forth in the chair.

'Who are you?' asked Don, calmly.

A torrent of words in a foreign language pelted from Ivalee's mouth — hard, harsh gutturals that carried the sting of abuse.

Molly said good-naturedly, 'Oh, get away, Ladislav . . . Silly creature — he's one of the bad ones. Always horsin' around.'

Jean said in a husky whisper, 'Is my father there?'

'Sure, he's here.'

'Can he speak?' said Don.

Molly's voice was doubtful. 'He'll try. He's not strong . . . .'

A second voice interrupted, a low gravel voice that rasped in Ivalee's throat; for a second or two both voices were speaking at once.

'Hello, Jean. Hello, Don.' The voice was distant.

'Art?' asked Don. 'Are you there?'

'Yes.' The voice was stronger. 'Can't quite get the hang of talking through a lady. Well, I'm over here safe and sound, in spite of Hugh's prediction . . . Now don't you folks grieve. It's a little lonesome, but I'm fine and I'll be happy.'

Jean was crying quietly. 'It was so sudden . . . .'

'That's the best way there is. Now don't cry, because you make me feel bad.'

'It's so strange to be talking to you like this.'

Art's dry laugh sounded in Ivalee's throat. 'It's strange for me too.'

'What's it like, Art?' asked Don.

'Hard to say. It's kinda hazy just now. It's something like home in a way.'

His voice faded, as if it were coming from a radio tuned to a distant station. Molly's voice came bright and cheerful. 'He's tired, dear. He's not used to life up here yet. But he's fine now, and we'll look after him. He wants to talk to you again.'

The voice changed in Ivalee's throat, becoming not Art's voice, but using Art's clipped intonations. 'Say, down there. You know where we were digging?'

'Marsile No. 1?'

'Yeah. Well, we stopped too soon. I just kinda pushed my head down and took a look. Don't quit, Don. Keep going, because it's there.'

'How far, Art?'

'Hard to say; things is a little confused. I've got to go. I'll be talking to you again sometime. Say hello to Hugh . . . .'

Molly's voice returned. 'Well, that's all folks,' she said brassily. 'He's a nice man.'

Don asked, 'Molly — can I visit this land where you are?'

'Sure,' said Molly. 'When you die.' And she chuckled. 'Of course, we call it "passing over".'

'Can I visit your country while I'm alive, here on Earth?' he asked.

Molly's voice faded, waxed and waned as if winds were blowing. 'I don't know, Donald. People like Iva visit us — but they always go back . . . I see that Ivalee's tired . . . So I'll be off about my business. Good-bye. . . .'

'Good-bye,' said Don.

'Good-bye,' said Jean, softly.

Ivalee Trembath raised her head; her eyes looked tired; the cheek muscles sagged around her mouth. 'How was it?'

'It was tremendous,' said Don. 'It couldn't have been better.'

Ivalee looked at Jean, still softly crying. 'What happened, Don?'

'Her father was killed tonight?'

'Oh. Too bad . . . Did you reach him?'

'Yes. He spoke. It was wonderful.'

Ivalee smiled faintly. 'I'm glad when I can help.'

'Thank you ever so much,' said Jean.

Ivalee patted her shoulder. 'You come to see me soon again . . . Do you still have the same plans?'

'Yes,' said Don. 'The same, only more of them. We'll start work as soon as we can.'

'Tell me about it next time,' said Ivalee. 'You're anxious to go now.'

'Yes,' said Jean. 'But I'm glad we came. Good night.'

5

Don and Jean drove along the Freeway, through swift bright-eyed shoals of automobiles; past phosphorescent tangles of neon, filling-stations with banners and signs, cafés, bars, creameries, hamburger-stands, used-car lots draped and festooned with electric light-bulbs — hundred thousand-watt effulgences along the street, like a row of monstrous incandescent jelly-fish. It was splendor familiar to Don and Jean, a vibrant agitation of light and color and life to be seen nowhere else in the world.

Jean said, 'I don't know Ivalee as well as you do . . . I'm sure she's honest.' She hesitated.

Don said, 'She's more than honest. She's completely transparent. She's the most guileless person I know. This is the fifth time I've sat at a seance with her. It was far and away the clearest and most direct.'

'I wasn't questioning her honesty,' said Jean. 'But — do you think that was really Father?'

Don shrugged. 'I don't know. It's possible that Ivalee unconsciously reads the minds of the people who visit her. That instead of spirits speaking through her mouth, she merely mirrors our own minds.'

'But about the oil well — he said there's oil, to keep on drilling.'

'I know. She wasn't mirroring my mind. Privately I've been skeptical of Marsile No. 1. Dowsers aren't infallible, no more than anyone else.'

Jean nodded. 'I've never believed there'd be oil . . . But now father, or his spirit — whatever it is — says there's oil. What shall we do?'

Don laughed grimly. 'Drill, I guess — if you're willing to risk it. If we can raise the money.'

'I'm willing to risk it . . . But there's Hugh to be considered.'

'Had your father made a will?'

'Yes. The property is divided equally between Hugh and myself.'

'There may be difficulties . . . Speaking of Hugh — look at that.' He pointed to an enormous billboard glaring under footlights.

This appeared in red and black, on a white background, in heavy portentous letters.

GREAT NATIONAL GOSPEL REVIVAL
Fight Three Great Evils
with
Fighting Hugh Bronny
Keep America
Clean, White and Christian
Fight Communism
Fight Atheism
Fight Blood Pollution
Massive Revival at the
Orange City Auditorium
Two weeks starting June 19

A picture depicted Hugh as a rock-jawed powerful giant, a hybrid of Abraham Lincoln, Uncle Sam and Paul Bunyan.

Don shook his head. 'I never suspected Hugh had come so far!'

'He's always been a worker . . . It's rather revolting, isn't it?'

Don nodded. 'I suppose people must come to listen to him.'

'Evidently.'

They arrived at Orange City, and were immersed in the inevitable melancholy details attendant on Art Marsile's death.

Art was cremated, his ashes buried in the orange grove, without funeral or formal ceremony, in accordance with his wishes. Hugh protested bitterly, until Art's attorney and executor of the estate brought forth the will, and indicated a paragraph giving explicit instructions as to the disposal of his body.

As Jean had informed Don, the estate was to be divided between Jean and Hugh, 'in any manner mutually agreeable to the legatees.' In the event that agreement could not be reached, the executor was instructed to sell the various properties of the estate at the highest possible figure and divide the proceeds between them.

Jean, Don and Hugh discussed the situation the night Art's ashes were buried. There were nine parcels of property: the house, the four hundred acres of desert, and seven orange groves of various acreage.

Hugh had prepared a memorandum of the value of the various parcels, and was ready with a proposal. 'I suggest that you keep the house, since my work takes me far afield, and I have no need of it. To compensate, I will take the Elsinore Avenue grove, which is roughly the same value. These other groves we can divide like this.' He explained his plan. 'The four hundred acres is worthless and I propose that we sell it and divide the proceeds.'

Don said, 'It's only fair to tell you, that we have reason to think there is oil on the property.'

Hugh frowned. 'What sort of reason?'

'A reason you may or may not take seriously. On the night Art died we stopped by the house of a friend, who is also a medium. While we were there, a voice, purportedly Art, spoke to us. The voice told us that there was oil on the four hundred acres, to proceed with the drilling.'

Hugh chuckled hollowly. 'And you are superstitious enough to give credence to this "voice"?'

'Superstition is belief in something non-existent,' said Don. 'This voice existed. I heard it. It sounded like Art. Jean and I are willling to take the chance it was Art.'

Hugh shook his great head slowly. 'I can't agree with you.'

'In any event,' said Don, 'I suggest that we sell one of the groves and use the money to continue drilling. It's a gamble, yes — but most of the bore is already there.'

Hugh shook his head once more. 'I have much better uses for money than pouring it into a hole.'

'Very well,' said Don. 'You take the Frazer Boulevard Valencias, we'll take the four hundred acres, and we'll split the other parcels according to your system.'

Hugh considered his list. 'Very well. I agree. I hope that I may be allowed to reside in the house during my stay in Orange City?'

'Of course,' said Jean. 'If you'll please take those posters and placards off the wall.'

Hugh rose to his full seven feet. 'As you wish,' he said coldly. 'It is your house.'

The division of the property was accordingly formalized. Don and Jean sold thirty-three acres of oranges, called the drill-crew back to work.

'Good money after bad?' inquired the foreman with genial good humor. 'Take my advice, Mr. Berwick, don't waste your money. This just ain't the right formation. We've passed the Granville Blue shales — that's where the Rodman Dome came in — and according to the geology you'll be hitting granite in another five hundred feet.'

'We want to see that granite,' said Jean. 'Drill on, Chet, and be ready to cap it when it comes.'

'Yes, ma'am.'

Three days later gas began blowing up the hole, and on the fourth day Marsile No. 1 came in.

Chet said sheepishly. 'I gave you good advice. You shoulda took it. But if you had, you wouldn't be millionaires like you're gonna be.'

6

At ten o'clock in the morning Hugh came into the living room, wearing a cream-colored suit, long pointed yellow shoes. Jean looked up from the armchair where she had been sitting, lost in thought. Hugh put his Panama hat gently on a chair, slapped his leg with a newspaper.

'Well, sister,' he said jocularly, 'oil on the property, after all. Why didn't you let me know?'

'You weren't here when the news came.'

'No. I was working with the Reverend Spedelius. It's wonderful, wonderful! God's gift to us. And we'll put it to God's work.'

Jean sat up in the chair, a faint cool smile on her face. 'What sort of fantasy is this, Hugh?'

'Fantasy?' He held up the newspaper. 'Surely this is true?'

'We struck oil on the four hundred acres, yes.'

'Then we're rich.'

'It was the four hundred acres you didn't want, Hugh.'

Hugh laughed hollowly. 'What's the difference? Perhaps I spoke unthinkingly — but I'm sure that our father intended us to share. That was the tone of his last will and testament . . . .' he looked around the room, picked up a book. ' "A Compendium of Supernormal Phenomena," by Ralph Birchmill.' He dropped it as if it were hot, glanced at Jean. 'I don't see the Holy Bible in the room,' he said, heavily jocose. He settled his great gaunt frame on the couch, knees almost as high as his chest. Don came in, sat down near Jean.

'Our father always insisted on an equal sharing of the good things,' said Hugh. 'I assume that we will continue to do so.'

'Not in this case,' said Jean. 'You're a moderately well-off man right now, with your orange groves.'

Hugh's hand slowly clenched on the newspaper. But his voice was gentle and low. 'True, sister. But I have a need for money beyond mere material needs. I'm pledged to the furtherance of God's will, to spiritual enlightenment of the people, to the Christian Crusade.'

'I'm sorry, Hugh. We've decided to put the money to other uses.'

Hugh held out his hands ingenuously. 'What use could be more important than spreading the Gospel?'

'It depends on your point of view. We plan to endow a research foundation.'

'You mean this black magic, devil worship, occultism stunt?'

Jean said impatiently, 'You know very well that we neither practice nor believe in black magic or devil worship.'

Hugh glanced meaningfully at the book on Don's desk. He rose restlessly to his feet, paced back and forth across the room. 'Exactly what kind of research do you intend, then?'

'I'll be glad to explain,' said Don politely. 'We want to bridge a very large gap in human knowledge. We want to attack what is commonly known as the supernatural with laboratory techniques. We want to make a large scale investigation of spiritualistic phenomena, with an eye to proving or disproving the existence of spirits, and perhaps the whole concept of the hereafter.'

Hugh stood back with an exaggerated gesture of alarm that nearly bumped his head on the door lintel. 'Proof of the hereafter? Isn't that rather beside the point? And presumptuous? Don't you read the Bible?'

'I don't care to argue theology with you,' said Don. 'You asked me a question; I answered you.'

Hugh nodded. 'Very well. I'll ask another question.' He strode across the room, looked down at Jean. 'This money, which you have acknowledged to be partly mine — do you intend to give it to me?'

'No, and I haven't acknowledged it as partly yours.'

Hugh nodded again. 'Do you have the effrontery to suggest that this hocus-pocus is more important than the Christian Crusade?'

Jean, leaning back in the chair, looked up at him coldly. 'Last night we went to your revival meeting. We listened to you. Do you know why?'

'Of course I don't know why. Unless —'

'No. We weren't planning to throw ourselves before the altar. We suspected that this matter would come up; we wanted to hear you with our own ears. We heard you.'

Hugh looked from Jean to Don, back to Jean. 'Well?'

'I'll speak with complete frankness,' said Jean.

'Of course,' said Hugh stiffly.

'There's no point beating around the bush. I think you're a fascist. You call yourself a preacher; you preach hate. You cloak your hatred in sanctimony, you bring out the worst in humanity. You asked people to come up and grovel, abase themselves for their sins — imaginary or otherwise. If there is a Creator, I'm sure you don't speak for him.'

Hugh said ponderously, 'That is not the truth. I preach the Lord's word.'

'Whatever you call it, you sickened me. I won't let you go hungry, but I'll never give a cent to your Christian Crusade.'

'Very well,' said Hugh. 'But what about the wishes of our father? He instructed us to divide the estate fairly between us.' He held up his great hand. 'I know what you're going to say. But surely you had secret information. You did not deal fairly with me.'

'I gave you every bit of information we had,' Jean said indignantly.

'You couldn't expect me to believe that story — about the medium,' bleated Hugh.

'We took our chances. You refused to take yours. As far as I'm concerned the subject is closed.'

Hugh danced back, stood with his fist in the air. 'Very well! I warn you that I intend to fight you and your blasphemous program in every possible way. The money came from the minerals God put into the earth; you should not use it to derogate the Word of God!'

'Why not let God do his own worrying?' Jean wearily asked. 'He can stop it anytime he wants . . . with a thunderbolt.'

'I am moving out of this sacrilegious place,' cried Hugh. 'I don't want your money. It stinks of the Devil!' He backed away. His voice boomed and rasped. 'You will know punishment, you will know death and the awful agony of the hereafter!'

'Please go, Hugh.'

Hugh departed. 'He's a madman' said Jean. 'Or — is he?'

Don was pulling Hugh placards off the wall. 'Filthy things
. . . I don't know.'

Jean put her arms around him. 'Don — I'm afraid of
Hugh.'

'Afraid? Physically afraid?'

'Yes . . . He doesn't care what he does.'

'I'm not so sure,' said Don lightly. 'I think he rather enjoys
these dramatic scenes . . . But — I hope we don't see too
much of Hugh. He's very wearing.'

7

At five o'clock in the evening the telephone rang. Jean
answered, turned to Don. 'It's a reporter from the Los
Angeles *Times*.'

'Let's talk to them. Publicity can't hurt us, and might do
us some good.'

Jean turned back to the phone and twenty minutes later
the reporter appeared at the front door. She gave her name
as Vivian Hallsey — a young woman of twenty-five, not quite
plump, with a round freckled face, alert eyes, a button nose
and dark red hair, tightly curled. She stood in the doorway,
looked from Don to Jean, smiled. 'You certainly don't look
as I expected you to look.'

'What did you expect?' asked Don. Vivian Hallsey shook
her head. 'Anything other than normality.'

Jean laughed. 'Why shouldn't we look normal?'

'I'm prejudiced,' said Vivian Hallsey. 'I understand that
you were led to drill this oil well by communication with the
spirit world. I've always thought that only neurotic old
women patronized mediums and fortune tellers.'

'Be that as it may,' said Don. 'Will you sit down?'

'Thanks. How *did* you find where to drill for oil? If it's
through a spirit, which spirit? Because I'd like an oil well
myself.'

Don explained the circumstances which led to the tapping of Marsile Dome.

Vivian Hallsey looked around the room and shivered. 'It makes me feel strange.'

'What makes you feel strange?'

'The idea of spirits — everywhere. The spirits of the dead. Watching you. We're never alone. It's as if we all lived in glass cages . . . It's embarrassing!'

'Not so fast,' said Don. 'We still can't be sure.'

'Sure of what?'

'That spirits exist. It's a pat answer.'

' "Pat answer"!' She looked at him incredulously. 'You tell me this? You're the one who just brought in an oil well, with the help of spirits.'

'I know,' said Don. 'That's the supposition. But it's possible there are other explanations.'

Vivian Hallsey clutched her head in exasperation. 'Exactly what *do* you think?'

'I don't know. We're going to spend the next few years finding out. Maybe the rest of our lives.'

'I never believed in life after death before. You convince me, and then the next minute you try to un-convince me.'

Don laughed. 'Sorry. But it just might not have been life after death.'

'I don't see how you can say that!'

'Ivalee Trembath might be highly telepathic. Without conscious effort on her part she might have been reading our minds — telling us things we wanted to believe.'

Vivian Hallsey was silent a moment. 'It all seems so fantastic . . . Isn't it more likely the other way?'

'I don't know. I'd like to know. If there is another world — it exists. That's just logic. If this other world exists, it exists *somewhere*! That's important. "The Land of Nod" for instance — a figure of speech, meaning sleep. It exists — nowhere. Perhaps the after-life is also a figurative expression — something like the "Land of Nod." But if it *does* exist, I want to learn the truth. I have a right to know. Humanity has a right to know.'

Vivian Hallsey looked doubtful. 'Human beings derive a great deal of comfort from the hope of an after-life. Isn't it cruel to take that hope away from them?'

'Possibly,' said Don. 'New knowledge always comes as an uncomfortable shock to many people. And of course it's perfectly possible we might prove the reality of an after-life.'

'You use the word "proof",' said Vivian Hallsey. 'Just how do you go about getting this proof?'

'The same way scientists try to get proof for any other matter in doubt.'

'But how do you start?'

'First with a little deep thought. The problem is how to get evidence — scientific evidence — and parapsychology is a hard field to get definite evidence in.'

'Why is that?'

'First, because the subject matter is so far out of reach. Second, good mediums are awfully scarce. Ivalee Trembath is one in a million. There probably aren't twenty people in the United States as sensitive as she is. Incidentally, please don't use her name, as she isn't a professional medium — just a gifted woman who is interested in the subject. Third, there are thousands of convincing charlatans, and even more thousands of unconvincing ones. Fourth, good mediums are sometimes jealous of their gifts and don't want anyone investigating. Others resent laboratory checks. They think it's a reflection on their integrity.'

'But surely there are mediums who'll cooperate.'

'Oh yes. With money anything is possible. There'll be lots of hard work involved, lots of sweat! If we got about a dozen mediums and held twelve simultaneous seances. . . . ' He paused.

'What would that prove?'

'I don't know. The results might suggest something. We've got to start somewhere.'

'Would these simultaneous seances prove or disprove the after-life?'

'So far as I know,' said Don, 'nothing a medium does or says has completely ruled out the possibility of telepathy, clairvoyance, precognition, telekinesis. These of course are paranormal — but they don't prove survival after death.'

'How about ghosts — and things like that?'

'Ghosts,' said Don. He looked at Jean. They both laughed.

'Why are you laughing?' Vivian Hallsey asked.

'Ghosts are how Jean and I became interested in parapsychology. It happened a long time ago . . . I wonder if the old Freelock place is still haunted. . . . '

'What happened?' asked Vivian Hallsey. 'Darn it, you're getting me interested. If I'm not careful — but never mind me. What happened at the Freelock house?'

Don told her.

'Do you think this ghost and the spirit which told you to drill for oil are the same sort of thing?'

'I don't know. I suppose they have certain qualities in common — assuming that the spirits aren't merely telepathic transferences. Even then there might be a connection. It's another thing we'll be checking. So far I haven't gone into it deeply. Various regions of the world have their unique type of ghosts. Very odd, when you consider it. You'd think a ghost in Siberia would be the same as a ghost in Haiti.'

'Unless, of course, they're all hallucinations.'

Don nodded. 'With that proviso, of course. The degree of evidence for English ghosts, for instance, is stronger than the evidence for Irish fairies. The were-wolf is confined to the Carpathians and Urals. Although there are were-tigers in India, and Southeast Asia, and were-leopards in Africa. Kobolds and trolls live in Scandinavia, duppies and zombies in the West Indies. The Onas of Tierra del Fuego knew a terrible thing called a 'tsanke'. Assuming that these supernatural creatures exist, or at least are seen — isn't this localization suggestive?'

'Of what?'

'You think about it.'

Vivian Hallsey laughed. 'Are you trying to make a new convert?'

'Why not?'

'All right. You've got one. I've got to write a story on all this. One more question: what will you call this research foundation?'

'There's only one name possible,' Don told her. 'The Marsile Foundation for Parapsychological Research.'

8

Eight more wells were sent down to tap Marsile Dome, and owners of adjacent property who had given up options and mineral rights gnashed their teeth in frustration. Representatives of six major oil companies approached Don and Jean Berwick with propositions of varying attraction. After six weeks of study and legal consultation, Don and Jean sold out to Seahawk Oil on a cash-royalty-stock transfer arrangement, and at last were able to devote their time to Marsile Foundation for Parapsychological Research.

But there were still other delays. The mechanics of organizing the Foundation were more complicated than Don and Jean had anticipated. To qualify for tax-exemption benefits, the Foundation was incorporated as a non-profit research institution, capitalized at a million dollars. 'At last,' sighed Jean. 'We can get started. But how? We still haven't decided on a thing. Not even on where to establish ourselves.'

'No,' said Don, thoughtfully. 'An institution with such an imposing name deserves an equally imposing headquarters — something concrete and glass, spread out over an acre — but how we'd use it at the present time — I haven't the slightest idea. . . . We'd better try to organize a staff, work out a systematic program, and then we'll know better what kind of facilities we'll need.' He picked up a letter from the table. 'We should get some help here. This is from the American Society for Psychic Research. They're interested in co-ordinating programs. One of their associates is coming out to see us.'

'That would be fine,' said Jean. 'Except that we don't

know their program. We don't even know our own.'

'But now we get down to business.' Don took a notebook and pen, then looked up as the doorbell rang. He jumped to his feet, opened the door.

'Hello,' said Vivian Hallsey. 'I was in Orange City and thought I'd drop by to see you.'

'Professionally or socially?' asked Don. 'Come on in, in either case.'

'It's a social visit,' said Vivian Hallsey. 'Of course, if you've done anything spectacular, like finding an Abominable Snowman or making contact with Lost Atlantis, I'd find it hard to restrain myself.'

'We're just shifting into high gear,' said Jean. 'Have some coffee?'

'Thanks. Sure I'm not bothering?'

'Of course not. We liked your story; you didn't make us out to be typical Southern California crack-pots. We're just now trying to organize a sensible program for ourselves.'

'Go right ahead. I'm interested. In fact, that's why I'm here.'

'Well, our first problem is deciding where to begin. There's plenty of literature, thousands of case-histories, bushels of more or less valid research — but we want to start where the others leave off. In other words, we're not planning to duplicate Dr. Rhine's experiments, and we don't want to make Borley Rectory-type studies. The field is enormous — ' The telephone rang, Jean answered.

'It's Dr. James Cogswell, from the American Society of Psychical Research. He wants to call on us.'

'Fine. Where's he phoning from?'

'He's in Orange City.' She spoke into the telephone, hung up. 'He'll be right out.'

Vivian Hallsey started to rise; Jean said, 'No, no, don't go. We like company.'

Five minutes later Dr. James Cogswell presented himself. He was sixty years old, a neuro-surgeon: short, plump, with coal-black hair, combed in precise dark streaks across his balding scalp. He wore elegant clothes; his manners were highly civilized. Don thought of him as representing the old-fashioned school of psychic research, a man who might have been colleague to Sir Oliver Lodge or William McDougall. Dr. Cogswell looked about with interest and a faintly patronizing air, which at first irritated, then amused Don. It was, after all, the natural condescension of a veteran for a group of enthusiastic, and undoubtedly naive, beginners.

'I understand that you plan to conduct a large-scale attack on some of our mutual problems,' said Cogswell.'

'That's our purpose.'

Cogswell nodded. 'Excellent. It's exactly what's needed — a well organized, well-financed — I understand that you're well-financed?' He looked searchingly at Don.

'Adequately so,' said Don. 'At least for all present possibilities and contingencies.'

'Good. We need a central agency, a permanent full-time trained staff working at a definite program. My own organization is loose and undisciplined; we're on our own so far as investigations are concerned. However we do have access to a large library, and perhaps I can save you some duplication of effort.' He looked around the room. 'Is this your headquarters?'

'Temporarily. Until we know what we need — which depends on our program.'

'And what is your program, may I ask?'

'We were just hacking it out when you arrived.'

'Am I interrupting you?'

'By no means. You can help us.'

'Fine. Go right ahead.'

'I was explaining to Miss Hallsey that we have no intent of duplicating either Rhine's work or repeating any of the classic studies.'

'Good. I approve heartily.'

'What we want to do is attack the basis, the lowest common denominator, of all parapsychological phenomena. The simplest, or most common, effect of course is telepathy. It's part of our everyday lives, although probably none of us are aware how much or how little we use it. Telepathy exists, it links minds. How? Action at a distance without a link — of some kind — is impossible.'

Dr. Cogswell shrugged. ' "Impossible" is a big word.'

'Not too big. Don't forget, Doctor, we're operating as scientists, not mystics. Axiom One: action at a distance is unthinkable. Axiom Two: an effect has a cause.' He raised his hand to quell Dr. Cogswell's objection. 'I'm familiar with the Uncertainty Principle. But doesn't it describe the limits of our investigative abilities, rather than the events themselves? We can't determine both the position and velocity of an electron simultaneously — but this does not presuppose that the two qualities are non-existent. So far as we know there is nothing to differentiate a stable radium atom from one which is about to disintegrate. To the best of our present knowledge the process occurs at random. But obviously, if we were able to compare the two atoms carefully enough, we could decide which was about to disintegrate. The lack is in our abilities, not the radium atoms. If they were exactly alike, exposed to identical conditions, then they must act alike.'

'I fear,' said Dr. Cogswell, a trifle pompously, 'that your analysis is based on human experience. You reason anthropomorphically, so to speak. Consider the increase in weight as an object approached light-speed. Such a concept is completely beyond our experience — yet it exists.'

Don laughed. 'Your analogy doesn't contradict me, Doctor. Remember, I'm not postulating that all events are determined by Newtonian physics. Light-speed physics works by its own determinants, so do sub-molecular reactions, and so do parapsychological events.'

'Very well,' sighed Dr. Cogswell. 'Continue.'

'We consider the varieties of parapsychological events: telepathy, clairvoyance, precognition, retrocognition, telekinesis, spirit action, poltergeists, house-haunting, sympathetic magic. With precognition and retrocognition, a sort of time-travel occurs. This aside, the phenomena all involve or occur in some sort of medium definitely beyond the sensitivity of our instruments. For the sake of the discussion, we'll call it mind-stuff. Super-normal continuum, if you prefer.'

'Mind-stuff suits me,' said Dr. Cogswell.

Don nodded, leaned back in his chair. 'So, it appears that our first objective is this mind-stuff, or continuum. What is it?'

Vivian Hallsey said, 'Heavens, we don't even know what our own matter consists of.'

Don nodded. 'Right. My question was rhetorical. I should have asked, how does it work? How is it related to our own matter?'

'What if there isn't any relationship?' suggested Vivian Hallsey airily.

'There *has* to be some relationship. The two states have too many qualities in common. Time, in the first place. Second, energy. Ectoplasm reflects light, and certain ghosts give off light. Anything which radiates or reflects light must have some sort of relationship with normal matter. Third, the fact that a great deal of parapsychological phenomena is generated inside an undeniably material brain.'

'Very well,' said Dr. Cogswell. 'So much is clear. Objective — mind-stuff. And how do you propose to proceed?'

Don smiled. 'If I wanted to learn something about Timbuctoo, how would I do it?'

'Go there.'

'And if I couldn't go there myself?'

'Talk to someone who's been there.'

Don nodded. 'Exactly. To this end I'd like to locate a dozen effective mediums of proved integrity, who don't object to scientific checks and corroboratory measures.'

'Ah,' said Dr. Cogswell sadly, 'wouldn't we all? There may not be that many in the whole United States.'

'After you get the mediums, after you contact the spirits — what do you ask them?' inquired Vivian Hallsey. 'And after they tell you, how do you check?'

Don said sadly, 'That's our first problem. And it's a hard

one. Don't forget, we still aren't at all sure that spirits exist. There's a strong possibility that the mediums are highly, if unconsciously, telepathic. We've got to rule out that possibility first. We want to determine whether a departed spirit can give first, information unknown to any human mind, living or dead; and second, information predicting an event in the future whose existence has been determined by pure chance, or at least by no human intervention, such as the fall of a meteor, a volcanic explosion, a sunspot.'

'Or two or three daily doubles at Santa Anita,' said Vivian Hallsey. 'That's what I need.'

Dr. Cogswell ignored her, rather pointedly. 'Those are the classic problems certainly,' he agreed. 'Personally, I know of no experiment to prove beyond dispute the existence of spirit control. There is always some combination of telepathy, clairvoyance, precognition or retrocognition to explain any apparently inexplicable knowledge.'

'I'd even be satisfied to learn the mechanisms behind telepathy, as a starter,' said Don.

'How about ghosts?' asked Vivian Hallsey. 'If you could authenticate ghosts, you'd prove the existence of spirits.'

'Not necessarily,' said Cogswell. 'Ghosts are probably the imprint of emotion on the supernormal continuum — about as alive as 3D movies.'

'But aren't there cases of ghosts acting with intelligence? Of responding differently to different circumstances?'

Cogswell shrugged. 'Perhaps. I can't think of any authenticated cases offhand. The Clactonwall Deacon, perhaps. Or the Wailing Lady of Gray Water.'

'Poltergeists,' suggested Jean.

'Yes. Poltergeists, of course.'

'There's one sure way to find out the truth,' said Don.

'Die,' said Cogswell.

'I think I'll be going,' said Vivian, 'before I get elected guinea-pig.'

'Perhaps I should have said two ways. The second is to go there — and return.'

Cogswell started to speak, then paused. Then: 'You mean, counterfeit death?'

'Something of the sort. Isn't it possible to die and be revived?'

Cogswell shrugged. 'There have been rather unusual rumors out of Russia . . . And some remarkable work being done at the local universities with low temperatures. The body can't take organic damage, of course. If large ice-crystals rupture the cells — finish. Then there's the matter of keeping the brain oxygenated. Ten minutes without oxygen — a man can never regain his sanity or reverse the massive brain damage. It's not an easy situation.'

'In the case of low-temperature catalepsy, is oxygenation so important?'

'No, not nearly . . . In fact — well, I'll admit it. I'm involved in some of these experiments myself. We've frozen a dog stiff, and revived him after twenty-two minutes.'

Vivian laughed. 'Now all you need is someone to be Bill the Lizard!'

Dr. Cogswell raised his eyebrows. 'Bill the Lizard?'

'A character in *Alice in Wonderland*. He was persuaded to perform some investigations with disastrous results.'

'These experiments are only the first phase, of course,' said Don. 'If the other world exists, perhaps we can set up channels of communication. Possibly even material transfer.'

Dr. Cogswell shook his head in respectful, if somewhat dubious, admiration. 'You have remarkable ideas, Mr. Berwick.'

'It's a remarkable world we live in,' said Don. 'Consider the sciences: astronomy, bacteriology, physics. Think how fantastic the contemporary scene would seem to the early researchers! And the older ideas of witchcraft and sorcery — how vastly more marvellous is our new knowledge! Our lives change every week — never the changes we expect. This work we're dabbling in now — it's the foundation of a new body of knowledge as important as all the rest together. The men of the future — they'll use the word "spiritualist" as

we say "alchemist", "astrologer." What we'll accomplish
— ' he shrugged. 'Who knows? We'll be lucky if we stumble
on a few of the right tools. Still — someone has to start.
Astonishing that humanity has waited this long.'

'Not astonishing, really,' said Vivian. 'The after-life, the
paranormal — they're part of all the superstitions, the
religions, and therefore taboo.'

'They still are,' said Dr. Cogswell. 'I care nothing for any
taboos, except those of the American Medical Association.
And there I've got to be careful.' He rose to his feet. 'Now
I must go. If I can be of any help, let me know.'

'You can put us in touch with a dozen effective mediums.'

Cogswell shook his head doubtfully. 'They're scarce as
hen's teeth. . . . Exactly how do you plan to proceed with
a dozen mediums? What do you hope to prove?'

'Mainly, I just want to see what'll happen. We'll try
simultaneous seances — the mediums separate, then the
mediums together. We'll try to send messages from medium
to medium through their spirit controls. We'll try for exact
knowledge of the physical nature of this after-life region.'

Dr. Cogswell shrugged. 'It sounds interesting and very
ambitious, but there are also difficulties. For instance, you'd
need optimum performances from all twelve mediums at the
same time — which in such an atmosphere would be
extremely lucky.'

'All we can do is try,' said Don. 'We'll never know
otherwise. Maybe this shot-gun technique will open up the
problem.'

Cogswell rubbed his chin. 'When do you propose to
begin?'

'As soon as possible. We'll call it — Exercise One.'

9

The day for Exercise One approached, arrived. At three
o'clock the participants began to arrive at 26 Madrone Place,
a large old house on the outskirts of Orange City, rented

for the occasion. First came members of the Psychical Research Society, observers from the psychology departments of local universities, Vivian Hallsey, with a somber-appearing man in a dark suit. She introduced him somewhat mysteriously to Don and Jean as Mr. Kelso. Don hesitated, then said, 'Are you a journalist, Mr. Kelso?'

'Of a sort, yes.'

'Our policy here is freedom of the press — in general. We see no reason why the public shouldn't be informed of any progress we make. But I do object to sensationalization, because it impedes us. It's difficult to persuade sensitive people to undertake these experiments. If they become notorious or the subject of ridicule, it's impossible.'

'I quite understand,' said Mr. Kelso. 'However I'm here today unofficially, an observer, a friend of Miss Hallsey's.

'Then you're very welcome.'

At five o'clock the mediums began to arrive, and were taken at once to separate rooms. The floors were bare; in each was a small wooden table, a couch and armchairs for the medium and the observers. Inconspicuous in each room was a microphone, the leads of which ran to a central bank of speakers and tape-recorders in the old living room, now known as the control room. Don had considered installing closed-circuit TV within each room, connected to a screen in the control room, but could think of no advantage to the scheme, and had abandoned it.

Of fourteen mediums approached, only eight had agreed to participate in the experiments. In general they seemed to be persons of average intelligence and education, ranging in age from Grandma Hogart, sixty-two, to her grandson Myron Hogart, eighteen. Myron showed a timorous excitement; Grandma Hogart's comments were caustic and skeptical; Alec Dillon held himself aloof — a pallid thin-featured man, austere and taciturn; Ivalee Trembath maintained her crystalline serenity. They showed little interest in each other — all except Grandma Hogart, who labelled the others frauds. To prevent friction and any possible collusion, conscious or unconscious, Don arranged that each medium be kept isolated from every other.

At seven o'clock the exercise was scheduled to begin; but Alec Dillon, unmarried, middle-aged, and temperamental, developed nervous attenuation and asked for time to gain composure. The delay irritated the others; there was grumbling. The exercise threatened to collapse even before it started. Jean and Dr. Cogswell scurried from room to room, apologizing, soothing, easing the tension.

Don sat in the control room tapping his fingers nervously, watching the signal panel, where seven lights signalled 'Ready.' Vivian Hallsey and Kelso sat quietly to the side. There was nothing to do but wait. Don turned to Kelso, 'Are you interested in this kind of thing personally or professionally?'

'Both,' said Kelso. 'It's frequently crossed my mind that telepathy, clairvoyance, etcetera, would confer a significant military advantage on the nation which systematized them.'

Don reflected. 'I suppose so. I hadn't considered that aspect of the situation. You're not a government official?'

Kelso shook his head. 'I work for *Life*. We recently ran a picture-essay on haunted houses. Did you see it?'

Don nodded. 'Beautiful pictures.'

Minutes passed. At seven twenty-five Alec Dillon sank with a sigh into his arm-chair, ready to summon his control; Sir Gervase Desmond. In the control room all eight lights glowed. Don hunched forward, eight intercom speakers in front of him; also eight microphones connected to light-weight headphones on the operators. By this means Don could give signals and instructions without disturbing the mediums.

Don spoke into a master microphone which took his voice to all the eight rooms. 'We're all ready. Remember, there's no pressure on any of us. This is for fun. We're not trying to prove anything; we're not trying to check on anyone — so everybody relax.'

From Room 2 came a resentful mutter; this would be Alec Dillon, who had a poet's aversion to exactitude and scientific method. If there were four firm contacts, thought Don, he'd consider Exercise One a success. Under conditions at 26 Madrone Place even four contacts would be remarkable. 'Let's go.'

He switched on the tape-recorders, leaned back in his chair, and prepared for a wait.

From Room 4, Grandma Hogart's room, came the sound of the Lord's Prayer; in Room 7 someone was humming a hymn; from other speakers came snatches of uneasy conversation, jokes, complaints.

Don waited. Jean came into the room, sat beside him.

'There won't be anything for five or ten minutes,' Don told Vivian and Kelso. 'They have to get in the mood to begin with.'

'Any chance of materializations, ectoplasm, things like that?' asked Kelso. 'I've got a Canon loaded with Tri-X that'll take stop-action of black cats fighting in a dark cellar.'

Don shrugged. 'Never can tell. Have it ready, if you like. None of these mediums, so far as I know, have ever materialized anything. An honest materialization is rare.'

'Can a spirit materialize without the help of a medium?'

'If you wait long enough,' Vivian told Kelso, 'you'll have all the answers on your own.'

Kelso laughed grimly, 'But I won't be able to sell the pictures. I might not even be able to have them developed . . . What about it, Don? Do these spirits ever materialize on their own?'

Don grinned. 'I've never been a spirit; I couldn't tell you. . . . So far as I'm aware — no.'

'But ghosts — they seem to come and go as they please. And poltergeists.'

'Ah,' said Don. 'A different matter. I'm referring to the class of spirits which communicate through mediums. Ghosts and poltergeists are two other classes. Three distinct classes in all — at least three classes.'

Kelso looked puzzled. 'Isn't that rather confusing? How do you know there are three classes?'

'They behave differently. The spirits — I'll use the word

to describe influences operating through mediums — the spirits act and think more or less as we'd expect the spirit of a human being to act. Ghosts seem to be mindless affairs, imprints of a great emotional disturbance on the parapsychological matrix, which reveal themselves under certain conditions — what these conditions are, no one knows. Poltergeists — "noisy ghosts" to translate literally — are invisible and mischievous. They occur principally in houses where adolescent children live — and it's possible that they're no more than an unconscious telekinetic process of the adolescent mind. That's just a theory — no more. Poltergeists don't seem to fit anywhere else into the picture.'

'Listen,' said Jean. A voice came from Room 3: the clear voice of Ivalee Trembath's Molly Toogood.

'Hello.'

'Hello,' said the voice of the Room 3 observer, a divinity student named Tom Ward. 'How are you tonight?'

'Very well. I don't think I know you.'

'No, we've never met.'

Jean signaled to Don; young Myron Hogart's wire, the line from Room 8 was coming alive; his control was rapping on the table. Almost at the same time a whistle came from Grandma Hogart in Room 4.

'Hello, sassy,' said Grandma Hogart. 'You're looking pert tonight — all cute in your little pink dress.'

'Yes, ma'am,' said the piping voice of a little girl. 'I'm all fixed up because I'm glad to see you.'

'This nice young man is Dr. Cogswell,' said Grandma Hogart.

'How-de-do,' said the control. 'My name's Pearl; I'm a little black girl; I was born in Memphis, Tennessee.'

The other speakers all began to sound; there was suddenly too much to listen to.

Jean said, in a hushed voice of astonishment, 'They've all made contact — every one of them!'

Two or three minutes passed. Chatter, gossip, greetings, small-talk came from the intercom speakers.

Don spoke into the subsidiary mikes, those which took

his voice to the operator's ear-buttons. 'Now — first question.'

They listened to Room 3, as Tom Ward, the divinity student, put the first of the rehearsed questions to Molly.

'What does it look like where you are now?'

The various responses came in over the speakers and were recorded on the tapes.

'Second question,' said Don.

In every room except No. 3 the question was asked, *'Do you know Molly Toogood? Can you see her now?'*

The answers came in slowly, dubiously, and were duly recorded.

As a second part of the same question, in all rooms except No. 2, the observer asked, *'Do you know Sir Gervase Desmond?'*

This was Alec Dillon's control; while the responses came in from seven rooms, Sir Gervase, a Regency Buck, criticized Alec in a nasal supercilious drawl. Alec, not completely in trance, defended himself, and they quarrelled until the amused observer intervened.

Listening to the quarrel, Don thought that the two voices of Alec and Sir Gervase mingled and spoke together; the tape recorder would corroborate his impressions. An interesting situation: two voices coming simultaneously from the same throat, the same larynx! Of course the diaphragm of any loudspeaker performed the same feat with no difficulty. But the vocal chords, the glottal passages, tongue, teeth and lips constituted a sound-producing mechanism rather more complicated than a diaphragm . . . Don shelved the line of thought; it had become too involved, and there was too much happening. He must guard against a marveling frame of mind, he told himself. Everything that he was seeing and hearing, everything in this universe and every other, had some kind of logic — some system of laws, some cycle of cause and effect. It might be far removed from classical physics and ordinary human experience — but the laws must be there, available for human brains to codify.

In the eight rooms the talk was becoming desultory.

'Third question,' said Don.

In each of the eight rooms the observer asked: *'What does our world look like to you?'* And after the answers were recorded, *'What does your medium look like?'* For the words 'your medium' the observer substituted the name of the medium.

The fourth question: *'Is ex-President Franklin D. Roosevelt present? Can you contact him at the present moment? What does he think of the present administration?'*

The fifth question: *'Is Adolf Hitler present? Is he being punished for his crimes on Earth?'*

The sixth question: *'Have you ever seen Jesus Christ? Mohammed? Buddha? Mahatma Gandhi? Have you ever seen Joseph Stalin?'*

Then the seventh question: *'In the year 3244 B.C. an Egyptian scribe by the name of Mahnekhe died in Thebes. Is it possible to communicate with him? Is he present now?'*

The eighth question: *'Do you think of yourself as a soul? A disembodied spirit? A person?'*

The ninth question: *How do you know when your medium is ready to make contact? Why do you respond?'*

The tenth question: *'Is there anything on Earth that you feel the need of? Can some living person bring it to you?'*

The eleventh question: *'Do you eat, sleep? What kind of food do you eat? In what kind of shelter do you sleep?'*

Twelfth question: *'Do you have a day and a night? Is it night or day now?'*

Thirteenth question: *'Does this type of questioning bother you? Are you willing to help us learn more about the after-life?'*

10

At 7:25 Exercise One began, with all eight mediums in touch with their controls. The questions were not necessarily asked or answered with consistent precision or timing. In many cases, the control chattered inconsequentialities, mumbled, refused to speak, or was otherwise uncooperative; there was no means by which the operator could enforce order. At Question 10 Sir Gervase Desmond, in a huff, left Alec Dillon, who fell into a deep sleep. At Question 11 Grandma Hogart's vitality waned, and her voice faded; little Pearl respectfully said farewell. After Question 10 only Ivalee Trembath, young Myron Hogart, Mrs. Kerr (a placid fat woman), and Mr. Bose (a thin Negro mail-carrier), still maintained contact with the other world. These four showed no signs of fatigue until after Question 13 and the end of Exercise One. The time was 9:45.

Room	Medium	Control	Identity	Apparent date of birth
1	Kenward Bose	Kochamba	Senegal Chieftain brought to New Orleans as slave	1830
2	Alec Dillon	Sir Gervase	English Nobleman	1790
3	Ivalee Trembath	Molly Toogood	Early California settler	1845
4	Grandma Hogart	Pearl	Little Negro girl	1925
5	Mrs. Kerr	Marie Kozard	Parisian demi-mondaine	1900
6	Mrs. Vascelles	Lula	?	?
7	Joanne Howe	Dr. Gordon Hazlewood	Massachusetts physician	1900
8	Myron Hogart	Lew Wetzel	Fiction character (?)	?

Grandma Hogart, Alec Dillon were asleep, to be joined at once by Mrs. Kerr; most of the others were relaxing with tea, coffee, beer or highballs.

Don and Dr. Cogswell stepped into each room, thanked the participants; Jean paid Mrs. Kerr, Grandma Hogart and Mrs. Vascelles their professional fees. Only Myron Hogart seemed interested in the results of the exercise; to the others it had been merely another seance.

By eleven o'clock the house was clear. Don, Jean, Vivian Hallsey, Kelso, Dr. Cogswell and Godfrey Head, a professor of mathematics at UCLA gathered in the library. The mood was convivial; the mass seance had come off with a success beyond the hopes of anyone.

'Don!' cried Dr. Cogswell. 'We've got to play back those tapes and do some computing.'

'If you like,' said Don. 'We can work up Question One tonight.'

The tape recorders were arranged in a row; the response to Question 1 was played back for each room in turn, and a list made of significant elements.

Question 1: *What does it look like where you are now?*

1. *Kochamba:* 'White plains' — 'golden ramparts, the host of the Lord' — 'shining in the pearly light of our Lord' — 'the golden towers, the lawns and flower gardens like the most wonderful park in the world, with statues of the angels, and everywhere the great glory of Kingdom Come.' — 'Off in the distance there's the lower-class places, but you can't see 'em so good, and not too far away there's Hell.' — 'No, Hell ain't down below — at least not too far down.'

2. *Sir Gervase Desmond:* 'Why naturally, it's the finest of places; would I be here otherwise? Everyone wears elegant clothes; the gentlemen and their ladies, I mean. It's like a great race course. No horses, of course, and nobody runs a book, more's the pity. But lovely, lovely, and all melting away into gold, and all the silver and pearly water; jewels for the taking, by Jove! Far too good for you, Dillon.'

3. *Molly Toogood:* 'Seems like it's all they're interested in nowadays. I told 'em once, but I'll tell 'em again: it's like your Earth, only much prettier. Of course we can see the old land anytime we want to look.'

4. *Pearl:* 'Now, Grandma, I don't know as I can describe

something like this, because it's too superior and wonderful for words. But we're all up here, all waiting for you; all the great men and women, all doing what they like to do. It's really pretty, all gold and green and off in the distance there's the great Light of God, and his wonderful city.'

5. *Marie Kozard:* (no reply)

6. *Lula:* 'Lovely, dear — I know you'd enjoy it. There's all the people, all walking around in balls of light, and the greater the man or woman, the brighter the light. And the gorgeous palaces, and sunrises and sunsets, like great peacock tails everywhere around the sky.' (In response to question: what costume do the great men wear?) 'Just the clothes they always wore. There's Napoleon in his cocked hat and white breeches, and there's George Washington — he's got powdered hair; he looks just like the pictures.'

7. *Dr. Gordon Hazelwood:* (no comprehensible reply)

8. *Lew Wetzel:* 'It's hard to say, because it's hazy-like. Everywhere you look, all the palaces and big buildings — they melt off into the haze. When I first came here it was different — there wasn't any of those big skyscrapers; it was more Frenchy-like. Now there's all these big streamlined steel and glass things.'

The first question was tabulated; the time was two o'clock. Don sighed, opened a can of beer. 'Let's see. What do we have?'

Godfrey Head looked down the list. 'The consensus seems to be that the after-world is a bright beautiful land full of palaces and golden castles, with people walking around in fancy clothes.'

'There's quite some talk of haze,' said Dr. Cogswell. 'Horizons melting away — and here: Lula says the skies are like peacock tails.'

'Why can't spirits take photographs?' asked Kelso, in

deep pain. 'Think of it: big picture-essay on the after-life. Think we'd sell that issue?'

'Another thing about Lula,' said Don. 'Notice how the people "walk around in balls of light," but the great men are the brightest.'

'Great men seem very much in evidence,' mused Jean. 'Still, it's really rather strange the different ways they see the after-life. There they are, all together in the same place — at least, so we assume — and each gives us a description similar, but just a trifle different, from the others. It doesn't make a lot of sense.'

'Well,' said Godfrey Head, 'we don't want to take everything literally; we've got to make allowances, to consider the subconscious bias of the medium, reconcile the various points of view, take the lowest common denominator, so to speak.'

Don drummed his fingers on his beer-can. 'I'm not sure that I agree — completely. I don't think it's good practice to select only the consistent statements. If we ignore whatever seems unreasonable, we're not learning anything, we're merely building our own picture of the hereafter — not the one which these controls have given us.'

'What about Wetzel's "skyscraper" — "streamlined shapes"? Incidentally, who was Lew Wetzel? The name's familiar.'

'A character in a novel. *The Deerslayer*, by James Fenimore Cooper, I believe.'

Head leaned back in his seat. 'Now this really demands consideration. How can a character in a novel have a spirit? . . . It hardly seems credible!' He looked at Dr. Cogswell. 'Are you convinced of this fellow's reliability? Do you trust him?'

'Perfectly.'

'Perhaps under the strain — the feeling of competition . . . .'

'No,' said Dr. Cogswell. 'I've heard Wetzel talk half a dozen times.'

'He's really the character from the novel?'

'That's right. I asked him about it. He says whatever or whoever he is he's there, and he can't account for himself any other way.'

'Of course,' said Jean, 'his character might have been taken from life.'

'Yes, that's possible. In fact, highly probable.'

'But what about these skyscrapers?' cried Head. 'Certainly we've got to exercise some selection!'

'We've got to be very careful,' Don insisted. 'We simply can't throw out items because they're inconsistent, or don't agree with *a priori* assumptions and theories.'

'But these people can't all be right!' protested Head. 'We've got to decide on a reasonable consensus — that's our function, after all!'

'They might be speaking from different parts of this after-world. To me Wetzel's comment about the skyscrapers is highly significant. It might mean that the after-world changes as our own world changes.'

'Or reflects this one,' said Jean.

'Or that the after-world and the control is nothing but the medium's subconscious fabrication,' grumbled Head.

Don nodded. 'That's certainly our big headache. The next question was designed to shed a little light.'

Jean read the question: ' "Do you know Molly Toogood? Do you know Sir Gervase Desmond?" '

'We'd still face uncertainties,' Don observed, 'even if Molly and Sir Gervase were described with great consistency — because we still reasonably might hypothesize telepathic communication between the mediums. It's not out of the realm of possibilities.'

'Certainly not an unreasonable explanation,' said Godfrey Head.

'As I recall,' said Don, 'the question gave us very little information; no one seems definitely to know anyone else.' He looked at his watch. 'It's late . . . Shall we call it a night?'

Head and Cogswell agreed. They rose to their feet. 'Incidentally,' said Head, 'have any of you been over to hear the Fighting Preacher at the Orange City Auditorium?'

'Not I,' said Cogswell. 'What about him?'

'Dill, from our Political Science department, took me to hear him. Dill is alarmed. He says this Hugh Bronny is an alarming phenomenon, a nascent Hitler. He's got a force, a gift of the gab, no question about it. But I only mention him because he's attacking "devil-inspired scientists who're fooling around with God's business!" He says that they're trying to produce life in test-tubes and also trying to sneak sinners into Heaven. He says places like the Parapsychological Foundation ought to be stopped — by force, if necessary. He really means business.'

Jean sat rather limp. 'He mentioned us — by name?'

'Oh, yes. In fact, he singled out the Parapsychological Foundation.'

'Anything to constitute slander?' asked Don lightly.

'He called you a Godless scientist, in league with the Devil. If you can show that he acted in malice and that your reputation is injured — you can sue.'

'First,' said Don ruefully, 'I'd probably have to prove I *wasn't* in league with the Devil.'

'Maybe we can take our stable of mediums to court,' suggested Dr. Cogswell, 'and materialize the Devil for a witness.'

'There'd be difficulties swearing him in,' Don remarked.

'That does it,' said Head. 'Good night all.'

Kelso, Vivian Hallsey, and Dr. Cogswell took their leave a few minutes later. Don and Jean were alone.

Don turned to Jean, took her hands. 'Tired?'

'Yes. But not so tired that — ' she stopped short, staring across his shoulder. Don turned. 'What's the trouble?'

'There's someone outside — at the window.'

Don ran to the door, opened it, went out on the porch. Jean came out behind him.

Don asked, 'Did you see his face?'

'Yes . . . I thought it was — 'she could not speak his name.

'Hugh?'

She pressed against his arm. 'I'm afraid of him, Donald. . .'

Don raised his voice a little. 'Hugh! Why don't you come

out, Hugh? Wherever you're hiding . . . . '

A tall shape materialized. Hugh stepped out onto the gravel path. The street-light shone yellow in his great angular face; shadows filled his eye-sockets and the pockets under his cheekbones.

Jean said in a sharp voice, 'Why don't you ring the doorbell, Hugh? Why do you look through the window?'

'You know why,' said Hugh. 'I came to see with my own eyes what goes on at this house.'

'See anything worthwhile?' Don asked.

'I saw evil men and women leaving this place.'

Don said in a voice that was dry and edged, 'I hear you've been including us in your invective.'

'I've been preaching the Holy Lord God's word as I understand it.'

Don studied him a moment, his mouth set in a disdainful smile. 'You may be a power-mad hypocrite, Hugh — or you may just be a plain fool. One thing you're certainly not — that's a Christian!'

Hugh stared back, his eyes like kettles of hot blue glass. He said in a heavy voice, 'I'm a Christian minister. I walk four-square down the Holy Path. And no sneering atheist like yourself can turn me aside.'

Don shrugged, turned to go inside.

'Wait!' commanded Hugh hoarsely.

'What for?'

'You spoke ill of me just now. You reviled me. You denied my Christianity — '

'Christ taught kindness, the brotherhood of man. You're no Christian. You're a demagogue. A rabble-rouser. A hate merchant and a fool besides. You're worse than any atheist.'

Now Hugh grinned, a painful uncomfortable grimace that showed long yellow teeth. 'You'll be sorry,' he said simply. Then he turned on his heel, his feet crunched down the gravel path.

Don looked back at Jean. 'Let's go home.'

11

Instead of driving home Don and Jean drove out on the desert, passing Indian Hill. Jean looked up toward the invisible hulk of the Freelock house. Don slowed the car. 'Want to go up and hunt ghosts?' he asked, facetious.

'No thanks,' said Jean decidedly.

'Scared?'

'No, not any more. I'm not afraid of the ghosts: it's the atmosphere which hangs around the house. . . .' She hugged his arm. 'I can't feel unkindly about the place — because that's where I decided to marry you.'

Don laughed. 'You probably thought you were picking a nice normal junior executive.'

'No,' said Jean. 'I knew you were nice and — well, sufficiently normal — but I knew you'd never be the sort of man to settle for security and routine.'

'Didn't you give up hope when the exaggerated report of my death came through from Korea?'

'In a way . . . But somehow I couldn't believe it.'

'That was a tough three years. I think I was half out of my mind the whole time . . . Mmf!'

'What's the trouble?'

'I've forgotten all the Russian and Chinese I learned so diligently. I doubt if I could ask for a drink of water now. . . .'

They turned off on a side-road, drove two miles into the dark desert, parked, got out of the car.

The night was clear and quiet; constellations rode across the sky, the air smelled fresh of sage and creosote bush.

'We should be in bed,' said Don.

'I know.' Jean leaned back against him. 'But I wouldn't be able to sleep . . . Not after tonight.' She looked up into the sky. 'Look, Don: all the stars, and the galaxies beyond — and beyond and beyond. Could the after-life world be as enormous as ours?'

Don shook his head. 'We'll have to ask the question at another mass seance.'

'And where is it, Don? In our minds? All around us? Off in another dimension?'

'All we can do is guess. I don't believe it's inside our minds, or in another set of dimensions. At least no dimensions with any formal or mathematical relationship to our own.'

' "If it exists — it exists somewhere"! — to quote that eminent student of the occult, Professor Donald Berwick.' Smiling, she looked up over her shoulder into his face.

'Right! Where that somewhere is, is the problem. Perhaps we'll have to go there to find out.'

She turned around, faced him. 'Now look here, Mr. Berwick — I don't want you toying with such ideas . . . Such as dying in order to make a personal investigation.'

Don laughed. 'No. I don't want to die for a while.' He kissed her. 'It's too much fun being alive . . . But maybe it might be possible to tiptoe along the borderline — during a period of extreme stupor, or unconsciousness. Even sleep.'

'Donald!' exclaimed Jean. 'Sleep! Dreams! Do you think — '

Don laughed. 'It *would* be amusing, wouldn't it? If every night everybody make little excursions into the after-world? . . . . It's not impossible, not unthinkable. Our dream-world certainly is a world of the mind. It's palpable, sensible — we feel, hear, see, taste. But dream-worlds — ' he thought, laughed. 'I was about to point out that dream-worlds are a function of individual experience, and couldn't possibly be the after-life . . . Then I remembered the results of Question One.'

Jean took his shoulders in her hands, shook him. 'If the after-world *is* the dream-world, I don't want you going.'

'Sure! But we always wake up safe and sound, don't we? But I'm not convinced of this dream-world — after-world equation. The dream-world shifts so rapidly.'

'How do we know that the after-world doesn't behave the same way?'

'We have the answers to Question One. And other reports, in the books of Eddy, Stewart Edward White, Frank Mason.

They — or I should say, the spirits they contacted — describe the after-world as Utopia — more beautiful, more glorious, more happy than our own.'

Jean nodded. 'That accords, more or less, with what we have heard tonight.'

'More or less. There are differences. Peculiar differences.' He took Jean's hand, they walked slowly along the pale ribbon of road. 'These men are honest and intelligent, and they've tried to be objective. Steward Edward White's Betty, Mason's Dr. MacDonald, Eddy's — I've forgotten his name — Reverend something-or-other; they give pictures of the after-world which are similar but not exact. Their hows and whys differ considerably.'

'I suppose we have to make allowances for the medium, the control and even the predisposition of the author.'

Don agreed. 'Another point: consider the curious way in which the afterlife seems to keep pace with contemporary sciences; never ahead, sometimes behind. For instance, Dr. MacDonald, a spirit, is asked to treat the medium Bib Tucker. He prescribes herbs which are unknown at the time. In 1920 when Mason asks him about the nature of electricity, Dr. MacDonald gives a contemporary answer — describes it as a phase of atomic energy. It's inconsistent and unconvincing — if we assume Dr. MacDonald to be a true spirit.'

They stopped. Don picked up a stone, tossed it out into the dark. 'If we think of Dr. MacDonald as a function of the author Mr. Mason, the medium Bib Tucker, and the other members of the particular group — he becomes more credible.'

'You mean that this Dr. MacDonald is an illusion — that Molly Toogood and all the others are illusions?'

'No. I think that they're real enough. Actually, I'm only speculating. But perhaps they've been created, brought into being . . . This may be the way ghosts, apparitions, spooks in general appear. Enough people believe in them — and suddenly they're real.'

Jean maintained a dubious silence. Don slipped his arm

around her waist. 'Don't like it, eh?' They started back toward the car.

'No,' said Jean. 'There's so much that your theory doesn't explain. The acts of free-will — like my father coming to us, telling us to continue drilling.'

Don nodded. 'True. But on the other hand, consider young Myron Hogart's control, Lew Wetzel. So far as we know, he never existed outside of a novel. Think of ghosts — the grotesque ones: the chain-rattlers, the women in shrouds, the luminous monks, carrying their heads in their arms. Isn't it reasonable to suppose that these are the product of minds? It may be possible.'

'Whatever they are,' said Jean, 'I don't really want to see any . . . I must admit, that in spite of my brave words, two-thirds of the time I'm scared . . . I suppose we should be starting back.'

'Cold?'

'A little . . . It's not the air . . . Sometimes the work we're doing frightens me. It's so remote from normal life. And death has such a close connection with it. I don't like death, Don.'

Don kissed her. 'I don't either . . . Let's go home.'

12

Don, Jean, Dr. Cogswell, Kelso, Godfrey Head and Howard Rakowsky, met at 26 Madrone Place at eight o'clock the next evening. Cogswell introduced Rakowsky, a short dark resilient man, active as a fellow member of the Society for Psychic Research from San Francisco. Don inquired as to Rakowsky's personal theories regarding spiritualistic phenomena, as he did of most people interested in the subject.

Rakowsky shrugged. 'I've seen so much I'm confused. Ninety-five percent is fake. But that hard five percent — ' he shook his head. 'I suppose I take it at its face value: communication from the souls of the dead.'

Don nodded. 'I'm a hard-headed Scot. I was skeptical until I had an experience that practically rattled my teeth. Our teeth, I should say. Jean and I saw a beautiful fiery ghost one night. I was startled enough to do some reading. I found lots of honest accounts — but none of them conducted under what a scientist would call test conditions. Our Exercise One the other night, so far as I know, is the first of its kind.'

'You were confounded lucky,' said Rakowsky. 'Good mediums are gold.'

'Not to mention cooperative controls,' said Cogswell.

'We did pretty well,' said Don, 'even though we still proved nothing.'

Kelso blinked. 'Surely you've proved some sort of post-death existence!'

'I'm afraid not,' said Don. 'In fact I'd like to discourage that particular emphasis. The average dabbler in para-psychology, when he strikes a bit of evidence, thinks he's proved that death isn't final; that he's demonstrated life beyond the grave. Being human, he's overjoyed. He doesn't worry about verification, or if he does, he interprets it to corroborate what he wants to believe.'

Rakowsky had raised his black eyebrows. 'You sound as if you yourself have doubts.'

'I don't think it's *proved*,' said Don. 'Not until there are no more alternative, equally consistent, theories.'

'I've heard lots of 'em,' said Rakowsky. 'By and large it's simpler to postulate an after-life. Especially,' he glanced impishly around the room, 'since that's what we all want to believe. Including Mr. Berwick.'

Don nodded. 'Including me.' He turned to the tape recorders. 'I'll give you another theory as soon as we finish tonight's work.' He looked at his list. 'Question Three: "What does our world look like?" '

Berwick turned on recorder No. 1. The voice of the observer asked the question; the rich heavy voice of Kochamba responded, as different from Henry Bose's dry husky tones as honey from vinegar. 'We have left your world behind,' said Kochamba. 'We rejoice up here at the feet of the disciples.' He said no more.'

'Now,' said Don, 'Sir Gervase Desmond, on No. 2.'

'*Your* world?' drawled Sir Gervase in contempt and astonishment. 'Well, I must say I haven't turned back a second glance. I assume it's still there — but I assure you, old fellow, I haven't a farthing's worth of interest. "What do you look like?" There you have me. I've never thought to notice . . . Ugly chap, now that I look. Face like a sick lizard.'

Molly, speaking through Ivalee Trembath, was kindlier. 'Why, just as it's always looked. And Ivalee herself — why, I hear her pretty voice; it comes to me along the vibrations, as they say, and the first thing I know I'm talking with strangers.'

Such was the pattern of response to Question 3.

Don paraphrased Question 4: ' "Is ex-President Franklin D. Roosevelt there? Can you see him, feel him? What does he think of the present administration?" ' He looked around the faces. 'The reason for the question is obvious. We want to find if a number of the controls can contact the same man simultaneously — and if they can, if they bring back identical messages from him.'

'Still proves nothing, one way or the other,' Godfrey Head pointed out. 'Nothing is proven until we can rule out telepathy. Which is hard to do, if not impossible.'

Cogswell laughed. 'If we ever turn up evidence that satisfies you — then we'll know we're on solid ground.'

Head said doggedly, 'We can't pretend to be scientists if we lapse into mysticism.'

'I quite agree,' said Cogswell ponderously.

'No argument on that point,' said Don. 'Well — let's listen to the answer. . . .'

He played the tapes. The responses were confused. Sir Gervase Desmond damned Alec Dillon's eyes for his insolence; other controls mumbled and muttered; Ivalee Trembath's equable Molly said that she saw him once in awhile, off in the distance, wearing a black cloak, usually sitting at a desk or in a chair.

'Is he still crippled?' the observer asked.

'He's a great man,' said Molly. 'Full of power.'

None of the controls reported Roosevelt's opinion of the current administration, nor showed any willingness to inquire.

The remainder of the tapes were played back, the data organized. Sometime after midnight the job was finished. The table was littered with beer-cans, ash-trays were full.

Don wearily took up the compilation, leaned back in his chair. 'In outline here's what we've got. "Is Hitler in the after-world?" Yes. According to two reports he appears as a shape of great solidity. Apparently he's being punished. Kochamba says he's in good old-fashioned Hell. Wetzel says he wanders the outer regions like a lost soul.'

'Contradiction,' muttered Head.

'Unless part of the time he's in Hell, and part of the time he wanders,' Rakowsky pointed out. 'Not impossible.'

Don continued. 'Question Six: religious leaders. Jesus is seen sometimes as a light of great radiance, sometimes as a man of great stature. He's wise, kindly, a great teacher. Mohammed, Buddha are also there, and seen in much the same manner. Gandhi the same. Now for Stalin the arch-atheist. There's two versions of Stalin apparently. One benign — the other evil. The benign shape, according to that little fragmentary sentence of Pearl's, is fading, dwindling; the evil shape is growing more solid. He seems to be enduring punishment, like Hitler.' Don looked around the room. 'I consider this significant. In fact, with the answers to the next question, it corroborates a suspicion that's been growing on me. . . .'

Rakowsky, Cogswell, Head and Kelso looked speculatively at him; Jean smiled faintly.

'Suspicion?'

'I have a theory regarding the after-life which I'll presently explain.'

'Theories are cheap,' said Radowsky.

'There may be a critical experiment to test this one. Well — let's go on. The Egyptian scribe. No one knows him.

No one can produce him — if we discount Lula's vague and rather facetious remarks.

'Eighth question. It arouses amusement in those who gave an answer. "Of course we're persons! Just like you!"'

'Ninth question: "How do you know when the medium is trying to make contact?" It's just like someone calling their name, so say Dr. Gordon Hazelwood, Molly and Pearl. Sir Gervase just knows.'

'Superior S.O.B.'

'Tenth question — they need nothing, want nothing.' Don was scanning the compilation rapidly.

'Eleven. Now they're starting to fold up. We rely on Molly and Wetzel mostly. They say that they rest, sleep; that they have houses. Molly lives in an old ranchhouse, Wetzel lives in a cabin; sometimes he camps in the wilderness. It seems that they live much as they lived in life on Earth. Eating isn't important — not a routine affair — but they seem to eat on occasion. Bodily processes they aren't clear on . . . Pearl giggles. Molly is shocked and offended.

'Twelve. No agreement. Apparently there's both darkness and light. Molly says it's always day. Wetzel says there's day and night. Marie Kozard says the time's always more or less evening.

'Thirteen: "Does investigation annoy you? Is it wrong for you to answer our questions? Do you want to help us learn more about the after-life?" No clear response. Molly says it's okay; she'll help. Wetzel doesn't want to be bothered; Kochamba thinks it's bad.'

'Too bad Joanne Howe isn't a better medium,' Cogswell grumbled. 'We could learn a lot from Hazelwood. He's the most intelligent one of the lot.'

Don threw the compilations down on the table. 'And that's it.'

'By and large,' said Cogswell heavily, 'an impressive mass of evidence. We've had excellent luck.'

Rakowsky grunted. 'It tells us nothing new . . . There's neither striking divergence nor agreement.'

'Well,' said Don, 'I'm newer to this game than any of

you — maybe a disadvantage, maybe not. It seems to me that we turned up all kinds of significant material — assuming, of course, that our mediums are honest.'

Cogswell eyed him patiently, Head shrugged. Rakowsky said, 'What's this theory you were talking about?'

Don settled himself in his chair, looked from face to face. 'You've all read Jung, naturally?'

'Naturally,' said Dr. Cogswell.

'You're all acquainted with the idea of Collective Unconscious.'

'Yes.'

'Jung uses the term to describe the reservoir of human symbols and ideas. I want to expand this phrase to take in all of human thought, memories, ideals, and emotions.'

'That's your privilege,' said Rakowsky. 'It's your theory.'

'I suggest,' said Don, 'that the so-called after-life is identical to the collective unconscious of the human race.'

13

The faces wore different expressions of surprise. Godfrey Head pulled his chin thoughtfully; Rakowsky blinked half-angrily; Cogswell's heavy mouth was twisted skeptically; Kelso appeared saturnine and disappointed.

'In that case, you definitely presume the absence of an independent after-life!' said Rakowsky.

Don grinned. 'I knew I wouldn't get any applause.'

Cogswell said sourly. 'Your "theory" is on its face illogical.'

Don's grin became a little pained. 'This "theory" explains spiritualistic phenomena without recourse to personal immortality. Does that make it illogical? Are we trying to get at the truth, no matter how cheerless it may turn out to be?'

'We want the truth, of course,' said Rakowsky. 'But so far —'

Cogswell interrupted. 'I maintain that the simplest

explanation is the best — the usually accepted theory — '

Head said impatiently, 'Let's hear Mr. Berwick out.'

They all looked at Don, faintly hostile.

Don laughed. 'Any theory that doesn't go on to prove after-life runs into trouble. Let's be honest with ourselves. Most of us can't swallow religious dogma — but we still want to believe in after-life. That's why we're involved in this kind of research. We're trying to *prove* something to ourselves — not disprove it. It's pretty hard to be dispassionate. But if we're not — if we don't lean over backwards, we're not scientists. We're mystics.'

'Go ahead,' growled Rakowsky. 'Let's hear some details to this theory of yours.'

'Hypothesis is probably a safer word. It makes a minimum number of assumptions. We need no occult propositions about the "purpose of life", "the pre-determined direction of evolution", "the Ultimate Unknowables". We can approach the problem with dignity, as self-determined men trying to systematize a mass of data, rather than humble seekers after an off-hand revelation or "divulgences".'

'A fine speech,' grumbled Cogswell. 'Go on.'

'Just one minute,' interposed Godfrey Head. 'I want to say that I heartily agree with Mr. Berwick in one respect. I've read some of the psychic research literature and a lot of it rather turned my stomach. Other-world beings are always making statements like "this much I have been instructed to tell you — ," "you are not ready to learn more — ", "you are hardly at the threshold of knowledge." I've always wondered, if they had any klnowledge to impart, why they didn't impart it.'

'Betty White described what she called "the unobstructed universe",' said Rakowsky.

Head nodded. 'So she did — with ostentatiously difficult terminology and ideas which she assured Mr. White were very, very difficult — and which Mr. White dutifully found difficult. They're really not so difficult. When Mr. White asks after matters which Betty thinks he's not entitled to ask about, he's reprimanded and told to keep to the subject . . . Excuse me for side-tracking. But it's a characteristic of spiritualistic writing which has always exasperated me.'

Don laughed. 'Me too. Well, to proceed. What does the collective unconscious contain? First, the actual contemporary scene: our cities, roads, automobiles, airplanes, the current celebrities. Second, imaginary places or localities distant in time and place which we're all more or less acquainted with: Heaven, Hell, Fairyland, The Land of Oz, the Greece and Rome of antiquity, Tahiti, Paris, Moscow, the North Pole. Third, famous men, or rather, stereotypes of famous men: George Washington as painted by Gilbert Stuart; Abraham Lincoln as on the dollar bill — or is it the five-dollar bill? Fourth, the concepts, conventions, symbols of the racial unconscious — as distinct from the collective unconscious. The American unconscious is naturally a part of the greater unconscious of the race. In turn it's built up of smaller blocks. The California unconscious is different from the Nevada unconscious. The San Francisco unconscious is different from the Nevada unconscious. The unconscious of the six of us is different from that of six people next door. So — we have this fabric. From a distance it appears uniform — the collective unconscious of Genus Homo. As we approach, it becomes variegated, till at its limit we find the unconscious mind of a single man. When a single man becomes aware of a person, the person takes his place as an image in the man's unconscious. The greater the number of men that know this person, the stronger their feelings toward him, the more intense becomes the image.

'Imaginary ideas become a part of the collective unconscious — such as ghosts, fairies. The images intensify with belief, until finally, under certain conditions, even people who don't believe can see these imaginary concepts.

'When a person dies, he figures strongly in the minds of the people who have loved him. By virtue of their devotion and faith the unconscious image gathers strength; he materializes, sends messages, and so forth. But we've got to remember that the spirit image is only a function of the living minds who knew the dead person. It talks and acts as the persons still alive think it should talk.'

'But look here,' cried Cogswell, 'there are a dozen authenticated cases of spirits giving information outside the knowledge of any living person!'

Don nodded. 'I'm hypothesizing that the spirits — call them spirits for lack of a better name — that they act by the personalities the living persons endow them with. Let's assume that John Smith is bad, in a hundred detestable secret ways. No one knows this. To his family and friends he poses as a man of benevolence and generosity. He dies; he's mourned by all. Statues are erected to him; his spirit sends back messages. But do these manifestations show John Smith's covert badness? No — they only corroborate John Smith's overt goodness.'

Cogswell shuddered. 'You picture a situation as detestable and incredible as the character of John Smith.'

Godfrey Head said with a grin, 'Dr. Cogswell is equating "detestable" and "incredible".'

Cogswell started to sputter; Don held up his hand for peace. 'We've got to be sure in our own minds why we're engaged in psychic research. If it's only to reinforce our hopes we'd better get out, go join a church. If we're after the truth — '

Cogswell was angry, his round face was red. 'Your theory is interesting, Berwick — but it's too pat. It's unconvincing.'

Rakowsky laughed. 'Take it easy, Doctor. Berwick's idea isn't unconvincing — what he says makes sense — but it just isn't in line with facts.'

' "Facts"?' asked Don. 'What facts?'

Cogswell pulled at his lips. 'Betty White has given us a very circumstantial picture of the after-life. The details she presented are — incontrovertible.'

'Well,' said Don, 'I don't want to argue the matter exhaustively . . . However, one point in regard to the "Unobstructed Universe" — Betty White's spirit spoke to White; but she spoke as the idealized version of Betty White.

She described the collective unconscious only as White and his friend Darby conceived it.'

'I must concede,' said Radowsky, 'that there are other accounts of after-life — and that Berwick's theory has ingenious elements to it . . . but like all the other theories, it gives no foothold for verification.'

'I'm not so sure.' Don rose to his feet. 'Suppose a person wanted to explore this collective unconscious, this after-life; how would he go about it?'

'The classic response is: die,' said Rakowsky.

'After he's dead — then what?'

'Then he's there.'

'True. But exactly as the people still alive remember him. He suffers whatever weakness and hardships they endow him with.'

'I see what you're getting at,' said Head. 'For a spirit — call it a spirit — to function at the optimum in this presumable after-life, he has to be remembered as a person with optimum qualities.'

'Right! Strong, intelligent, resourceful, for example!'

Jean grinned. 'He's got to be curious — so that he'll want to investigate. Also he must be endowed with the will to communicate back.'

Dr. Cogswell stuck his fist into his palm. 'What about Houdini? He had all these qualities. He was well-known. But he never showed himself.'

'It's a good point,' said Don. 'But I think it can be circumvented. How was Houdini known? What was his reputation?'

'He was known as an intelligent resourceful man, certainly.'

'Yes,' said Don. 'But he was known as a profound skeptic — a man who claimed that spiritualism was 100 percent falsity.'

'Well, yes.'

'A few men and women expected to hear from him. The public was beset by Houdini's own skepticism. Houdini to this day roams the after-life as the eternal embodiment of skepticism, believing nothing, not even in his own existence.'

Cogswell gave Don a look of grudging admiration. 'You talked yourself out of that one.'

Don said, 'I'm not just giving glib answers. I'm trying to show that my theory can meet objections.'

'It hasn't met all of them. Just what, precisely, do you plan to do?'

'I want to explore the after-life. That means, I want to explore the collective unconscious. No doubt dangers exist: bogey-men, dragons, demons, television horrors, all the stereotypes of terror. They may even be dangerous; I don't want to go as a weakling.'

'Don!' said Jean, genuinely alarmed.

' "Go"? What do you mean "go"?' asked Rakowsky. 'In the classic sense?'

'Good heavens no!' said Don. 'I'm not planning to kill myself. I'm talking about heavy unconsciousness, drugged or otherwise. Of course there are methods to kill a body — to make it legally, finally dead — and then revive it. Dr. Cogswell knows more about the subject than I do.'

Dr. Cogswell spoke with care. 'These processes exist —but they're purely experimental. We've only killed and revived dogs so far; no human volunteers have been available.'

Don said, 'Naturally we'll try the least drastic methods first . . . Incidentally, would anyone else care to make the journey? I'm only putting myself forward from a sense of responsibility.'

'The honor's all yours,' said Godfrey Head. 'At least, so far as I'm concerned.'

'What's the best way for attaining a deep stupor, the metabolism just barely ticking, the brain inert?' Don asked Dr. Cogswell.

'There's a new anesthetic, which may meet your requirements.'

'Do you have any objection to using it?'

'No. None whatever. When do you wish to — go? Is "go" the right word?'

'It serves the purpose. Do you think we could be ready

as soon as next Saturday?'

'I'll be in surgery Saturday,' said Dr. Cogswell. 'It would have to be Sunday.'

'All right, Sunday, then.'

Kelso broke in. 'I don't understand this. When you awake from the anesthetic, do you expect to remember your experiences?'

'No,' said Don. 'Whatever is discovered must be reported through the controls of three or four of our most dependable mediums — Ivalee, Myron Hogart, Mr. Bose, Mrs Kerr. If I am able to leave my corporeal body and wander around the after-world, perhaps Kochamba or Molly Toogood or Lew Wetzel will notice. I hope so anyway.'

'It sounds interesting,' said Kelso. 'I suppose there's no way you could take a camera along?' he added hopefully.

'You think of a way. I'll take it.'

Kelso shook his head helplessly. Dr. Cogswell said, 'We'll have to make certain preparations . . . The hospital would be most convenient. But there I'd fear for my professional reputation. . . .'

'Eventually the Foundation will own the proper equipment,' said Don. 'But in the meantime if we can perform the experiment here, so much the better.'

'It'll cost money,' said Dr. Cogswell.

'No trouble there,' said Don. 'Whatever it costs, we're good for it.'

14

At eleven o'clock Sunday morning all was in readiness. In three of the upstairs bedrooms Ivalee Trembath, Myron Hogart and Mrs. Kerr sat relaxed, eyes closed, trying to make contact with their controls. With them were Godfrey Head, Rakowsky and Tom Ward. On a couch in the living room Don Berwick lay, with Jean sitting close beside him. Contacts were fixed to his chest, wrists and neck; his respiration, heart action and blood pressure were registered on nearby instruments. Dr. Cogswell had arranged his equipment around the room: various drugs, hypodermics, an oxygen mask, oxygen tank and anesthetic. He had hired a professional anesthesiologist for the occasion, a mystified young woman who was unable to understand why a healthy man wanted to be rendered unconscious on a fine summer morning.

'Ready?'

'Ready.'

Vivian Hallsey, at the control table, flashed signals to the upstairs rooms. Dr. Cogswell administered the hypodermic; the anesthesiologist applied the mask.

In five minutes Don lay inert. Dr. Cogswell sat beside him, watching the dials which registered his vital processes. Respiration was shallow and slow; pulse and blood pressure were low.

Vivian Hallsey grimaced toward Jean, motioned above-stairs, shook her head. Ivalee Trembath had failed to contact the dependable Molly Toogood; Mrs. Kerr's Marie Kozard was off somewhere on business of her own. Only Myron Hogart had entered a trance. He lay almost as quiet as Don, lips twitching, fingers jerking.

Godfrey Head spoke, quietly, gently. 'Is Lew Wetzel there, Myron? Can we talk to Lew Wetzel?'

From Myron Hogart's lips came a cackle of harsh gibberish. Then a deep easy voice laughed. 'Hear that? That was an Injun talking.'

'Hello, Lew.'

'Hello, mister. You understand that Injun talk?'

'No, I'm afraid not, Lew. How's everything up above?'

''Bout as always. Nice day today.'

'Do you see my friend Don Berwick there?'

'Don Berwick. Scout, is he? Or trapper?'

'He's from my own time. He's a scientist trying to learn things.'

'Don't see him around.'

'I guess he hasn't passed over to you yet. He's unconscious now, and will be up there temporarily. Look for him.'

'Can't be bothered with them off-again gone agains. Why don't he handle himself more carefully?'

'He wanted to see you. He wants to shake hands.'

'He's welcome, he's welcome.'

'Look around for him, will you, Lew?'

'Can't worry too much about him, mister,' said Lew fretfully. 'If he hasn't passed over, he'll be hard to find. It sucks all a man's vitality out of him living down there with you folks . . . Yeah, there's someone here. He's pale and wan — too weak to talk.'

'Ask him what his name is.'

'He says his name is Donald Berman.'

'Donald Berman, eh? Are you sure?'

'Course I'm sure, you scalawag.'

'It wouldn't be Donald Berwick, would it?'

'I've heard enough of you, mister, and your doubtin' ways. I ain't talkin' no more to you.'

Godfrey Head pleaded and cajoled, but Lew Wetzel remained obstinately silent. Myron Hogart twitched, whimpered, gave a jerk, opened his eyes. 'Did you talk to Lew?'

Godfrey nodded. 'He came; we talked a bit.'

'Learn what you wanted?'

'He was a little touchy today.'

Myron sighed. 'He gets that way sometimes.'

In the other rooms Ivalee Trembath and Mrs. Kerr still sat. Mrs. Kerr sang hymns, but Ivalee was quiet. Their controls refused to appear.

Two hours later Don returned to consciousness, assisted by a few whiffs of oxygen. He lay looking up at the ceiling, deep in thought, then turned his head, searched the faces standing over him.

'Do you remember anything?' asked Jean.

Don frowned. 'It's like coming out of a dream. There were shapes, lights. There was a face; a man with pale blue eyes. He seemed to tower over me, as if I were a child. He wore fringed buckskin . . . Lew Wetzel?'

Jean nodded. 'He's the only one who came through.'

'What did he say?'

'You tell us what you saw first.'

'That's all. Except I seemed to fly . . . It's completely vague. Like last week's dream.'

15

'Well, we can't expect dramatic successes every time,' said Don. 'Today was just a teaser . . . Damn that Lew Wetzel!'

The group sat at the back of the old Marsile house in Orange City. Charcoal glowed in the barbecue pit; steaks marinated in oil, garlic, herbs and wine.

Kelso asked Dr. Cogswell, 'Do you think some other anesthetic might work better? One of the hypnotics?'

Dr. Cogswell shook his head. 'I'm sure I don't know. We're just prodding around in the dark.'

'How about opium?'

'Opium? You mean — opium?'

'Yes. According to the lore, it turns the mind out to canter through flowering fields. Or perhaps mescaline?'

Dr. Cogswell shook his head doubtfully. 'Opium and mescaline induce hallucinations, true, but the mechanism is purely cerebral.'

Don sighed fretfully. 'Doctor, how much effort would be involved in setting up a simulated-death tank at 26 Madrone?'

'Considerable effort, a great deal of money.'

Jean turned away quickly, went to fork the steaks out over the coals.

Dr. Cogswell's eyes took on a thoughtful glint. 'Our present equipment is obsolete. We've a dozen ideas which we'd like to introduce into a new system. However, funds are short, and my colleagues would be delighted if I reported that funds were forthcoming.'

'Okay,' said Don. 'You can take over the old dining room and kitchen — make any alterations you like.'

Kelso asked, 'You're seriously planning to try this artificial death, Don?'

'I don't plan to check out the new equipment, no. I want to see it tested backwards and forwards first. If they "kill" and revive a dozen dogs, a dozen primates, including a few orang-utans, I might then want to take a chance.'

Kelso considered. 'Isn't there any other way, one that doesn't incur any risk?'

Jean looked hopefully over her shoulder.

'You name it, we'll try it.'

Kelso rubbed his chin. 'If we could train a chimpanzee —'

Don snapped his fingers. 'A question we should ask: "Are there animals in the after-world?" Excuse me; what would we train the chimpanzee to do?'

Kelso shook his head. 'Darned if I know.'

Don turned to Dr. Cogswell. 'How long will it take you to set up a new tank?'

Dr. Cogswell considered. 'Oh, about a month and a half — in that neighborhood.'

'And allow another two months for testing — say a total of three or four months. Right?'

Dr. Cogswell nodded.

'We can put the time to good use,' said Don. 'Kelso, maybe you can help us out here.'

'I'll be glad to try.'

'Granting my theory, that the mass unconscious generates an after-world in the matrix of mind-stuff, that the characteristics of a spirit are determined by reputation; that notoriety and fame strengthen the spirit — conceding all this to be true, it might benefit me to be planted in the public mind as a man of, say, ingenuity and effectiveness.'

Kelso nodded thoughtfully. 'In other words — you want publicity?'

'Of a certain sort: as much as possible. The public should think of Donald Berwick as efficient, resourceful, insatiably curious, given to traveling to strange places, with a faculty for emerging unscathed. They must think of him as a lucky daredevil who always wins.'

'Well, well, well,' said Kelso. He ran his fingers through his hair. 'I wouldn't dare work a hoax.'

'You wouldn't need to,' said Jean in a muffled voice. 'If you just printed a few facts.'

'Facts? About the Foundation here? I'd like to. I've been kicking myself for not getting pictures of the mass seance — which of course we could re-enact.'

Jean shook her head. 'I'm not referring to the Foundation . . . Tell him about your escape from the Chinese prison-camp, Don.'

Don grinned sheepishly. 'It's a long story. It'll take awhile.'

'Let's hear it.'

'The steaks are done,' Jean said. 'We'd better eat first.'

Over coffee Don self-consciously settled himself in his chair. 'I'm warning you, this is wild. At the time it seemed perfectly normal, but now — ' he shook his head. 'I still look at the photographs just to convince myself.'

'Toward the end of the Korean War I was captured, and for reasons best known to the Chinese shipped to a camp in Manchuria, near a town called Taoan, along with ten other Americans. We weren't listed with the Red Cross, and were never repatriated after the war. I think we were intended for special brain washing, with an eye to making secret agents out of us.

'I was a prisoner for two years. I knew that if I got bored, I'd be lost, and to protect myself I learned Russian and Chinese. Studied hard at it — nothing else to do. They were glad to help, thinking their techniques were taking hold.

'The two years were tough. Six of the fellows died. Two were killed trying to escape, three died from disease and malnourishment, one from a disciplinary beating. One day a Russian colonel visited the camp. He looked a bit like me . . . To make a long story short, I killed him, hid the body under the barracks, walked out in his uniform. In his jeep I drove to a place called Tsitsihar, on a feeder-line to the Trans-Siberian Railway.

'By this time there was a hue and cry. I ditched the jeep, bluffed my way aboard a west-bound train. I stayed aboard two days and a night — past Chita, to a place called Ulan Ude, near Lake Baikal. Near Genghis Khan's Karakorum, as a matter of fact. Here my luck ran out — I was having visions of riding into Moscow and strolling to the American Embassy. I ran into a "colleague", and gave him the wrong salute. I jumped off the train, ran through the yards. They were hot on my trail — a Keystone Kops sequence, but not very funny. I jumped into a cab of a locomotive, pushed a gun into the engineer's back, and hid while the search-party ran past. We started back down the line to Chita. I couldn't see any way out. Twenty miles out of town I tied the engineer and fireman hand and foot, drove the locomotive into Chita. When we reached the yards I throttled down to about ten miles an hour, jumped out, let the train make its own decision. A hundred yards farther it ran into a yard engine.

'Here the story gets confused. I'll merely say I was chased through the streets of Chita. I hid in a bordello, stole a suitcase and some civilian clothes, mingled with a group of eighty Russian engineers, on their way to Harbin in a truck convoy. I couldn't get away from them; I was put to work installing machinery in a cement plant.

'I stole a car, drove north to a town near the Siberian border — Kiamusze on the Sungari River. I hid aboard a barge, was taken to Tunkiang on the border. I stole a skiff, paddled across the river into Siberia, and rode a local bus to Khabarovsk. At Khabarovsk, after a month of intrigue, I managed to scrounge an air passage to Sakhalinsk on Sakhalin Island. I walked south to Korsakov, sneaked onto a fishing boat. When the fisherman appeared, I made him take me south. He set me ashore on Hokkaido one very early morning. I went to the police station; they took me to an American Army camp. In brief,' said Don, 'that's the story.'

Kelso asked in a hushed voice: 'You're giving it to me freely?'

'If it'll do any good. I've got a few photographs that I took along the way. It was a Russian camera, not too good, but — they're pictures.'

Kelso examined the pictures. 'If this doesn't make the Great Adventure series, my name isn't Robert Kelso.'

'Wait till you hear the details,' said Jean. 'You've just got the outline.'

Donald Berwick appeared on the cover of *Life* wearing a Russian colonel's uniform. He was depicted gazing at a wall-map of East Asia, the path of his escape-route marked in black. His stance suggested capable masculinity; his acute hatchet-faced profile gave the impression of incisive virility. *Lucky Don Berwick* read the caption. He conspicuously carried a Polaroid camera, an incongruous note on which Kelso had insisted.

'If there's anything in this wildest of all schemes,' said Kelso, 'I want pictures of it. You've got to appear in the after-life wearing a camera. Because I want pictures!'

'What good are pictures?' argued Head. 'He can't mail 'em back.'

'He's got to materialize. I want him to show himself, holding out photographs like a man selling postcards. I'll have a cameraman ready, and if *Life Magazine* doesn't weep for joy, I'll jump in the ocean.'

'Will he dare print the pictures?'

'Who could resist?'

'Don't forget to emphasize somewhere that the camera is self-developing,' said Don. 'Also, that I always carry it loaded; otherwise it won't do any good.'

Jean brought him the issue. 'Here — look it over. You're famous.'

Don groaned ruefully. 'Lucky Don Berwick.'

'You should read the story.'

Don turned to the article, read. 'Oh, Lord . . . they make me out a combination of Chairman Mao, and Tarzan.'

'Excellent!' said Jean. 'Just what you want.'

Don looked up with an embarrassed grin. 'I suppose

it's what I was asking for. But now — I feel a fool.'

'You've made an impression,' said Jean. 'Look. Here's an article in the *Orange City Herald* — about "Lucky Don Berwick, local hero!" '

Don read the article, grinning and blushing. 'Here I'm a high school athletic prodigy, a war hero, a student who just barely missed a Rhodes scholarship, a petroleum engineer of uncanny ability.' He ran his hand through his hair. 'I feel the pressure of this contrived personality . . . It's gathering weight!'

Jean put her hand on his, squeezed. 'It's not really as contrived as you might think. You really are like that.'

'*Rats.*'

'The picture is exaggerated — but it's you. Also — look at this.' She pointed to a column on the other side of the page. Hugh Bronny's face stared challengingly forth at Don.

EVANGELIST ENTERS
POLITICAL PICTURE

Bronny Declares for Governorship
'Christian Crusade' as Third Party

Hugh Bronny, evangelist, and leader of what he calls the 'Christian Crusade,' today announced his candidacy for the governorship of California. At a press conference called at his Orange City headquarters he displayed a petition which he claimed bore the signatures of a million voters — enough to arouse attention and respect from both Democrats and Republicans. 'I plan to make old-fashioned Christian principle the basis of government,' declared 'Fighting Hugh' Bronny. 'The Christian Crusade is marching to bring the nation back to the fundamental idea of God — a clean white American God. We'll sweep the state elections this year; in two years we'll send Christian Crusade Congressmen to Washington and by 1968 we'll have a Christian Crusade President in the White House!'

'The man's off his rocker,' said Don.

'Surely there can't be any chance of Hugh *becoming* governor!' protested Jean.

Don shook his head. 'I imagine there's still more sane people than lunatics in California.'

'I keep thinking of Hitler,' said Jean. 'How the Germans voted him into power, on something of the same basis.'

'Yes. It's a good analogy. Hitler appealed to the worst instincts of the Germans; Hugh does the same for us.'

The doorbell sounded. Don went to the window. 'Speak of the devil. It's Hugh!'

Jean started to the door, then paused. 'What on earth can he want?'

'Let's find out.'

Jean opened the door. With a laugh that was half-hysterical, she cried out, 'Hugh — you've got a new suit!'

Hugh was wearing a double-breasted black coat with great padded shoulders, gray flannel trousers, limp black shoes.

'What of it?' asked Hugh grimly. 'I'm the next governor of the State, and I've got to look the part.' He swung his eyes suspiciously from Jean to Don. 'What's behind all this publicity you're getting? War hero! Fantastic escape! It's dishonest.'

'You're wrong,' said Don.

'You mean to say that all that stuff is true?'

'I mean that the facts speak for themselves.'

'Come on,' said Hugh scornfully. 'Let's have some details. I've known you too long, Don. You can't pull the wool over my eyes.'

'It's the truth,' said Don. 'Take it or leave it. Do you think they'd print anything they couldn't verify?'

'Humph!' Hugh snorted. 'Aren't you going to invite me in?'

'Hugh,' said Jean, 'you get crazier every time I see you.'

Hugh's eyes glistened. 'You're talking to a very important man, sister.'

'What do you want?'

'Well — ' Hugh hesitated. 'As you know, I'm entering politics. I need money — you've got money that belongs to me. I want it.'

'It doesn't belong to you and you won't get a cent,' said Jean.

'What do you do with all the God-given money?'

'We're planing to build a laboratory and research center.'

'For your Foundation of Atheistic Blasphemy?'

'Call it anything you like.'

'What are you doing with all those animals at Madrone Place? Dogs, monkeys, apes?'

Don asked, 'How do you know about these things, Hugh?'

'I keep my eyes open. What are you doing with them?'

'We are developing a new medical technique.'

'You're killing them and bringing them back to life!'

'How do you know?' Don asked suspiciously.

'As I said, I keep my eyes open. I want to know why you're doing this? Are you going to try this unholy game with a man?'

'Haven't you asked enough questions?'

Hugh lowered his great head archly. 'Just friendly interest.'

'You're no friend of ours.'

'I'm friend to all men. All God-fearing, clean-thinking men.'

'I don't fear anyone. And you're no friend of mine. Perhaps you'll do us the honor of leaving?'

Hugh serenely inspected the cuffs of his glossy new white-on-white shirt. 'I came to visit my sister and my old home — which is my right. I came here — taking valuable time — to get some information.'

'If it concerns money,' said Don, 'you've got it. You don't get any.'

'I'll sue.'

'On what grounds?'

'You knew the oil was there. You asked me to accept half of the property, because you knew it was due to me.'

'How did we know oil was there?' asked Don.

Hugh looked at him blankly.

Don said dryly, 'Evidently you concede that your father's ghost directed us to continue drilling.'

'No,' said Hugh without moving a muscle of his face.

'Spirits of the departed worship God, or suffer in Hell. They do not concern themselves in earthly affairs. And however you learned of the oil, the money is mine. And now I need it.' Jean said slyly, 'Surely a candidate for governor has better things to do than stand on front steps wheedling money from his sister.'

'It's my money,' said Hugh doggedly. 'If you think you'll keep it with impunity — you're wrong. Because I will fight back. Do you think I am called Fighting Hugh Bronny for nothing?' He fixed them in turn with a blue glare, then turned, stalked away.

Jean watched him go. 'He's a different person, Don . . . It's something to do with changing his clothes . . . He's important now.'

Don nodded. 'He's building his own niche in the collective unconscious. Fighting Hugh Bronny . . . Let's go over to Madrone Place.'

They drove across town, to the old frame building. From within came sounds of activity. An electric drill whined, a power-saw rasped through wood.

Don and Jean entered, walked through a new metal door into a large bare bright room. White-enameled cabinets lined one wall; opposite were oxygen tanks, an iron-lung, high frequency electrical equipment. Through the floor came pipes, leading to a refrigeration unit in the cellar. A long glass-walled tank rested on a stainless steel box in the center of the room.

Don nodded to the tank. 'There it is. Ferry to the after-world . . . What did Charon call his boat? Cerebus? No, that was the dog.'

Jean's fingers were clenching his arm. Don looked down at her with a wry grimace. 'What's the trouble?'

'I'm worried.'

'It's Hugh. He's upset you.'

'He's a maniac!'

'I suppose he is . . . Sometime I'm going to take an hour off and try to visualize the world as he must see it.' He

looked through a door into the next room. A man wielding
an electric drill at the instrument panel nodded. He was
about forty-five, round-bodied but sturdy, with a blond
forelock hanging into his eyes. He finished drilling, came
into the outer room.

'Doctor Clark,' said Don, 'I didn't expect to see you
installing your own equipment.'

'Just a small refinement,' said Dr. Clark. 'Everything's
working beautifully — better than we had hoped.'

'Then there's no danger?' asked Jean anxiously.

'No fatalities since our first two days. Last night we held
a chimpanzee under for an hour and a half. She's bright
as a dime this morning.'

Don peered into the tank. 'Make it comfortable,
Doctor — I've a long way to go.'

16

The room was the same; the night was two weeks later.
Nine men and three women sat or stood in their assigned
positions.

Doctors Clark, Aguilar and Foley stood beside the glass-
walled tank. Godfrey Head, Howard Rakowsky, Kelso,
Vivian Hallssey and a cameraman sat in chairs to one side
of the door; to the other sat Jean and Ivalee Trembath.
Doctor James Cogswell stood by the foot of the tank and
with him was Donald Berwick.

Don wore a blue terry-cloth bathrobe. His face was
composed but the skin at his jawline shone pale. He turned
his head, met Jean's eyes. He smiled, uttered to Cogswell,
crossed the room, took her hand.

'I can't help but worry,' she whispered.

'There's nothing to fear,' said Don. 'The technique has
been practiced on dogs and chimpanzees till they can do it
in the dark.'

'I've heard that when men return to life, they're not
always — sane.'

'Nothing like that's going to happen.'

'Another thing — that article in today's paper. Won't it prejudice some people, after the archetype?'

Don shrugged. 'Perhaps, perhaps not. It makes the archetype more exactly me. It focuses a lot more attention. . . .'

At this moment Fighting Hugh Bronny stood in the Orange City Auditorium, reading the article to seventeen thousand rapt followers. He leaned his gaunt body forward over the podium, spoke with the sly breathless relish of a dog stealing garbage. As he read he raised his head to glance across the auditorium. To his eyes the scene appeared as an over-exposed photograph — burnt by glaring lights, marked by shadows and smoky air, and the mosaic of pale faces was blurred, out of focus. He no longer thought of the audience as human beings. They comprised a unique substance, malleable as candle-wax, but with a responsive fiber that stimulated and excited him like a bath-brush on his bony back.

Fighting Hugh Bronny read in triumph. He finished the article. The audience was silent; Hugh could sense the seventeen thousand pulsing hearts, the prickle and minuscule multitudinous shine of thirty-four thousand eyes. He felt a great glow of power. These people were waiting for him to tell them, to lead them; he could fix and form their minds, whip them back and forth like a fisherman dry-casting.

'I'll read the article again,' said Hugh in a throaty voice. 'And as I read, ponder the audacity of these hermetic imps.' He looked around his audience, raised his voice to oboe pitch. 'These atheists.' He peered into the blur of faces. 'These nasty vandals, breaking a way even in God's own Heaven.' He paused. Even the sibilant sound of breath and stirring cloth had stopped. There was as deep a hush as is possible when seventeen thousand people gather under a roof hung with bright lights.

Hugh's voice dropped an ominous octave. 'If your blood doesn't boil like mine — then never call me Fighting Hugh

Bronny, and never call yourselves Christian Crusaders.'
He bent his head over the clipping and read.

Lucky Don Berwick
To Plumb Psychic Region
by Vivian Hallsey

'Three months ago Lucky Don Berwick was a man known to comparatively few people; today his name is on everyone's tongue. Wherever men and women get together, chances are they're talking about Lucky Don Berwick. Now comes news of an adventure to pale all the fabulous exploits in Berwick's fabulous life — if it works. Tonight at nine o'clock Donald Berwick will be killed. By every medical and legal definition he will be dead. His heart will be stilled. His lungs will pump no air. There will be no sign of life in Berwick's body; there will be no spark of life in Berwick's body; he will have passed "beyond".

'At nine-thirty Drs. Cogswell, Clark, Aguilar and Foley of Los Angeles Medical Research Center will attempt to revive Donald Berwick by techniques conceived during World War II, improved upon, and now said to be perfected. At ten o'clock it is hoped that Lucky Donald Berwick will be lucky enough to be once more alive.

'What is the purpose of this experiment? Hang on to your seats, ladies and gentlemen; this is a jolt. Donald Berwick has volunteered to undertake the most daring exploration of his existence (although it's a journey all of us must make). He will endeavor to bring back a report on the land beyond the grave, if there *be* any.'

Hugh looked up, carefully crumpled the clipping into a ball, cast it away with a gesture of revulsion.
'There, Christian Crusaders, you have it. You say with wrath in your hearts, God will punish these men. I say to you, God will certainly punish Donald Berwick and his kind! He has sent me — ' Hugh soared to his full height, arms stretched high; his voice a trumpet. 'He has sent me! He

has sent me as his strong right arm!' And in Hugh's voice was the sudden certainty, and every heart felt a pang, every throat contracted, gulped for air, expanded in a great guttural moan. 'He has sent me! — and I will lead! — first against the Devil's Imp Berwick! — then against the vile forces that seek to befoul and destroy this dear America of ours! I can't tell you, go to 26 Madrone Place, make your wishes known. I can't urge you — as I might wish — to tear that cursed haunt of evil stone from stone. No! They'd say I was inciting you to riot! I can't say that! No, brothers! All I can say is that's where I'm going! Now is the time for Christian Crusaders to ask themselves to enforce the will of God. By fighting? Or by reading in the papers of blasphemy and sacrilege? The address, brothers and Crusaders! 26 Madrone Place. I will be there!'

17

Don looked at his watch. 'Time grows short . . . I suppose I should be more alarmed, but I'm not.' He grinned. 'Just another dull evening.'

Head said dryly, 'You're starting to take the exploits of Lucky Don Berwick seriously.'

Don grinned. 'It's hypnotic; I can't help it. The synthetic personality is taking me over.' He caught Jean's glance, laughed. 'I'll resist it.'

Clark and Aguilar were giving the tank a final cursory inspection.

The cameraman walked here and there taking photographs.

Don glanced around the faces, meeting the eyes that watched him with covert speculation. 'Everybody looks comfortable.' He prodded Cogswell's plump ribs. 'Cheer up, Doctor. After all, it's me that's being killed.'

Cogswell mumbled unhappily. 'Do you think there'll be time for materialization?'

'I'll do what I can.'

Dr. Foley touched Berwick's elbow. 'Come on, Lucky; take the dive.'

Don slipped out of the bathrobe. He wore the Russian colonel's uniform to identify himself as completely as possible with the archetypal image of himself in the mass mind. A Polaroid camera hung around his neck; at his hip, a holster held a .45 army automatic.

'Take a good look,' said Don. 'And remember — Lucky Don Berwick! Concentrate on it! The "Lucky" part especially.' He stepped into the tank, stretched out.

Foley started a timer; Clark and Aguilar gave him intravenous injections in the right and left thighs, then the right and left shoulders. At one minute Foley threw a switch; motors under the tank began to whine. The glass was quickly frosted, Don's shape became indistinct.

At two minutes Clark and Aguilar repeated the injections, while Foley clamped a soft band around Don's wrist, looped a metal ribbon around his neck. Dials on the panel indicated pulse and body temperature. The pulse indicator quivered, sank: 60, 55, 50, 45; the temperature gauge hovered at 98.6 for thirty seconds, then began to dive. When it hit 90 degrees Foley threw in another switch; the motors below the cabinet sang.

Don was now unconscious. His pulse sank swiftly: 20 — 15 — 10 — 5 . . . It quivered to a stop. The temperature gauge began to plummet: 80°C — 70° — 60°. Dr. Clark and Dr. Foley reached into the tank, flexed Berwick's legs, arms. The temperature dropped: 50° — 40° — now far below room temperature.

Dr. Aguilar worked a knob; the motor sound declined in pitch. The temperature gauge moved more slowly, came to a halt at 34°.

Drs. Foley and Aguilar slid a glass cover over the tank, Clark opened a valve; there was a sound of pumps.

Dr. Cogswell turned to the spectators. 'At this time —

he's essentially dead. The pumps are drawing the air out of his lungs; the tank will be refilled by an atmosphere of nitrogen.'

Foley reached through a port, rubber gauntlets over his hands. He put a bracket against the waxy temples, pressed contacts against various parts of Don's close-cropped scalp. Aguilar watched a dial muttering, 'No — no — nothing. No activity.' Cogswell turned to the others. 'He is now officially dead.'

Kelso said, 'Okay to take pictures of the tank?'

Dr. Cogswell nodded shortly.

Kelso motioned to the photographer.

Jean was looking at Ivalee Trembath. 'No . . . Not in here. There's too much infringement — disturbance.'

'Want to leave the room?' Rakowsky asked her.

'Yes, please.'

Rakowsky and Jean took her to one of the upstairs bedrooms. Suddenly conscious of noise, Rakowsky looked out the window. He touched Jean's arm. 'The street — it's full of cars.'

The cars crowded bumper to bumper along the street, like glowing-eyed black fish. They roared and groaned and choked to a halt. The doors opened; men and women with twisted faces squeezed out, struggled and sidled to the sidewalk. They started to chant — off-key, off-beat. The tune suddenly emerged.

'Listen,' said Jean.

' "Onward Christian Soldiers", ' said Rakowsky.

Jean shuddered. 'It sounds weird — music from the future . . . What are they doing here? . . . a convention? A gathering?'

'A demonstration,' said Rakowsky.

'An attack,' said Ivalee Trembath.

The voices rose into the night, the faces looked up, pale as clamshells. A tall figure, larger and more definite than the faceless crowd, stalked to the door.

Rakowsky muttered, 'I'm going to call the police.'

Hugh's bony knuckles echoed on the door. 'Open up,

open up, in the name of the Lord God Most High. Open
this cursed door!'

Jean suddenly snapped out of it to find Ivalee's hands
clutching her. Ivalee was crying. 'Jean! Jean! Don't!' Jean
had a heavy earthenware vase in her hand; the window was
open in front of her. She stopped struggling, put down the
vase. 'What a horror!' she whispered. 'I would have killed
him . . . . '

The knocks were sounding again. 'For the last time!'
blared Hugh's voice; then the door swung open. Godfrey
Head's calm voice rose up.

'I have called the police. You're disturbing a delicate
scientific experiment. I advise you to leave before you get
in serious trouble.'

'Anti-Christ!' crackled Hugh's voice. 'Stand aside.' He
put a great hand on Head's thin chest, pushed. Kelso stepped
out on the porch. Hugh attempted to thrust him aside. Kelso
swung a bony fist into Hugh's mouth, sent him reeling off
the porch.

From the distance came the eery moan of sirens. It seemed
to stimulate the crowd, to heighten their mood.

Hugh staggered around, faced them. His mouth oozed
black blood, his shirt was torn. 'They have drawn my blood!
In the name of my blood, forward! The time is now! We
will kindle a fire to carry us over the world! Onward, you
Crusaders, you soldiers of Christ! With fire and
sword — onward!'

The crowd roared, surged. Jean caught a horrifying
glimpse of Godfrey Head being yanked by his necktie, flung
down from the porch, disappearing under the dark rush.

An enormous baby-faced young man with side-burns
wearing a leather jacket charged into the hall, clamped
Kelso's arms; they fell heavily, Kelso on the bottom.

Hugh stalked forward, kicked. The young man jumped
up, kicked too, again and again with booted feet.

Hugh looked about him, majestic, flaming-eyed. 'Fire and
sword!' came the cry behind him; and a woman who looked
like a consumptive stenographer began keening 'Onward

Christian Soldiers!' And the baby-faced young man yelled, 'Kill the devils! Kill the atheists!'

At the foot of the staircase, the institute's cameraman snapped pictures — one, two, three — then prudently retreated down the hall. Hugh ignored him. The four doctors came forward, so cool and inquiring that Hugh was momentarily taken aback.

'Will you kindly get that beastly mob out of here?' asked Dr. Aguilar testily.

Rakowsky marched forward. 'I'm placing you under arrest. If you attempt to escape, I'll shoot you.'

' "Escape"?' roared Hugh. 'Stand aside!'

The doctors were disconcerted; the authority which served in hospital and laboratory had failed; they suddenly became ordinary men. They fought.

In the living room there was a sudden crackle, a roar and babble of voices. Hugh sidled against the wall, fended off Dr. Aguilar with one great hand. Jean met him at the door; he slapped her face, she staggered back.

Hugh stood a moment in the doorway. Cogswell, his face twisted by fear, lurched forward. 'Go away, get out of here!'

Hugh looked contemptuously from Cogswell to the tank. Donald Berwick lay cold, impassive, dead. The dials showed no pulse. The temperature was 34°.

Jean stood with her back to the tank; Ivalee Trembath gripped a chair to one side; to the other Dr. James Cogswell stared at Hugh like a hypnotized frog.

'Get out of here, Hugh,' whispered Jean. 'I'll kill you. . . .'

Hugh's eyes blazed. 'No one can stop me . . . I am the new Messiah!' He took a step forward. Cogswell, screaming hoarsely, charged. Hugh swung his long lank arm, slapped Cogswell's red cheek. Cogswell thumped to the wall, slid down to the floor. Hugh stepped forward.

Jean ran around behind the tank. Ivalee swung the chair. Somebody behind Hugh fended it off.

Jean slid back the glass cover, seized the automatic from Don's holster; the cold stung her hands. She aimed it, pulled the trigger. Nothing happened. Hugh laughed. He reached under the tank, heaved. The tank was bolted to the floor. Hugh grunted foolishly. Jean looked at the automatic, frantically fumbled, threw off the safety. She aimed. Hugh raised his foot, kicked. Glass tinkled. Hugh reached, seized Don's cold arm.

Jean fired. The bullet struck Hugh's shoulder; he flinched, but seemed to feel no pain. He tugged at Don. With a sliding rush the body slid out on the floor.

Jean took a step forward, aimed, fired. Hugh clutched his abdomen in surprise. Jean pulled the trigger, firing steadily. Hugh's knees sagged. Blood suddenly spouted from a hole in his neck. His knees buckled; he toppled. Jean aimed her gun at the faces in the doorway, the shapes behind Hugh. They scuttled and ducked like beetles.

'Jean,' said Ivalee, 'the house is on fire.'

'Fire!' came a cry from the hall. Ivalee went to Cogswell, tried to pull him to his feet. He lay limp, his breath coming in stertorous gulps. There was a shuffle in the hall, a curious lull. Then a sudden terrified sound of feet, a scream, not so much of pain as terror.

Ivalee ran out into the hall; Jean saw the flicker on her face. For an instant the silver of her hair and ice of her face were alloys of gold. She turned back to Jean. 'We can't get out the front.'

Jean ran to the body of Donald Berwick. She knelt beside it, rubbed the cheeks. They were cold and damp from condensed moisture.

'Jean', said Ivalee gently, 'Don is past all that.'

'But Iva — we can do something — we've got to do something . . . The doctors — they could revive him . . . .'

The flames poured into the room, bringing clouds of smoke. 'We've got to get out of here,' said Ivalee.

Jean looked down aghast at Don's body. 'We can't —' she began in a tired voice.

Ivalee lifted her to her feet. 'We can't help him now, Jean. . . .'

'But — he's really alive. Iva . . . The doctors can bring

him back to life! It's so horrible! I can't abandon him!''

'He's dead, Jean . . . The doctors could bring him back to life in the tank . . . With the right timing and their drugs . . . Don is dead, Jean. And so is poor little Cogswell.'

'Dr Cogswell — *dead*?'

'Yes, dear. Come, we can't stay any longer . . . . '

By force she dragged Jean out into the hall. Sheets of flame blocked the way to the front door, and filled the rear hall.

'To the second floor,' said Ivalee. 'It's our only chance.'

They ran up the stairs, pursued by hot smoke, stumbled into the front bedroom. Ivalee went to the window, while Jean leaned against the wall, numb with grief.

'The street is full of cars,' said Ivalee. 'The firemen are bringing hoses in from the corner. Listen, the mob is still chanting. They don't know that Hugh is dead.'

From one end of the street to the other the voices quavered, swelled in a chant of triumph. Jean tottered to the window. 'Can we jump?'

'It's too far,' said Ivalee.

Searchlights played on the house. Firemen hauled hoses down the sidewalk, running, shouting, pushing people aside. The nozzles were dry; no water came. The firemen turned, looked back along the line in rage, dropped the nozzles, ran back along the hoses.

'The service stairs,' said Jean. 'Maybe they're still open.'

They ran to the rear of the house. Behind them a gust of flame roared up the main staircase. Jean opened a door on the service stairs, closed it quickly on the wave of flames and blast of smoke.

Ivalee went to the back window, a heavy old stained-glass piece, tried to open it, without success.

'We're worse here than we were up front.' They turned, looked back down the hall. The main stair-well acted as a chimney; flames were consuming the upper banisters.

Jean picked up a chair, threw it at the stained glass. It broke, but lead held the pieces together. The air was very hot, and rasped their throats. Smoke seemed to seep from her lungs into her blood, into her brain. Vision swam in Jean's eyes, her knees began to sag.

Behind her she heard a sound, felt a blast of cool air; she felt a strong arm. She looked up. 'Donald!' She could not hold on to her senses. Slowly she fainted; and when she awoke, hours later, and she lay in the emergency hospital, Ivalee Trembath was in the next room.

The nurse had no information.

The next day when she and Ivalee Trembath were discharged, they took a taxi to the old Marsile home across town. Two reporters were waiting. Ivalee sent them away; they were alone.

Jean stood, hollow-cheeked, dry-eyed. She said, 'Iva — just before I passed out — I saw him. Donald. Alive.'

Ivalee nodded. 'He carried us out.'

'But how? He was — dead.'

'I saw him too. . . .' Ivalee sat down in a chair. 'Let's see if we can find him — or get news. . . .' She covered her eyes with a scarf.

Newspapers throughout the United States ran an account of the fire at 26 Madrone Place. The headlines read:

LUCKY BERWICK
RUNS OUT OF LUCK
ENDS CAREER IN RELIGIOUS RIOT

Sometimes in the same story, sometimes in a different column the death of Fighting Hugh Bronny was reported:

Members of the Christian Crusade revel in a saturnalia of religious ecstacy. Only an hour before his death Hugh Bronny exhorted his followers: 'Rally to the Crusade; I am the new Messiah!'

According to the Reverend Walter Spedelius, Hugh Bronny's passing follows the Christ-pattern. 'Christ died to show humanity its sins; Hugh Bronny died to lead us out of the mire to purity. He was a great spirit, a saint, a prophet, and we shall follow him in death as we did in life.'

18

Donald Berwick lay down in the tank. He felt the weight of the camera on his chest, the mass of the automatic at his side. Overhead were the faces of Clark, Aguilar and Foley. He turned his eyes, glimpsed Jean through the glass. Then he felt the sting of the hypodermics, the clamp of the gauges. The motors whined below him; the air suddenly grew cold. He closed his eyes. When he tried to open them, he could not — already his muscles were numb.

He felt life leaving him, like the tide receding from a shallow shore. He felt chilled, then suddenly warm and numb; then for a last transparent interval, freezing cold, through and through. Feeling left him and he died.

He had no feeling of leaving, no sensation of drawing away from his own frame. Another phase of Donald Berwick existed, and it seemed always to have been. Now it came into its own.

From a new and strange perspective, Donald Berwick looked around the room. There were other shapes present; after a moment he recognized them. They were diaphanous, and stood swaying like seaweed, their feet anchored in small man-shaped pellets. One small cold pellet lay near his own feet, quiet and detached: the old Donald Berwick.

The new Donald Berwick felt a pang of pity, then took stock of himself. He had memory; he recalled the whole of his life. Suddenly he realized there had been a great oversight in his preparations. Building the archetype 'Lucky Don Berwick' in the collective unconscious, he had ignored a prime source of power. Who could know Donald Berwick himself? He examined his form: the uniform, the gun, the camera. All there. He compared his watch and camera. The camera was harder, brighter, more solid. Twice as hard, thought Berwick.

Jean — he picked out the supple waving shape that was Jean. Her eyes were on him. This was Jean: composite of her own unconscious and that of all who knew her. Different in small ways from the Jean he knew, but not greatly . . . Ivalee Trembath: her ice and silver composure was less noticeable; her mouth was soft and wistful. And the others — but later, later. First a picture to test the dream-camera. He set the aperture, aimed, snapped the shutter. Now — we'll quickly look over this after-life country — then back . . . How did time go? Fast or slow? He looked at his watch. The hands waggled, spun back and forth . . . Well, thought Don, evidently it's whatever time I think it is . . . Now, I'll step out into the street . . . .

The walls went dim; he moved his feet, he stood in the street. It looked much as he recalled it; cars moved like phantoms, in and out of his vision unless he concentrated . . . The street was suddenly full of cars.

Don thought, now — up! If I am a thought, I travel like thought! And he passed through walls and floated in the dark sky. Below was the city; around him in all directions spread the carpet of lights . . . But this was not the city of reality; this was the composite of a myriad imaginations; the lights glowed softer, like crystal balls; the distance melted into nothingness.

And I'm a thought — then north! And mountains were below him, clad in dark pines, and ahead was a granite ridge, white and gray; and strangely it was early morning; Berwick stood on a peak and looked in all directions, separately and at once.

China! He felt no movement; he was a thought; he was in China. This was not the China of reality, it was the composite China, the stereotype, or rather, the paradoxical set of stereotypes that made up the collective unconscious: the drabness of Communist China, the splendor of the old empire. He remembered his Polaroid; he pulled the tab, looked at his first positive. Fair. Not bad. He tucked it into his pocket.

He set the aperture, photographed a pagoda, a comic-opera rickshaw nearby. In the background were the hazy mountains and graceful willows of old Chinese paintings. Below he could see other faces and shapes.

He thought himself to the ground. This was the old Bund, in Shanghai. He willed himself to see it; suddenly it took form and full solidity. He stood in the street. A coolie in flapping blue denim trotting toward him, halted, stepped aside, looked back.

Hey, thought Don, I have materialized. . . . It seems easy . . . I'll return to Orange City and materialize at Madrone Place.

He thought: up. Drift slowly. Over the Pacific. . . . He spied the moon. Should he dare? But of course, it was now his nature; he was Lucky Donald Berwick, who dared anything!

He thought: moon. And he was on the moon. Faster than light, as fast as thought. He stood on a silver and black plain; a scene from an imaginative painting.

He pulled the China photograph from the Camera, aimed his camera at the moonscape. It occurred to him to wonder about his organic processes. . . . Was he breathing? he felt pressure in his chest; then suddenly he materialized; he stood on the stony reality of the moon's surface. His skin pulsed, his eyeballs bulged, cold struck up through the soles of his shoes. He had time for a brief thought: he was already dead; where would he go now if he died?

He let himself drift back into the unconscious. And the moon became the unconscious stereotype . . . Don scanned the sky. Mars!

Quick as thought, faster than light!

He stood on a dim red desert, the thin wind hissing past his ears. The sea-bottoms of ancient Barsoom? He turned his head; there in the distance was a ruined city — a tumble of white stone, a movement of the weird hordes of green warriors. He looked again; there seemed to be tall nodding vegetables behind, like dark dandelion fluffs. . . . He took a picture, then thought of the canals. . . . He stood beside a wide channel full of gray water. Ah! thought Don. The

canals of Mars did exist! He laughed at his own foolishness
. . . All in the mind, all the collective unconscious. Was he
on Mars at all, or was he merely a thought? He concentrated
his attention; he stood on cold dry sands, under a dark
brilliant sky; and this was Mars indeed. How had he arrived?
Were mind and universe one? Was the 'real' world only
another place of unreality, with mind and matter interacting?

He glanced at his watch. What time was it? He had stepped
into the tank at 9 o'clock. The watch read 9 o'clock. He had
surely been dead ten minutes . . . Now it read 9:10. Or had
it only been a single minute? And the time was 9:01. The time
was whatever he chose it to be. Very well then. Back to Earth.
At this rate there would be ample time for exploration.

He was in space, diving for Earth — a glorious sensation
of freedom! Don sang in exultation. It was fun to be dead!
Earth — lovely familiar old Earth. There it was, laden with
its billions of souls!

Was it Earth, or was it a thought? . . . For the first time
it occurred to him to wonder: where were all the other souls?
The spirits of all the dead? The angels? Jesus Christ?
Mohammed and his houris? And he vibrated up into a
fantastic golden land, flowered with white clouds. There
indeed walked radiant winged beings, and there, off in the
distance, was a shining city of glass and gold; and there was
an effulgence, a blinding bright figure with a merciful face
. . . . Only an instant. Then an image of a great garden, with
lawns and flowers and marble pavilions, rows of cool cypress
and poplar, turbaned shapes sipping sherbets, sublimely
beautiful maidens . . . Don thought, there is no false religion;
whatever Man believed, *was*; whatever stage of abstraction
Man could conceive, he could attain . . . . Religion was, God
was. But they were functions of Man; the mind of Man was
the Creator.

Where was Molly Toogood, Ivalee's control? And the
wandering spirits of the dead? . . . . He saw Molly, a
pleasant-looking woman: perhaps not as bright or hard-
format as he was. She nodded. He sensed other shapes,
flimsier than Molly. Where was Art Marsile? He looked

around him, and — wonder of wonders — he stood in front of the old Marsile home under the pepper trees. He walked up to the door. Art looked out. 'Hello, Don. I been waiting for you. Got time for a chat?'

Don looked at the house, half-expecting to see Jean come running out, blonde and fresh and pretty. 'No,' said Art. 'She's not here, Don. It's not her time yet. Maybe you'd better go check. There's trouble down there, Hugh — as usual.'

A flicker of thought. Don stood on the porch of 26 Madrone Place. In the street were numerous pellets of human beings, with their souls attached like frail balloons. All except one. Don recognized it: Hugh Bronny. Bronny's soul was tall, broad, and glowed with fiery intensity. The pellet of Hugh Bronny came up to the house; the soul — call it a soul, for lack of a better word — looked Don in the eye.

'Go away,' said Don.

The soul opened its mouth, but the pellet ignored the message, knocked on the door.

Don thought himself into the laboratory. He watched while the Hugh Bronny pellet marched into the room; he tried to speak to the lovely wraith anchored in the Jean pellet, but she was too absorbed and upset.

The pellets moved, like shining quicksilver. He examined his body. Dead — but with the potential for life. He tried to slip his feet back into the cold pellet, but there was no purchase; he slipped away.

The Hugh Bronny pellet destroyed the Don Berwick pellet. Jean's wraith shimmered and twisted. Her body pellet seized the gun.

Don heard the shots as dull clicks, stones tapped under water. Hugh's soul seemed to bulge, to sparkle, to take on mass. It was a monstrous ominous presence — it looked like Hugh, but it was strong and tough and muscular. The face was Hugh's face as Hugh must have conceived it: hard, fervent, unyielding.

The Hugh pellet was dead. The Hugh Bronny soul was free. It came toward Don. They looked eye to eye an instant.

Hugh reached out his powerful arms; Don knocked them aside. The contact was solid, but elastic, like two pieces of heavy rubber colliding.

Hugh moved off, and was gone. Don looked back to the house. It was in flames. The men who had worked with him — where were they? Cogswell — 'Hello Doctor,' said Don to the pale soul which stood beside him. 'I see you're dead.'

'Yes,' said the soul of Dr. James Cogswell. 'It's very easy, isn't it?' The soul looked Don over with a trace of surprise. 'My word, you look hard and strong. It's amazing.'

'We worked enough for it,' said Don. 'Lots of people believe in me.'

'Not too many believe in me!' said Cogswell in wonder. 'Yet here I am!'

'You believed in yourself, didn't you?'

'Yes, of course.'

'That's the most important.'

'Interesting,' said Cogswell. 'This is a most fascinating place. Well, I must be off to explore.'

'See you around,' said Don.

The house was in flames. The wraiths of Jean and Ivalee Trembath shifted, as Jean and Ivalee ran around the house.

Jean's wraith looked at Don beseechingly.

'Of course,' said Don gently. He dropped low, stood inside the room. He concentrated, materialized.

The women were dropping like flowers at twilight. The fire crackled behind him.

Jean raised her head, looked into his face with vast surprise. He lifted her — how light she was! — went to the window.

A problem! He was now a material body, and subject to the material laws of gravity . . . He could no more descend the thirty feet to the ground than could Jean.

Don thought himself to the roof. He materialized, tore down the ancient radio aerial, lowered it past the window, let it hang.

He materialized again inside the room, and now the smoke

was thick. He wrapped Jean and Ivalee with drapes from
the windows, looped the aerial first around Jean's body,
lowered her to the ground. He thought himself down,
released her, repeated the process with Ivalee Trembath.
Then he carried the two of them through the back entrance
to the alley.

He motioned to a man driving past in a car. The man
ignored him. Don materialized in the seat beside him. The
man's jaw dropped, strangled words came from his throat.

'Stop the car,' said Don. 'There are people hurt back
there.'

The man gasped out his acquiescence. Don put the two
women in the back seat.

'Take them to emergency, City Hospital.'

'Y-yes, sir.'

Don relaxed his clutch on reality, expanded away into the
after-life.

19

The police jailed as many Christian Crusaders as they could
identify; the next day they were fined, lectured by the judge
and released. Tramping out of the court house they defiantly
broke into their hymn, 'Onward Christian Soldiers.'

The Reverend Walter Spedelius attempted to rent Orange
City Auditorium, but was turned down. He called a mass-
meeting on the farm of one Thomas Hand, at the outskirts
of the city. And there in a great square framed by eight
bonfires, the Reverend Spedelius took up Hugh Bronny's
torch.

'Verily, brothers,' he cried in the brassy sing-song
monotone of the evangelist, 'our brother Hugh lived and
died like a Christian saint — like a crusader of old! He gave
all his earthly life to show us the way — just as many years
ago Jesus Christ, yea Jesus Christ, did the same — and
brothers, I say unto you, Hugh Bronny, Fighting Hugh
Bronny, is here with us tonight — and I say unto you,

brothers, we won't let him down — we'll fight in the name of Jesus and Moses and the Prophet Elijah and the Prophet Hugh Bronny — and we'll fight till we bring the Kingdom of God to this wonderful land of ours. . . .'

The Christian Crusaders were news; reporters and photographers were on hand, and the papers and news-magazines throughout the United States announced the new crusade. Segregationists, anti-Semites, America-Firsters thronged to ally themselves with the movement.

The opposition stirred. A dozen liberal organizations denounced the movement, editorials appeared in the great newspapers, bitterly critical of Fighting Hugh Bronny, Walter Spedelius and the Christian Crusade. In the tumult Lucky Don Berwick was almost forgotten. He was no longer news.

20

In the region beyond time, Donald Berwick lived and moved. He became aware of a tug, a pull; and since he was no more than a thought, dwelling in the massive composite of all the thoughts that ever were, he responded.

Ivalee Trembath was calling him. She and Jean sat in the living room of the old Marsile house.

Don looked into the face of the swaying soul that stood with feet anchored in Ivalee's body-pellet. The soul spoke, 'Release me, Donald, and take my place for a while, and I'll roam; and when you want to leave, I'll be back. . . .'

It was strange speaking with Ivalee's mouth, hearing with her ears. Sight and muscle coordination, at the moment, seemed impossible.

'Hello, darling Jean,' said Don.

'Hello, Don. How are you?'

'I'm very well. Things over here are just as we expected. I've got pictures for Kelso.'

'Don — I miss you terribly.'

'I miss you too, Jean . . . .'

'You helped us out of the fire. You materialized.'

'Yes.'

'Is that hard?'

'It wasn't then. I was at the height of my intensity. I'm not so strong now.'

'I don't understand, Donald.'

'I don't either. The stronger I am, the easier it is for me to materialize.'

'Are you weaker — because people aren't thinking about you so much?'

'Yes. I believe so. More or less.'

Jean's voice quavered. 'Then Hugh must be very strong.'

'Yes,' said Don. 'I've seen him. He glows with strength. You'd never recognize him.'

'Is he — as wretched as he was on Earth?'

'He's different. He's as evil. But the smallness, the petty detestable part of Hugh has dwindled. Hugh is now something magnificently evil.'

'What happens when he sees you?'

Don paused, then said matter-of-factly. 'He tried to kill me.'

'Kill you!'

'Sounds odd, doesn't it? I'm already dead. But that's how it works.'

'How can he kill you? You're immaterial — a thought?'

'A thought can overwhelm another thought out; reduce it to oblivion, make it something furtive and ethereal — despised.'

'Hugh is trying to do that — to you?'

'Yes.'

Jean was silent a moment. Then: 'You know what's going on down here?'

'Not altogether. I've been — out, away.'

Jean explained, and Don was silent for several minutes.

'Don,' said Jean diffidently, 'are you still there?'

'Yes. I'm thinking.'

There was another minute of silence. Jean sat tense,

watching the limp form of Ivalee, her hands twisting and
knotting a strand of ribbon.

'Jean.'

'Yes, Don.'

'The battle is between a pair of ideas. Hugh represents
one, I represent another. I must fight Hugh. Kill him or
kill the *idea* of Hugh.'

'But Don — are you strong enough?'

'I don't know.'

'How can you fight?'

'Just as on Earth. Tooth and nail, fang and claw.'

'If you lose — will I ever see you again?'

The voice was fading, indistinct. 'I don't know, Jean.
Wish me luck. I can see Hugh now . . . He's coming.'

Ivalee Trembath twitched, mumbled, then lay quiescent.

There was a sudden roar in the room, like a train passing
through. The roar subsided to a rumble, faded.

'Iva', said Jean gently. 'Iva.'

No response. Jean listened. The air was very still but
seemed to crackle like cellophane.

Jean slowly got to her feet, went to the telephone.

Hugh Bronny stood over Donald Berwick. They were
on a featureless expanse, a plain without end; it might have
been the Ukrainian Steppe, or the distorted perspective of
a surrealist painting.

Hugh was wearing his black double-breasted coat. His
enormously muscular arms filled out the shoulders. His eyes
blazed like electric arcs, his face was the size of a shield;
his legs were knotted with strength.

'Donald Berwick,' said Hugh, 'I've hated you on Earth,
and I hate you here.'

'You could not help but hate me,' said Don, 'because
you're the personification of hate — here as you were on
Earth.'

'No,' said Hugh, 'I was a great religious leader; now
I am a saint.'

'Words can't conceal fates.'

Hugh took an ominous step forward. 'I will expunge you,

you miserable pap-mouthed coward.'

Jean telephoned Godfrey Head. 'Godfrey — I must see you.'

'Sorry, Jean, can't make it . . . I'm bound for a meeting of the Faculty Association. Two of the University Regents have become Crusaders; can you believe it?'

'Godfrey — I've just talked to Donald. He's fighting Hugh Bronny right now. We've got to help him.'

The telephone line buzzed with silence. Then: 'Help him? How?'

'Let me come with you to your meeting . . . I take it you're all anti-Bronny?'

Godfrey Head snorted. 'Naturally. But what can you do?'

Jean laughed bitterly. 'I'm several times a millionaire. There's a lot I can do.'

Hugh snatched out, caught hold of Don's shoulder. Fingers dug into flesh like tongs into a bale of hay.

A sword, thought Don, and he held a sword. He swung, hacked; the blade clanged against Hugh's neck. Hugh reached out his hand, seized the blade, snatched it from Don.

'I will cut you to infinitesimals,' he chanted, 'I'll smear you into smoke, I'll blow your memory out of time. . . .' He lashed out with the sword. Don sprang back; the blade hissed past his chest, leaving a red groove.

He thought sword, and held in his hand another sword.

Hugh bellowed out a gust of mocking laughter. He took a stride forward, slashing with his sword.

Godfrey Head diffidently addressed assembled members of the University Faculty Association.

'A friend of mine wishes to speak to the meeting. I want to warn you in advance: be prepared for a surprise. What you will hear may strike you as unprecedented and unsettling. But, remember, we presume ourselves as intellectual elite, and we've got to shoulder the responsibilities which go with the status — or else admit ourselves to be the academic equivalent of fast-talking four-flushers.' His mild face glowed; he glared at the surprised audience as if they had challenged him.

'This meeting was called to establish a position in regard to the Christian Crusade. What Jean Berwick will tell you bears on the subject.' He motioned Jean up to his side. 'This is Jean Berwick. Listen carefully to what she says, and think carefully, because I think a time has come for us, and all other intelligent people, to make a choice.'

Jean stood up on the podium, frail and intent. 'My name is Jean Berwick. My husband Don Berwick died recently, in what might be called the first armed aggression of the Christian Crusade. He is dead, but he is still fighting — in spirit.' She smiled wanly. 'In spirit, he needs our help.'

'I have a proposal to put to you — one of far greater scope than any of you had expected to hear tonight. Why do I come to you? Because you are the first large group of influential and intelligent people I could reach, and because you understand the implications of the Christian Crusade. I want to crush the Christian Crusade, grind it into oblivion. It is not enough to jail one or two demagogues; the Christian Crusade is an idea. We must organize a counter-idea, stronger and more inspiring, to smother it.

'Exactly what is this so-called Christian Crusade? It is hate, enforced conformity, authoritarianism, race bigotry. Are the Crusaders Christian? They make a rite of submission to a malignant and vengeful God, who rewards his friends like a ward-boss and sentences his opponents to torture in Hell. Christ would turn away in disgust from this God. What is the counter-doctrine? A crusade for human dignity and the right — the obligation — to nonconformity, as passionate as Bronny's crusade for his orthodoxy! A declaration of independence from religiosity and the assertion that men are masters of their own destinies. These are the issues: human values against superstition; civilization against barbarism; faith in man against faith in dogma.

'What do I expect of you here tonight? I want you to rise to the challenge that our knowledge of right and wrong has set before us. I want you to endorse the manifesto I have outlined, to set it as standard to which intelligent men and women can rally.

'We are on the verge of space; already we can tap unlimited energy. There is the outer threat of Communism, less dangerous than this internal threat symbolized by the Christian Crusade. These are problems *and* opportunities. How shall we meet them? With the mill-weight of the past around our necks? Or as proud, questing, self-reliant men of the future?

'What is your answer? If you're with me, clap . . . If you're not — ' she smiled. 'Then you can hiss.'

She waited. There was ten seconds of silence, in which the churn of minds was almost palpable; honest enthusiasm tugging at conventional caution.

There was a sudden sound of clapping. It grew in volume. It filled the hall.

Jean relaxed against the podium. 'I am not speaking to you. I'm not an orator. It's Donald Berwick speaking through me. If Hugh Bronny symbolizes the past, then Donald Berwick is the standard of the future.'

Hugh laughed at Don. 'Strike. You cannot cut me. Your sword is dull.'

Don looked. The sword had turned to dull gray pewter. He saw a glint, ducked. Hugh's blade whistled over his head.

Gun, thought Don, and he held his .45 automatic.

Hugh's sword became a monstrous revolver, shooting yellow projectiles the size of hand-grenades.

Don aimed, fired.

There was discussion. A brisk sharp-featured man said, 'Do you propose that we issue a Manifesto of Atheism?

We can't do that. There are many Christians among us, as well as Moslems, Jews, a few Buddhists, Orthodox Hindus — in addition to the free-thinkers, Unitarians, agnostics, and atheists.'

'No,' said Jean, 'I don't ask you to endorse atheism, or any other belief. We merely accept and proclaim that there's an elemental mystery to the universe and to the why of things. Everyone is free to speculate. I speak not for atheism, but against compulsory theism, or compulsory dogma of any kind, even our own.'

'I see. In that case you have my whole-hearted support.'

Godfrey Head addressed the chairman. 'I move that we adjourn the meeting, that we immediately convene as the Society for Intellectual Freedom — with the purpose of drafting the Declaration Jean Berwick has proposed.'

Don pulled the trigger of his gun. The bullet smashed into the barrel of Hugh's great weapon. The projectile buzzed past Don's ear, exploded somewhere behind.

Hugh sprang forward, they grappled. One enormous arm circled Don's throat. Hugh pressed his weight against Don, trying to force him over backwards.

Don swung up a desperate fist, struck Hugh on the nose. He felt the cartilage crush; then Hugh's weight pushed him back. He landed with a boneshaking jar. Hugh's hands went to Don's throat.

'I'l tear your head off,' hissed Hugh. 'I'll strip you arm from arm. . . .'

The Society for Intellectual Freedom became known to the nation and the world, on the following day. It was bitterly attacked by certain of the organized religions; by the Christian Crusade in particular, and hailed with joy by people uneasily aware that anxiety and uncertainty had driven them to accept doubtful dogma.

And who was Jean Berwick? The wife of Lucky Don Berwick — who had been killed resisting the Christian Crusade!

By a tremendous racking effort, Don threw Hugh off him. They rose to their feet, stood facing each other. Hugh had lost something of his overpowering confidence, but he was possibly more ferocious. Don grew larger, more solid.

They both glowed with a cool blue light. The background had shifted; they stood in a valley between two ranges of low black hills.

'Hugh,' said Don, 'I could kill you with my hands . . . But I prefer to demolish you with my mind.'

Jeffrey Hannevelt, President of the Unitarian Association, executive chairman of the Society for Intellectual Freedom, told reporters, 'We could take Walter Spedelius, Casper Johnson, Gerald Henrick to court — we might get them indicted for conspiracy. But that's not enough. We've got to discredit them. We're modern men, in charge of our own destiny. We're moving into a new era of civilization, setting up a whole new culture pattern. It's up to us how it'll turn out. How do we want it? The kind of world men dream and hope for? Or a world of groveling subservience to authority — political, religious, or otherwise? You know what the answer is. We can advance to a state where humanity proudly accepts and asserts responsibility for its own actions, where each man is proud to be a free-willed individual.'

'Would you say, sir, that it's a case of rational versus the irrational? Good versus bad?'

'It's too big to compress into words,' said Jeffrey Jannevelt. 'To call it science against superstition would be about as close as you could come.'

Hugh thought a war-club into his hands, and leapt forward to strike. Don retreated, projecting a glass dome over Hugh.

The dome swiftly contracted, fitted around Hugh, then would constrict no more. There was a struggle; Don thought another stronger glass skin around Hugh. Hugh blinked it away. The glass cracked, split. Hugh stepped out like a moth from the chrysalis.

Hugh thought a flame-thrower; in the split-second before the flame reached him, Don thought a metal wall. The flame spattered back.

Only Hugh's upward glance warned Don; he thought himself a mile back; a lump of iron, the size of a small asteroid, crashed into his footsteps.

On Hugh's right hand, Don conceived a mass of uranium shaped like a bucket; on Hugh's left hand he conceived a mass shaped like a plug. They darted together; Hugh saw them coming; they did not appear to be aimed at him. He stepped back with contempt.

The pieces joined. Don thought himself a thousand miles away.

Thought is faster than radiation; thought is faster than any shock-wave. The great glow dazzled Don's eyes; otherwise he was unharmed.

Where Hugh had stood was a glowing crater.

21

On the terrace of Godfrey Head's beach cottage ten miles south of Santa Barbara, Jean, Ivalee Trembath, Godfrey Head and his wife, Howard Rakowsky sat quietly. It was a warm evening. The Pacific lay flat and calm, glistening under a half-moon.

'Did you see that?' said Jean suddenly.

Godfrey Head looked around the sky. 'What? Where?'

'A flash! A great light!'

'I didn't see anything,' said Head.

Rakowsky shook his head; Ivalee said nothing.

'Might have been an atom-bomb explosion in Nevada.'

The telephone range; Godfrey Head answered. They heard his voice: 'How many? . . . Really . . . That's wonderful. It looks as if we did some good after all . . . . '

He returned to the terrace. 'That was Claiborne in Los

Angeles. The Christian Crusaders put on a huge rally out in Gardena.'

'Really?'

'Three hundred and twelve people showed up. There's also a warrant out for Spedelius. Misappropriation of funds.'

'I guess that does it,' said Rakowsky. 'Funny how these movements come up — and seem so important and critical. Then suddenly when they burst like a balloon, when they're past, how weak and paltry they seem in retrospect.'

Godfrey asked Jean, 'What of the parapsychological research?'

'We'll get started up again. As soon as possible. We've barely scratched the surface. What is mind-stuff? That's the basic question. Did it exist before man, before life on Earth? Did intelligence adapt itself to a pre-existing ocean of mind-stuff, or did intelligence generate mind-stuff? If there is intelligent alien life on other planets, do they use the same mind-stuff as we do? How do the material processes of the brain engage the non-material processes of the mind-stuff? What is the mechanism? Where's the linkage?'

Rakowsky held up his hand. 'Enough to keep us busy several months right there.'

'Of course it won't be the same . . . I don't want to go back to Orange City . . . Maybe we can build a research center somewhere up here, along the ocean. . . .'

She rose to her feet. 'Excuse me, I'm going to take a walk down the beach.'

'Like some company?' asked Head.

'No thanks.'

They watched her go. 'Poor kid,' said Rakowsky. 'She's been through a lot.'

Ivalee smiled. 'Something very wonderful is about to happen to Jean.'

Jean sat on a half-buried length of timber. She looked up — a man stood before her. She jumped to her feet, stepped back.

'Don't be frightened, Jean.'

The blood was pounding in Jean's ears. 'I'm not frightened.'

He took her hands, kissed her. His face felt warm; there was a stubble of beard on his cheeks.

'Donald,' she sighed. 'You feel real.'

'I am real.'

'I wish you were, Donald. . . .'

The surf roared quietly; the stars fulfilled the ancient patterns. Her voice sounded thin and far away.

'Sit down. I'll explain. It won't take long.'

She slowly sat on the log. 'How — how long can you stay?'

'Till I die.'

'But — you're already dead.'

'And now I'm alive again.'

'Don, don't tease me, if it's not true.'

'It's true. I died. I was a thought — hard and intense and definite. I materialized. Remember? But I was not hard and definite enough — not true matter. I slipped back. Then as the thought lost intensity I became weaker. Until I fought Hugh Bronny. At first he was very strong — a giant.'

Jean nodded. 'At the same time we were fighting the Crusaders — and they were strong at first. But we won — just tonight.'

'Tonight I killed Hugh Bronny.'

Jean sighed, laughed wearily. 'A dead man being killed.'

'He's not utterly destroyed. Because the cycle goes on in the after-life. What's left of Hugh is the thought of his thought — a poor shambling wraith.'

'I don't understand, Donald.'

'I don't either . . . But suddenly I was strong — intense as I never had been before. More than anything I wanted to be with you. And here I am.'

'Are you real? All of you? Not just your outside feel and look?'

'Look at me — touch me.'

She did. 'Mightn't it be — well, illusion?'

'I am real. Perhaps because it's the simplest way. A

material body must move; what's more rational than muscles to move it? Material muscles. And what more rational than material blood to nourish the muscles? And what's more rational than functioning material lungs and a functioning material stomach to feed the blood? Is there an easier way to simulate a normal human being than to *be* a human being? There's nothing mystic or occult involved. . . . It's common sense. Carbon atoms crystallize into a diamond, not because a diamond is pretty or because a diamond has occult significance — but because that's the way carbon atoms fit together. The simplest way. The same way with me.'

'Don — can you stay here — forever?'

'Until I die. I'm material now.'

Jean looked up the beach, toward the lights of the beach-cottage. 'Shall we go back — and tell the others?'

'Let's not . . . Where's your car?'

'Up the road.'

'Let's go.'

'But Howard — Godfrey — Ivalee — '

'We'll telephone from Orange City.'

Jean laughed softly, patted his cheek. 'Shall I get my suitcase?'

'You'd better get your check-book,' said Don. 'I should have materialized a satchel-full of twenty-dollar bills.'

'That's counterfeiting,' said Jean. 'How are we ever going to explain this?'

'My return? Lucky Don Berwick staggered out of the burning house, had an attack of amnesia, finally came to myself.'

'It'll have to do.' She turned away. 'Can I trust you not to de-materialize?'

'Yes . . . I'll wait in the car.'

Five minutes later she returned to the car with her suitcase. 'Donald?' She looked into the car. 'Don! Where are you?' A sudden terrible fear gripped her.

'Right behind you. What's the trouble?'

'Nothing.' She got in, slammed the door. 'I was just . . . afraid.'

'There's nothing to be afraid of.' He started the motor, turned on the lights. The car moved out to the highway and turned south toward Los Angeles. The tail-lights became a pair of red dots, a glimmer, and then were lost.

Afterword

All events, personalities, and places in this novel are fictitious, with the exception of Los Angeles. The seance sequences are modeled after actual occurrences; the general tone of spirit communication as described accords with actual instances. Theories and speculation are the author's own, although he assumes that other people, considering the same subject, have drawn similar inferences.

The author is no enemy of Christian ethical doctrine, as he has tried to make clear. But he cannot disguise his opinion of certain forms of evangelism. Hugh Bronny represents an unfortunate possibility of the 'hard sell' technique in that direction, rather than any specific case. Thus a similarity exists here with Sinclair Lewis' *Elmer Gantry*.

Captious readers may raise their eyebrows at the last few pages. Even the author's credibility is strained. Still — on the other hand — who knows? Perhaps such things happen all the time. Stranger things do.

— Jack Vance

THE ENCHANTED PRINCESS

JAMES AIKEN RECOGNIZED THE MAN standing at the reception desk as Victor Martinon, former producer at Pageant. Martinon had been fired during the recent cutbacks, and the headlines in *Variety* sent chills down every back in the industry. If flamboyant, money-making Martinon went, who was safe?

Aiken approached the desk, puzzled by Martinon's presence at the Krebius Children's Clinic. A versatile lover, Martinon never stayed married long enough to breed children. If Martinon were here on the same errand as his own . . . well, that was a different matter. Aiken felt a sharpening of interest.

'Hello, Martinon.'

'Hi,' said Martinon, neither recognizing Aiken nor caring to indulge a stranger.

'I worked on *Clair de Lune* with you — built the Dreamboat sequence.'

Clair de Lune was Martinon's next to last picture.

'Oh, yes. Quite an effort. Still with Pageant?'

'I'm in my own lab know. Doing special effects for TV.'

'A man's got to eat,' said Martinon, implying that Aiken now could sink no further.

Aiken's mouth tightened, reflecting mingled emotions. 'Keep me in mind, if you ever get back in pictures.'

'Yeah. Sure will.'

Aiken had never liked Martinon anyway. Martinon was big and broad, about forty, with silver hair pomaded and brushed till it glittered. His eyes were vaguely owlish — large, dark, surrounded by fine wrinkles; his mustache was cat-like; he wore excellent clothes. Aiken had no moustache; he was wiry and dark. He walked with a slight limp from a war wound, and so looked older than his twenty-five years. Martinon was suave and smelled of heather; Aiken was abrupt, angular and smelled of nothing much in particular.

Aiken spoke to the nurse behind the desk. 'My sister has a little boy here. Barry Tedrow.'

'Oh, yes, Barry. Nice little boy.'

'She came to visit him yesterday, and told me about the film you were showing. I'd like to see it. If I may, of course.'

The nurse looked sidewise at Martinon. 'I don't really see any objection. I suppose you'd better speak to Dr. Krebius. Or if Mr. Martinon says it's all right —'

'Oh.' Aiken looked at Martinon. 'Some of your stuff?'

Martinon nodded. 'In a way. The films are, well, experimental. I'm not sure we want anyone checking them just yet.'

'Here's Dr. Krebius,' said the nurse placidly, and Martinon frowned.

Dr. Krebius was stocky, red-faced, forthright. His hair was whiter than Martinon's and rose from his scalp like a whisk broom. He wore a white smock, and gave off a faint odour of clean laundry and soap.

The nurse said, 'This gentleman heard about the films; he wants to see them.'

'Ah.' Dr. Krebius looked at Aiken with eyes like small blue ball bearings.

'The little stories.' He spoke in a heavy accent, gruff and deep in his throat.

'You are who?'

'My name is James Aiken. My sister saw the films yesterday and told me about them.'

'Ah ha,' growled Krebius, turning to Martinon as if he might clap him on the back. 'Maybe we charge admission, hey? Make money for the hospital!'

Martinon said in a measured voice, 'Aiken here works

in a film laboratory. His interest is professional.'

'Sure! What of it? Let him look! He does no harm!'

Martinon shrugged, moved off down the hall.

Krebius turned back to Aiken. 'We show not much. Just a few little stories to please the children.' He glanced at his wristwatch. 'In six minutes, at two o'clock precisely. This is the way we work here, precise on the second. That way we cure the sick little legs, the blind eyes.'

'Oh,' said Aiken. 'Blind children too?'

'My specialty! You know of the Krebius Clinic in Leipzig?'

Aiken shook his head. 'Sorry.'

'For ten years we do tremendous work. Far ahead of what you do here. Why? There is more to do, we must be bold!' He tapped Aiken on the chest with a hard forefinger. 'Two years ago I give up my wonderful hospital. There is no living with the Communists. They order me to make lenses, soldiers to see better down the guns. My work is to heal the eyes, not putting them out. I come here.'

'I see your point,' said Aiken. He hesitated. Martinon's attitude had given him the uncomfortable sense of interloping.

Krebius looked intently at him under bristly eyebrows.

'Incidentally,' said Aiken, 'as Martinon says, I'm in the special effects business. I'd like to see anything that might be new.'

'Of course. Why not? I have no interest in the film; it is not mine. Look as you please. Martinon is the cautious one. Fear is caution. I have no fear. I am cautious only with the tools of my work. Then!' He held up his blunt hands. 'I am like a vise. The eye is a delicate organ!'

He bowed, walked off down the corridor. Aiken and the nurse watched him go. Aiken, grinning a little, looked at the nurse, who was grinning too.

'You should see him when he's excited. I was raised on a farm. The old kitchen range used to get red hot. When water spilled on it . . . .'

'I'm a farm boy myself,' said Aiken.

'That's Dr. Krebius. You'd better go. He wasn't fooling. We work by the split-second around here. Right down the end of the hall, that's the ward for today's films.'

Aiken walked down the corridor, pushed through the swinging door into a large room with curtained windows. Crippled children occupied beds along the walls, wheelchairs down the centre of the room. Aiken looked around for Barry, but saw him nowhere. A table near the door supported a sixteen millimetre projector; on the far wall a screen hung. Martinon stood by the projector threading in the film. He nodded curtly at Aiken.

The clock on the wall read half a minute to two. Martinon flicked on the projector's lamp and motor, focused the image. A nurse went to sit under the screen with a big red book.

At exactly 2 P.M., the nurse stood and announced, 'Today, we watch another chapter from the life of Ulysses. Last time, you'll remember, they were trapped by a terrible one-eyed giant called Polyphemus, on the island that we call Sicily today. Polyphemus is a horrible creature that's been eating up the Greeks.' A delighted shudder and buzz ran around the room. 'Today we find Ulysses and his men plotting an escape.' She nodded. The lights went out.

Martinon started the projector.

There was a chattering sound. The white rectangle on the screen quivered, shook. Martinon switched off the projector. The lights went on. Martinon bent over the projector with a worried frown. He banged it with his knuckles, shook it, tried the switch again. The same chatter. He looked up, shook his head despondently. 'Don't think we're going to make it today.'

The children sighed in unison.

Aiken went over to the projector. 'What's the trouble?'

'It's been coming on a long time,' said Martinon. 'Something in the sprockets. I'll have to take it to the repairman.'

'Let me take a look. I've got the same model; I know it inside out.'

'Oh, don't bother,' said Martinon, but Aiken was already investigating the mechanism. He opened a blade of his pocket knife, worked ten seconds.

'She'll go now. The sprocket holding the drive gear was loose.'

'Much obliged,' muttered Martinon.

Aiken took his seat. Martinon caught the nurse's eye. She bent over the book, began to read aloud. The lights went out.

The Odyssey! Aiken was looking into a vast cave, dim-lit by firelight. Hoary walls rose to fade into high murk. Off to one side lay a great manlike hulk. At his back a dozen men worked feverishly, and in the vast smoky volume of the cavern they were miniatures, manikins. They held a great pointed pole into the flames, and the red firelight played and danced on their sweating bodies.

The camera drew closer. The features of the men became visible — young, clean-limbed warriors moving with passionate determination, heroic despair.

Ulysses stood forth, a man with a face like the Sistine Jehovah. He made a sign. The warriors heaved the spear to their shoulders. Crouching under the weight, they ran forward against the face half-seen in the dimness.

It was a lax, idiotic face, with one eye in the middle of the forehead. The camera drew away showing the length of Polyphemus' body. The Greeks came running with the flaming pike; the eye snapped open, stared in wonder, and the pike bored into the centre — deep, deep, deep.

Polyphemus jerked his head, the spear flung up, the Greeks scuttled into the shadows, disappeared. Polyphemus tore in agony at his face, wrenched loose the spear. He lunged around the cave, groping with one hand, clasping his bloody face with the other.

The camera went to the Greeks pressing back against the walls. The hairy, towering legs tramped past them. A great hand swept close, scraped, grabbed.

The Greeks held their breaths, and the sweat gleamed on their chests.

Polyphemus stumbled away, into the fire; the logs scattered, embers flew.

Polyphemus bellowed in frustration.

The camera shifted to the Greeks, tying themselves under the bellies of monstrous sheep.

Polyphemus stood at the mouth of the cave. He pushed the great barrier rock aside and, straddling the opening, felt the back of each sheep as it passed between his legs.

The Greeks ran down to the golden beach, launched their galley over the wine-dark sea. They hoisted the sail and the wind drove them off-shore.

Polyphemus came down to the beach. He picked up a boulder, flung it.

Slowly through the air it flew, slanting down toward the Greeks. It crashed into the sea, and the galley was tossed high on a fountain of water and bright white foam. Polyphemus stooped for another boulder. The scene faded.

'And that's all for today,' said the nurse.

The children sighed in disappointment, began to chatter.

Martinon looked at Aiken with a peculiar sidelong grin. 'What do you think?'

'Not bad,' said Aiken. 'Not bad at all. A little rough in spots. You could use better research. That wasn't any Greek galley — it looked more like a Viking longboat.'

Martinon nodded carelessly. 'It's not my film; I'm on the outside looking in. But I agree with you. All brains and no technique, like a lot of this *avant garde* stuff.'

'I don't recognize any of the actors. Who made it?'

'Merlin Studios '

'Never heard of them.'

'They've just organized. One of my friends is involved. He asked me to show the film to some kids, get their reaction.'

'They like it,' said Aiken.

Martinon shrugged. 'Kids are easy to please.'

Aiken turned to go. 'So long, and thanks.'

'Don't mention it.'·

In the hall, Aiken met Dr. Krebius, standing with a pretty

young blonde girl. Krebius gave him a genial salute. 'And the film, you liked it?'

'Very much,' said Aiken. 'But I'm puzzled.'

'Ah ha,' said Krebius with a fox wink at the girl. 'The little secrets that we must keep.'

'Secrets?' she murmured. 'What secrets?'

'I forget,' said Krebius. 'You know none of the secrets.'

Aiken looked intently at the girl, glanced quickly at the doctor, and Krebius nodded. 'This is little Carol Bannister. She's blind.'

'That's too bad,' said Aiken. Her eyes turned in his direction. They were a wide, deep Dutch blue, mild and tranquil. He saw that she might be a year or two older than he had first imagined.

Krebius stroked her silken-blonde head as he might pat a spaniel. 'It's a pity when lovely young girls can't see to look and flirt and watch the boys' hearts go bumping. But with Carol — well, we work and we hope, and who knows? Someday she may see as well as you or I.'

'I sure hope so,' said Aiken.

'Thank you,' the girl said softly, and Aiken took his leave.

In an unaccountably gloomy mood, he returned to his lab and found himself unable to work. For an hour he sat musing and smoking, then, on a sudden inspiration, called a friend, who was legman for a famous Hollywood columnist.

'Hello, Larry. This is Aiken.'

'What's up?'

'I want some information on Merlin Studios. Got any?'

'Nothing Never heard of 'em. What do they do?'

Aiken felt like dropping the whole thing. 'Oh, they've made a few snatches of film. Fairy tales, things like that.'

'Any good?'

Aiken thought back over the film, and his wonder revived. 'Yeah,' he said. 'Very good. In fact — magnificent.'

'You don't say. Merlin Studios?'

'Right. And I think — just think, mind you — that Victor Martinon is in on it.'

'Martinon, eh? I'll ask Fidelia.' Fidelia was Larry's boss. 'She might know. If it's a tip, thanks.'

'Not at all.'

An hour later Larry called back. 'I've learned three things. First, nobody in the trade knows anything about Merlin Studios. It's a vacuum. Second, Vic Martinon's been doing some fancy finagling, and he has been heard to use the words 'Merlin Studios'. Third, they're arranging a sneak preview tonight.'

'Tonight? Where?'

'Garden City Theatre, Pomona.'

'Okay, Larry. Thanks.'

Aiken watched five minutes of feature film, which was immediately followed by a slide reading:

Please do not leave the theatre.
You are about to witness a
SNEAK PREVIEW
Your comments will be appreciated.

The slide dissolved into a title: a montage of coloured letters on a silver-green background:

VASILLISSA THE
ENCHANTED PRINCESS.
A fantasy based on an ancient
Russian fairy tale.
THE MERLIN STUDIOS.

The silver-green background dissolved into orange; bold gray letters read: *Produced by Victor Martinon.*

There were no further credits. The orange dissolved into a blur of grey mist, with wandering hints of pink and green.

A voice spoke. 'We go far away and long ago — to old Russia where once upon a time a young woodcutter named Ivan, returning from the woods, found a dove lying under a tree. The dove had a broken wing, and looked at Ivan so sorrowfully that he took pity on it. . . .'

The mist broke open, into the world of fairyland, a landscape swimming in radiance, richness, colour. It was real and it was unreal, a land hoped-for but that never could be. There was a forest of antique trees, banks of ferns with the sun shining through the leaves, moist white flowers, beds of violets. The foliage was brown, gold, rust, lime and dark green, and down through the leaves came shafts of sunshine. Beyond the forest was a green meadow sprinkled with daisies, buttercups, cowslips, cornflowers; far away down the valley the dark wooden gables of a village; the onion dome of a church could be seen.

The story proceeded, narrated by the voice. 'Ivan nursed the dove back to health, and received a malachite casket for reward. When he opened the casket, a magnificent palace appeared on the meadow, surrounded by beautiful gardens, terraces of ivory, statues of jade and jet and cinnabar.

'The Czar of the Sea, riding past, saw the palace. Angry at Ivan's presumption, he set Ivan impossible tasks — cutting down a forest overnight, building a flying ship, breaking an iron stallion to the saddle.

'The dove came to Ivan's aid. She was Vasillissa, a beautiful maiden with long honey-blonde hair. . . . '

The fable vaulted from miracle to miracle, through battles, sorcery, quests to the end of the earth, the final defeat of the Czar.

There was no sound from the audience. Every eye stared as if seeing the most precious part of their lives. The landscapes glowed with marvellous light: pink, blue, black, gold. The scenes were rich with imagery; real with the truth of poetry. The Czar, a great swarthy man, wore a scarlet robe and over this a black iron corselet embossed with jade. Chumichka, his steward, hopped around on malformed legs, glaring wildly from a pallid sidelong face.

The story swarmed with monsters and creatures of fable: griffins, hedgehounds, fish with legs, fiery birds.

And Vasillissa! When Aiken saw Vasillissa, he stirred with surprise. Vasillissa was a beautiful golden-haired girl, gay as any of the flowers. Vasillissa was as much a thing of magic as Ivan's wonderful palace. Like the fairy landscapes, she awakened a yearning. In one scene she came down to the river to catch a witch who had taken the form of a carp. The pool shone like bottle-glass, shadowed by black-green poplars. Vasillissa stood looking over the water. The carp jumped up in a flurry of silver spray. She turned her head suddenly and her blonde hair swung out to the side.

'I must be completely mad,' said Aiken to himself.

Vasillissa and Ivan finally escaped the raging Czar. 'And they lived happily ever after, in the palace by the Dorogheny Woods,' said the voice. And the picture ended.

Aiken drew a great breath. He joined the applause of the audience, rose to his feet, drove back to his apartment at breakneck pace.

For several hours he lay awake. Magic Vasillissa! Today he had seen her as a blind girl, with silky blonde hair; slight, thoughtful, rather shy. Carol Bannister — Vasillissa. She was and she wasn't. Carol was blind. Vasillissa had bright blue eyes and could see very well indeed. What a strange situation, thought Aiken, and lay tossing and dozing and dreaming and thinking.

James Aiken was hardly a handsome man, although he had an indefinable flair, a concentration of character. His mouth drooped at a harsh saturnine angle; he was thin and angular; he walked with a limp. He smoked and drank a good deal; he had few friends, and made no great play for women. He was clever, imaginative, quick with his hands, and the Aiken Special Effects Laboratory was doing good business. He aroused no great loyalty from his employees. They thought him cynical and morose. But a cynic is a disappointed idealist; and James Aiken was as tender, wistful an idealist as could be found in all Los Angeles.

Vasillissa, the Enchanted Princess!

He brooded about Carol Bannister. She had not acted Vasillissa, she *was* Vasillissa! And the magic longing rose in his throat like a sour taste, and he knew nothing else in his life was as important.

At quarter of ten next morning he drove north on Arroyo Seco Boulevard, up winding Lomita Way to the Krebius Children's Clinic.

At the desk he gave his name, asked to speak to Dr. Krebius, and after a short wait was ushered into an austere office.

Krebius rose to his feet, bowed stiffly. 'Yes, Mr. Aiken.' No longer the bluff and genial doctor of yesterday, he now seemed stubborn and suspicious.

Aiken asked, 'May I sit down?'

'Certainly.' Krebius lowered himself into his own chair, erect as a post.

'What do you wish?'

'I'd like to talk to you about Carol Bannister.'

Krebius raised his eyebrows inquiringly, as if the choice of topic had surprised him. 'Very well.'

'Has she ever done any acting? In the movies?'

'Carol?' Krebius looked puzzled. 'No. Never. I have known her many years. My sister is married to the cousin of her father. She has done no acting. Perhaps you are thinking of her mother, Marya Leone.'

'Marya Leone? Carol's mother?'

Krebius indulged himself in a wintry smile. 'Yes.'

'I feel even sorrier for Carol.' Marya Leone, a long-faded soubrette, was known along Sunset Strip as a confirmed and unregenerate alcoholic. A fragment of long-dead gossip rose into his mind. 'One of her husbands killed himself.'

'That was Carol's father. Four years ago. That very night Carol lost her vision. Her life has been clouded by great tragedy.'

Krebius pushed himself back in his chair, his white eyebrows came lower down over his hard blue eyes.

Aiken said in a conciliatory voice, 'Do you think there's a connection? Between the blindness and the suicide? Shock perhaps?'

Krebius spread his hands in a non-committal gesture. 'Who knows? They were on holiday in the mountains, in a lodge that Marya Leone at that time still owned. Carol was fourteen. A thunderstorm came one night. There was quarrelling. Howard Bannister shot himself, and in the next room a bolt of lightning struck through the window near young Carol. She has seen nothing since.'

'Hysterical blindness. That's the word I was thinking of. Could she be suffering from that?'

Krebius made the same non-committal gesture. Aiken felt in him a lessening of suspicion and hostility. 'Perhaps. But I think not. The optic nerve no longer functions correctly, although in many ways it reacts like perfectly healthy tissue. Carol is victim to a unique disability. The cause, who knows? Electricity? Shock? Terror? In the absence of precedent, I must strike out for myself. I attempt to stimulate the nerve; I have devised special equipment. I love her as my own child.' Krebius leaned forward, pounded the desk for emphasis.

'What are her chances of seeing again?'

Krebius leaned back in his chair, looked away. 'I do not know. I think she will see — sometime.'

'Your treatments are helping her?'

'I believe and trust so.'

'One more question, Doctor. How does Victor Martinon fit into the picture?'

Krebius became subtly uncomfortable. 'He is her mother's friend. In fact — ' His voice trailed off. 'In fact, it is said at one time — '

Aiken nodded. 'I see. But why — '

Krebius interrupted him. 'Victor is helping me. He is interested in therapy.'

'Victor Martinon?' Aiken laughed in such sardonic disbelief that Krebius flushed. 'I can hardly see Martinon playing in a Salvation Army Band.'

'Nevertheless,' said Krebius, 'he assists me in giving treatments.'

'To Carol?'

'Yes. To Carol.' Krebius was once again stubborn and hostile. His eyes glared, his white eyebrows bristled, his chin thrust out. In an icy voice he asked, 'May I ask your interest in Carol?'

Aiken had been expecting the question, but had no easy answer ready. He fidgeted uncomfortably. 'I'd rather not answer that question. . .You can think of it as a romantic interest.'

Krebius' busy eyebrows rose in surprise. 'Romance? Little Carol? A child yet!'

'Perhaps you don't know her as well as you think you do.'

'Perhaps not,' muttered Krebius deep in thought. 'Perhaps not. The little ones grow up so fast.'

'Incidentally,' Aiken asked, 'does Carol have any sisters? Or a cousin who looks like her?'

'No No one.'

Aiken said no more. He rose to his feet. 'I won't take up your time, Doctor. But I'd like to talk to Carol, if I may.'

Krebius stared up truculently as if he might refuse, then shrugged and grunted. 'I have no objections. She must not leave the hospital. She is in my care.'

'Thank you.' Aiken left the office, went to the reception desk. Martinon was just coming in through the main entrance. At the sight of Aiken his pace slackened.

'Hello, Aiken. What are you doing here?'

'I might ask the same of you.'

'I have business here.'

'So have I.' Aiken turned to the nurse. 'I'd like to speak to Carol Bannister. Dr. Krebius gave me permission.'

'I'll ring for her. You can wait in the reception room.'

'Thanks.' Aiken nodded to Martinon, went into the reception room which opened off the lobby, across from Krebius' office.

Martinon looked after him, turned, walked into Krebius' office without knocking.

Time passed. Aiken sat on the edge of his chair, his hands moist. He was extremely nervous, and correspondingly annoyed at himself. Who would come through the door? Carol Bannister? Vasillissa? Was he confused, mistaken, making a fool of himself? The minutes passed, and Aiken could no longer sit still. He rose to his feet, moved around the room. Through the open door he saw Martinon come into the lobby followed by Dr. Krebius. Martinon was pale and obviously nervous. Krebius looked surly. They marched up the corridor, neither speaking to the other, and disappeared into a room next to Krebius' office, marked *Laboratory*.

The corridor was now empty. Aiken went back to the couch, forced himself to sit quietly.

A nurse appeared in the doorway. 'Mr. Aiken?' she asked briskly.

'Yes.' He rose to his feet.

Carol came into the doorway, felt her way past the jamb. In her white blouse and grey flannel skirt she looked like a college freshman; her honey-coloured hair was brushed till it shone. She seemed slighter and more fragile than Aiken had remembered, but of course his recollection was coloured by the image of Vasillissa, agile, vital, reckless.

She looked uncertainly in Aiken's direction, with wide, blank, Delft-blue eyes.

'Hello.' She was puzzled.

Aiken took her arm, led her to the couch. The nurse nodded briefly at Aiken, disappeared. 'My name is James Aiken. I spoke to you in the hall yesterday.'

'Oh, yes. I remember now.'

Aiken was studying her face. Was this Carol? Or Vasillissa? And if she were Vasillissa, how did Carol see? He made up his mind. It was definite. There was something unmistakable. This was Vasillissa. But she lived in a new country, in a new time, unable to use her magic. The dove with the broken wing.

She moved restlessly. Aiken hastily said, 'I suppose you're wondering what I want.'

She laughed. 'I'm glad you came. I get lonesome.'

'Dr. Krebius tells me you lost your sight in a lightning storm — '

Her face went instantly blank and cold. He had said the wrong thing.

'He says that it's very likely you'll see again.'

'Yes.'

'These treatments — do they do you any good?'

'You mean, the Opticon?'

'If that's what they call it.'

'Well, up to three or four months ago I thought I saw the colours. You know, little flashes. But I don't see them any more.'

'How long has Martinon been working with you?'

'Oh, a few months. He works differently from Doctor Krebius.'

'How?'

She shrugged. 'He doesn't do very much. Except read to me.'

Aiken was puzzled. 'What good does that do?'

'I don't know. I guess it keeps me amused while the machine is turned on.'

'Do you know that Martinon used to be a motion picture producer?'

'I know he used to work in the movies. He's never told me exactly what he did.'

'How long have you known him?'

'Not very long. He says he used to know Mother. Mother was in the movies.'

'Yes, I know. Marya Leone.'

'She's quite a drunk now,' Carol said in an even voice which might or might not conceal deep feeling. She turned her blank eyes toward him. 'May I feel your face?'

'Certainly.'

Her fingertips felt his hair, forehead, brushed over his eye sockets, nose, mouth, chin. She made no comment.

'Well?' said Aiken.

'Are you a detective or something like that?'

'I'm a frustrated artist.'

'Oh. You're asking so many questions.'

'Do you mind? I've got a lot more.'

'No. If you'll answer some for me first.'

'Go ahead. Ask.'

She hesitated. 'Well, why did you come to see me?'

Aiken smiled faintly. 'I saw a movie last night, called *Vasillissa the Enchanted Princess.*'

'Oh? The fairy tale? I know that one very well. About Ivan and the wicked Czar of the Sea.'

'In this movie Vasillissa was a very beautiful girl. She had long silken hair like yours. She had blue eyes like yours. In fact —' Aiken hesitated over the fateful phrase ' — in fact, she was you.'

'Me?'

'Yes. You. Carol Bannister.'

Carol laughed. 'You flatter me very much. I've never acted, not even in grammar school. Watching Mother emote killed any urge I had.'

'But it *was* you.'

'It couldn't be!' She was smiling, half-worried, half-amused.

'The film was produced by Victor Martinon; Martinon's been hanging around here. You live here. The coincidence is too great. There's something going on.'

Carol was silent. She was thinking. A queer look came over her face.

'Yesterday I saw another film,' said Aiken. 'Part of *The Odyssey.*'

'*The Odyssey* . . . Victor read *The Odyssey* to me. Also *The Enchanted Princess.*'

'This is very strange,' said Aiken.

'Yes. And these last few days . . . .' She was blushing, blushing pink scarlet.

'What's the matter?'

'He's been saying some rather awful things. Asking questions.'

Aiken felt the skin at the back of his neck slowly going taut. Carol turned her head, as if she could actually see him, swiftly put her hand up, touched his face. 'Why, you're angry!'

'Yes, I'm angry.'

'But why?' She was puzzled.

The words spilled out of Aiken's mouth. 'You may or may not understand. I saw this picture last night. I saw Vasillissa — this may seem very strange to you — but everything she did, every angle of her head, every motion of her head — they meant something to me. I sound like a school boy, but I fell in love with Vasillissa.'

'But I'm not Vasillissa,' she said.

'Yes, you are. You're Vasillissa under a spell. Vasillissa frozen in a block of ice. I want to help you, to make you the free Vasillissa again.'

Carol laughed. 'You're Ivan.'

'At heart,' said Aiken, 'I'm Ivan.'

She reached up again, touched his face, and the touch had a different texture. It was less impersonal. 'You don't feel like Ivan.'

'I don't look like Ivan, either.'

A figure loomed in the door. Carol dropped her hand, turned her head.

'Mr. Aiken,' said Krebius, 'I would much appreciate a word with you in my office.'

Aiken slowly rose. 'Just one minute, Doctor.'

'Now, if you don't mind.'

'Very well.' Aiken turned to Carol, but she had stood up. She was holding his arm.

'Doctor,' she said, 'does what you want to talk about concern me?'

'Yes, my child.'

'I'm not a child, Dr. Krebius. If it concerns me, I want to be with you.'

He looked at her in bewilderment. 'But Carol, this will be men's talk.'

'If it concerns me, I want to know.'

Aiken asked, 'Are you planning to warn me off? If you are, you can save your breath.'

'Come with me!' barked Krebius. He turned, stamped across the lobby to his office, flung the door open.

Aiken, with Carol holding to his arm, started to walk through; Krebius put out his arm to bar Carol. 'To your room, child!'

'You'll talk to us both, Doctor,' Aiken said in a low voice. 'And you'll tell us both the truth, or I'll go to the Board of Health and demand an investigation! I'll charge you with malpractice.'

Krebius' arm dropped like a wet sack. 'You threaten me! I have nothing to hide! My reputation speaks for itself!'

'Then why do you allow Martinon to use Carol as he has?'

Krebius became stern and stiff. 'You speak of matters you know nothing of.'

Carol said, 'I know nothing about them either.'

'Come in, then,' said Krebius. 'Both of you.' He turned, stopped short, staring at his desk. Four glossy 8×10 photographs were lying face up. Krebius stumped hastily across the room, snatched the photographs. His hands were shaking; one photograph fell to the floor. Aiken inspected it quizzically, lit a cigarette. Krebius grabbed up the photograph, furiously pushed it into a drawer with the others.

'It's not true,' he said hoarsely. 'It's a fraud! A fake!' He jumped to his feet, banged his fist on the desk. 'It's nonsense of the worst sort!'

'Okay,' said Aiken. 'I believe you.'

Krebius sat down, breathing heavily.

'Tell me,' said Aiken, 'is Martinon blackmailing you with these pictures?'

Krebius looked at him dully.

'They're nothing to worry about,' Aiken said. 'If he showed them to anybody, he'd get in worse trouble than you would.'

Krebius shook his head. 'I want you to leave this hospital, Mr. Aiken,' he croaked. 'Never come back.'

'Doctor, tell us the truth. How did Martinon make those pictures? Somehow, he's been photographing Carol's thoughts.'

'My thoughts?' Carol drew a deep breath. '*Photographing my thoughts?*' She considered a minute or two. 'Oh, my god!' She hid her face in her hands.

Krebius was leaning forward on his desk, hands clenched in his hair. 'Yes,' he muttered. 'May God forgive us.'

'But, Doctor!' cried Carol.

Krebius waved his hand. 'I found it out when I first tried

the Opticon. I noticed images, very faint. I was amazed.'

' "Amazed" is not the way I feel,' said Carol, bitterly.

'I built this machine for you alone, my dear. You had a unique handicap — all the equipment for sight, but no vision. The Opticon was to stimulate the optic nerve. I fired bursts of coloured light into your retina and observed the results. I was astonished to find images on your retina.'

'But why didn't you tell me?' Carol demanded.

'You would have become self-conscious. Your thoughts would not flow freely. And it was only in you, one person in all the world, in whom I could see these marvels.' Dr. Krebius sat back in his chair. 'We knew vision always as going one way. Light strikes the retina, the rods and cones send electric messages to the visual center. In Carol, the one way is cut off. But in her the process is reversed. The energy from the brain forms an image on the retina.

'I took some photographs. They were scientific curiosities. I went to your mother's house to ask for money. She pays me nothing. I am not wealthy. I met Victor, and we drank whiskey.' Krebius narrowed his eyes. 'I showed him the photographs. He wanted to experiment. I saw no great harm. There might be money for all of us. For you, Carol, for you most of all. I said yes, but the treatments must continue; no compromise with the cure!'

'But actually you don't know what Victor's been doing?'

'No. I thought there was no need.'

'He hasn't been giving any treatments.'

Krebius sat silently.

'He doesn't want Carol to see,' said Aiken. 'She's a gold mine for Victor.'

'Yes, yes. I see this now.'

'Also, she gave him a club over you.' Aiken turned to Carol. 'Did Victor ever ask you about Doctor Krebius?'

Carol's face was pink with embarrassment. 'He asked some awful questions. I couldn't help but think about what he was saying.'

'Carol has a strong visual imagination,' said Krebius mournfully. 'It's not her fault. But these pictures. . . .'

'They'd never stand up in court.'

'No, but my reputation!'

Aiken said nothing.

Krebius muttered, 'I've been a fool, a wicked fool. How may I expiate my weakness?' He rose, lurched over to Carol. 'My dear girl,' he faltered. 'I will cure you. You will see again. You have a good retina, you have a healthy optic nerve. Stimulation! We will make you see!' And he said softly, 'If only you will forgive me!'

Carol said something in a muffled voice. Her face was pinched, constricted. She seemed dazed.

Aiken said, 'I'd like to call in somebody else for consultation. Doctor Barnett.'

'No,' said Krebius. 'I have forgotten more about eyes than any man in California knows.'

'But do you know anything about the brain?'

Krebius was silent for a moment. Then, 'You are obsessed with psychology. Today, all is psychology — miracles. And good old-fashioned surgery goes out the window.'

'But certainly you've seen cases of hysterical blindness,' Aiken protested.

Carol said faintly, 'I'm not hysterical. I'm just angry.'

'In wartime, in the front lines,' said Aiken, 'when something terrible happens, sometimes men can't walk, or hear, or see. I've seen it happen.'

'I know all this,' said Krebius. 'In Leipzig I have treated several such cases. Well, we will try.' He took a deep breath, took Carol's hands. 'My dear, do you agree to an experiment? It might be unpleasant.'

'What for?' she asked in a low voice.

'To help you to see!'

'What will you do?'

'First, a little injection to quiet the brain. To make it easy for you to talk.'

'But I don't want to talk,' she said in a stony voice.

'Even if it will help you see?'

For a moment a refusal seemed to be on her lips, but she bit it back and said, 'Very well. If you think it will help me.'

'Hello!' said Victor Martinon from the doorway. He looked from Krebius to Aiken to Carol, and back to Aiken. 'You still here, Aiken? Must be wonderful to have time to waste. Let's go, Carol. Time for exercises.'

'Not today, Victor,' said Krebius.

Martinon raised his handsome eyebrows. 'Why not?'

'Today,' said Krebius, 'we try something different.'

'Oh, so?' said Martinon in a tone of mild wonder.

'Come, Carol,' said Krebius. 'To the Opticon. We will try to photograph the beast that rides your brain.'

Carol rose stiffly, walked through the door. Aiken followed. Out in the hall Martinon said, 'I'm sorry, Aiken, but I don't think Doctor Krebius wants strangers watching his treatments. Do you, Doctor?'

Krebius said stiffly, 'Aiken comes if he likes.'

Martinon shrugged. 'Whatever you say. I won't answer to Carol's mother for the consequences.'

Carol said, 'Since when has Mother cared two cents one way or the other?'

'She's very fond of you, Carol,' Martinon said patiently. 'And she's a sick woman.'

Carol's face took on a bleak look. 'Probably only a hangover.'

Aiken said conversationally, 'I didn't know you were still seeing Marya Leone.'

'I've known her for years,' Martinon said with simple dignity. 'I gave her her last part — in *They Didn't Know Beans.*'

Krebius pushed open the laboratory door. Carol went in, walked directly to a heavy black ophthalmologist's chair, seated herself. Krebius unlocked a cabinet, rolled out a heavy device with long binocular eye-pieces. 'Just one moment,' said Krebius, and left the room.

Martinon seated himself in a chair at the far wall, crossed his legs with an expression of patient boredom. 'Apparently everybody figures me for the bad guy.'

Aiken said, 'I can't speak for anybody else. As for myself — '

Martinon made a careless gesture with his cigarette. 'Don't bother. The trouble is, you don't see what I'm trying to accomplish.'

'Money?'

Martinon nodded slowly. 'Money, of course. But also a new way of making pictures. There's a whole new industry ready to spring to life.'

Martinon fell silent.

Aiken patted Carol's hand. 'You look scared.'

'I am scared. What's going to happen?'

'Nothing very much.'

'Do you think I'm crazy? And that's why I can't see?'

'No. But there may be something in your mind that doesn't want to see.'

'But I do want to see! If I want to see, why can't I? It doesn't make sense!'

'Theories come and theories go,' said Martinon in a tired voice.

After a moment Carol said, 'I'm afraid of that Opticon. I'm afraid to think.'

Aiken glanced at Martinon, who met his eyes blandly. 'I imagine you would be.'

'You lack the scientific outlook,' said Martinon.

'You lack something too,' said Aiken.

Krebius came in with a loaded hypodermic.

'What's that?' Aiken said.

'Scopolamine.'

'The truth drug,' said Martinon.

Krebius ignored him. He swabbed Carol's arm with alcohol. 'Now, Carol. A little prick. And pretty soon you'll relax.'

Half an hour passed in dead silence. Carol lay with her head back, a small pulse showing in her throat.

Krebius leaned forward. 'How do you feel, Carol?'

'Fine,' she said in a leaden voice.

'Good,' said Krebius briskly. 'Now, we make our arrangements.' He laid her arms in her lap, clamped her head gently between two foam-rubber blocks, wheeled the Opticon close, adjusted it so that its sensors pressed against her eyes. 'There. How does that feel?'

'All right.'

'Can you see anything?'

'No.'

'Do you want to see?'

There was a pause, as if Carol were groping for several different answers. 'Yes. I want to see.'

'Is there any reason why you can't see?'

Another pause, longer. 'I think there's a face I don't want to see.'

'Whose face?'

'I don't know his name.'

'Now, Carol,' said Dr. Krebius, 'let's go back five years. Where were you?'

'I was living in Beverly Hills with Mother. I was going to junior high school.'

'You could see?'

'Oh yes.'

Krebius pressed a switch; the Opticon began to hum and click. Aiken recognized the sound of film winding past a shutter. Krebius reached to the wall, turned out the lights. A faint neon night-light glowed ruby-red beside. Otherwise, the room was nearly dark.

Krebius said gently, 'Do you remember when you went to the lodge by Holly Lake, up in the Sierras?'

Carol hesitated. 'Yes. I remember.' She seemed to gradually become rigid. Even in the dark Aiken could sense her hands tightening.

'Don't be frightened, Carol,' said Krebius. 'No one will hurt you. Tell us what happened?'

'I don't remember very well.'

'What happened, Carol?'

Tension began to build; everyone in the room felt it. Krebius' voice was sharper; near the night-light, Martinon had stopped smiling.

Carol spoke in a low voice. 'Mother was desperate. Her last picture was a flop. The studios wouldn't take up her option . . . she was drinking heavily.'

'What happened the night of the thunderstorm?'

A pause of five seconds. A chair creaked as Martinon leaned forward.

Carol's voice was a husky whisper. 'Mother had a friend visiting. Her lover. I never knew his name. They were in the kitchen mixing drinks and laughing. . . . My father drove up. . . . I loved my father; I wanted to stay with him, but the court . . . .Outside it was thundering. The wind howled — first loud, then it died altogether. And the clouds came in, you could feel them pressing down.'

Martinon said, 'You're scaring the poor kid to death!'

'Shut up!' Aiken said softly.

'Go on,' said Krebius. 'Go on, Carol. Tell us. Get it off your chest. Look the truth in the face.'

Carol's voice began to rise. 'Daddy walked in. I told him what I had seen. He was very angry. Mother came out laughing, staggering. Daddy said he was going to take me away, that Mother wasn't fit to keep me. Then he saw Mother's friend.' Carol was wailing now, in grief and terror. 'Outside was lightning. And the lights went out.' She screamed. 'He shot Daddy. I saw him during the lightning flashes. And then — there was the most terrible sound. The whole world exploded . . . .' Her voice rasped, she panted. 'And the flash of lightning — right in my eyes . . . .'

Was it Aiken's imagination? Or did he see white light flicker from Carol's eyes? Carol had sagged. She was inert.

Krebius rose to his feet. 'My God!' he muttered, 'that is awful. All this time she carried this knowledge deep in her little head — her father murdered before her eyes!'

'And goes blind, so she won't have to look at her mother's face,' said Aiken.

Martinon said, 'Aren't you jumping to conclusions? Maybe the lightning made her blind. Maybe she'll always be blind.'

'We'll soon find out,' said Aiken. He felt Carol's forehead; it was hot and damp with sweat; the hair clung to his fingers.

Krebius turned the lights on dim.

Martinon went over to the Opticon. 'In any event, it's an interesting session. I'll develop this film; I'd like to see what's on it.'

'No,' said Aiken suddenly. 'You keep away from that film.'

'Why should I?' Martinon asked. 'I've provided the film for this machine. It belongs to me.'

'They're evidence,' said Aiken. 'Bannister never killed himself. You heard what Carol said. He was murdered. The man's face is on that film.'

'Yes,' said Krebius, 'I'd better take charge of the film, Victor.'

'I hate to insist,' said Martinon. 'But they're my films. You can see them whenever they're developed.' He busied himself at the Opticon.

Aiken came forward. 'I also hate to insist, Martinon, but I want these films. I'm anxious to see who the murderer was.'

'Keep your distance,' said Martinon levelly.

Aiken pushed him away from the Opticon. The film came with Martinon; the roll clattered to the floor, unwound in lazy coils.

Martinon said, 'Now you'll never see the man's face!'

Aiken could no longer bear Martinon's look of complacent self-possession. He threw a punch at the neat grey mustache. Martinon blocked it expertly, struck back, sent Aiken sprawling among the coils of film.

'Gentlemen, gentlemen!' cried Krebius. 'We must act like gentlemen!'

Aiken rose to his knees, crouched, butted Martinon, who staggered across the room, flung his arms out against the wall to catch himself. At this moment Carol's eyes opened. Victor was in front of her.

She stared into Martinon's face and screamed, a hoarse, cracked cry of fear. She struggled from the chair, pointing at Martinon.

'I know your face! You shot my father!'

'Well,' said Martinon, 'I've got a nasty job here now.' He reached into his pocket and came out with a knife. He pressed at the handle, the blade snapped out. He moved toward Carol.

'Martinon!' cried Aiken. 'You're crazy!' He pushed the Opticon into Martinon, it crashed over on top of him. Aiken stepped on his wrist; the knife clattered over the floor. Aiken grabbed the knot of Martinon's tie, twisted, ground his knuckles into the jugular, banged Martinon's head on the floor.

Presently Martinon lay still. Aiken released him. 'Call the cops.' He got to his feet. Martinon rolled over, groaned, lay limp.

Krebius ran out into the hall. Aiken turned, looked at Carol. She was crouched, her legs drawn up on the chair, her eyes wide.

Aiken said, 'Hello, Carol. You can see, can't you?'

'Yes. I can see.'

'Do you know me?'

'Of course, you're James Aiken.'

Then: 'Who's that?' she whispered, looking at the man on the floor. 'Is it — Victor?'

'Yes.'

'All this time he's worked on me . . . .' Her lids fell shut. 'I'm so sleepy and tired. . . . '

'Please don't go to sleep yet.'

'I won't . . . .'

A squad car squealed to a stop outside the door, and Victor Martinon was taken away.

In Krebius' office Carol drank black coffee. 'Now I don't want to go to sleep. I'm afraid I might wake up blind.'

'No,' said Aiken. 'Never again. The spell is broken. Vasillissa is free.'

'Magic!' said Carol. She looked at him, smiling. And suddenly she was the real Vasillissa, as gay and clever and daring as the enchanted princess. She reached out, took his hand.

'Magic,' said Aiken. 'Magic.'

JACK VANCE

ARAMINTA STATION

Travel out along the galaxy's Perseid Arm. Branch off to follow the ten thousand stars of Mircea's Wisp. Eventually you will come to the Purple Rose System — three stars, Lorca, Sing and Syrene, that seem about to drift away into the void.

Three planets circle Syrene. On one, Cadwall, there is Life.

Long ago the Naturalist Society of Earth had listed Cadwell as a natural preserve. An administration centre had been set up and staffed to protect the planet from all exploitation.

Araminta Station.

Now, centuries later, the young Glawen Clattuc is beginning to wonder about what the future may hold for him in the hierarchic, carefully ordered hereditary society that is life on Cadwall . . .

'Piquant cultures, cool, somewhat ruthless heroes, labyrinthine plots and bizarre passion. *Araminta Station* offers many delights'

Locus

HODDER AND STOUGHTON PAPERBACKS

JACK VANCE

THE AUGMENTED AGENT

These are the worlds of Jack Vance . . .

Complex and strange worlds. Exotic alien landscapes, future technologies: worlds of the future. Yet peopled with all-too-human heroes, struggling for sanity and survival . . .

Over the decades, Jack Vance has been hailed as one of the masters of science fiction. His award-winning stories are marked by intelligence, wit and a boundless imagination.

Included here are classic tales of fantasy and adventure. Stories certain to satisfy the devoted Vance fan — and to open the eyes of the first time Vance-discoverer.

'Vance at his quirkiest and most charming'
Publishers Weekly

A Royal Mail service in association with the Book Marketing Council & The Booksellers Association.
Post-A-Book is a Post Office trademark